Sara heard a scrambling noise as the gully dwarf climbed out of the crater, then her attention flew back to the horax. They were scuttling closer from several directions. She stamped and shouted and waved her knife, and for a moment they seemed to hesitate. One edged warily into the glimmer of light from the lichen, and for the first time, Sara was able to see her pursuers. Her breath caught in her throat. The thing in the greenish light was long and low to the ground, shiny black, and segmented like an armored centipede. It had six pairs of legs and short but powerful-looking mandibles that moved slowly back and forth as if the creature were tasting the air.

"Fewmet, hurry!" she shouted.

DRAGONLANCE NOVELS

Bridges of Time Series

SPIRIT OF THE WIND
Chris Pierson

LEGACY OF STEEL
Mary H. Herbert

THE SILVER STAIR
Jean Rabe
(Available January 1999)

DragonLance® NOVELS

LEGACY OF STEEL

BRIDGES OF TIME SERIES

MARY H. HERBERT

LEGACY OF STEEL

Distributed to the book trade in the United States by Random House, Inc. and in Canada by Random House of Canada, Ltd.

Distributed to the hobby, toy, and comic trade in the United States and Canada by regional distributors.

Distributed worldwide by Wizards of the Coast, Inc. and regional distributors.

Cover art by Jeff Easley
First Printing: November 1998
Library of Congress Catalog Card Number: 97-062373

9 8 7 6 5 4 3 2 1

ISBN: 0-7869-1187-5

8392XXX1501

U.S., CANADA,	EUROPEAN HEADQUARTERS
ASIA, PACIFIC, & LATIN AMERICA	Wizards of the Coast, Belgium
Wizards of the Coast, Inc.	P.B. 34
P.O. Box 707	2300 Turnhout
Renton, WA 98057-0707	Belgium
800-324-6496	+32-14-44-30-44

Visit our website at **www.tsr.com**

To Mary Alice Wojciechowski,

My friend, fan, baby-sitter, coffee supplier, sympathizer, cheerleader, and fellow fantasy devotee!

Chapter 1

The pain came again in the deep hours of the night. It began as a dull ache of despair in the center of her heart, where it found her own grief and joined with it, opening her old wounds and thrusting her back into that raw, quivering emptiness. She tossed and turned under her blankets; tears trickled down her sleeping face, but still she could not draw away from the bitter sadness.

The pain increased in the course of her dream and radiated outward toward her arm and back. The dull ache turned into a throbbing agony that burned like acid across her upper body.

Help me. An inhuman voice cried from a long distance away. *Help me!* The plea filled her mind with need. The voice struck a chord of familiarity, yet such as this creature
had not spoken to her in years.

A persistent pounding suddenly filled her dream. "Help me!" The words were repeated but the voice was different—human this time.

"Sara! Sara, please, I need your help!"

The dream voice dwindled into the darkness. The pain drained away, leaving only a residue of tension in her back muscles. Sara woke up and dragged herself upright. She was in her own bed, in her own cottage. Night lay thick and cold around her. The human voice without cried again, "Sara! Are you there?"

"Yes, yes, Jacobar. I'm coming," she answered. Through the haze of weariness and the sadness left behind by the dream, Sara stumbled across the dirt floor to the door. She flung the door open to greet her night visitor.

A young man, tall and brawny and very worried, rushed in. "Sara! Thanks be. You've got to come. It's Rose. She's delivering, and I think the babe is stuck."

Sara summoned a patient smile from somewhere within her. She was getting quite used to these nocturnal visits. Her reputation for skilled care was rapidly spreading through the countryside. While Jacobar paced by the door, Sara hastily threw on her work clothes: an old pair of men's pants, boots, and a clean but worn tunic. Grabbing her cloak and her healer's bag, she hurried out into the blustery night after the young farmer.

The cold air struck her like a blow. Although it was nearly spring, the past few days had been tempestuous and unseasonably chilly from a storm that moved in from the north. Sara pulled her cloak tighter and shivered. She just hoped the laboring mother was in a warm place.

Close on Jacobar's heels, she hurried with the man along the village road to a path that led east past the common pastures to a small cot and barn that sat huddled in a shallow dale. The house was small and neat and surrounded on two sides by a hedge of trees that grew as a windbreak. Pens and corrals clustered around the barn.

For a moment, Sara feared the farmer was leading her to one of the muddy pens—she had delivered more than one baby in the mud before—but Jacobar veered toward the barn and threw open the door. Lamplight spilled out into the windy darkness, and the sheltering walls of the barn welcomed her. Sara indulged in a small sigh of relief and stepped into the barn.

Her patient lay on her side in a bed of clean straw, her great flanks quivering with her effort. Rose was a plow horse of mixed breeding, thus not worth a great deal to anyone but a farmer. To Jacobar, she was priceless for her gentle disposition, her strength, her patience, and mostly for the fact that he could not afford to replace her. To him, she was everything.

"Can you help her?" he asked anxiously as Sara stripped off her cloak.

The woman nodded. "I think so. Bring me some hot water and soap if you have it."

Gladly Jacobar ran out to fetch what she needed.

Sara carefully laid her tools on a clean cloth, then methodically inspected the mare. She was pleased to see Jacobar had not waited too long to fetch her. Others had put off the call, not wanting to pay her fee, and finally ended by summoning her in a panic when it was often too late to save both the foal and the mare. This time Jacobar had recognized the mare's difficulties and acted swiftly. Sara gently patted the mare's brown head and murmured encouragement in her ear.

Jacobar soon returned, a lump of gray soap in one hand, a bucket of steaming water in the other. Sara went to work washing her hands, then lubricating her arms from a jar of sweet-smelling ointment. Fortunately the colt was not twisted or lodged in its foaling bed; it was simply trying to come forth backward. The mare, who had strained for a long while, was too tired to continue alone.

Sara carefully inserted her arm into the mare's birthing canal, found the foal's hind feet, and slipped a soft noose around the tiny hooves.

"Now," she told Jacobar, handing him the other end of the rope. "Pull gently only when she pushes. I'll help guide it out."

Perhaps encouraged by the human help, Rose made a new effort to push out her baby. As Jacobar pulled and

Sara gently helped, a glistening wet bundle eased out of the mare and slid to the straw.

Sara swiftly cleared away the amniotic sac, cut the umbilical cord, and wiped out the baby's nostrils. "It's a fine colt," she announced. The young farmer grinned his delight.

Rose climbed to her feet and began to lick her baby from diminutive muzzle to fly-whisk tail.

Sara watched, feeling the glow of satisfaction spread through her. It helped dispel some of the vestiges of the dark dream that still clung to her mind. She stretched her aching muscles and slowly made her way to her feet.

"Are you all right, Sara?" Jacobar asked suddenly. He peered at her in the dim lamplight, concern on his plain face.

"Yes. I just didn't sleep well. Bad dreams."

"Then come to my house. I have no wife, but I can cook a fine breakfast," and without further persuasion, he led her to his cottage and made her a huge meal of corn cakes, sausages, eggs, and toast. Sara discovered she was ravenous and pleased Jacobar mightily by eating a large breakfast and complimenting him frequently on his cooking skills.

By the time she left for home with a basket of eggs for her fee, the sun had risen behind a ceiling of gray clouds, and Sara felt considerably better.

She hurried through the village—or tried to. Several people called her over for news about Jacobar's mare, and others waved and greeted her, pleased as always to see her.

Sara did not try to put them off. She liked the villagers. They had readily accepted her when she wandered into their village seven years ago, and after only a brief period of adjustment, they embraced her ability to treat animals. Life in Connersby was simple and hard, but it was also quiet and satisfying after her previous existence.

When Sara finally reached her own cottage, she closed

the door behind her and took a deep breath. The morning had barely started and already she felt as if she had been working half the day. Her unmade bed looked very inviting, but there were too many other things to do. Instead of moving, though, Sara leaned back against the door and contemplated her house.

The cottage she called hers was a simple one of stone, timber, and thatch, with two rooms, a loft, and a single fireplace. The largest room served as her living space. She had a rope bed and a clothes chest on one side, a kitchen on the other, and a single table and chairs in the middle. The second room held her herbs and medical supplies and her loom. Many years ago, in another lifetime it seemed, she had been a weaver in a tiny farming community much like this one. Until a Dragon army officer named Kitiara erupted into her life and changed it forever.

Deep in thought, Sara walked to her clothes chest and opened it. She plunged her hand in amongst the clothes and linens and pulled out a sword scabbarded in leather and fleece. This morning, instead of closing the chest as usual, Sara knelt and began to dig through her clothes and belongings. At the very bottom of the chest, something hard wrapped in an old blanket met her fingers. She paused, her fingers still resting on the bundle. The voice from her dreams came back to her, imploring, grief-stricken, frightened. She thought she knew the source of the voice, but how could it be possible she could hear it after all those years? And why now?

"No!" she snapped to herself. "It's only a dream." Almost frantically, she threw her things back into the chest, burying the bundle out of sight.

She snatched up her sword and hurried out the back door to the trees that hemmed in her cottage. Behind her home rose a tree-clad hill, part of a ring of hills that protected the valley where the village was located. Sara climbed the hill on a path she knew by heart and made her way along a ridge to a small glen that angled down the ridge to the east.

There in the narrow confines of rocks and scrub trees, along the banks of a stony stream, Sara pulled her sword from the scabbard and drew herself up into a defensive posture. One after another, with meticulous care, she completed every sword exercise she had ever learned, from thrusts and parries to undercuts and blocks. When she was finished with the right hand, she repeated every exercise with the left. Every day, rain or sun, she had performed these exercises, sometimes adding changes of her own, but always completing the entire regime.

She had begun this practice to maintain her skills for self-defense. She continued it now out of habit. No one in the village imagined she did this; no one in the village knew what she had been or what she really was.

Sara wanted it that way. If any word had leaked out that an exile from the Knights of Takhisis lived in the village of Connersby in Solamnia, the Dark Knights and the good Knights of Solamnia would have swarmed all over this region to find her.

Or at least they would have several years ago. But the old world had been lost and a new world had been found in the Second Cataclysm only two short years ago. In that bitter, flaming summer, most of the knights of the light and the dark had perished together in a brutal war against Chaos, the Father of All and of Nothing. Chaos had been defeated, but in his retreat, he had forced the other gods to go with him, leaving the world of Krynn bereft of its gods, their magic, and most of the finest warriors in Ansalon. Only a few scattered remnants of the two orders remained, and Sara doubted they would be very interested in seeking out old deserters accused of treason.

Still, Sara kept her secret. The life she led until seven years ago was over and not one she recalled with joy. Only the memories of her adopted son, Steel Brightblade, kept that life alive in her memories.

Sara lifted her face to the pale sky and sent her thoughts winging back to the day when the dark-haired woman, Kitiara Uth Matar, thrust her baby into Sara's arms and rode away, never to return. From that moment, Sara Dunstan considered herself Steel's mother, and she devoted her entire life to his welfare.

It was he who had led her into the dark knighthood, and it was in the hope that she could turn him back from that path that she betrayed the Knights' Code and put her own life in danger by trying to lure him away from the goddess, Takhisis. She would have sacrificed anything for him—something his own mother never did.

Even now, two years after Steel's death in the last battle against Chaos, Sara mourned him as deeply as a blood mother could for her own son. The only comfort she found lay in the fact that Steel had died a hero, sacrificing his own life for the sake of his world. Looking back on her life, Sara did not begrudge a single moment she had spent with Steel, or for him.

The woman wiped her face with the hem of her tunic and sat down on a rock. She sighed, glanced down at the weapon in her hands. The sword exercise, if nothing else, had kept her strong and youthful beyond her fifty-one years. But, she laughed ruefully, her age was beginning to tell. Her knees ached and her reflexes were slower. Her eyesight was not as sharp as it once was. Her hair, once light brown, had turned prematurely gray and now hung in a silver braid down her back. And her mind tended to wander too often over old memories.

One day she would have to give up this swordplay and birthing horses and trimming cows' hooves and all the hard, difficult labor she performed and leave it all to someone younger and stronger. One day. Until then, there was lots to do and not enough time to do it all. Already the late winter day was passing.

Rested, Sara sheathed her sword and hurried home to

her loom and her chores. She put her dreams and memories aside for another time. What were they, after all, but mere phantoms of the past? There were far more practical things to think about in the light of day.

Like all days, though, the day drained away into darkness, and that night Sara's dream came again. It was an odd dream, for it had no images, no light or color. There was nothing but impenetrable darkness, the pain of body and soul, and the voice crying its misery to anyone who could hear.

Sara woke to find her pillow soaked with tears and her back stiff and sore from the tension. She lay awake the rest of the night, staring at the ceiling. The next day she looked wan and felt exhausted.

"It will go away," she told herself. "It's only a dream. I don't need to worry about it."

But the voice did not go away. For three more nights, the piteous cries echoed in her sleep until Sara woke screaming, "Leave me alone!"

On the fourth day, Sara was so weary she fell asleep over her loom, and she dreamed again of the darkness and the voice. This time the dream changed. A dim light filtered through the gloom, revealing stone walls and a sand-covered floor. The voice still cried, softly and steadily like a miserable child. Its tone rose and fell as if its maker was half-asleep. Then something moved into Sara's vision and confirmed her suspicion. Two forelimbs, muscular and taloned, stretched out on the sand before her. The pale light gleamed on faded blue scales.

The dragon, as if sensing her presence, raised its head and looked around. Through its eyes, Sara saw the length and breadth of its body. She gasped in her sleep. The dragon was emaciated, its color dull and dry. Its right forearm seemed bent at an odd angle, and a long, seeping wound stretched across its shoulders. It dropped its head back onto the sand and whimpered.

Sara sighed with resignation. "All right," she said

aloud. "I'm coming." The dream abruptly snuffed out.

Perhaps her acceptance was all the dragon needed, for that night, after Sara packed her gear and readied her cottage to leave, she slept through the night without a single dream.

Chapter 2

Sara left her cottage early the next morning. After leaving word with her nearest neighbors that she would be gone for a while, she slung her pack and a bow over her shoulders and marched west toward the coast.

To be sure, she had little idea where to look for the blue dragon, only a few guesses. Since there were none of the deserts blue dragons preferred in Coastlund, the sandy floor she noticed in her dream probably indicated the dragon was somewhere near the coast in a cave. There were, of course, thousands of miles of coastline in Ansalon, but Sara reasoned the dragon had to be near for its feelings to influence her dreams so powerfully. What it was doing alone, so badly hurt, in a cave in Solamnia, Sara could only imagine.

She traveled as quickly as she was able. The road, little more than a cart track, wound westward past scattered farms and small villages. The sky was overcast, and a stiff wind blew from the west. A light rain dampened her cloak; mud caked her boots. She camped one night in the open and went on early the next day.

By late afternoon, she reached the fishing village of Godnest on the coast. She made her way to a run-down inn near the docks for a meal. As she ate a rather thin meat pie, she debated which way to go. There were only two choices. She could go south toward Hargoth or northeast toward Daron. Either way, the coast was rather barren and rugged enough in places to have sea caves large enough for a blue. But which way? She hated to waste the time and strength searching in the wrong direction. This was winter, after all, the month of Deepkolt, and not the best time to be traveling on foot alone searching for something.

Sara raised her mug to her lips and sampled the watery ale while she surreptitiously glanced around the common room. Asking directions was out of the question. The mixed group of villagers and fishermen would be suspicious about vague queries about caves, and they would not be pleased if she explained that a wounded blue dragon was hiding somewhere near them. Nor did she think she could take a nap, summon her dream, and ask the dragon for directions.

Frustrated, she paid the innkeeper and walked outside into a steady rain. A short distance away, several fishing boats were hurrying back into the small harbor before the teeth of a rising wind. The roof of clouds thickened and darkened with every passing moment.

"Bad storm this afternoon," observed a villager behind her. "Best stay here tonight." He brushed past her to hurry down the path to the houses that clustered securely on a low bluff by the harbor.

Sara shivered under her wet cloak. The man was probably right. It was ridiculous to wander aimlessly around the beaches in this kind of storm. The gods only knew where— She checked herself abruptly. No. The gods would not know. Not anymore. They were gone, with their moons and their magic, leaving behind a world reeling from the loss. There was no one to pray to, no one to guide, no one to listen.

What if I did find that dragon? Sara mused. Could I heal it? Should I? What would I do with a large blue dragon bereft of its health and its purpose and, quite likely, its rider? Whom could I ask? Who would care? Perhaps it would be better just to go home. The beast will probably die before I find it anyway.

Annoyed with her thoughts and unanswered questions, Sara turned around and went back into the inn. She rented a tiny room, purchased some bread and wine, and retreated to the solitude of her thoughts.

For the remainder of the afternoon, she lay on the bed, listening to the wind roar around the eaves and the rain pound on the roof. She thought for a long time about loss and grief and pain and the comfort of companionship.

The gods were gone; there was nothing to do about that. Their help and succor, their guidance through the ages, had passed on, leaving their children behind. The only thing Sara firmly believed anymore was that if those children were going to survive on their own and make anything of their world, they would have to rely on each other, no matter who those children happened to be. She sighed. And if that meant slogging up and down the coast to find and help a desperate dragon, then that's what she should do. The future would fall into place as it would.

Sara fell asleep to the music of the storm and dreamed of the dragon. The images that came this time were stronger and sharper than before, revealing more details of the dragon's surroundings. Through its eyes, she saw the dark stone walls of a large cave and the faint outline of a long, low opening that led out to a beach. Through its ears, she heard the pounding of the surf, the howl of the wind, and the distant cry of seabirds outside. She heard, too, the dragon's harsh breathing.

Who are you? whispered a voice in her mind. *You have plagued my dreams for nights.*

And you mine! Sara sent a rejoinder, then she added in a gentler tone, *Where are you?*

Go away. No one can help me now. I am dying.

You called for help for days.

That was then. Go away.

Where are you? Sara called, but her plea met only silence. The pain came then, just as before—the grief that sliced her heart and the physical pain that flayed across her back. She writhed under her thin blanket and sobbed until someone pounded on her door and told her to be quiet.

When morning came, she was sore and exhausted, but somewhere in the throes of her dream, she had detected the direction of the dragon's cave. She would go northeast up the coast toward Daron.

The wind still whipped the surf to a rage and blew fitful showers of rain across the landscape; a heavy veil of cloud still obscured the sky. The worst of the storm had passed, though, and Sara found travel was not too difficult. Following a tip from the innkeeper, she sought a footpath that ran parallel to the beach and skirted the low hills through clumps of thick shrubs and tall, wind-cured grass.

After giving the matter some thought, Sara bought an old pack mule from a farmer and loaded her gear on its back. To her own supplies, she added bundles of firewood, a fishing pole, and a large cooking pot. The farmer looked on with curiosity until she told him flatly she was going to hunt for dragons.

Leading the mule, Sara headed up the coast along the narrow path. After several hours of slogging through the mud puddles, being alternately soaked and buffeted, and seeing nothing but low sand hills cloaked in mist, she began to wonder if she was going in the right direction. There was nothing along this stretch of the coast that could hide a gnome, let alone a dragon. Yet her dream had said north to her consciousness, and her heart agreed. So she kept walking and hoping her intuition was right.

At noon, she stopped for a quick meal and to rest the old mule. While she ate, she noticed the daylight seemed to be getting brighter. The rain had slowed, and now it stopped altogether as the clouds lifted. The wind whisked away the mist and the drizzle, and in just a short while, Sara could see along the coast from horizon to horizon. She sat up abruptly and stared north. There it was, she thought. It had to be. Far ahead, almost lost in the haze of distance, was what looked like a dark line of rugged bluffs at the edge of a high headland.

Excited now, Sara hurried through her meal and urged the mule back on the path. As she hoped, the low-lying hills beside her rose higher into a range of tree-clad slopes that led upward to the towering bluffs. The trail forked near a small creek, one path pointing upward to the hills, the other leading to the beach. Sara took the beach path and came down among the sea grass and dunes. Gray waves rolled noisily onto shore at her left. A sea gull glided silently overhead.

The cliffs loomed up before her, dark with rain. A flock of white seabirds roosted on the sheer walls and made an endless racket of calls and cries. Sara did not see anything that resembled a cave at this end of the headland, so she and the mule made their way to the base of the cliff and worked their way along the narrow strip of sand left by the high tide. The storm had pushed the tide up higher than normal, and in some places waves had washed up against the stone. Fortunately the tide was receding, and Sara was able to search along the entire length of the high, irregular cliffs.

Several haphazard piles of sand finally helped her locate the cave. The piles were scattered about the base of a cliff wall that sat slightly forward from the main bluff and was edged by a narrow, rock-strewn glen. A small creek tumbled down the glen in a series of delicate waterfalls before tumbling into a small pool on the beach and flowing into the sea. Just to the left of the waterfalls lay a snag of driftwood and the piles of sand. At first Sara saw little else until she crossed the creek and climbed up the sand.

There it was—a long low opening into the rock worn away by eons of storm tides. It looked like a tight fit for a dragon, even with much of the sand removed from the entrance. The blue must have had to dig its way in.

Sara looked around carefully. She did not see any sign that the dragon had left recently. The sand was washed smooth by the rain and unmarred by tracks. Beside her, the mule tossed its head nervously. Its nostrils flared at the strange scent coming from the cave; its tail flicked its agitation. Sara took it away from the cave mouth to the other side of the creek, gave it a long drink of fresh water, and tied it to a snag of driftwood. Away from the frightening cave, the mule settled down immediately.

Sara removed her cloak and hung it over the driftwood to dry. Then she pulled in a deep breath and summoned all her courage. On their best behavior, blue dragons tended to be willful, arrogant, and stubborn. Wounded blues were downright dangerous in their pain and unpredictability. If this dragon had set his mind on death, he would not appreciate her intrusion and could easily remove her from his cave with a single bolt of his lightning breath.

The only things she could rely on were her years of experience dealing with dragons and her inner hope that this one still wished to live. Her face set in a calm mask, she walked to the cave entrance. She gave her eyes a moment to adjust to the gloom.

"I am here," she announced boldly and strode inside.

The cave Sara entered was large and roomy by human standards, but for an adult blue dragon, it was small and cramped, a last resort for a sick and wounded dragon. Sara had walked barely ten paces inside when she came to a stop in front of a large mound of sand that extended back into the rear of the cave. A smaller mound lay slightly to one side of the larger pile.

Two baleful eyes stared at her out of the sand. "Go away!" hissed a voice in the language of dragons.

But Sara, who had trained dragons for the late Lord Ariakan, replied in Common tongue, "No. I am here to help."

Sand exploded in all directions. A dragon head, lean and fearsome, reared up out of the mound on a long, scaly neck and loomed over the woman. "Go away!" it roared, and it drew back its head to loose a bolt of lightning.

Chapter 3

The dragon suddenly jerked in midbreath, his eyes grew huge and smoke leaked from his nostrils. "I know you!" snarled the blue.

"Cobalt!" gasped Sara in genuine surprise.

"I thought you were dead," they said in unison.

A long silence fell as the two stared at each other. Sara knew Cobalt could still blast her with his dragon's breath. The dragons loyal to Takhisis and the Vision were as strict in their code of justice as their human counterparts. Although few of the knights stationed outside Storm's Keep knew of her crime, Lord Ariakan had condemned Sara to die for her treason to the knighthood. Any Dark Knight or blue dragon had a duty to kill her on sight.

But so many things had changed since the Summer of Chaos. The Knights of Takhisis no longer existed as a viable organization. Only Cobalt's sense of loyalty to a dead cause could persuade him to kill Sara now. She fervently hoped another loyalty would be stronger. Cobalt had been the nestmate of Flare, the blue Sara had loved and trained and eventually left with Steel. She had trained Cobalt, too, for a while, before turning him over to a new rider, a handsome young knight named Vincit. Old friendships faded slowly in blue dragons. Perhaps this one would remember.

"Blast it," murmured Cobalt, and his horned head

sank slowly to the sand. "I'm too weak to kill you now."

"Well, that's fine," Sara said matter-of-factly. "In the meantime, I'm going to make a fire and have something to eat. It was a long hike over here to find you, and I'm quite hungry."

The dragon's breath slipped out in a long, ragged sigh. His eyelids slid shut. "Do what you want. Just leave me alone."

Sara knew better than to push her attentions on the blue. Cobalt could be terribly stubborn when confronted. It would be far safer to encourage him to accept help willingly.

Trying to look as casual as possible, Sara unloaded her mule and brought her packs and the dry firewood into the cave. Against one wall, near the entrance, she built a fire ring of stones and laid a fire. As soon as the flames were hot, she set the caldron filled with water over the heat.

Fishing pole in hand, she walked to the opening. "Keep the fire going for me, will you?" she called over her shoulder.

Cobalt did not answer. Sara hadn't expected him to, but besides being stubborn, he was also curious. There was a good chance he would keep her fire burning just to see what she intended to do. Since he had not killed her yet, she suspected the dragon's strong sense of survival had not totally faded. Perhaps his stomach was hoping for something to eat.

Sara fished for several hours in the cold surf by the cliff. She was not very good at it, being a farm girl herself, and she missed a catch more often than not. But the water swarmed with fish rising to feed after the storm, and with only a few curses and tangled lines, Sara was able to catch enough fish to make a meal for a dragon.

She made three trips into the cave with her catch, trying not to pay too much attention to her fire. As she hoped, the flames burned hot and the water gently boiled. She cleaned the fish in full sight of Cobalt, where the wind could carry the smell to his nose. She left the heads and entrails in a pile on her cleaning stone and carried the tidbits to him. Without a word, she laid the stone in the sand by his head and went back to her fire to make the soup.

Pieces of fish, a little salt, and some bits of seaweed Sara knew to be high in nutrients went into the caldron to simmer. The results looked nasty to her, but it would be nourishing and tempting to a starving dragon.

While the soup cooked, Sara sat back against the wall and studied Cobalt. Although it was difficult to see much through his covering of sand, Sara could tell the blue was in bad shape. Just as her dream revealed, he was emaciated from starvation and illness, and he appeared to be favoring his back. His normal vivid blue coloring was faded to a dull gray; his brilliant eyes were lackluster and full of pain. His horns and the spiky frill around his head were flattened tightly against his skull. The torn ruins of a dragon saddle dangled from his chest.

Cobalt stirred. "Why did you come?" he asked suddenly.

Sara saw his yellow eyes upon her and she returned his gaze, unblinking. "I dreamed of a blue dragon in trouble. I did not know it was you."

"Would you have come if you had known?"

"Yes."

"Even knowing I could kill you?"

Sara smiled slightly, remembering her earlier reluctance. "Yes."

He clicked his teeth together. "Huh. Doesn't matter now. Oaths to a vanished goddess aren't much good. Who is going to listen? Everyone is dead."

"We are not."

"I will be soon."

"You do not need to be. I can help you. The world has lost enough blue dragons."

"Not without Vincit." The eyes closed again, and he slipped into sleep.

Sara removed the caldron from the fire and set it in the sand to cool. She cooked some fish for herself, checked the mule, and retrieved her cloak. Night had come by then, filling the cave with dense darkness. Sara hauled the caldron close to Cobalt and curled up by her fire for some much-needed rest. She slept well and deeply, without dreams or distress.

In the morning, Sara woke to find Cobalt buried in the sand again. However, the fish soup and the pile of fish entrails were gone. She smiled to herself and went fishing again.

The next few days followed much as the first. Cobalt remained stubbornly embedded in his mound of sand, refusing to move or talk or cooperate in any way except eating. Silently, when Sara was out of the cave or asleep, Cobalt ate whatever offering she left for him.

Encouraged by his willingness to eat, Sara used most of the daylight hours finding things to tempt an ailing dragon. She fished, set snares in the hills for rabbits, raided birds' nests, caught crabs, and collected seaweed and clams. Every day her catch was thrown in the soup pot, simmered for a few hours, and left by Cobalt's head at night. Every morning the pot was empty.

In the evenings, Sara sat by her fire, eating her own meal and talking to the dragon in her firm, melodious voice. She told him about her village and the years she had spent there; she told him stories about Steel and Storm's Keep; she talked about anything that came to mind just so he could hear her voice. Although he did not respond, he kept an ear cocked in her direction, and he didn't once ask her to be quiet.

On the fourth day, as Sara stirred her soup, she felt the dragon's eyes upon her. She turned and saw Cobalt gingerly stand upright on his three good legs. Sand cascaded off his back and wings and fell from his sides in damp clumps. He stood just long enough to free himself from his blanket of sand, then pulled his wings close to his body and sank back down to his belly.

Sara wordlessly brought him the soup and watched with satisfaction while Cobalt slurped the pot dry.

"Humph," snorted the dragon. "Can't you do better than this? I'd like something with more meat."

Sara grinned. "Let me see your back and I will try to find something tastier."

"Oh, if you insist. You won't do any good though," he groaned. "It's an old wound and it's festering."

Sara didn't stand still to argue with the irascible dragon. She hauled her pot to the creek, scrubbed it clean, filled it with water, and lugged it back to her fire. Then she brought out her medicine bag and laid out its contents on a blanket.

Cobalt watched her listlessly.

Sara began her examination at the dragon's wedge-shaped snout and worked her way, scale by scale, back to the tip of Cobalt's blunt tail. The dragon had grown some in the years he had been with Knight Vincit, not only in length but also in breadth and mass. He was about forty-five feet long, muscular, and well built. Healthy, he would have been a handsome figure of a dragon. Sick as he was, his condition tore at Sara's heart.

One problem was several deep parallel lacerations across his shoulders where the dragon saddle usually sat. From its appearance, Sara guessed the wound was at least several weeks old. Under normal circumstances, a dragon's rider or trainer or even the dragon itself would have treated the wound and kept it clean while it healed. But Cobalt had no human help, and his own head could not pivot around far enough to reach his damaged shoulders. The injury, unattended, had become infected, and now it oozed pus from a black, swollen mass on his back.

The other critical problem was his right foreleg. It had apparently broken, and without splints to keep it straight, it was healing at a bad angle. His right wing, too, had suffered some damage. There were minor tears in the delicate membranes and several large, raw scrapes that looked as if the dragon had fallen heavily on that side.

Sara had seen enough. "I'll be back," she informed her patient, sliding down his side to the ground. She hurried outside to the beach.

After days of clouds and gloom, the wind had finally died, and the sun broke through to bestow its radiance on the sandy white beaches. Sara paused a moment to savor the balmy afternoon, then she hurried down to a cluster of rocks half submerged in the receding tide. Somewhere in one of those tidal pools, she hoped to find a creature particular to Solamnia's western coast, a small, insignificant creature she had seen only a few times.

She searched carefully under the water in the shelter of the rocks until she found two prickly brown things that reminded her of fist-sized cockleburs. Using a stick, she gently pried them loose from their watery perch and pushed them to the edge of the water, where she tipped them upside down and speared their soft underbellies with her dagger. She carried the dead creatures into the cave and laid them out before her fire.

"What are those?" Cobalt snorted.

"Numbtouch sea urchins," Sara replied as she broke off the spines one by one. "They produce a slime on the points of their spines that is a very effective painkiller."

"So?"

"So I am going to use these little points on you while I clean your wounds and . . ." Sara paused to cast a quick glance at the cave entrance. If Cobalt objected violently to her remedy, she wanted a clear way out.

"And what?" Cobalt prompted suspiciously.

Sara took a deep breath and said hurriedly, "Reset your leg. You see, it's crooked. I shall have to rebreak the fracture, set it properly, and splint it, or it will never hold your weight." She stared up at the dragon's head and waited for his reaction.

"That seems like a great deal of trouble for nothing," he said in a mournful tone. "I am so empty. Vincit is gone. Everything is wasted. I don't want to stay in this world anymore."

Sara crossed her arms and glared at the blue. "Things are different, but by no means is everything gone, Cobalt. Vincit was a good rider; I remember him well. He cared for you very much. Do you think he would want you to waste away when there was help and food close by? I can promise you he would never forgive me if I let you die."

Cobalt's head dropped to the sand and his eyes closed. "Do what you want, then," he muttered.

The woman set to work before Cobalt changed his mind. She did not like the heavy mood of depression that gripped the dragon, and she hoped that fixing his body would help revive his spirits. Blues could be very touchy when their riders died; some she knew had allowed themselves to die rather face the loneliness and grief. Cobalt, though, had not tried to kill himself, and despite his listlessness and misery, there were flashes of life in his choices.

She dragged her pot of warm water beside his shoulder. With her healer's tools and the sea urchin spines, she started her first task of cleaning the infected wound on the dragon's back. First she cut away the remains of the harness and tossed the saddle aside. Prying apart the dragon's tough scales, she inserted a row of urchin spines into Cobalt's skin and muscles beside the lacerations. The anesthetic took effect immediately.

Alternately washing and trimming the wound, she was able to remove much of the ruined scales, dried blood, pus, and dead tissue. She was relieved to see that the injury was not as deep or as damaging as she feared. When the wound was cleaned to her satisfaction, Sara slathered a liberal coating of an antiseptic ointment over the whole area and laid clean strips of cloth on top to protect it from dirt and sand.

Next she cleaned and treated his wing injuries. His leg she saved for last, partly because of her own nervousness and partly because if he took serious objection to what she had to do, at least his other wounds were already treated.

With one cautious eye on the dragon's fearsome teeth, she inserted urchin spines above the break in his foreleg and below it.

Cobalt lay very still, his eyes closed. Only one ear swiveled in her direction.

Sara started talking to him in a low, reassuring voice. "This may feel very odd. Please don't move. I am going to try to pull the break apart again. Fortunately it is a simple break, and the set hasn't solidified yet. I hope it will part easily." She continued to talk, describing everything she did and planned to do. As she hoped, the fracture in the bone separated easily under pressure, and Sara was able to manipulate the two ends back into proper alignment. She splinted his leg with driftwood and strips of cloth. Only then did she pull out the urchin spines.

Cobalt let his breath out in a long sigh. A moment later he was asleep.

Chapter 4

The next several days remained pleasantly cool and sunny. Sara was able to fulfill her promise to Cobalt for something meatier. She brought down a buck with her bow and carried it back to the cave on the back of the old mule.

Cobalt grabbed for the deer so greedily he almost snatched the mule. The mule squealed in terror, kicked up his heels, and bolted down the beach at a speed that belied his age.

Sara spat a curse and ran after him. By the time she returned with the mule, Cobalt slept happily in his sand nest, a few broken bones lying scattered around him. She smiled and shook her head. Whether he knew it or not, the blue had taken the path to healing.

She brought him several more deer in the following days and continued to cook the fish and seaweed soup. He ate everything she gave him. His leg took the new set and slowly healed as straight as before. The tears on his back remained clean and free of further infection. New flesh began to grow and the wounds gradually closed. Sara knew he would always have scar tissue marring the beautiful symmetry of his scales, but his muscles worked well enough and he still had the full range of movement of his wings.

His color improved, too. From a dull, tarnished metallic appearance, he brightened to his usual shimmering blue. Sara had forgotten how handsome he could be when he was healthy. She stood in the entrance to the cave one afternoon and watched the setting sun bronze his shining body. His scales gleamed a bright sapphire blue along his head, neck, and back, then his color deepened down the extremities of his body until his feet and tail were a dark, almost greenish blue—thus the origin of his name. In the golden light of sunset, he looked as if an artist had overlaid a gilt patina over molded enamel.

Sara smiled at him. He cocked an eye at her and shook the rough spiny frill around his head.

"I heard what happened with you and Steel," he said abruptly.

The woman nodded once. She sat down in the warm sunlight by the entrance and stretched out her long legs. "I freely admit I never wanted my son in Takhisis's dark knighthood—"

Cobalt interrupted her. "And you tried to get him out. Flare told me."

"And I tried," Sara repeated softly. "I am glad now I failed. Steel was where he needed to be. He died as he wanted, courageously, with honor, doing what he thought was right. Even his father, Sturm, could not ask for more than that."

The dragon stirred in his nest. His eyes glowed like fire in the light of sunset. He dipped his head and looked at Sara with his fiery eyes. "Why did you try to take him away from Takhisis? Why did you yourself join if you did not believe in her Vision?"

Sara knew these questions from Cobalt were inevitable. He had been a knight's dragon, after all, a servant of the dark goddess. She realized, too, that the only way she had a hope of earning his trust was to tell him the truth.

"I do not believe in the sovereignty of evil," she replied firmly. "There is more to this world than darkness and tyranny. Ariakan lured Steel into the dark knighthood against my wishes with promises of glory, riches, and power. I was desperate to get Steel out. I went with him to stay near him, to try to protect him. I endured years as Ariakan's mistress and servant just to be with Steel. I trained dragons, learned the ways of the knighthood, and stayed at Storm's Keep long after Ariakan was finished with me, hoping to find some way to convince my son to leave before he took the final oath. I failed in that. I even kidnapped him and took him to the High Clerist's Tower to see his father's tomb. Unfortunately his birthmother's blood proved stronger that day."

Sara hesitated, her face creased in a sad frown. Cobalt watched her closely.

"Now you know the truth about me," she said with a small shrug of her shoulders. "I am no minion of Takhisis and never will be."

"But you like blue dragons," he said, a faint undertone of hope in his voice.

She laughed softly. "Some of them."

The dragon flipped his wings in his version of a shrug. "There is no more Queen of Darkness to obey. Ariakan's knighthood is dead. My rider is dead. There is only you and me now." He tilted his head and peered down at her. "I see no problem we cannot work through."

Sara met his gaze eye for eye, pleased more than she imagined she would be. "You do not have to stay with me if you do not want to. There are probably real knights out there who would be pleased to have you for a partner."

"You are the one who came to help me," he pointed out. He dropped his head back to the sand and scratched his chin on a small rock. "We will see when I am stronger."

Sara crossed her arms. "Now it's your turn. Tell me about Vincit. What happened to you two?"

Cobalt hesitated, reluctant to put the past into words. But he had started this conversation, and he realized he owed Sara his tale. "We were with a wing in Northern

Ergoth, laying siege to the Solamnic fort at Gwynned during the Summer of Chaos. That's why we were not part of the final assault on the Abyss. After we lost the Vision and all contact with Lord Ariakan, our officers abandoned us. The remnants of our group tried to stay together, but the entire population turned against us. Even the kender from Hylo hunted us through the Sentinel Mountains. We tried to leave the island, only to fall into an ambush. Most of our companions were killed. Vincit and I barely escaped. We could have left then—should have, I suppose. Vincit was consumed with rage. He wanted revenge, so we attacked a small party of Solamnic Knights near the coast. Stupid, really. One had a silver dragon with him." Cobalt fell silent, remembering the aerial battle that day.

"A silver dragon did this to you?" Sara prompted.

"I was weak from hunger. The silver was bigger, stronger, faster. It wounded Vincit in the second pass. I fled with the saddle dangling from my shoulder. Vincit was still alive, still clinging to me, but he died before I found a place to hide. I made my way across the water and eventually found this cave."

"So now we both know what has happened to the other. What do we do now?" Sara mused, more to herself than to the dragon.

"Eat?" he suggested.

Sara laughed. Her robust sound of merriment filled the cave and fell pleasantly on Cobalt's ears. He would not tell her, not yet, but he liked her laughter and the sound of her voice when she talked to him. Her voice helped fill the aching emptiness in his thoughts and soothed his sadness. He lifted his head from the sand to watch as she lugged her fish pot within his reach.

"Eat well," she ordered. "Tomorrow you are going outside to stretch."

Cobalt obeyed.

The sun shone warm on the sand the next day when

Sara urged the dragon out of his nest and into the light. He chose a sheltered place by the stream to bask in the sun, and he looked so comfortable stretched out on his belly, Sara patted his side and bade him good-bye.

"I need supplies from the village south of here," she told him. "I should be back by dark. And don't eat the mule." She shook a finger at him.

"Humph," he snorted. "That old thing is too stringy."

"Good. Just remember that," she said, shouldering her bow and quiver.

She left him soaking in the sun and hiked south along the faint path back to Godnest. In the village, she purchased a loaf of bread, some cloth for bandages, a new blanket, a round of cheese, and for a bucket of clams she picked along the way, she got a small bag of potatoes. She enjoyed a mug of ale at a different tavern, then put the sea to her right and walked back north.

It was nearly dark by the time she reached the cliffs with her supplies and a brace of rabbits she had brought down along the trail. She saw Cobalt's place by the stream was empty. She hurried past the waterfalls and climbed the mound of sand before the cave. Halfway up, a sound froze her in midstep. A guttural voice whispered something. Sara did not catch the words, but she recognized the tongue. Goblins.

Vile little scavengers! She dropped to the sand and peered cautiously over the top. A dark, squat shape hunkered in the darker shadows by the opening. At least three, maybe four, shapes hovered close by. Their attention seemed to be focused on the interior of the cave. Sara listened and thought she heard the soft snoring of the dragon. If Cobalt was asleep, the goblins probably intended to sneak in and steal whatever they could find.

Sara curled her lips back in disgust. She hated goblins ever since her stay at Storm's Keep. Nasty, sniveling, boot-licking, conniving . . . her list was endless. She would be strung out on an ant nest before she'd let those brutes near the blue.

She dropped her bundles to the sand and silently strung her bow. Fitting an arrow to the string, she took aim at the shape by the door.

At that moment, the other three crept cautiously into the cave's mouth.

The woman loosed the string. Her arrow sped true and pierced her target before it could utter a cry. The goblin collapsed to the sand. Sara sprang up and over the top of the mound, slithered down to the cave entrance, and crouched by the stone wall. A second arrow waited in her bow.

How many more are there, she wondered. The stench of the dead goblin filled her nose. Her throat, irritated by the smell, tickled a warning.

"Cobalt! Goblins!" she yelled before a sneeze could give her away.

A loud squawk and a squeal erupted from the blackness in the cave. All at once the darkness was splintered by a crack of lightning, the blue dragon's breath weapon. In that flash, Sara saw three goblins caught in the brilliant explosion of light. They stood immobile, frozen in the blinding radiation.

The light flicked out. The goblins yelped and bolted for the entrance. Sara waited as they charged past her, then she fired at the nearest fleeing form. It toppled face first into the sand. A second blast of lightning arced out of the cave and caught one more goblin in the back. The other vanished into the night.

Sara hurried into the cave. A terrible stench hit her like a blow. "Cobalt, could you start the fire? I want some light."

Another bolt of lightning seared from the blue and ignited a roaring fire in her fire ring. The flames illuminated the front of the cave, revealing the source of the horrid smell. A goblin Sara had not seen before had caught the full force of the dragon's lightning. It lay sprawled on its back, its short, red corpse smoking gently.

"Ugh," Sara managed to gasp. She did not bother to say more until she had hauled all the dead goblins away from the cave and left them where the tide would carry them away.

She came back wiping her hands and looking disgusted. "Well, the mule is gone, and there are several tracks leading up into the hills," she said. "That must have been a small raiding party."

Cobalt huffed a cloud of steam from his nostrils. "Little thieves probably thought I had treasure or something in here. As if I'd ever let any of them have it!"

The woman dropped her bundles by the fire. "But now we have a problem. At least one escaped and probably made it back to the main camp. If he didn't get a good look at this cave, he may convince the others to come back here to check it out. Goblins can be very tenacious."

"I can handle goblins," Cobalt said with a ring of derision in his voice.

"Of course you can," Sara responded, patting the big dragon on the neck. "When you are healthy and strong and not trapped in a small cave. But both of us are familiar with some of their nastier weapons. What if they threw a pot of scavenger mold in here? Neither one of us could escape it."

Cobalt looked thoughtful. "I am too weak to fly yet. What if I walked? We could find another cave."

Sara examined his splinted foreleg then climbed up to look at his back. The lacerations were healing nicely. "I know of several near my home," she told him. "I could take you there to recover your strength until you make up your mind what you want to do."

He grumbled deep in his throat. "I do not like to run before goblins. It is not seemly."

Sara said with a laugh, "Then consider it simply an

expedient move. I should be closer to home anyway. I have crops to plant and things to do."

She fixed his soup with the rabbits and ate her own meal of cheese and bread. Before she went to sleep in her blankets, she strung a trip wire across the cave's entrance and added extra wood to the fire.

Despite her casual tone to Cobalt, the presence of goblins in the vicinity of the cave worried her deeply. Although goblins were minions of Takhisis, they would not be reluctant to kill a blue if they realized the dragon was injured. And they'd certainly have no compunction about killing her for her blankets or her bow or the bits of gear she had in the cave. She needed to get Cobalt back on his feet and strong enough to travel soon!

She roused the dragon at dawn and urged him outside to walk in the sand while she fished for his breakfast. This time she did not have to cook the soup; she simply tossed the fish to him, and he scooped them up as fast as she unhooked them. When he was finished eating, she urged him into the water and had him swim back and forth until he was so tired he could barely stand upright. She left him basking in the sun and went to hunt for meat. Wary of goblins, she stayed near the cave and hunted in the hills nearby.

She found more goblin tracks and considered following them to see if her hunch about a larger raiding party was right. Then common sense returned, and she veered off the path to stay close to the bluffs. One woman wouldn't stand a chance against a pack of goblins.

She brought down a wild cow for Cobalt and, cursing the theft of the mule every step of the way, butchered the beast and dragged it, piece by piece, back to the dragon.

Cobalt devoured every scrap, belched his thanks, and went to sleep.

Sara settled down on the sand and leaned back against the dragon's warm shoulder. She was so tired after her exertions to feed the big lummox, she also promptly fell asleep in the sun. She hadn't napped very long when a sound intruded upon her peace.

"Sara," whispered a faint voice. "Sara, they're back."

The woman stirred, startled awake by the urgency in the voice. Her eyes flew open.

"Don't move. They think I am still asleep. They're in the rocks by the waterfall. They do not see you."

Sara stayed still and slouched lower behind the dragon's back. She glanced around, saw it was late afternoon. The sun's rays slanted nearly horizontal across the white-tipped waves. "Are they moving?" she hissed.

"Not yet. They are just watching. I think there are only two."

"Scouts."

"Do I blast them?"

"I think you'll have to. If you tried to move from here, they would see immediately that you are hurt."

"With pleasure." Cobalt leisurely lifted his head and looked in the general vicinity of the lurking goblins. A fierce blast of lightning seared from his mouth and exploded on a cluster of rocks midway up the waterfall. Pieces of rock and debris flew everywhere. Something shrieked, and a small reddish figure bolted out of the cloud of dust and scrambled up the glen.

Cobalt loosed his lightning again. Another thunderous blast exploded into the hillside. When the dirt and rubble settled down, the glen was still.

The dragon heaved himself to his feet and limped slowly over to the creek to examine his accuracy. Sara hurried after him and climbed up among the shattered rocks to make certain the two scouts were dead. She found them—or what was left of them—and after a cursory check, she hurried back down.

"They're just like the others. Flat faces, pointy ears, sharp teeth, and all. And look at this," she said, thrusting something under Cobalt's nose. "They all had bits of stolen armor and old clothes, but every one of them had this badge on his chest."

The dragon tilted one eye to study the patch she had torn from the goblin's uniform. It looked black, with a red hatchet crudely painted in the center. "Only a large tribe with a recognized leader bothers with badges," he remarked. "They are going to be curious when their scouts do not return."

"Yes," Sara affirmed. "We don't have much time left. How do you feel?"

The dragon stretched his wings out as far as they would go and gently flapped them in the evening breeze. "I am stiff and sore, but I feel stronger. You feed me well."

"Do you think you will be able to leave in a day or two?"

"Yes." He suddenly bobbed his head and rumbled a dragonly chuckle. "Think how disappointed they will be when they find only an empty cave."

The next day was a repeat of the previous one. Sara spent the morning fishing for Cobalt and accompanying him while he swam, then she hunted in the afternoon. They saw no goblins that day and Sara went to sleep that night hoping fervently that the goblins had decided the dragon in the cave was not a good prospect for looting.

On the following day, though, Sara realized they would have to leave the cave, goblins or no. When she returned that afternoon with a hunk of freshly killed deer, she looked out over the ocean and saw storm clouds massed on the western horizon. Her heart sank.

Cobalt sat on the beach, his head into the wind, his nostrils flared. "The air is changing," he said to Sara. "That storm smells big."

Sara could not judge a storm by its smell as easily as Cobalt, but she didn't have to for this storm. The signs were very clear. She studied the towering masses of clouds that piled up like battlements across the sky; she saw the distant lightning flicker in the stormheads; she felt a new damp chill in the wind; and she knew he was right. She also realized that the tide was running out. By the time the storm hit, the tide would be coming in and their cave would offer little protection from the rising surf.

"We need to leave," she told the dragon. "If we go now, perhaps we can find other shelter before the storm breaks."

Cobalt agreed. He ate his meat and waited for her outside while she hurriedly packed her gear, her blankets, and some dry tinder in her pack. She buried her fire ring, then, as an afterthought, buried her pot, too. The goblins got her mule; she wasn't going to give them her pot.

The clouds had obscured the sun by the time Sara emerged from the cave. The air was noticeably colder, and the wind beat against the cliffs with gusty enthusiasm.

She debated about climbing the bluffs to look for shelter in the more rugged hills, but she thought about Cobalt's leg and his bulk and changed her mind. He didn't need to be climbing rocky slopes or plowing his way through trees. She took, instead, the more open southern direction. There wasn't as much cover that way, but the going was easier for the dragon.

With Cobalt close on her heels, she waded out into the edge of tide and led the way back along the headland. The waves would obliterate their tracks and, with luck, throw off the goblins.

Cobalt still limped on his front leg, but he made no complaint about the pain in his leg or the stiffness across his shoulders. He followed Sara through the shallow water as best he could and kept a close watch on the approaching storm.

They had progressed about two miles along the beach when Sara turned up onto dry land and led Cobalt through the tall sea grass and dunes to the path that paralleled the shore. She walked past several clumps of tangled shrubs and vines, came down a gentle slope, and was about to jump over a low, wet spot in the trail when she looked up and stopped so quickly that Cobalt nearly stepped on her.

The dragon choked on a snort of surprise. There, not more than ten paces away, was a large band of goblins coming along the path toward them.

The leader of the goblins saw them about the same time. He slid to a stop, startled. His band screeched to a halt behind him, half of them crashing into each other to keep from hitting him.

For the space of two heartbeats, the two groups merely stared at each other.

The goblin leader made the first move. In a blur of motion, he yanked up a loaded crossbow and released the bolt directly at Sara's chest.

Chapter 5

"Down, Sara!" bellowed the blue dragon.

Sara dropped to her face in the mud just as a sizzling bolt of lightning shot from the dragon and burned into the milling troop of goblins. The leader fell, his rusty breastplate split in two and his leather jerkin smoking. Others fell, too, seared by the fiery heat. The band burst apart as goblins scattered, screaming, in every direction.

Cobalt sent bursts after them to speed them along.

Suddenly a horn, sounding rather bent, sounded from some nearby bushes. "To me!" bellowed a harsh voice. "Grishnik to me!"

Sara lifted her head. "Leave the dragon!" she yelled in the deepest, most guttural Goblin syllables she could manage. "To the cave! The cave is unguarded!"

Goblin voices rose excitedly out of the grass and undergrowth. "To the cave!" a second voice took up the idea. Loud rustlings came from the bushes where the horn had called. "To the cave," agreed the harsh voice. There was a sudden burst of commotion as the goblins sprang out of their hiding places, and before Cobalt could draw breath to blast them again, they disappeared into the thick grasses.

The dragon heard a strange hacking noise at his feet. He dropped his head and peered at Sara, still lying flat in the mud. Her entire body shook from head to boot. "Sara?" he asked worriedly. "Are you all right?"

She rolled over onto her back, and the laughter she had contained in the mud burst out of her in a long peal of hilarity. "It worked!" she gasped between fits of giggling. "I can't believe they fell for it."

Cobalt curled his lips, revealing his white teeth. Humans called it a dragon smile. "What is the most obvious choice for goblin honor? Stay and fight a blue dragon on foot or go search a cave they think might have something valuable in it?"

The woman picked herself up out of the mud and tried to brush herself off. "Let's go before they realize the cave is empty."

"Maybe if we're lucky, they will stay in there awhile digging for buried dragon treasure and get trapped by the storm."

"We can but hope."

They hurried on as fast as Cobalt's leg would allow. Sara knew they would be approaching Godnest soon and its outlying farms, and she kept a close watch on their surroundings to avoid contact with anyone. She did not want to draw undue attention to the blue or scare anyone out of his wits.

Eventually she left the path and led the dragon east. She hoped that by going cross-country and traveling at night they could cross the low-lying coastal plains and reach her village near the mountains undetected. They were in Solamnia, after all, where blue dragons were not welcome.

They did not go far, however, before the mass of clouds overtook them and the wind began to roar. The first drops of rain splattered on the ground; thunder rumbled overhead.

"Over there!" Cobalt called, and he pointed with his nose to a place Sara could not see. He rumbled forward past her and limped to a copse of trees that stood dark in the gathering storm. Sara did not notice until she was nearly among them that the trees hid the ruins of an old farmhouse. The roof had collapsed at one end of the stone building, but there was just enough shelter left for Sara and some of Cobalt.

The dragon tore out the collapsed section of the roof, knocked over the remains of a wall, and made himself comfortable. His back end stuck out into the rain, but he didn't mind as long as his head and shoulders remained dry.

Sara scrambled into the roofed section of the house just as the rain let loose in a drenching downpour. The woman climbed gratefully among the debris to a seat near the stone wall. Night had fallen with the storm, and the house was black within. Sara could see nothing until the vivid bursts of lightning lit her surroundings for a second or two at a time.

Using the dry tinder in her pack, she started a tiny fire, just enough to see by. She quickly found plenty of wind-blown tree limbs, old furniture, and some pieces of firewood still lying by the ramshackle fireplace to add to her fire. In a dry spot near the stone wall, she built her fire to a roaring blaze and set a small pot of water near the heat to boil for tea. While her tea brewed, she changed her muddy tunic and hung it outside to wash off.

"Do you suppose the goblins are still in the cave?" Cobalt asked sleepily.

Sara sipped her hot tea and grinned at the darkness. "Sweet dreams, Cobalt."

* * * * *

By slow, short stages, traveling at night, Sara led the dragon toward the Vingaard Mountains. They passed many farms and a few villages on the fertile lowlands, but most of the humans were asleep, and any night creature that saw them did not bother to make a fuss.

Each day Cobalt seemed a little stronger and his limp grew less. Sara left his splint on during the night to give his leg more support while he walked, and when they found shelter for the day, she took it off to check his skin and give his limb a rest. Every evening before they started, Cobalt spread out his wings and practiced flapping to strengthen his muscles. Sara knew it would not be long before he could be airborne once more.

The trek seemed to do him good in other, more subtle ways, too. The dark shadow of depression gradually eased from his mind. He still bore the scars of his loss and his grief, and Sara knew from experience that he always would. Yet since the evening they had talked in the cave about their past, he seemed more himself. He ate heartily, took interest in his surroundings, and lost the tendency toward sickly self-pity. He told Sara tales about Vincit and their adventures, and he often revealed a sense of humor his nestmate, Flare, had never had.

The only real problem she had with him, and this had the potential to be a big one in the regions near her village, was his complete disregard for ownership. Cobalt did not think twice about snatching an ox or a horse or a cow from a farmer's field at night. If he was hungry and the animal was available, he took it.

Blue dragons in Lord Ariakan's service were taught the concepts of his dark honor and the dishonorable nature of theft from friends and allies. But Cobalt did not consider the people of Solamnia his allies, and therefore their stock was fair game. Sara worried that his thievery would alert the residents to their presence and send a party after them. She admonished him several times and tried to explain her reasons, but he simply shrugged and ate his catch. Sara knew full well she would have to find a way to impress him with the importance of hunting wild animals, or he wouldn't be able to stay long in Coastlund.

As it happened, her point was made for her by an unexpected source. Just one night's journey from Sara's village, they stopped at dawn and took refuge in a tall stand of evergreens. Cobalt made a nest in the fallen needles and was about to tuck his head under his wing when he sensed something coming, and coming fast. His head reared up to scan the sky.

"What is it?" Sara asked, then she, too, felt it, a gathering fear that weakened her legs and sent her body shivering. Instinctively she ducked under a tree and pressed her body down into the undergrowth.

Cobalt curled into a tighter ball. "Khellendros," he hissed fearfully.

Sara managed to look up through the trees and saw a tremendous blue dragon winging slowly overhead. The rising light of morning gleamed on his underbelly and sparkled on the iridescent blue scales of his back and neck. Sara knew Khellendros had returned to the north and claimed the Northern Wastes as his own, but she had not yet seen him flying over Coastlund until now. She swallowed through a dry throat. By Huma's shield, he was huge! The largest blue dragon ever to darken the skies of Krynn.

She watched as he flew lazily overhead. Was he looking for them? Or was he just surveying the landscape? She cast a quick look at Cobalt and was relieved to see he was staying huddled in his nest, perfectly still.

Finally Khellendros veered away and flew west toward the coast. Sara watched him go until the sapphire of his shining hide was lost in the blue of the sky. Her breath blew out in a gusty sigh of relief.

"That is the other reason I do not want you to draw attention to yourself," she said fervently. "Khellendros would kill you in an instant if he thought you were a threat."

Cobalt turned his amber eyes toward her. "I knew he was back," he whispered, "but I didn't know he was so close to us."

"He has several lairs in the Northern Wastes; he rarely comes here. But let's not give him a reason to!" Sara crawled over to Cobalt's side and put her hand on his folded wing. She knew when to push home a point. "When we find a cave for you in the Vingaard Mountains near my home, you must promise me you will not take farm animals or do anything to terrify the people. There are plenty of deer and elk and other large animals for you to hunt. No one needs to know you are there. Agreed?"

Cobalt took one more glimpse at the sky. "I promise."

The next night they reached the village of Connersby. Sara recognized the familiar landmarks of the creek and the huge willow that grew near the bridge, the farms, and the tavern at the edge of the common fields. She made a wide berth around the village and hiked up into the high foothills to the east. She found the path over the ridge that led to her practice area, and from there she struck north and east, deeper into the mountains. In the years that she had lived in Connersby, she had explored extensively the mountain region beyond the village, not only because she wanted to familiarize herself with possible escape routes but also because she enjoyed exploring and hiking. She knew well the faint game trails and the paths made by travelers of all descriptions. She knew where to find water and shelter and where the best berry patches grew.

She also knew the location of a large isolated cave, seldom used by anything but mice and an occasional bear. The cave was a long walk from her cottage, but its seclusion was better suited to the blue dragon than the caves closer to her home. Unerringly she led the dragon down the ridges, up rocky slopes, and through woods, dense with evergreen and pine, to a deep valley far from the regular mountain trails.

Cobalt checked the cave from end to end and pronounced his satisfaction by settling down on a dry, flat place near the opening and promptly going to sleep.

Sara rubbed her hands along his steel-colored horns in farewell before she sought her own cottage and bed.

* * * * *

She left before dawn the next day to visit Cobalt, taking her sword and bow with her. She practiced her swordplay under his interested gaze, and to her surprise, he made several astute suggestions about her footwork and the angle of her blade in two different parries.

"I used to help Vincit," he told her.

Afterward they went hunting, and Sara brought down two elk. Cobalt carried them back to the cave, where he ate one and saved the rest "for later." He complained about the hardness of his bed and the itches in his healing skin.

Sara spent the remainder of the morning treating his wounds and oiling his itches. She promised to bring some hay for his bed the next time she came.

She hurried home to clean house, set up her loom, and fix something to eat. A farmer came late in the evening and asked her to attend a laboring cow. By the time Sara fell into bed after midnight, she was exhausted.

Her days fell into a hectic pattern as the winter gave way to spring. She quickly decided to purchase an old but spry bay horse, who could carry her to the dragon's cave in half the time or carry bales of hay or meat when needed. The horse soon learned the dragon would not harm him, and he stayed in Cobalt's company with only a halfhearted show of nervousness.

While the horse helped shorten her traveling time, he could not help Sara with her countless other tasks. She divided her time between her cottage and her garden, the village's animals, and the dragon. The farmers often wondered at her constant absences, but any time they asked, she told them she was hunting, or looking for herbs, or trapping, or anything else she could think of at the moment.

She also spent time at her loom. She was still a weaver by training, and she supplemented her income by weaving rugs, wall hangings, and fanciful cloth for clothes. Much of her work she sold in local markets, but the better items she stored in her loft for a trip she planned to make someday to the markets in Palanthas, where she knew she could get higher prices. If she ever had time to go.

Meanwhile Cobalt healed and thrived in his mountain retreat. As soon as his wings were strong enough, Sara encouraged him to fly, asking only that he restrict his flying to the hours at dusk and dawn or on nights when the single pale moon lit the sky. He squawked a little at the limited time until she reminded him that Khellen-dros was still making his flybys. Since the big blue was nearly four times larger than Cobalt, the smaller blue swallowed his pride and obeyed Sara's orders.

Once in a while Sara would fly with him. She had to rig a crude dragon saddle out of strips of leather, heavy padding for his scarred back, and a cobbled horse saddle, but she was pleased with the results. Once it was in place and she climbed up behind his neck ridges, the saddle held her firmly in place while he spiraled upward into the evening sky and dipped and swirled and flew to his heart's content.

Sara loved those brief hours in the air. She did not real-ize how much she had missed the feel of a powerful dragon beneath her, or the flow of the wind in her face, or the incredible vistas of land that spread below them. She reveled in the powerful upbeat of Cobalt's wings and in the incredible freedom of his flight. Now she did not have to worry about avoiding other dragons swoop-ing around them, teaching battle strategies, or fretting that someone else could get hurt. All she had to do was sit back in her saddle and experience the joy of the ride.

Cobalt seemed to pick up some of her pleasure, for he flew longer, higher, farther, better when she was with him.

Spring came and went in a blur of planting and lamb-ing, and summer waltzed in with a long stretch of warm days and balmy nights. The anniversary of the Battle of the Rift came on a hot day in Fleurgreen, and the village took the opportunity to celebrate the day with music, festivities, and a bonfire. Sara observed it quietly with Cobalt in the cool shade of his glade.

As summer passed, Sara continued her busy days, often working late into the night. She sometimes wondered how much longer she would be able to keep up such a heavy load of responsibilities. The constant labor was beginning to wear thin.

The uncertainty plagued her, too. She did not know how long the dragon would or could stay with her, and the thought of losing him bothered her intensely. He was content where he was for now, but how soon would it be before he changed his mind and left her, or a wanderer stumbled across his lair in the woods and spread the alarm, or Khellendros caught him unaware and killed him?

Deep in her heart, Sara knew the course of her present life would change—perhaps drastically. It was only a matter of time.

Chapter 6

Autumn came in its time and brought with it the days of harvest and gathering. Everyone worked hard, from the grannies who shelled beans to the youngest children, who could pick nuts and gather apples. After the blistering hot summer of three years before when the crops withered on the vine and the people went hungry the following winter, no one wanted to miss a single opportunity to put food aside for winter.

With the balmy winds of autumn, however, came a chilling frost of dark tidings and evil rumors. Connersby was not close to any of the major roads through Coastlund, and news sometimes took a while to reach the village. Thus it was autumn before the people heard the first real news of the dragon, Malystryx. Vague rumors had drifted through Ansalon during the year of a great red dragon that landed on Misty Isle, but most people considered the story of a dragon from another land a mere fireside tale. That autumn showed them differently.

Other news, equally as foreboding, trickled into the village as the season passed, news of troubles and disasters, of a strange new bard known only as the Herald, of the growing activity of frost wights in the south and the increasing influence of Khellendros to the north. The war with Chaos was over, but Krynn's troubles seemed to move on, with or without the gods.

Sara had been so busy during the cool days of autumn,

she had heard little outside news of any sort. That changed one evening with the arrival of the traveling cobbler.

Known in the region only as Bootjack, the cobbler was a small man with a pointed beard and agile fingers. Some said he was part kender, because of his broad smile and love of talk. Others thought he was part dwarf because of his short stature and the wonderful ability of his fingers. He never told. He made any kind of footwear from slippers to fancy dress boots, and his workmanship was unequaled. He traveled in a small red wagon through the villages of Coastlund, the Vingaard Mountains, and the plains of Solamnia, gathering news and sharing tales and making shoes.

He came up Sara's lane near dusk, leading his cart horse, a little plump mare favoring her front leg. Sara saw him coming and came to greet him.

"How did you know I needed boots?" she said, smiling at him as she swung open the gate of a small corral.

"How did you know I needed help for my horse?" he replied with a laugh.

It was a trade easily done. Sara provided the leather for a pair of boots, and Bootjack provided the labor. While she examined his mare, he leaned over the fence and launched into his latest news.

"I just came back from Palanthas," he said, shaking his head. "The place just isn't the same since that sorcerer came in and leveled the Tower of High Sorcery. Can you believe that?"

It wasn't a real question, Sara knew. Bootjack rarely gave his listeners time to make a reply. He launched into a long recital of the city's woes from the dropping population and shrinking trade to the disappearance of the books from the Great Library of the Ages and the destruction of the Tower of High Sorcery.

"Many of the temples are empty, too," the cobbler said, shaking his shaggy head. "A few clerics hold out, but with the magic gone and the gods vanished, most don't feel it's worth the effort." He clicked his tongue loudly, drew a small flask out of his vest, and took a long swallow to lubricate his dry throat.

"That big, evil-sucking dragon doesn't help either. He's lurking up there in the north, scaring off the locals, and giving the shipping fits. I hear tell he's spreading the northern wasteland farther and farther south. Some say he's just waiting to pounce on Palanthas."

Sara ran her hands down the mare's leg. The well-trained animal calmly lifted her foot for Sara's inspection. Although the woman looked busy, her attention was focused almost entirely on Bootjack's words.

"Of course, that isn't the worst of it. I heard from some Dark Knights in the city a few stories that will curl your hair. That red beast of a dragon, Malystryx? She charred the Misty Isle. Burned everything to a crisp. Then last spring, I heard, she crossed over to the Dairly Plains. It's anyone's guess what she plans to do there."

"Sounds as if this dragon is more than just a rumor," Sara managed to say as she drew a hoof-pick from her belt and began to clean the mare's hoof. The news of the dragon was disheartening, but something else he had just said sent an electric spark sizzling through her mind.

Bootjack threw up his hands. "More than a rumor! I wish to the absent gods she was just a rumor. I heard tell she's bigger than Khellendros and twice as wicked. No one can stop her. And what if there are more like her? One of those knights I talked to said even Riverwind has gone to the Dairly Plains to see this dragon for himself."

Sara gently dropped the mare's hoof to the ground and straightened. There, he had said it again. Almost fearfully, she asked Bootjack, "You said 'Dark Knights' told you all of this. What knights? I thought all the Dark Knights had left Palanthas during the Summer of Chaos."

He started, surprised by her question. "What? Oh! Not really. A few Solamnics are there and some of the

Knights of Takhisis. They have an unspoken detente at the moment. Both groups stay out of sight and don't cause trouble." He paused and rubbed his whiskery cheek. "Come to think of it, things look to get a little tougher for the Solamnics. Seems I heard a rumor that most of the Knights of Takhisis are leaving Palanthas for Neraka."

Sara stiffened. Her hands tightened in the mare's stiff mane. "Why there?" she asked. Why at all? her mind thought.

"The Council of the Last Heroes gave the knighthood control of the area around Neraka, you know. Seems they may be regathering there."

Sara leaned against the mare's warm side and tried to stifle the sudden chill that settled in her stomach. "I thought they no longer existed as a group. Their leader is dead, their queen is gone. Most of their ranks were slaughtered." Despite her wish to sound casual, her voice rose higher with every word.

Bootjack lifted his skinny shoulders in a shrug. "Well, that's true enough. But there are a few still lurking around. In fact, I heard tell they have a new headquarters and are looking for recruits. Can you believe it?" He glanced at Sara and saw in surprise that she had turned as pale as milk. He patted his round belly, pleased he had spread some news that elicited such a response. It wasn't often he got to shock someone down to her bootstraps.

Sara didn't want to believe it. The world had suffered enough from the Knights of Takhisis. Let them stay dead and buried. And yet what if Bootjack was right? Could it be possible someone was reorganizing the dark knighthood?

The thought plagued Sara through the dinner she served Bootjack and remained with her for days afterward. Her mind roved far on the news she had heard, and she pondered its portent in her silent thoughts. She wondered if she should talk to Cobalt about her fears, then decided against it. She wanted to be certain of her facts before she brought up the subject. There would be time to talk to him later.

Six days after Bootjack dropped off her new boots, fetched his mare, and went whistling on his way, Sara dragged herself out of bed from another miserable night of internal debate and made a decision. Wearily she rode her horse back into the mountains to tell Cobalt her plans. She found the dragon absorbed in digging up a large tree for no more reason than he wanted the exercise. While he dug and tore at the roots and played in the dirt, she ran through her sword drills and tried to find the words that would explain her emotions without angering her friend.

It was hard enough trying to explain them to herself. She felt beset by a complicated welter of feelings about the Dark Knights—anger, resentment, frustration, intense dislike, even outrage that they would consider reforming their sinister organization. She firmly believed the knighthood should have died out with its founder, Lord Ariakan. But how could she explain all of this to a blue dragon, a servant of Takhisis?

Maybe—if the rumors were not true—she wouldn't have to.

When the tree finally crashed down and Cobalt stood over it like a triumphant gladiator, Sara laughed and put away her sword.

"Come talk to me," she said, wiping her forehead and sitting on a flat boulder.

Cobalt flopped down on the ground beside her. A coating of dirt and bark covered his legs and chest, and a branch with a few leaves still clinging dangled from his horns. He bent his neck to take a close look at her. "You look worried, Sara. What is bothering you?"

"I've heard some disquieting news," she said, each word deliberately slow. "I need to go to Palanthas for a few days to learn more."

"I shall go with you."

"No, not this time. I don't want you anywhere near Khellendros. I plan to go as a craftswoman to sell my weaving. If all goes well, I'll be back within two weeks."

The dragon's head dropped lower, and his eyelids slid halfway down to hood his golden eyes. "What is so important that it sends you across the mountains to Palanthas?"

"I have heard that the Knights of Takhisis may be regrouping in Neraka. I want to know for sure."

"Why? Surely you do not wish to rejoin them."

"I just have to know. For my own peace of mind." Sara decided not to say any more than that now. Once she knew the truth, she could decide how much of her feelings to tell him. It was possible he would take offense at her attitude and leave her. That possibility truly worried her. She had become quite used to his companionship and would miss him horribly if he left.

Cobalt's gaze locked into hers, and he studied her for a long time before he replied. "Be careful, Sara. If you are not back in two sevendays, I will come looking for you."

She nodded, her heart grateful for his concern. "You be careful, too. No stealing cows while I'm gone. And stay out of sight." She reached up and scratched his eye ridges gently. "I'll miss you," she added in a voice barely above a whisper.

He crouched on his belly and watched her mount the old horse for the ride back down the trail. He continued to stare at the spot long after she had ridden out of sight.

"I'll miss you, too," he said sadly.

Chapter 7

Sara packed carefully for her trip to Palanthas. The rugs, shawls, scarves, cloth, and wall hangings she had woven and saved for several years were brought out of her loft, shaken out, and folded into the horse panniers she borrowed from a neighbor. Seven days of trail food was added to the baskets, as well as several changes of clothing. She topped one pannier with her cloak and a blanket and filled the other with a nose bag, an extra halter, and a bag of grain for the horse.

She debated taking her sword before she realized that it was simply her nervousness trying to influence her. No mere weaver would have a sword among her belongings. She contented herself with her short hunting bow, a dagger at her belt, and a second long, slim blade tucked into the calf of her new boot.

Dawn had not yet lightened the sky when Sara loaded the panniers on the horse and left her cottage. Although it was early and she had slept little, she didn't want to be distracted by curious villagers or farmers needing help with an animal. She just wanted to get moving and finish this trip as soon as possible.

Unfortunately, while Palanthas was due east of Connersby as the dragon flies, there was no direct land route from the village over the mountains to the city. Sara had to go north to Daron, then take the trail southeast past the iron mines and on to Palanthas. It was a dangerous trip for a woman alone, but Sara hoped to find other travelers in Daron who would not mind another person joining their group.

She reached the port town by evening and found an inn on the outskirts near the trail to Palanthas. The inn, named the Widow's Walk, was a large, prosperous establishment befitting a town as busy as Daron. It was owned by a woman—the widow, Sara imagined—who kept it well. The stables were clean, the inn courtyard was neat, and the long, tall building was in good repair.

Sara decided to splurge on a room. If there were travelers leaving for the city, this would be a good place to find them. She left her horse in the care of a young lad and paid extra to store her packs.

The common room was busy—another good sign— filled with local fishermen, sailors, merchants, a few local farmers, and a group of dwarves. Most of the customers were engrossed in their own food and conversation. Only a few looked her way when Sara entered.

That was to Sara's liking. She had deliberately dressed in a plain, drab skirt and tunic to ensure her presence was not memorable. Her silver hair had been rolled into a bun, topped by a loose hat; her dagger was tucked out of sight under a voluminous vest. Her face was pleasant, but at her age, not enough beauty remained to attract casual eyes.

After a few words with the lady innkeeper, she learned what she wanted to know. A party of merchants was leaving for Palanthas in the morning. When she approached the men dining near the fireplace, they eyed her up and down for a mere moment and nodded agreement. For a small fee, she could join their party.

Sara was satisfied. The fee was not exorbitant and was only to be expected. The merchants had five armed guards traveling with them and a train of pack animals. Few bandits or lone ogres would dare attack a party that large.

They left the Widow's Walk after breakfast in a long, noisy caravan and took the trail into the rugged Vingaard Mountains. The trail, while not a maintained high road, had been traveled enough to be fairly wide and, on the lower slopes of the mountains at least, easily negotiated. The morning was cool and rainy, and the towering peaks of the range stayed veiled behind clouds of mist.

Leading her horse, Sara stayed in the rear of the caravan with several other hangers-on and the servants.

That night the rain blew itself out and a stiff wind dried the trail. The sun rose into a brilliantly clear sky at dawn and turned the snow on the high peaks into dazzling mantles of purest white.

The merchant train found its stride in the following days, and to Sara's relief, the miles fell quickly behind her. Three days out of Daron, the caravan crossed over the pass and began the downward descent toward the Bay of Branchala. Five days out, the caravan topped the last ridge and wove down the steep road into the broad sheltered basin of Palanthas. She drew aside at the top of the trail to let the others pass. Her eyes followed the long line of pack animals down the switchbacks to the valley below and her gaze filled with the walls and towers and buildings that once had been the shining center of Solamnia.

The rays of the late afternoon sun touched the rooftops of the sprawling city and illuminated the streets Sara had known well so many years ago. The light sparkled on the waters of the bay where the docks bustled with activity. It gleamed on the windows of the great palace in the center of the city and it gilded the walls of the massive Great Library of the Ages.

Sara knew the city had suffered damage from the backlash of energy from the Abyss that opened in the ocean to the north. From the looks of things, much of the obvious damage had been cleared away or repaired, leaving just a few razed streets along the bay and some tumbled ruins in abandoned lots.

Only one obvious landmark was missing from her view of the city, and its absence glared like a wound on unprotected skin. The awe-inspiring black Tower of High Sorcery, with its bloody minarets and its fearsome Shoikan Grove, was gone, wiped from the face of Palanthas in one horrifying stroke. No one knew exactly what caused the disaster or what happened to the tower and its contents. All that remained was a pool of a shining obsidian substance and an echoing emptiness.

"Better not stand there all night," someone called to her. "The shops close at six chimes, and the city guards still impose a limited curfew."

Sara tugged her weary horse into a walk and trod the final distance into the city.

The chimes, hanging in the clock tower in the Temple of Paladine, were just ringing six when Sara left the merchants' caravan and strode into the city on her own. Six strikes from the clock marked the end of the business day in Palanthas and were accompanied by much slamming of shutters and locking of doors and bustling about in the streets.

It had been a long time since Sara had been in Palanthas, and she walked slowly to see everything, pleased to be back in the city. With no real destination in mind, she simply wandered where chance took her. Old memories assailed her, memories of Steel as a small boy walking hand in hand with her through these very streets. She remembered his dark, curly head and his vivid gaze and the rapt attention he gave to the stories she used to tell about knights and honor and courage.

With the good memories came the bad ones, too: her growing fear that Kitiara would come to claim her son, the grief she felt over the battling darkness she saw in Steel's soul, the terror of the fires in the city that destroyed their home. And worst of all, she remembered that dark night when Steel was twelve years old when the black riders appeared at her door and Lord Ariakan lured Steel into his evil order.

Sara shivered with a cold that was not in the air. In her mind's eye, she saw again the cold visage of the dark lord and the determined, proud face of her son. She had begged and pleaded and cried for him to stay, but Steel was entranced by the promises of Ariakan and determined to go. Sara felt her eyes burn with unshed tears. The passersby around her faded into a blur of colors and distant movement.

She had tried everything, and finally all she won was the chance to accompany him to Storm's Keep. For her, it may as well have been a prison. For years, she cooked and cared for Ariakan's recruits and trained his dragons, and when he desired, Ariakan took her to his bed. The only things that kept her going through those long, brutal years were Steel and the dragons.

Then, just before he was to take his final vows, she violated the knighthood's Code by kidnapping Steel and trying to turn him back to the light. Her plan did not work, and she lost him at last.

Sara stopped so abruptly that her horse bumped into her back. Fiercely she wiped her eyes with her sleeve to erase the evidence of her pain. Those years were long over, she told herself. There was nothing left worth crying about.

She forced herself to move again. She didn't want to stand around all night like a lost child. Without conscious thought, her feet carried her through the streets past the gatehouse in the Old City Wall and into the older section of Palanthas. Lights flickered in many houses around her as night settled over the city. Before her thoughts had caught up with the present, Sara found herself standing by the edge of a wide expanse of green lawn that flowed comfortably, like an invitation, toward an elegant building built of white marble. Sara recognized it immediately: the Temple of Paladine.

A slow smile spread over her face. She had been to this temple before to give thanks for salvation, and once or twice to find Steel. There was a bench, a marble seat, he had loved. It used to sit . . . over there, under a tree. Sara could not see it in the dark, but she knew where it should be.

Leading the horse, she walked across the smooth, grassy lawn to the aspen tree she remembered and tied the horse to the gray trunk. The stone bench still sat there, unchanged, unmoved by the years that had passed.

Weary with the ache of her memories, Sara sank down on the cool stone. Her hand touched the back of the bench and felt the outline of the frieze carved into the marble. It was that simple, rather crude carving that Steel had liked so much, perhaps because of the simplicity of emotions it portrayed.

Nothing in Steel Brightblade's life had been simple—not his birth, not his childhood, not his maturity. From the moment of his birth, he had been torn by the conflicting desires represented by his blood mother, the Dragon Highlord Kitiara Uth Matar, and by his father, the Solamnic Knight and hero Sturm Brightblade.

Sara saw the struggle of the light and the dark in his soul every hour of every day. She did not know what happened that last day when Steel met the god Chaos and died; she only hoped that by then her beloved child had found his peace.

Her fingers lightly traced the outlines of the carving that portrayed the funeral of a knight. The frieze pictured the knight lying on a bier, his arms folded across his chest. His shield leaned against the side of the bier. Twelve knightly escorts stood on either side of the knight's body, every one stern and solemn.

Steel had never told her what he saw in those simple images, but Sara guessed it was the honor paid the dead knight, the courage implicit in his life, and the peace of his death—things she hoped Steel found for himself in the Battle of the Rift.

Sara smiled to herself in the darkness, a sad, slow smile of remembering.

Her horse by the aspen snorted in alarm and lunged back against his rope. The tree swayed, showering Sara with bits of bark and a few twigs.

A voice, cool and pleasant, said, "Good evening. We did not mean to startle you."

Sara raised her head and saw two figures standing in the darkness, perhaps ten paces away. There was just enough starlight for her to see that one was a handsome man of indeterminate age and solid build. The other was a woman, slender, elegant, as beautiful and enduring as the temple itself.

Sara recognized the woman immediately, the Revered Daughter Crysania, High Priestess of the Temple of Paladine, leader of the god's faithful on Ansalon. The other she had never seen before. Sara rushed to her feet and hurried to her horse's head, too embarrassed to speak.

The old bay jerked on his rope, his eyes rolling white with nervousness.

The man bent toward his fair companion and spoke softly in her ear. She nodded, leaning into his support with warm familiarity.

"Forgive us for startling you," the priestess said to Sara. "So few come to the temple anymore. I was pleased to know someone was making use of our grounds. It is getting late. Is there anything I can do for you?"

Sara hesitated, unsure of what to say.

Crysania stood, waiting patiently, her hand lightly resting on the man's arm. Her eyes, blind to the world of men, gazed sightlessly into the darkness. "My friend says you are a woman, and I hear your light step and the rustle of your skirts. Do I know you?"

"Not well, Revered Daughter," Sara said faintly. "I met you once or twice many years ago when I lived here with my adopted son. My name is Sara."

Lady Crysania spoke softly to her companion, who inclined his head. He smiled at her, then kissed her hand and walked away, leaving the two women alone in the darkness. The priestess walked to the stone bench, found the edge with her fingers, and sat down. She gestured for Sara to join her.

Closer now, Sara could see how little Crysania had changed since she saw the priestess for the first time nearly twenty years ago. Her hair was still black, netted in silver, with little gray to mark the passage of years. Her pale skin, though etched by the trials of her past, remained ageless, as enduring as the marble of the temple.

Sara sat down on the edge of the bench. She wasn't afraid, but she felt uncomfortable, almost guilty, to be sitting so close to the High Priestess of Paladine's temple. While she had never accepted the precepts of Takhisis or taken the blood oath, she had served Lord Ariakan for years and still carried the uncleanliness of those years in her soul. Although Paladine was gone, Sara couldn't help but feel the blessedness of his temple and the grace of his cleric, and she wondered what Crysania would think if she knew Sara's past.

"What brought you to these grounds, to this particular bench?" asked Lady Crysania softly.

The thought of lying to the priestess never crossed Sara's mind. "Memories. My son, my adopted son, used to come here to sit on this bench. He would sit and daydream. . . ." Her voice tapered off.

Sara caught a glint of a smile on the lady's face. "I know you now," Crysania said. "You were the mother of Steel Brightblade. Sara . . . Sara Dunstan." She hesitated, her sight turned inward. "Steel came here that horrible summer. He and Palin Majere." She laughed quietly, her voice musical. "They did not intend to. They were looking for the Tower of High Sorcery."

Sara tried to stifle a gasp and failed. She leaned forward, eager to hear more. "Why the tower?"

"You don't know?"

"I know very little of Steel's last five years, Revered Daughter," Sara replied, the regret obvious in her words. "After I . . . failed him, he took the oath of the dark knighthood, and for both our sakes, he did not try to contact me again."

The priestess smiled, her expression warm and comforting. "You did not fail him. Nor he us."

Sara stiffened. "How do you know?"

Crysania laid a hand over Sara's cold fingers. "I have listened and learned much since that night Steel was here, and I have come to the realization that what Steel did in the Abyss was not for Takhisis or Paladine, but because he felt it was the right thing to do. And that, I think, he got from you."

Sara sat stiff and silent. She had never learned the details of Steel's death, only that he had died a hero. Her tears, already close to the surface, brimmed over her eyes and slid silently down her cheeks. "Tell me," she whispered.

The priestess's fingers tightened over Sara's, and she began to tell her about the night Steel and Palin made their way to the Shoikan Grove and the Tower of High Sorcery. "Palin was Steel's prisoner, and for his ransom, he was to take Steel to the tower and open the Abyss." With those words, Crysania took Sara through the terrible days of the Chaos War to the last day when the sun burned endlessly in the sky and the ocean boiled and a fearsome battle waged between the Father of All and of Nothing, his immortal godchildren, and the peoples of Krynn.

"Palin told me about that day. He said Steel and a few of his men were the only survivors of Lord Ariakan's mighty force left at the ruins of the High Clerist's Tower. They joined a remnant of Solamnic Knights and flew their dragons to the rift to challenge Chaos, knowing this battle would be their last." She felt Sara move slightly and she paused, waiting for her companion to speak.

"He died the way he wanted to," Sara murmured. Deep in melancholy, she swallowed hard against her tight, dry throat and whispered, "If only I could do the same."

Crysania turned her sightless eyes to her companion's face. Her inner sight, sharpened by years of struggle, looked beyond Sara's words to the recesses of her heart. "You do not wish to die. It is not in you."

Sara shifted her shoulders in a slight motion of denial. "I feel so empty. Since Steel died, there has been nothing for me to believe in."

"Perhaps you are not ready yet to accept something else. Keep your mind open. Even without the gods, things have a way of working out."

Sara barely nodded.

The two women sat silently together in the darkness, each examining her own thoughts. Behind them, the old horse had finally settled down. He whiffled his nostrils and shifted his weight from one hind leg to the other. To the east, the single pale moon shed its silvery light on the tops of the eastern peaks.

"Lady," said Sara after a while, "I came to Palanthas to learn the truth about a rumor I heard concerning the Knights of Takhisis. Perhaps you know. Are they regrouping?"

Crysania turned a troubled face to Sara and replied, "I've heard those rumors, too. Those and more. But I cannot say for a certainty that they are true. The Council of the Last Heroes did grant the knights control of the land around Neraka, and I know some Dark Knights have been leaving Palanthas to go there. It is probably the only safe place left for them these days. Beyond that, I do not know. Perhaps," she added with a half-smile, "someone should go to Neraka to find out."

"Perhaps," Sara echoed faintly.

"But for now—" Lady Crysania rose, "—let me offer you the hospitality of our house. There is room for your horse in the stable and ample room for you in our guesthouse. Many rooms in our temple buildings stand empty now. Do not feel you are putting anyone out."

"Thank you, Revered Daughter," Sara said gratefully. "I will accept."

The priestess rose gracefully to her feet and waited while Sara untied the horse and patted his neck. Unerringly she led Sara and her horse across the temple grounds to the rear, where the stable, kitchen, and dormitories were located. There she bade Sara good night and left her in the care of an elderly cleric.

* * * * *

Sara spent eight more days in the city by the bay. She found a booth to rent in the market district and set up her wares to sell. Although the quality was good and the craftsmanship excellent, people were not buying luxury items readily.

Bootjack was right, Sara quickly discovered. Palanthas was not quite the same. Too many people had left or died; too many businesses had closed. Because the great library was virtually empty and the temples were redundant without gods to serve, the influx of visitors, students, and those seeking work in the city had slowed to a trickle. Without a growing population to support the economy, the city's treasury, already strained by the war and expensive repairs to the docks and major buildings, was running low. People were cautious, careful of their money and their words.

Nevertheless, Sara stuck with her intentions. By day, she opened her booth, and while she had to drop some of her prices, she slowly sold all but a few items. In the evenings, she went from one inn to another, to taverns and public parks, to the docks and the playhouses, listening and asking guarded questions to garner any bit of information she could about the Knights of Takhisis. Here, she had little success. Few people wanted to talk about the Dark Knights. Mostly she heard complaints and bitter accusations levied against the occupation force that had held the city until the Battle of the Rift or against individual knights who had turned to banditry and murder since then. No one seemed to know or care if the knights were re-forming in Neraka.

Eight days after she arrived in Palanthas, Sara realized with a start of disappointment that she had been gone thirteen days. She had promised Cobalt she would be back in fourteen; now she would be late, and there was no telling how he would react. She wasn't certain whether to be discouraged or relieved at her lack of information. Was no news good news? Or were the knights keeping their dark secrets carefully hidden?

That evening she closed her booth and packed her belongings in the panniers. She knew it would be safer to leave Palanthas with a caravan again, but she couldn't find any merchants or travelers who were leaving for Daron the next day. She made up her mind to go anyway and hope she could find someone on the trail.

Early the next morning, with Crysania's blessings and a stocked food bag, Sara led her horse out of Palanthas and hurried north on the trail for home.

Chapter 8

A cold, blustery wind swept up the mountain trail, sweeping golden aspen leaves and dust before it. Sara put up with it for a few hours, then changed out of her skirts into a pair of durable pants that were not only warmer but also easier to wear on the steep slopes. With her hair braided under her loose knit hat and a heavy cloak over her tunic, she looked more like a man than a woman.

She had seen no one else that day but a few shepherds with their flocks in the distance and a small party of travelers trekking south to Palanthas. There was no one in sight going north. Sara mentally shrugged and pushed on. Cobalt was waiting, and she didn't want to worry the dragon into doing something stupid.

The day passed uneventfully, and Sara found a sheltered place to camp for the night. She passed the iron mines the following day, and still she found no other travelers heading toward Daron.

Except for the possibility of danger from thieves and highwaymen, Sara actually preferred solitary travel. She liked picking her own pace suitable to her horse and herself; she liked the dust-free air and the tranquility of the mountains, without shouting drovers, bellowing beasts of burden, complaining merchants, and whining servants. She did not have to carry on meaningless conversations with companions she did not like or waste endless time waiting for the caravan to get ready to move. The only thing she missed was the time spent by the camp-fires at night, when instruments were inevitably brought out and musicians played rollicking tunes for hours to enliven the cold mountain nights.

She crossed the pass safely during an afternoon of gathering clouds and gusty winds, and that night a light snow began to fall. Snow was still falling in the morning when Sara packed her gear and fed her horse. She eyed the sky warily, for no one in her right mind wanted to be caught on the open mountain trails in an autumn snow-storm. Fortunately the clouds seemed tattered and the wind brisk, leading her to hope the snow showers would end soon.

She filled her water bag from a nearby stream and loaded one of the panniers with dry firewood from a sheltered deadfall. If she were forced to stop somewhere unprotected, she wanted to be prepared. Clucking to her horse, she headed down the mountain.

The snow did end soon, several times. It was one of those days when the sky was a swiftly moving panorama of brilliant sun and dark clouds and intermit-tent showers of sparkling snow. Cloud shadows scud-ded over the mountain faces, pushed by a capricious cold wind.

A snow shower had just ended, as abruptly as it began, when the hairs on Sara's neck began to prickle in that uncanny warning she well remembered. Someone was watching her.

Sara's head went up, and her eyes moved along the stony slopes around her. She was walking on an open section of the trail that hugged the side of the hill. There were no trees or large stone outcroppings for cover. There was nowhere she could hide, and nowhere anyone else could hide to ambush her. Yet she still felt the pres-ence of someone close by.

Her pulse quickened. Her right hand slid closer to her bow that hung from one of the panniers. She kept walking beside the horse, trying to look casual, as if she had no hint of danger. The sun burst out of the clouds at that moment, its bright light dazzling after the snow squall.

Something moved to Sara's right. She spun around in time to see a patch of snowy grass and vines suddenly thrown aside to reveal a hole dug in the earth. A man in dirty armor burst out of the hole and lunged at her, a sword in his hand. He was too close for her to use her bow, so Sara snatched her dagger from its sheath, and before the man could lay a hand on her, she flipped off her cloak and slid beyond his reach. Her reflexes may have slowed from age, but her speed and her balance were finely tuned from years of practice.

Her attacker, expecting slow, easy prey, met instead a furious dagger-wielding opponent. His heavily bearded face registered surprise. Then he sneered and moved in to disarm her. Pulling his lips back over broad, yellow teeth, he raised the blade of his sword and brought it whistling around to strike her arm.

Sara heard shouts behind her from several directions, and she realized she needed more than a mere dagger to defend herself. Instead of ducking her assailant, she slipped under his blade, dipped her shoulder, and crashed into his belly. He grunted in surprise. His sword whistled over her head.

Her blade slipped under his armpit, where the breastplate ended, and rammed deep into his flesh and muscle. Sara wrenched it out and stabbed again. The man howled with pain.

Sara rolled over him as he crashed to the earth, then bounced to her feet, snatched the sword from his weakened grasp, and spun on her heel to meet the other attackers.

There were three more, all as lean and hungry as wolves, all dressed in ill-kept armor. Shocked by the fall of their comrade, they slunk forward, studying Sara warily.

"Look," one of them shouted in surprise. "It's a woman!"

Sara dodged behind her horse and grinned wickedly at the men. Her hat had been knocked off in the struggle with the first brigand, and now her braid swung loose like a silver horse's tail.

The old bay, panicked by the shouts and the smell of blood, reared in fright. One of the men tried to grab his headstall, but the gelding whipped his head aside and bolted away down the trail. Sara was left facing the three men.

They slid to a stop and slowly edged around her until she was surrounded.

"Come on, be a good girl and give us that sword," the shortest man wheedled.

Sara glared at the men, her eyes narrowed, her lungs breathing hard. Their armor was rusty and dirty and badly dented, but beneath the grime, she could make out the death lily, the emblem of the Knights of Takhisis.

"Swine," she hissed. "Groveling in dirt for those lilies you wear. How many backs did you stab to get those?" She rose on the balls of her feet and crouched forward, her bloodied dagger in one hand, the sword in the other. Her blade sliced the air to keep the men at a distance.

Two of the men laughed. The third, a tall, dark-haired half-elf, studied her moves with a sense of growing recognition. He was about to say something when a shadow passed over their heads.

Everyone looked up simultaneously. A powerful downdraft abruptly smote them all, and a ferocious roar reverberated in the air. Blue wings sailed overhead.

"Cobalt!" Sara cried in delight.

The blue dragon roared again. His teeth snapping, he dropped like a sapphire fury out of the sky and landed with an earth-shuddering thud beside Sara. The three men were too terrified to move. With a snarl, he snatched the shorter man in his front talons. He tore the man to shreds with tooth and claw, then grabbed at a second. He was about to rend that man, too, when Sara cried, "Wait, Cobalt!"

The red fire faded from his eyes. Keeping his prey pinned under his claw, he lifted his muzzle at her command. Blood dripped from his jaws onto his panicked victim, who screamed once and promptly fainted.

The third brigand, the half-elf, stared at Sara in shocked realization. He saluted almost frantically. "My lady, we had no idea you were a dragon rider."

Sara tossed her attacker's sword on the ground. She wiped her dagger on the wounded man's pant leg and thrust it back in her belt before she bothered to answer. The action was meant to look cold and commanding, but Sara also wanted a moment to find her voice and still the trembling of her hands.

"You didn't exactly take the time to ask," she said frostily. "If you had, I would have told you I am Knight Officer Sara Conby." It was a slight exaggeration, but it made the brigand's eyes bulge.

"We didn't think . . ." the half-elf stammered. "I mean, we never guessed you . . ."

Sara sneered. "You didn't think. Well, who else would travel the mountain trails alone but someone quite capable of dealing with scum like you! What are you doing up here? Is this any way for Knights of the Lily to behave?"

"Yes, Knight Officer. I mean, no. We're going to Neraka to rejoin our order. But we had no supplies or transport, and winter's coming. We thought a few travelers here and there would get us enough food and coins to go south."

A bolt of anger and hatred shot through her and, in spite of herself, flicked across her face. She quickly drew her brows together before the man caught her expression. "Neraka? I have not heard of anything happening there. I have been hiding my dragon in the mountains.

We do not hear news often."

The half-elf, eager to please, plunged on. "Yes, my lady. We heard through our sources in Palanthas that the general has put out a call to all surviving knights to come to Neraka. There are plans to rebuild the order. The city is safe for us because the knights rule there. You and your dragon would be welcome. Come with us. We would be glad for your company."

I bet you would, Sara thought sourly. Glad for the dragonfear spread by Cobalt that would help you murder and steal your way to Neraka. Keeping her face impassive, she merely said, "Who is this general you speak of?"

"General Mirielle Abrena, my lady. She has taken over command of the order since Lord Ariakan's death. She plans to restore the power of the knighthood." Sara felt Cobalt move abruptly, as if startled. The name was not familiar to Sara. Perhaps Cobalt knew. Not that it was important. She had at last the verbal confirmation she wanted.

Suddenly Sara felt stone cold all the way to the core of her being. All she wanted to do now was go home. "I have things I must deal with here before I leave," she said, her tone short and brittle. "Perhaps I will see you in Neraka."

The half-elf bobbed his head and practically bowed. "We apologize, Knight Officer, for the inconvenience."

Sara jerked her head toward the wounded man groaning on the ground. "You will have plenty of time to consider your actions while you deal with your comrades." She laid a hand on Cobalt's forearm and said to the dragon, "Let him go."

The dragon rumbled deep in his throat and let the man drop several feet to the ground.

She climbed up Cobalt's leg to his shoulders and carefully sat down on his back. Her perch felt very precarious without a dragon saddle to hold her on the thick scales. "Go easy," she whispered. "I don't want to fall off in front of them."

Cobalt obeyed. Instead of springing upward, he took two running leaps downhill, unfurled his wings and glided smoothly into the air. He soared down the mountainside until he caught a weak thermal that lifted him higher into the sky. He curved gently around and slowly flapped his wings until he was following the trail down the mountain.

"See if you can find the horse," Sara suggested wearily. Now that the fight was over and the men were lost from sight, she felt her energy drain away. She leaned forward, threw her arms around Cobalt's neck, and hugged him tightly. "I forgot to say hello. And thank you. And what are you doing here?"

"You also forgot something else. You are late!" admonished the dragon. "You said fourteen days. It's been seventeen. And look what happens?" He snorted in disgust, wisps of steam flying from his nostrils. "I can't let you go anywhere without me!"

Sara laughed. It felt wonderful to be on his back and to know he had worried about her.

"There he is," Cobalt said, and he glided downward toward a wide patch of grass near the trail. There stood the old bay, head down, his sides heaving. He barely flinched when the dragon landed nearby.

Sara slid off and hurried to the old horse's side. His coat was slick with sweat; steam rose from his heaving flanks. She ran her hands down his legs and was relieved to see he had not hurt himself. He was just exhausted. She threw one of her blankets over him so he wouldn't cool too quickly, then she gently urged him back on the trail. He had to walk out his sweat or he would founder.

Cobalt looked on with ill-concealed impatience. "Do we have to take that old bag of bones back? It will take forever. Couldn't I just eat him? I can carry your gear."

Sara threw a frown at him and vehemently shook her head. "You will not eat this horse. He is my friend. If you are hungry, go find an elk or a few deer." She curled a lip and pointed to the blood splattered on his chest from the man he had killed. "And while you're at it, find a lake and wash that off. We will follow this trail, so it will be easy to see us when you're finished."

"All right, I will. It took me a long time to find you, and I am very hungry."

Sara grinned and waved him away. She had no fear that he would go far.

Cobalt came back within the hour, sucking bits off his teeth and looking very satisfied with himself. He flew in low, lazy circles over Sara's head until she found a place to camp for the night.

By that time, the bay horse had cooled and rested enough to want to graze. Sara hobbled him in a sheltered nook by a rock wall where enough grass had escaped the early frosts to satisfy his appetite. She built a fire close to a low overhang and cooked her supper.

Cobalt stretched out where he could watch her, his yellow eyes half-lidded. "Did you find what you wanted to know?" he asked after a while.

"Yes. And no."

"That's helpful."

Sara sighed, her gaze on the hot flames of her fire. "Yes, I learned that the rumors I had heard were true, but I do not know how accurate they are and how far the truth extends."

"And do you need to know that, too?"

She lifted her face to meet the dragon's unblinking gaze. She knew full well what that mission would entail, and the thought scared her silly. "I'm not sure yet," she answered truthfully, then she asked him a question. "Did you recognize the name of Mirielle Abrena?"

A sneer pulled back Cobalt's lips. His horns pressed flat on his head, a sure sign of his disapproval. "She commanded the wing in Northern Ergoth where Vincit and I were sent. As soon as word reached us that Lord Ariakan was dead and the Battle of the Rift was over, she took her personal staff and left the rest of us to fend for ourselves." There was a bitter rumble of resentment in his voice.

"She is ambitious," Sara mused.

Cobalt snorted. "She is dangerous." He bent his head down closer to Sara. "Are you thinking of going to Neraka?"

"I don't know."

"When you decide, you tell me, because I will not let you go away again without me. I have lost one friend and rider. I will not lose another."

Sara did not reply. She could not. No words could escape past the tightness in her throat. She banked her fire for the night, collected her blanket, and settled down against the dragon's warm side to sleep. That was all the answer he needed.

Sara felt stiff and sore the next morning, the result, she knew, of not practicing with her sword for two weeks and sleeping on the ground. The old bay did not feel much better. His gallop down the trail was the most exercise he had had in years. Together they walked gingerly along the trail until their muscles grew limber and the sun warmed their backs.

Cobalt huffed and grumbled at the delay, then he went off to hunt.

His departure was most propitious, for as soon as he was out of sight, a party of travelers from Daron appeared at the top of a hill. Sara pulled off the trail and waited for them to pass.

There were five, four men and a young woman, bound for Palanthas—to visit family, they told Sara. They waved to her and remarked on the fact that she was traveling alone.

She just grinned and warned them to watch out for thieves. But their presence on the trail reminded her that it would not be safe for Cobalt to fly about the mountains in broad daylight. While a few travelers could not hurt him, news could spread to the wrong ears, including those of Khellendros. She had heard in Palanthas that the huge blue was killing dragons of all colors in the territory he considered his, and she did not want Cobalt's skull added to his pile.

When the blue returned, she insisted they stop and travel only at night. Cobalt irritably asked again if he could eat the horse.

Instead of getting angry, Sara just patted the smooth scales of his neck. "I lost one dragon when Flare left me," she said. "I do not want to lose you."

Cobalt backed down and did not grumble again the rest of the journey home.

It took Sara three more days to lead the old bay home, traveling at night and skirting around Daron to avoid any confrontations between humans and the dragon. During those nights, she had ample time to think about the Knights of Takhisis and the news she had heard.

The thought that the order was rebuilding bothered her far more than she thought it would. She believed the world had suffered enough injustice and cruelty and evil at the hands of the Dark Knights. Now that Krynn was entering a new age, Sara did not want to accept the possibility that the Knights of Takhisis could have an important place in it. Their influence was dead; let it stay dead! she thought over and over.

So, what if the brigands were right, that a new, ambitious general had taken over the knighthood and was planning to restore it to its former power? Was she as strong and capable as Lord Ariakan? Or was she simply a usurper who would topple in short order? Were there enough knights left to make this attempt successful?

Someone should go, Crysania's words echoed in Sara's thoughts. Someone should go see what was going on.

But Sara's mind rebelled. "I can't," she said to the horse plodding by her side. "I have a new life now. I have responsibilities and friends. I have a home where people need me, a house and garden that need tending. The potatoes should be dug before a freeze. My loom must be restrung. I can't go back among the knights. If just one of them recognized me, they'd kill me. I am too old. I couldn't pull it off."

The old horse just flicked an ear at her and kept quiet.

But if her horse was quiet, a small voice in her heart was not. Yes, such a journey to Neraka to investigate the knights would be dangerous, it told her. They could discover who she was; they could kill her as a spy or a traitor. But who else would be better to go than a woman who had spent ten years learning the original organization from bottom to top? If she could keep her wits about her and no one recognized her, there was no reason the knights would be suspicious of her. She could slip into Neraka, blend in for a short while, learn all she could, and slip out again. She could take her information to the Solamnic Knights, if she could find them. Or maybe Caramon Majere would know whom to contact. It would take a few weeks at the most, if Cobalt flew her there and back. This could work, the little voice said. Someone should go.

Her internal debate lasted the entire trip home and for days after. She dug her potatoes and restrung her loom, tended the villager's animals, and took care of Cobalt, but her thoughts were always elsewhere, and even the most obtuse farmers noticed she was terribly distracted. Her friends tried to ask her what was wrong, but she refused to talk to anyone.

Then the inevitable happened. Someone spotted Cobalt in the mountains and brought the news back to the village. A shepherd had taken his dogs into the high hills to track a rogue wolf that had been killing his sheep. Instead of the wolf, he found dragon tracks and the scattered bones of deer, elk, and, to his horror, sheep. In the distance, on a high promontory, he saw the blue dragon sleeping in the sun. The shepherd was furious and scared and smart enough to know he needed help to rout the dragon out of the region. He called off his dogs and raced back to Connersby to sound the alarm. Word spread quickly, and the villagers began to gather near the village well to make their plans.

Sara heard the news that evening while she was putting a poultice on a cow's sore leg. It took every bit of her self-control to keep her voice bland and her hands from shaking. Quietly she tied the cloth that held the poultice and patted the cow's tan hip.

"You're coming, aren't you, Sara?" the farmer asked excitedly. "We're meeting to decide how to deal with the brute. We can't have the likes of that dragon lurking around here and eating our stock."

"No," she answered slowly, "you certainly can't."

Ignoring the farmer's curious gaze, Sara put her things back in the bag. "Change the poultice in the morning and keep the wound clean," she mumbled, and she walked out without another word.

She walked home lost in a daze of thoughts and emotions, and worry for the dragon. After the door closed behind her, she leaned against the cool wood and drew in a deep breath. Now there was no more time to debate or procrastinate. She had known somehow, from the instant Crysania spoke those words in the night, that she would eventually go to Neraka. All she needed was some impetus, a kick in the pants, to get her over the threshold of her fear. The danger to Cobalt—and the villagers she liked so much—was impetus enough.

She knelt by her clothes chest and dug down through the clothes and the linens to the hard bundle that lay at the bottom. It was heavy and cumbersome, and she dumped nearly all the contents of her chest on the floor before she hauled the package out and laid it on her bed. One after another, she untied the strings that held the bundle together. The covering fell away to reveal something deep blue trimmed with black fur. It was a cloak, a gift long ago from Lord Ariakan. She unwrapped the cape and pulled out several more items, laying them side by side. Gloves, a helm, boots, and leather breeches—the kit of a dragon rider.

One more item fell into her lap, a large brooch wrought in mother-of-pearl, another gift from the late, unlamented Lord Ariakan. Sara picked it up and turned it over in her hands, almost loath to touch its four gleaming petals. It was a black lily, the emblem of the Knights of Takhisis. She curled her lip and almost flung the brooch into the cold fireplace. But, no, it and the blue dragon could be her passport into Neraka. With deliberate care, she pinned the brooch to the blue-black cloak and began to pack.

Chapter 9

Her gear was ready. Her cottage was barred and prepared for winter. If all went well, Sara thought, she would come back in a month or two after the furor over the dragon died down in the village. She would find a new cave for Cobalt and let her life return to normal. Everything would be all right.

So why did she feel like she was lying to herself?

She loaded her packs, her weapons, and the dragon saddle on the bay and hurried him up the trail behind her cottage into the trees. Dusk had turned to dark night, for clouds obscured the sky, but Sara knew the trail so well she didn't need extra illumination. Her feet followed the familiar contours of the trail without mishap, and in just a few short hours, she and the horse entered the clearing before the cave.

"Cobalt!" she called to warn him of her presence.

Silence met her cry. She peered in through the entrance and sensed the cave was empty. Cobalt was not there.

Impatiently she unpacked the horse, stacking her gear close to the cave. The dragon would be back soon; he was probably out hunting—she hoped. As soon as the horse was unloaded, she removed his harness and the lead rope, leaving only the halter. A quick slap on the rump sent him trotting toward home. The old bay knew the trail so well, she had no doubt he would make his way back to the cottage, where someone was bound to find him. That done, she sat down to wait for Cobalt.

Her wait was a long one. It was just past dawn when Sara heard the rush of wind in dragon wings and looked up to see the familiar shape of the blue wheeling down to land in the clearing. He rumbled happily to see her.

At that same moment, she heard unmistakably the distant keen of a hunting horn.

"Oh, bleeding moons!" she snapped. "Cobalt! Where have you been?"

Ignoring the horn and the urgent tones of Sara's voice, Cobalt carried something under his forearm into the cave. There came the sound of digging and stones being moved.

Sara strode into the cave, her gray eyes flashing. "Cobalt! We must leave, now! What are you doing?" In the deep gloom of the cave, she could see nothing, but she could hear the dragon industriously digging in the far end of the cavern. "You're burying something." Her voice was an accusation.

"Just a few little things I picked up from some hill dwarves," he muttered.

There was no time to argue this. Sara strode forward and grabbed the first part of his anatomy she reached, his blunt tail, and tugged hard. "Cobalt, if you have a stash here already, fine. I don't care. Just bury it well. We will be gone from here for a while."

The dragon paused, for her worry had reached him at last. "Why?"

"There are people from my village coming to look for you. I don't want them hurt."

"Where are we going?"

"Neraka," she replied flatly.

Cobalt's eyes gleamed gold in the darkness. "Why?"

Sara was exasperated. "Is that all you can ask?"

"I want to know. You've been stewing over Neraka for days."

Sara tried to sort through the jumble of her feelings,

and it was out of the jumble, not from any reasoning process, that she said, "Because I have to."

What the dragon made of that he did not say. He only shoved the dirt back in his hole, tossed on a few rocks, and trampled it all down. Then he nudged Sara out the opening.

For the moment, they said nothing more, postponing for a breathing space anything else that needed to be said. Sara hurriedly harnessed the dragon saddle to Cobalt's back and strapped on her packs.

In the quiet of the coming morning, they heard clearly the bay of dogs and the muffled shouts of approaching men.

She donned her cloak and gloves and, without further hesitation, pulled the helm down over her silver hair. It was time to go. Cobalt bent his foreleg to help her up, and she swiftly climbed into the saddle.

As soon as she was strapped in, his powerful hind legs thrust them up into the cold, clear air. His translucent wings unfurled, blue sails against a cerulean sky.

The sun lifted above the eastern peaks just in time to gild his scales with pale gold. He gleamed like a blue diamond caught in a beam of light.

From below came more shouts and angry cries. Sara glanced down and saw several dozen men running through the trees below. They carried flails and pitchforks, a few old swords, and bows. One man even had a lance. Sara knew they wouldn't have stood a chance against a dragon like Cobalt. She did not know whether to admire them for their courage and determination or laugh at their idiocy. Briefly she saluted them before the dragon carried her away out of sight.

They flew south for a time, paralleling the range of peaks in the Vingaard Mountains. The day was crisp, the air crystal clear, and the winds aloft were just strong enough to provide lift for Cobalt's wings—perfect flying weather. The blue stretched out his neck. He flattened his horns and reveled in the joy of flight.

Strangely, Sara was able to share in his pleasure. She had left her work, her home, her friends, and perhaps her future behind to face dark intrigue, evil, and dismal danger in the days ahead. And yet she felt relieved, almost excited. A terrible tension in her mind, one she had not even recognized, was gone, shattered with the strength of her final acceptance of her duty. This journey was right. She knew it with every fiber of her being, and if she died or failed in her attempt, at least she had made the effort and not languished in Connersby, always wondering if she should have.

Sara smiled to herself. Steel would have been proud of her actions whether or not he approved of her intentions.

She let Cobalt fly for most of the morning before she suggested he find a place to hide and rest.

He did not argue, since he was already tired from a night of hunting and chasing hill dwarves, and he banked down to a narrow canyon where a creek provided water and a cliff offered an overhang just large enough to shelter a blue dragon.

Sara cut some pine boughs for a bed and, weary from her long night, wrapped herself in her cloak and went to sleep. Nothing disturbed her, and she woke several hours after sunset feeling refreshed, if a little stiff from the unyielding ground.

Get used to it, she told herself. There was no telling what lay before her in the days ahead. To be honest, Sara did not know exactly what she planned to do when she reached Neraka. Ideally she wanted to hide on a high vantage point overlooking the city and just watch what was going on without stepping foot in its foul streets. When she had seen all there was to see, she and Cobalt could slip away unsuspected. That was the ideal.

But Sara knew from long experience that life was rarely ideal. Scouts or flying dragon guards could spot her; she and Cobalt could be captured, possibly executed as spies. And if she did not go into the city, she would miss a wealth of detailed information about the knights: their organization, their leaders, their strength, their plans.

Lord Ariakan had studied everything he could about the Solamnic Knights before he formed his own order for the Dark Queen. Know your enemy, he used to expound to his men, and his precepts had worked. The knights had been highly successful against the Solamnics—until the god of Chaos turned against them all.

Yet if she went into Neraka itself, there were dozens of new difficulties to think through. She had never been to Neraka before. What was it like? Could she get in undetected? If she was questioned, how would she explain her presence to the authorities? How would she get out? Should Cobalt go with her? Would he want to go?

When she asked the blue that question, he cocked his head to one side and repeated what he had told her earlier in the mountains near Daron. "I've already lost one rider. I do not want to lose another."

"Will you keep my identity secret from the other dragons?"

He huffed a cloud of steam. "Since they would kill you if they knew, of course I will." He thought of something else and added, "What if one of the older knights recognizes you?"

"I thought of that. I think a little change in appearance would not hurt."

"A disguise?"

"Nothing so obvious. Just a little alteration. Even eight years ago my hair was long and gray. People would remember something like that. So I'll try shorter and lighter." She dug into her pack for a small packet she had thrown in at the last moment. "Camomile and basil," she chuckled, throwing the packet into a pot of water she had heating on her small fire. "Camomile to lighten the gray. Basil to add body and shine. If it does nothing else, it'll make me smell like a salad."

By the light of the tiny fire, she used her dagger to cut off her silver braid just above her shoulders. She tried not to sigh as she tossed the braid on the fire. Her thick, full hair had been a source of quiet pride for years and had not been cut since Steel was a boy, before her brown tresses turned prematurely gray.

She washed her hair in creek water with a sliver of soap and rinsed it several times in the infusion of camomile and basil. While it dried, she ate a quick meal, packed her gear on Cobalt, and buried her fire.

The dragon curled his neck around to look at her critically in the dim starlight. "You look different. Younger. Your hair is curly."

"It is?" Sara's hand flew to her newly shorn hair. To her surprise, she felt waves in her hair—nothing like corkscrews, but there were definitely soft curls that had been released from the weight of the long braid. She tied it back behind her head with a strip of leather and grinned. "I should have done this sooner."

On the skirts of a west wind, they crossed over the mountains and flew westward above the night-dark lands of Elkholm. They passed over the Vingaard River and into Heartlund, and at dawn they sought shelter in a strip of forest not far from the edges of the Dargaard Mountains. In the dense woodland, they spent the day resting and poring over Sara's map and planning their approach to Neraka.

Since she did not know what to expect, Sara left many of their decisions as open as possible. She did not want to commit themselves to a plan that could prove untenable the moment they laid eyes on the city. "Whatever happens," she told Cobalt, "just follow my lead."

After nightfall, Cobalt flew Sara over the edge of the grasslands into the hills and the desolate Khalkist Mountains of the old Taman Busuk. The mountain peaks rose like a series of ragged saw blades interspersed with wide valleys of grassy wasteland. Snow robed the summits and lay thick along the gray-black granite slopes. A powerful wind swirled among the peaks and set plumes of ghostly white trailing from their crowns.

To rise safely over the mountains, Cobalt had to fight against the icy winds that threatened to send him tumbling sideways or sweep him into a cliff wall. He stretched out his long neck and blunt tail, and strained with all his strength to keep his wings moving and his direction true. He did not want to be swept off course if he could help it.

Sara clung to his back and tried to keep her cloak tightly wrapped around her. She was very thankful for the leather boots and flying gloves that kept her feet and hands from freezing.

Both of them breathed a sigh of relief when they reached a valley and could fly lower into the warmer, quieter air.

They flew over three distinct splintered ranges before they reached the dense heart of the Khalkists, where the volcanoes steamed like sleeping giants and the valleys disappeared entirely. Below Cobalt's wings, as far as Sara could see, stretched a vast, bleak realm of barren peaks and stony ridges.

She shivered as much from the cold as the bleakness of the land beneath. Although she had never been near Neraka, she had heard descriptions of it from other knights at Storm's Keep. Yet that did not prepare her for the harsh, almost cruel character of the landscape surrounding the city.

I shouldn't be surprised, she thought. The city was founded by Queen Takhisis and had been the location of the Temple of Darkness. It seemed only fitting the Dark Queen would choose a place in the midst of a massive natural stone fortress.

Sara grimly held on to the horn of her saddle. She forced her mind to tramp down any tendrils of fear that tried to grow. Cobalt was close to Neraka, if her map was right, and she needed to stay alert.

Daylight glimmered on the eastern horizon when Cobalt spotted pinpoints of light on the ground far ahead. He dropped lower in altitude and skimmed along the flanks of the mountains toward the lights. They skirted a smoking volcano, turned south slightly, and glided to a landing on the top of a tall, steep-sided ridge in the highlands north of the city. In the shelter of a rock outcropping, they looked down into the basin of Neraka and watched silently while the rising sun brought the city of the Knights of Takhisis to life.

At first there was nothing to see but the city's torches and lamps clustered around the central fortress. The rest of the valley was shrouded in dense darkness. Little by little, though, the sky grew brighter and shed its pale gleam on buildings, walls, tents, and barracks. Details became clearer; colors returned. The mountain's shadow still loomed over the valley, but slowly the shade retreated as the sun rose higher.

Sara took a long, contemplative look and thought the city looked better in the darkness. The opal light of dawn could do nothing to improve the scene below.

The city of Neraka had sprung up in a wide, flat basin that reminded Sara of a piece of old, worn crockery. The valley floor was brown and barren, cracked with fissures, and any trees that may have grown on the floor or on the slopes were long gone, cut down to fuel the endless fires that burned within the city. Around the bowl loomed massive volcanic peaks that steamed and smoked and added their own fumes to the pall that hung over the city.

The city itself consisted of three main areas, one within the other, like concentric rings. In the center was the heart of Neraka, the fortified inner keep that sheltered within its confines a large open square. In the square was a crater, a deep black hole that at one time had been the foundation of a huge building. Nothing reflected off its black emptiness, and no amount of sunlight could enhance the evil gloom that hunkered over the sunken stone.

Sara knew without asking that the ruin was the Temple of Darkness, destroyed by the forces of good nearly thirty-five years before.

Outside the inner keep was the inner bailey, crowded with buildings of all descriptions. A second, higher wall, strengthened with massive watchtowers, surrounded this part of the inner city, and at its base was the outer bailey. This, too, was jammed with buildings and streets, stables and markets. Even in the early morning hours, the streets crawled with activity.

Outside the walls was the second ring of the city proper, if "proper" was a term that could be applied to the warren of brothels, bars, shops, slave pens, huts, and hovels that clung close to the fortress walls like so much fungus.

The last ring of Neraka belonged to the Knights of Takhisis and was shaped by orderly sections of barracks and tents arranged in a circle around the city. The area looked frightfully organized and busy with troops hurrying back and forth. The wall of tents reminded Sara not so much of an organized military establishment as a prison wall meant to keep inhabitants of the city in and intruders out.

Guards marched everywhere, on the fortress battlements, at the gates, in the busy streets, around the tent quarters. She could see sunlight glint off their weapons and armor and hear the distant echo of their horns. A dozen dragons, mostly blues, flew lazy circles over the valley floor, keeping a close watch on the four roads that led into the city.

Apparently the Knights of Takhisis had already built up a sizable force in the three short years they had occupied the land around Neraka. The thought made Sara shudder.

"Well," she said to Cobalt, crouched beside her. "Do we stay here, sneak in, or knock on the front door?"

Cobalt suddenly lifted his head and swiveled around to look at the ridge behind them. His nostrils flickered, and he grunted, "I think we'd better knock."

Sara sprang to her feet, her hand automatically reaching up for her sword strapped to her back. She didn't see what disturbed the dragon at first, but then she spotted them, a squad of draconians loping across the top of the ridge toward them.

"Wyrmsbreath, that was fast!" she muttered irritably. "Where did they come from?"

"Do we fight?" Cobalt asked hopefully.

"No. Not yet. Since they know we're here, that rules out secrecy." She untied her blue-black helm from the saddle and pulled it decisively over her silver-blond hair. "Come on. We'll knock. You are now the mount of one Knight Warrior Sara Conby."

"Knight Warrior?" Cobalt snorted. "Last time you were an officer."

"I don't want to push my luck," she said briefly. Ignoring the rapidly approaching draconians, she climbed to the saddle. Cobalt spread his wings and leapt aloft.

Ever alert, the dragons flying above the city spied the blue immediately and abruptly veered toward him.

Cobalt paid scant attention. Huffing to himself, he glided over the ridge until he was over the squad of draconians. There were six of the big brutes, all heavily armed and clad in crude black tunics. They turned their reptilian heads upward to glare at the dragon.

He chuckled to himself, a sound Sara always found disconcerting. Forewarned, she tucked her seat deeper into the saddle, wrapped her hands around the leather of the padded horn, and leaned forward. Cobalt suddenly snapped in his wings and dived straight for the draconians.

Their mouths fell open to reveal yellow, snaggled

teeth, then surprise turned to fear, and they stood rooted to the ground as the dragon plummeted toward them. The blue sent a blast of dragon lightning scorching into the ground beside them. The draconians suddenly found their feet and scattered in all directions. As skillfully as an eagle, Cobalt swept over their heads, altered his wing angle, and pulled up into a smooth ascent.

Sara's head snapped back from the force of his turn. Bemused, she rubbed her neck while he spiraled upward. She would have bet any number of steel coins he was grinning.

Satisfied with himself, Cobalt veered back toward Neraka and all at once came snout to snout with three suspicious dragons. Three more quickly circled behind him and effectively cut off any escape. Three of the blues carried helmed riders—knights, by the look of their armor. They waved lances at Sara and gestured fiercely toward the city.

Sara and Cobalt understood the message. Meek now, the blue dragon followed their escort into the valley and winged downward toward the approaches to the teeming streets of Neraka.

Chapter 10

The dragon escorts led Cobalt to the broad, open field in front of the main gate and landed on either side of him, their stance threatening, their yellow eyes hooded in suspicious stares.

Two of the three riders slid off their mounts and strode with wary purpose toward Sara.

Sara closed her eyes for just a heartbeat, a silent prayer on her lips. She had no idea if any god or immortal being could hear her, but this time she did not care if it seemed foolish to pray to an empty firmament. She had to put her hopes and fears into some form of expression that let her soul reach out beyond her own limitations to something more potent, more powerful than she. She would command her own actions and decisions, but if some deity wanted to throw a little luck her way, she just wanted him to know she would be grateful.

She then swallowed once to sooth the dryness in her throat and slid off Cobalt to the parched, hard-packed ground.

The two knights stopped in front of her. Their hands rested on their sword hilts. Their armor gleamed from hours of careful polishing; their weapons were honed and in good repair, and their boots were new.

Sara felt her stomach lurch from a flash of memory that exploded in her mind like a crack of lightning: two knights, wearing armor decorated with the skull and the lily of Takhisis, walking up the path to her house—Lord Ariakan and his guard coming to take her son away.

Sara stiffened her back and saluted with a mix of feigned arrogance and stifled hatred. "I would like to see your commander," she demanded before the other two could say a word.

They exchanged a glance. Their gaze slid to Cobalt, then back to Sara, their eyes unreadable behind their own helms.

"Your sword, please," one ordered.

Sara handed it over grudgingly. "Take care of it."

"This way." The man indicated the main gate with a gloved hand.

Sara nodded curtly. After a quick pat to Cobalt's neck, she followed her guide to the massive gateway leading into Neraka's fortified inner city.

Cobalt yawned to show his curved teeth to the other dragons, flipped his wings neatly to his sides, and made himself comfortable in the sun to wait.

At the gateway, the knight stopped Sara with a curt signal. The huge iron gates stood open like the maw of some great stone beast. On the battlements, horns blared a signal to the guards, and flags of black and blue fluttered in the wind.

The captain of the guard left the gatehouse to meet Sara's escort. He ran his eye speculatively over her riding gear, her sword in the knight's hand, and the lily brooch that gleamed on her cloak.

"This dragon rider wishes to see the general," the guard informed him.

The captain, a human mercenary of muscular proportions, jerked his head toward the interior of the fortress. "The general is in the temple square."

The guard behind Sara pushed her forward through the iron gate.

Sara immediately wished she could turn around and go home. The view of the city from the heights had shown her the temple ruins, a fortress, and the helter-skelter growth of buildings and tents inhabited by a busy, motley populace. What it did not prepare her for was the squalor, the stench, and the rowdy crowds.

Neraka had been captured and held by the Solamnic Knights for a while, and they had made some effort to rebuild and strengthen the walls, erect permanent buildings, and clean the streets. Unfortunately most of their good efforts had vanished in the three years since the Knights of Takhisis moved back.

The narrow streets were jammed with decrepit wooden edifices and hastily erected buildings that looked ready to collapse at the first hearty sneeze. Humans, tall brutes blithely ignoring the winter cold, draconians of every description, ogres, goblins, and hobgoblins clogged the walkways and passages. Some marched in guard patrols or ran about looking purposeful. The majority crowded into the countless brothels, bars, and gaming rooms and engaged in brawls at every opportunity. Gully dwarves scampered underfoot like rats, eating the refuse in the streets and stealing anything that wasn't tied down. Among the crowds, Sara also saw slaves of every race that had been brought to serve the denizens of the city and provide for any need or pleasure.

A chill queasiness crept through Sara. Although the sun was shining, none of its warmth and little of its light seemed to get past the high walls. The air inside the fortress was still, cold, dank, and gloomy.

She and her escort hurried along the paved road through the Queen's Court and into Temple Square. Automatically Sara's eyes went to the ruins of the evil temple. At one time, the black, twisted Temple of Darkness rose like an obscene growth out of the barren earth of the Neraka vale, until the Heroes of the Lance, aided by the gemstone man, Berem, brought about its destruction.

Thirty-four years later the ruins remained as a tremendous crater in the temple compound. The innermost walls around the Temple Square were nearly leveled in the blast that had turned the temple into a cloud of shards.

Sara noticed the crater had been barricaded by a wall built of rubble. Through a break in the walls, she saw a gang of draconians supervising slaves inside the barrier in some labor Sara could not yet determine. A group of high-ranking knights in blue and black uniforms stood close to the wall in close consultation with a dark-robed cleric.

The guards escorting Sara took her across the square and stopped several paces away to await their commander's notice. The brief respite gave Sara a chance to look over the wall. She wished she hadn't.

A cold, bitter chill emanated from the shadow that shrouded the crater. The hole plunged downward out of sight into the dark bowels of the temple's foundation. The draconians she saw carried whips, which they used mercilessly on a long line of slaves that trailed down into the depths like a worm crawling into a corpse. A second line toiled out, carrying chunks of broken stone and buckets of broken mortar and dirt, which they added to an ever-increasing pile. The slaves trembled and staggered, the fear plain on their filthy faces. But the draconians drove them at their work until they collapsed and others were forced to take their places. Sara saw a heap of bodies dumped at one end of the barricaded wall.

"Who are you?"

A voice, sharp and authoritative, brought Sara out of her appalled appraisal. She swiftly erased any expression from her face and slowly pulled off her helm. Thankful that none of them looked familiar, she saluted the officers, three men and two women. "Knight Warrior Sara Conby."

A woman stepped away from the group. Tall and lithe, she moved with leonine grace to stand before Sara. They stood almost eye to eye, which gave Sara an excellent opportunity to study the woman's face. It was almost impossible to tell her age. Her skin revealed she was past the bloom of youth, but no lines or wrinkles marked her even features. She was beautiful as a lioness is beautiful—golden, powerful, streamlined. Her eyes blazed a brilliant blue, as hard and calculating as a predator's. Her gold hair, cut short to wear beneath a helm, clung to her strong-boned head in a thick, golden cap.

She studied Sara like a lioness, too, slowly and very deliberately.

Sara did not flinch or waver. She had been sized up by fiercer predators than this one. She remained motionless and kept her eyes straight ahead.

"A Knight of the Lily," the woman said thoughtfully. She flicked her gaze over the few dragon scales glistening on Sara's leather breeches. "A dragon rider, too."

"She and her dragon were up the Firewalk Heights," the guard reported. "They were watching the city. A patrol of draconians spooked them out."

"Watching the city," the woman repeated. Her eyes bore into Sara's calm gray ones. "Spying? That is an offense we take very seriously."

"And well you should," Sara responded coolly. She saw the other officers and the cleric hanging back respectfully to watch the woman, and she knew now who confronted her. "However, General Abrena, the Code states a knight shall have the right to evaluate an unfamiliar situation or terrain before acting. My dragon and I arrived just before dawn. To come flying into Neraka before I had seen the lay of the land would have been foolish."

The general suddenly smiled a feral grin that pulled up the corners of her mouth, but did not touch the detachment in her eyes. "Where did you serve?"

Sara remained impassive, her tone matter-of-fact. "Storm's Keep, for many years. I was a dragon trainer for Lord Ariakan. Then I transferred to Qualinesti to fight the elves." Far away, on the edge of her attention, she heard the draconian whips crack, the groans of the slaves, the rumble of stone dropped on the heap. She ignored it, ignored the officers standing in speculative silence, and concentrated on keeping her face emotionless. She sensed that even the slightest tick of fear or hesitancy would be recognized instantly by this eagle-eyed general.

Mirielle paced around her. "What have you been doing since the Chaos war?"

"Hiding, mostly," Sara answered. There was truth enough in that. "My own dragon was killed. I found this one wounded and cared for him until he regained his strength."

The general's golden eyebrows rose. "Indeed. And what happened to your first dragon?"

"My wing was sent north toward Palanthas to help fight the war. We were ambushed by firedragons. The others were slaughtered. I was knocked unconscious, but my dragon hid me and died defending me."

"Interesting. You seem to instill a firm loyalty in your dragons."

Sara did not reply.

"Why did you come to Neraka?"

Sara felt on safer ground when she did not have to lie. "I was near Palanthas when I heard the knights were regathering here. I came to see for myself. Cobalt and I are tired of hiding."

"Do you wish to rejoin the order?" the general asked.

"She's rather old," one of the officers put in.

Sara shot a glance at him and understood his remark. He looked barely twenty, and already he wore the insignia of a junior officer—a hard, forceful young man, by the look of his eyes and the forward stance of his body.

"That's enough, Targonne," Mirielle said without bothering to look at him. "Sometimes age and experience more than make up for youthful exuberance. Or," she went on, and her voice dropped into a mild warning, "family connections."

The young officer closed his mouth, disconcerted.

"He's right," Sara said. "I am no longer in the prime of my strength. But I can train dragons, fight, tend sick or wounded animals, and cook."

"But do you want to rejoin the order?" repeated Mirielle.

No! screamed every strand of Sara's emotions. She wanted no more of this evil knighthood, no more of their cruelty and unwavering desire to control. No more!

"Yes," said her mouth before her emotions got the better of her. She had come this far on this strange quest; she couldn't back out now. Besides, if she said no, they'd probably kill her.

Mirielle Abrena nodded in satisfaction. "We need all the experienced knights we can find, Knight Warrior Conby. The tasks ahead of us are enormous." Her long fingers reached out to touch the night lily brooch on Sara's cloak. "That is a beautiful piece."

Sara thought of the man who had given it to her. Out of his armor and behind closed doors, Lord Ariakan had been charming yet arrogant, gentle yet demanding, as dark and handsome as the gift he had given her. Without a second thought, she unpinned the brooch and gave it to Mirielle. "It was a gift from a man long dead. I think he would have approved of you."

For a moment, General Abrena was too startled to move. She was accustomed to fawning sycophants and gifts given in hopes of personal gain, yet Sara's expression expected nothing and her gesture was freely given. Mirielle took the brooch in her hand with a small nod of thanks and pinned it to her own cloak.

"Take her to Lord Knight Cadrel," she told the guards. "Tell him to find a place for her. I suggest one of the training talons. Her experience will help guide the younger knights."

Sara saluted the general, then the officers behind her, and marched after the guards out of the compound. She let her breath out in a long sigh, but it was hardly relief. For the second time in her life, she had voluntarily joined the Knights of Takhisis. What had she gotten herself into now?

Chapter 11

Sara followed the guards out of the fortress toward a cluster of wooden buildings just to the northeast of the main gatehouse. Several of the ramshackle edifices were civilian—a tavern, a brothel, and a shop specializing in knives. But the tallest and most imposing building had guards standing by the doors and a shield nailed above the lintel.

"In there," one of her escorts said brusquely. "Lord Knight Cadrel is in command of recruitment, and if you want to remain in Neraka, do not look at his hands or face." On that helpful remark, he and his companion took her inside.

The first floor of the building was bisected front to back by a wide hallway. Rooms led off the hall to the left and right, and everywhere Sara looked there were scribes, slaves, and young knights bustling around in a constant stream of activity.

They entered the first room they came to, a room made dim with shuttered windows and not enough lamps. A large desk took up most of the space, and behind it sat a man in the uniform of a lord knight. He was a man of massive size, who once had the bulk and muscle to fit his frame. Now his body had shrunk inward, leaving his skin to sag over prominent bones. He wrote busily on a parchment with one hand. The other hand lay on his lap, hidden out of sight. His head, loosely covered with thinning brown hair, tilted over so Sara could not see his face.

One of the guards cleared his throat. The lord knight lifted his head.

Even with the guard's warning, it took all of Sara's concentration to relax the muscles in her face and keep her breath steady when she saw the ravaged ruin of Lord Knight Cadrel's visage. It had to be a disease, she thought, for an old wound would have scarred or at least shown some indication of healing. This affliction was slowly rotting away his face, feature by feature, inch by inch of skin. His nose was already devoured into discolored holes, and the open, gnawing sores covered his lips, one cheek, and his left temple. The remaining skin looked dull white, as if it had already died.

He sat expectantly, almost daring someone to say something. When no reaction came from Sara or the guards, he cocked an eyebrow at them. "Well?" His query came out dry and raspy.

"Lord Knight, General Abrena sends this knight to you for reinstatement and suggests one of the new talons."

"Does she," Cadrel said, sounding slightly irritated. Stacks of scrolls and parchments littered his desk. He had to lift his left hand from under the desk. Sara saw it, too, had been devoured by the disease. Two fingers were gone, and a third was rotted to the second joint.

He shoved a few piles aside and shuffled through a stack until he found the list he wanted. "What are your strengths, woman?"

"Training dragons, healing, cooking," Sara replied briefly.

"Good. We need dragon trainers." He snorted. "By the rift, we need everything! I do not know how she expects me to fill every talon and wing she wants when we have so few." He had a deep voice and formed his words with deliberate care. Even so, his speech came out slightly slurred due to the damage to his mouth. His meaning was clear enough to Sara, though, to distract her from her dismay and pity.

According to all those tents and barracks out there, she pondered, the general's army had reached an impressive strength. Why does he complain?

The lord knight consulted his lists once more and said, "Report to Knight Officer Guiyar Massard, Red Quarter. He needs a second-in-command." He pushed his maimed hand out of sight and went back to work without waiting for a reply.

Sara and the guards saluted and retreated outside.

"What is it?" she asked as soon as they were out of earshot.

"Morgion's Curse," one guard replied, looking peaked. "I can never get used to seeing it. He was struck with it during the Summer of Chaos when the gods left us. Without the healing magic, no cleric has been able to help him, and no herb can even slow it. He is hoping for war soon to avoid a long and lingering death."

Sara rubbed her cheek. She had heard of Morgion's Curse, named for the god of decay and disease, but she had never seen such an advanced case of it. Those unfortunates who were afflicted used to seek the help of clerics for healing. Now there was nothing left for the sick and wounded but herbs, witches' brews, and folk medicine once thought redundant.

The guard returned her sword, then pointed east toward a section of tents. "The Red Quarter is that way. Look for the red flags," he told her, a hint of scorn in his voice. "Knight Officer Massard is probably still there. He is supposed to be drilling his recruits today, but he stayed at the taverns quite late last night."

The second guard said something sharp and irritable in a language Sara did not recognize, and the two strode away to return to their dragons.

Cobalt ambled over to join his rider. "The dragons told me they were glad to see me. They said the knights are very shorthanded."

"So I am beginning to see," Sara said thoughtfully.

Cobalt fixed an amber eye on her face. "Are you here to stay?"

She laid a hand on the warm scales of his leg. "Only until I learn what I need to know and can figure out a way to get away from here unscathed. If you change your mind and decide to stay with the knights, I will not try to stop you."

"There is nothing here I crave." He chuckled. "Except perhaps, someone else's coins or treasure. No, when you go, I go."

They walked together in companionable silence toward the quarter where the red flags flew. At the edge of the tents, more guards stopped her and questioned her. As soon as they heard who she was looking for, they smirked and jerked thumbs toward a section of large canvas tents set up before an open quadrangle.

"There are herd beasts in a pasture east of here set aside for the dragons," they told her. "Your dragon will have plenty of time to feed if he wishes."

Cobalt did wish, and with a grin, Sara unsaddled him and sent him on his way.

Curious, she made her way toward Knight Officer Massard's tent. What was it about the man that sent everyone sneering and smirking? Five paces from the tent, she found out. A loud, rumbling snore issued from the open flaps; a pool of drying vomit covered the dirt by the entrance.

Sara gingerly stepped over the mess and pushed open the flap. Fumes of vomit, unwashed body, and old ale filled her nostrils. Skull-splitter ale, she realized, holding her nose. If the man sprawled out on the cot had spent a night drinking that, it was no wonder he passed out. She curled her lip in disgust.

"He's been like that for hours," said a young male voice behind her.

Sara backed carefully out of the tent and turned to meet the speaker. Her eyes widened and her breath caught in her throat. For one precious moment, she thought Steel had returned to her. Then her common sense returned and her eyes looked closer, and the image of Steel faded softly away.

The young man who stood on the path was as tall and dark-haired as Steel had been. His skin was tanned from years of work in the sun, and he grinned at her with a crooked smile so like Steel's it wrung her heart. But there the resemblance ended. As Sara stared at him, she noticed his eyes were green, like the grasslands on a spring day; his face was long and narrow set, with features slightly too large to be very handsome. Thick, dark eyebrows shaded his eyes, and a newly healed scar marred his left cheek. He wore the black tunic and pants trimmed with blue that seemed to be the latest uniform of the order, as well as a chain mail shirt and a light cloak. He had a good sword strapped to his waist.

He tilted his head at her silent appraisal and asked curiously, "Were you looking for him or just wondering what the racket was?"

"I am supposed to report to Knight Officer Massard," Sara said. "Is that . . . ?"

"The one and only, thank the gods. Commander of the Sixth Talon. All five of us."

Sara glanced around at the tents. "Five?" she echoed in surprise. A talon usually had nine.

The young man waved a hand at the tents around them. "Most of these are empty. Set up for future recruits, I guess."

Or to fool a spy looking down from the heights, Sara added mentally. She introduced herself.

"Derrick Yaufre," he returned. "No offense, but you must be one of the original knights."

Sara laughed. She liked this man's slightly irreverent and honest outlook. "None taken. And you're close. I joined more years ago than I care to remember."

"Good. We need some experience. Massard is an original, too. One of the survivors of the war. Now he spends most of his time drinking or sleeping it off. The rest of us are so new our armor still squeaks. Come on, I'll introduce you."

In a chivalrous gesture that made Sara smile, Derrick relieved her of the saddle and packs and hoisted the load over his own broad shoulders.

She followed him around the quadrangle to a cluster of tents, where a group of young people—very young people, to Sara's eyes—sat upon stools or wooden boxes in a bored-looking group. They looked up as Derrick joined them, and in the hope of something more interesting, they rose collectively to their feet and greeted Sara.

Sara eyed them one by one. Three men, including Derrick, and two women made up the Sixth Talon. As a group, they were all well conditioned, hard as dragon scales, and eager to learn. As individuals—well, Sara would have to see what characteristics were revealed by time and trial. She quickly explained who she was and what her assignment was to be.

The group perked up immediately. "Then you can take us out!" one of the women exclaimed. "Knight Candidate Marika Windor, ma'am," she added hastily. "We were supposed to go on a training flight this morning, but Massard is dead drunk."

The others nodded, looking none too pleased by their commander's indisposition.

Sara considered them. There was no real reason for them to sit about doing nothing when she could take them on their assignment. How difficult could a training flight be? She had ridden dragons in dozens of them. It would also give her a chance to get to know these warriors without the company of their sodden leader.

"Do you all have dragons yet?"

They nodded eagerly. "We were assigned dragons last

week," Derrick assured her.

"Last week," Sara said, amazed. "Have any of you passed your test?"

They looked at each other, their thoughts passing plainly between them. "We haven't taken it yet. We're all still squires," Marika told her.

"But . . ."

Derrick held up a hand. "I know. We're rather old to be just squires. Most of us joined just a few years ago, after the order was decimated by the war. General Abrena was willing to accept anyone of reasonable age, and they've rushed us through the training. We will all take the test sometime after New Year."

Sara shook her head. In the past, the knighthood hadn't accepted anyone over the age of fourteen for candidacy. They usually took boys and began their training and indoctrination by age twelve and made them squires by age fifteen. These young people looked to be five or six years older than that and had only been in training for a few years. The order was desperate for recruits if the older ranking officers seriously considered letting these novices take the Test of Takhisis this soon.

She filed that piece of information away for later and said, "Get your riding gear. We'll call in the dragons."

Whooping with excitement, the five split off to their tents to grab their equipment. Derrick eyed Sara's make-shift saddle, then tossed it and her gear into an empty tent. He came back a few minutes later lugging his own dragon saddle and a spare one that he gave to Sara.

"This one was Tamar's," he said. His face darkened and he finished sadly, "He died last week when he failed his test."

The saddle was well crafted of fine leather and strong bindings. Sara took it with a nod of thanks and wondered at Derrick's tone. Most squires would have reviled a candidate who died in failure. Derrick did not. He seemed truly grieved that his companion was dead.

The others came dashing up to join them, anticipation shining from their faces. Sara led them out of the tent quarter to a wide, empty field where there was ample room for dragons to land.

She lined them up and stood in front of them, her arms crossed, her expression stern. "Now, before we call the dragons, I want all of you to give me your names so I will know who to yell at when you do something wrong."

They shifted on their feet and exchanged sly grins. They caught her slight bantering tone and responded to it like children suddenly released from an onerous duty.

Derrick, she already knew. Marika was a stocky, muscular girl with a long brown braid and eyes as earthy as her laugh. Kelena, the second woman, had cut her dark red hair into a halo of curls and sported a band of freckles across her narrow face like a banner. She was from Sanction, she told Sara, and had joined the order to follow in the footsteps of her older brother, who had died in the rift.

Saunder, the oldest of the young men, wore his dusty blond hair long and tied back in an intricate knot. He was tall and rangy and quiet to the point of reticence.

The youngest of the talon—all of seventeen years, he told Sara proudly—was Jacson. He was voluble enough to make up for Saunder's silence and energetic enough to keep them all entertained. He reminded Sara of a kender who viewed the world with wide-eyed enthusiasm and grabbed for everything he could get out of a moment. He was of slight stature for a knight candidate, yet he was deceptively strong and very quick-witted.

Sara studied them all, and to her surprise, she felt the slightest niggling doubt. Not a one of them looked like the burning zealots she remembered caring for at Storm's Keep. Those squires had been truly dedicated to a religion and a way of life and worshiped a goddess who revealed her power in every part of their lives. These five men and women seemed to lack that religious fervor. Was it any wonder? Takhisis was gone; her Vision was dead. What was left for them to worship with all their hearts and souls?

She pushed that notion aside. Not everyone in the world felt as empty as she did or looked on the disappearance of the gods as abandonment. Perhaps she was just letting her own confusion color her impressions.

She forced her seeds of doubt aside and automatically reached for the lily brooch that used to hang on her cloak. Only when her fingers touched the soft fabric did she remember she had given the brooch away. A long time ago she had used the brooch as a focal point to summon dragons. Now she would have to do it the hard way.

"Call your dragons," she ordered the talon.

Derrick and Saunder stepped forward and produced slender whistles hanging from chains around their necks. When they blew the whistles, Sara heard no sound. A dog barked somewhere nearby. Then there was a rush and flap of large wings and two blue dragons landed in the field close to the talon.

Sara glanced around quizzically, waiting for the other three.

"That's all," Derrick said with a shrug. "There are so few blues left after the war, our wing commander only assigned two to us. We have to take turns."

"Take turns," Sara muttered. "How can you learn aerial tactics if you have to take turns on two dragons?"

"Massard said we would get more later," Jacson said. "If you can believe him."

"Well, we'll make the best of it." She marched up to the two dragons. They were both young, maybe fifty years, of similar coloring, and both were shorter than Cobalt. "What are your names?" she asked. Howl and Squall, they told her in unison. Obviously nest mates.

She quickly sent Howl, named for the raucous tone of his voice, out to the herd fields to fetch Cobalt.

The big blue arrived, snorting and grumbling, and promptly dumped the bloody carcass of a cow on the ground in front of Sara. "I wasn't finished yet. You said I had plenty of time," he complained.

His rider ignored his grumps. "So hurry up. I changed my mind."

He cast a warning growl at the younger dragons and hunched protectively over his meal. With his sharp teeth, he tore the carcass to pieces and gulped it down, indulging in a lot of slurping, gnashing, crunching, and other unnecessary noises.

The five squires watched him in sick fascination. Sara hid a smile. Obviously they hadn't paid much attention to the eating habits of their dragons.

As soon as Cobalt had spat out the last bone, Sara saddled and climbed onto his back. "Derrick, you and Marika ride first. We're going to play catch."

She explained what she meant and dispatched the other riders to spread out across the field. The object of the game was for a dragon and its rider to hover over the field and "catch" one of the people on foot—carefully, Sara emphasized. The "prey" then had to be carried to a holding pen—a red flag stuck in the ground—and rider and prey exchanged places. Cobalt played games master.

The young squires took to the game immediately. Shouts and laughter filled the chilly air. The dragons enjoyed it, too, and dipped and swooped after their running quarry and roared their frustration when someone escaped their clutches. The racket drew other knights and squires, who came to watch. Some brought their dragons until there were so many in the field, Sara was afraid the dragons would hurt themselves. She divided them into teams.

There were a few bumps and bruises and a cracked head, but no one was seriously hurt in the melee, and while the dragons and riders gained valuable practice maneuvering close to the ground, Sara was able to observe her recruits and learn something about them.

Derrick, she saw, was the natural leader of the group. He encouraged the others and kept them going with his example and his optimism.

Saunder was as tough as dragon hide and had a quiet cunning that let him stay back until the right moment, then he urged his dragon on and caught his prey more often than not.

Jacson laughed his way through the game, cracking jokes and hurling good-natured insults at everyone.

Red-haired Kelena bulled her way into the thickest skirmishes and gave way to no one. As fast as a sprinter, she could not be caught on the ground until she decided it was her turn to ride. Marika, although not a good runner, was probably the best rider. She pulled a few stunts in the saddle that left Sara gasping.

When the game broke up, the Sixth Talon regathered, laughing and joking among themselves. Sara was pleased. She released the dragons and led the riders back toward the tents for a well-earned meal

They had no sooner entered their own section of the Red Quarter when they heard a scream of pain coming from Massard's tent. Another scream and another shattered the quiet, and as one group, Sara and the squires raced for the tent.

Chapter 12

"Where are they?" bellowed a hoarse voice. *"Tell me now!"*

Behind Sara, the five squires slowed perceptively as soon as they realized the one in pain was not their vaunted leader. Knowing him as they did, they had no wish to become his next target.

A faint crack, then another screech of pain, met Sara at the tent's entrance. She threw back the tent flap and strode inside.

A large, truculent-looking man lifted his head and glared at her.

Sara felt her heart contract. She knew that face. It was heavier, more florid, and red-veined from drinking, but she knew it. At one time this knight had been at Storm's Keep. She tensed, waiting for the recognition to burn in his eyes and the denouncement she knew must come. Yet it did not.

He glowered at her furiously, shook the whip in his hand, and shouted, "What do you want?"

Something whimpered on the ground.

Sara spotted a small goblin cowering at Massard's feet. He raised a whip and brought it down across the goblin's back with vicious force. The goblin screamed again and groveled at his feet.

Goblins were not Sara's favorite creatures. She hated their ugly faces and the way they stole from the dead. But she hated injustice more. She took one step forward, plucked the whip out of Massard's hand, and said in a level voice, "If you are looking for your talon, we were at the practice fields doing our training rides."

Massard looked flabbergasted at her audacity. "Who are you?"

"Knight Warrior Sara Conby. I have been assigned to you as second-in-command."

The man rubbed the stubble on his jaw. He looked dreadful and smelled worse. Sara doubted his clothes had been changed or washed in days. His eyes were bloodshot, and his graying hair was a gully dwarf's nest.

The goblin, seeing the whip out of Massard's hand, scampered behind Sara. "No hit," he whined. "Message. I only have message."

"Why didn't you say so? Get on with it, you pea-brained street refuse!" roared Massard. "Do something right."

"Knight Warrior Conby is to join the general for dinner tonight at sunset," the goblin blubbered, bobbing his head. "At general's quarters."

"The general, huh," Massard grunted at Sara. "Already boot-licking, I see." He hurled a boot at the cowering goblin. "Well, get out of here, you worthless filth. The next time I want an answer out of you, you'd better give it to me, or I'll use something more persuasive than a whip."

The goblin squealed and bolted out of the tent. The five young people stood at attention and watched it all, wide-eyed.

"You can't very well beat something out of him if he doesn't know it," Sara said reasonably. Her consternation faded somewhat as she realized he did not recognize her. In its place grew intense contempt.

"As for you," he snarled, ignoring her remark, "I should write you up for dereliction. You failed to report to me in a timely manner and—"

"Dereliction," Jacson cried, stepping forward impulsively. "When you were—"

Derrick clamped a hand over his arm and hauled him back into line. "Sir," he said in the same calm manner Sara used. "Knight Warrior Conby did report to you, and when she saw that you were . . . unavailable, she took us on our assigned training." His emphasis on the word "assigned" was not lost on the officer.

Massard knew he would have some explaining to do if he disciplined his new junior officer officially. The man subsided to something closer to his usual bad temper. "Bring me some ale," he growled, and he sagged onto the edge of his cot.

"Would you rather have some hot water and a meal?" Sara suggested. "The squires must attend to their duties, and I would like to know my responsibilities."

"Get me the ale, woman, and shut your infernal chatter!"

Sara's lips tightened to a thin line. She sketched a salute and left Massard to his own foul company. She found the others studying her in amazement.

"Why did you do that?" Kelena asked her.

"Do what?"

"Stop Massard from beating the goblin. He has a terrible temper. He could have turned that whip on you."

Sara lifted her chin. "A knight does not abuse his power by inflicting cruelty and pain on the innocent. It is one thing to whip a goblin who has stolen from you or attacked you. It is another to beat him for something he does not know. It is a matter of justice."

She gave the recruits a minute or two to absorb that. "All right, now. Jacson, run to the nearest tavern and get the knight officer his ale."

The irrepressible young man grinned. "If he stays drunk enough, maybe he'll stay out of our way."

Sara ignored that. It was too close to the wish she had, that if he stayed drunk enough, he may not recognize her. But she knew he had to sober up eventually. The knights were shorthanded, but not so much that they would tolerate an officer who was perpetually drunk. Massard had to be fulfilling his responsibilities somehow.

"Meanwhile," she said, "let's get something to eat and a pot of hot water. I would really like some tea." They went to their tasks, grateful to leave Massard to nurse his hangover alone.

Sara soon learned the knights in Neraka had no central mess hall. There was a supply building where the recruits and knights could get the basics. Beyond that, they were responsible for feeding themselves. They could eat in the city, which Saunder pointed out was too expensive on a squire's pay. They could use a communal kitchen set up in their quarter, or they could cook over campfires outside their tents. Everyone had a small brazier in his tent and supplied his own pots and pans. Sara decided she would have to do a little scrounging.

Derrick showed her the tent where he put her gear and, with the group's consent, gave her the brazier from Tamar's possessions. The dead squire must have been from Abanasinia, Sara guessed when she saw it. The brazier was small and beautifully wrought, with an interwoven design of fanciful animals and intertwined knots. She thanked them all and then discovered one reason for their generosity. None of them liked to cook.

Resigned, she helped them put together a quick meal of bread and cheese and baked apples, and she set a pot of soup to simmer in the low coals during the afternoon so the recruits would have something while she dined with the general.

The young men and women were pleased that their junior officer had been chosen to eat with General Abrena. They rarely saw the general, let alone had the chance to accept an invitation from her.

Sara did not have time to give it much thought. Evening was hours away, and there was still much to do. Derrick, Saunder, Jacson, Marika, and Kelena left to attend to their duties as squires to five of the ranking knights in Neraka. Sara was left to unpack and deal with Massard.

Fortunately the man spent most of the afternoon in his tent drinking the ale Jacson had brought him. The respite gave Sara a chance to do some exploring on her own. She walked around the perimeter of the ring of tents to see for herself just how empty it really was. She talked to other recruits, to several goblins who acted as messengers and servants, and to a number of knights who were off duty. It became clear to her that, while the tent city was busy, it was nowhere near filled to capacity.

She found a number of other talons-in-training and spoke to their officers. Those talons, like the Sixth, were being rushed through training, and if the younger knights liked it, the older ones did not. The few original knights she talked to bemoaned the traditions ignored and the precepts of Lord Ariakan that were being forgotten. The day proved to be very informative.

To her intense relief, not a single knight recognized her or doubted her authenticity. To them, she was simply one of the lucky few who had survived. For the moment, it seemed the only ones she had to worry about were Massard and General Abrena. If the ale fumes ever cleared from Massard's head, Sara feared he could remember her.

The problem with Mirielle was just the opposite. Sara knew from the intense scrutiny she had received under the blue gaze of the general that Mirielle was very astute and too observant. She would catch the slightest slip, the first wrong word, the moment's hesitation. She might not know of the renegade dragon rider who once called Steel Brightblade her son, but she would certainly know how to treat an imposter and a spy.

By the time Sara returned to the Red Quarter, the sun was setting behind a dense bank of clouds. The wind whistled mournfully around the tents, and the torches in the quadrangle danced in the gathering darkness.

Massard heard her steps and came out to meet her. His walk was stronger, and his eyes watched her keenly. Only his disposition had not improved. "There's a clean uniform for you in your tent, and that sniveling little goblin is back," he said in a growl Sara thought was probably habitual. "You are to report to General Abrena. When you are finished, you will come back and stand your watch on guard duty. Is that clear?"

"Yes, sir."

His eyebrows lowered like thunderclouds. "What did you say your name was?"

Sara licked her lips, suddenly tense. "Knight Warrior Sara Conby."

He snorted through his large nose. "Bring me some of that soup before you go." Turning his back on her, he stamped back into his tent.

She obeyed in silence. It was better not to draw undue attention to herself too often. She brought him a steaming bowl of soup and backed out before he thought of anything else.

As he said, the goblin was waiting for her in her tent. Gritting her teeth, she took a quick inventory to make sure everything was where she left it in the sparsely furnished shelter, then lit the tiny lamp that hung from the tent pole.

The goblin stood huddled in his torn, filthy tunic. His dull red skin looked like blood in the lamplight. "Message," he mumbled. "Must take you to general."

"Thank you. If you will step outside, I will change my clothes. Then I will come with you."

The goblin was so unaccustomed to polite requests that he simply stared at her, his flat nose quivering.

"Go! Outside. Wait." Sara put it in as simple terms as she could. This time the goblin bobbed his head and scuttled out.

Sara quickly pulled off her own clothes, leaving them in a pile to wash, and put on the black clothes brought by the goblin. The uniform was designed to be worn under armor or alone, to be practical, durable, and generic. Stylish it was not. The black tunic had long sleeves and quilted padding across the chest and shoulders. Blue trim adorned the neckline and the sleeves. The pants laced at the legs and tied at the waist and were too baggy for Sara's taste. She hoped fervently she would not have to wear these too many days.

She shoved her feet into her rider's boots, strapped on her belt and its dagger, and went outside, where the goblin sat picking his nose.

When he saw her, he bounced to his flappy feet and bobbed his head again. "Nice clothes, Knight Warrior. Nice boots. Nice shirt. Look good! Nice—"

"All right!" Sara cut him off rather sharply. "Thank you. May we go?"

Nodding and mumbling to himself, he led Sara across the open field to the main gate of Neraka and into the streets of the inner city. If it were possible, the streets in the evening were even busier and more crowded than in the morning as the laborers and the soldiers finished their work for the day and came to spend their coins. Only the merchants closed their shops before sunset, leaving the streets to the patrons of the houses of pleasure and entertainment. Gangs of draconians roamed from street to street. Ogres jostled for room with mercenaries in the taverns, and goblins seemed to be everywhere.

The small goblin paid scant attention to the throngs. He took Sara through the Queen's Way to a section of Neraka built on the east side between the huge inner walls and the outer wall. Loosely named His High and Mighty's Grandiose Playground of Pleasures by the locals, the area was actually one of the nicer and cleaner sections of Neraka. There the buildings were larger and better constructed, and the streets were relatively quiet.

Most of the buildings had been built by the self-styled

Lord Mayor of Neraka—His High and Mighty, a draconian of vile architectural taste—soon after the fall of the Temple of Darkness. The Solamnic overlords had removed the worst of the lord's attempts at "beautification" and had left the main buildings with plain facades, simple columns, and clean windows. Only the lord mayor's personal palace remained a garish eyesore of loud colors and inappropriate decoration.

The Knights of Takhisis under General Abrena had been granted the use of several of the buildings in the "playground." The general promptly moved into one of the larger homes, dubbed the Pink Palace. Her officers took over the municipal buildings for their headquarters, and her personal guards kept the area free of troublemakers. The most recent lord mayor complained a little, but he didn't have the power or the men-at-arms to remove them.

The goblin waved a clawed hand at one of the guards and passed through the gateway into the playground without stopping. He took Sara through the calm torchlit street directly to the general's house. Torches in sconces lit the plain face of the broad two-story building, one of the few built of stone, and the only one built of pink stone—one of the reasons for its name. Lights burned in every window, and guards paced by the wide front door.

Sara turned toward the entrance, but the goblin grabbed her pants leg and tugged her away. "No, no. Front door for guests. You go in back."

Sara protested. "You said I was to join General Abrena for dinner."

"Yes, yes. General need you." He pulled her around the back and took her in through the spacious kitchen.

Sara slowed to take an appreciative appraisal. The recruits and knights in Neraka may have had to fend for themselves, but General Abrena and her staff ate quite well. Drudges were turning a calf on a spit in a huge fireplace; several roasted pigs sat on platters, ready to be served. Cooks prepared bowls of steaming vegetables, and bakers pulled pans of newly baked bread out of the brick ovens.

Sara took a deep breath of the rich odors and felt her mouth begin to water. Her stomach rumbled in anticipation.

All at once the steward, a tall, wraith-thin man, rushed into the kitchen. He saw her and threw up his hands. "There you are! You're the last. Get inside now. And you, you sniveling little worm eater. What took you so long?"

The goblin immediately ducked his head and started whining, "I didn't do it. It was her fault. She started it."

Sara shook her head in disgust and walked away.

The steward hurried after her. "You will be serving the general tonight. It is a great honor, so you must know what to do."

"Slow down," Sara insisted. "What am I doing here? The goblin said I was to join the general for dinner."

The steward rolled his eyes. "That good-for-nothing sewer scum. Why does the general keep him around? General Abrena ordered you to serve as her squire tonight for a dinner she is having for some important officials."

Sara laughed. She should have known it would be something like this. Generals did not usually share meals with their common soldiery.

The steward glowered at her and hurried her through a covered walkway into the main body of the house and to a large hall that served as council room and occasional dining room.

On this night, a large black wood table had been set before a stone fireplace, where a comfortable fire cast a cheerful glow on the silver utensils and glass goblets. Fifteen chairs sat around the table, and at each chair but one stood a squire in black or a servant dressed in colorful robes. They waited silently, unmoving and expression-less. Only one looked her way and winked.

Sara stifled the urge to giggle. It was Jacson, looking fit to burst in the stuffy atmosphere. She hurried to take her place behind the general's chair at the head of the table before she did something undignified.

The steward quickly explained to her about pouring the wine, keeping the finger towels available, and serving the food from the left and the drink from the right. He showed her where to find the salt cellars and the napkins. Sara, who knew all too well how to serve generals, merely nodded.

At that point, the doors of the hall opened and General Abrena and her guests arrived. Instantly a troupe of musicians began to play soft music from the gallery and the squires pulled out the chairs. Laughing and chatting among themselves, the general, her staff of officers, and six civilians found their seats and sat down.

Mirielle inclined her head in a brief greeting to Sara as she took her seat. The woman had left her armor behind and came dressed entirely in sleek black leather trimmed in gold and adorned with the black lily brooch. The results were ravishing and appeared to be having some effect on the lord mayor, who sat to her right. His eyes rarely left her, and his attention never wavered from her presence.

For the next few minutes, Sara was too busy pouring wine into the general's glass and serving the first course to pay attention to the other guests. But as the dinner progressed, she was able to take brief glances at the other occupants of the table. One surprised her. She thought only senior officers were present, but at the opposite end of the table sat the young officer who had commented on her age, Knight Officer Morham Targonne. Beside him was a heavily built, older version of himself dressed in rich robes and bedecked in jeweled rings and heavy chains. His father, Sara presumed. The elder Targonne was deep in discussion with another man in the desert robes of the Khur barbarians.

Two men sat across the table from them, and Sara guessed from the conversation that they were from Jelek, Neraka's nearest neighbor. Those two listened and watched their dinner companions and contributed little to the conversation.

Interspersed between the civilians sat Mirielle's staff officers, who did their best to make the affair pleasant and reassuring.

The one notable person missing from the table was the Lord Knight Cadrel. Sara knew by rights and by ranking, Cadrel should have been present. But whether he excused himself or Mirielle kept him away, the leprous knight was not there to spoil appetites.

The ensuing hours passed slowly for Sara. She grew hungrier by the minute, and the long night and busy day were taking their toll. She was so tired and hungry she could hardly keep from swaying as she stood silently behind Mirielle's chair through the long and tedious dinner. Jacson caught her eye several times and grinned at her from behind his knight. The other squires and servants ignored her entirely.

At long last, the dessert was finished and the last dirty dishes were whisked away. More wine, a dark, rich red, was served. The guests leaned back in their chairs, warm and replete from the excellent meal. The conversation slowly moved to the subject of Neraka and the knighthood's place in the government.

Sara shook her woolly head and tried to pay attention. To give herself something to do, she fetched a tray of sweetmeats from the steward and set the bowls out on the table. An argument was going on between the lord mayor and the general, a disagreement that seemed to be an old one.

The lord mayor, a retired mercenary with his own ideas about Neraka, was saying, "We in the city appreciate the presence of the knights, of course, General. But you were only granted jurisdiction over the land around the city. We have been governing Neraka alone for years now. There is little that would interest you in the day-to-day tedium of running such a small city."

Mirielle leaned forward. Sara had the thought that if the woman really were a cat, her tail would be twitching by now. She looked ready to pounce.

"On the contrary, your lordship," the general said smoothly. "There is much here to interest us. The flourishing black market, the slave trade, the mercantile empire of the Targonne family." She nodded toward the elder Targonne. "The mere fact that our queen's temple lies within your boundaries is enough to draw our attention."

"But it is in ruins. Your slaves have done little more than empty out a few lower chambers and corridors. What good will it do you when your goddess is gone?"

Mirielle curled lips into a smile. "She has left us for now, but I think she will return, and when she does, I will be ready. Neraka is my first step." She pushed a bowl of sweetmeats toward the mayor without a pause in her speech. "With the city firmly in our grasp, we can rebuild the knighthood to its former glory. Once we are strong again, we will find a way to bring our queen back and spread her influence over the whole of Ansalon."

The mayor popped a few sweetmeats into his mouth and chewed them before answering, "You are highly ambitious, General Abrena, and I would be happy to assist you in any way I can. But the city of Neraka wishes to retain its autonomy. Perhaps we should put together a treaty to finalize the relationship between the Knights of Takhisis and the citizens of Neraka."

Mirielle lounged back in her chair, her arms draped over the armrests. She watched the mayor from under her long lashes and finally said, "I don't think that will be necessary."

Something in her tone set off a warning bell in Sara's

mind. She snapped alert, the tray clutched in her hands, and following Mirielle's unblinking gaze, she turned her eyes to the burly lord mayor.

A shining sweat broke out on his forehead. His swarthy face abruptly paled to a sickly yellow. All at once he bellowed and lunged to his feet.

"What have you done, you witch!" he screamed. A violent paroxysm of pain bent him double. He groaned and fell to his knees by Mirielle's boots.

The other guests bolted to their feet. The squires and servants looked helplessly shocked. The two men from Jelek hastily put their sweetmeats back on the tray and pushed away from the table. The general's officers looked on with interest.

It was their knowing expressions that told Sara this had been planned. Disgust roiled in her stomach, and she moved around the chair to try to help the mayor. Mirielle watched impassively.

The man gasped for air. "Kill her!" he wheezed to his servant, and he collapsed to his side.

Before the general realized what he was doing, the mayor's servant slipped his hand into his sleeve and pulled out a slender throwing knife. As fast as an assassin, he hurled the knife at Mirielle's chest.

Sara witnessed his hand move from his sleeve, and she saw the flash of steel in the firelight. Without thinking of the consequences, she lunged forward and shoved the wooden tray in front of the general like a shield. The knife struck deep and quivered in the wood.

One of the lord knights moved in quickly behind the servant to prevent his escape, wrapped his hands around the man's head, and, giving a single jerk, broke his neck.

"Lord Knight Gamarin, I told you to search these people for weapons," Mirielle said irritably.

On the floor, the mayor's body jerked twice and shuddered to a deathly stillness.

The men from Jelek stared at the body, horrified, then one of them pointed a shaking finger at Sara. "You . . . you poisoned him!" he cried.

All eyes turned to Sara, standing beside the body, her eyes downcast. She turned the tray over in her hands and studied the knife stuck in the bottom.

"She did not kill him," Mirielle said, refilling her glass. "I did. That is the only treaty I will make with his sort. Remove the bodies," she snapped to her steward. To her officers, she said, "It is time. Follow your orders."

The knights saluted her and hurried out together, their squires trailing along in confusion. The remaining civilians shuffled nervously and waited for the general's next move. The room grew very still.

Mirielle enjoyed her moment. She sat back in her chair and sipped her wine while the remaining guests fidgeted and the servants scurried in to carry away both bodies.

"Aconite," Sara said into the silence.

The general started. "How do you know?"

Sara turned slowly on her toes and met Mirielle's speculative gaze. "I have studied herbs. Aconite is a deadly poison. It's also called wolfsbane. A tiny dose of its infusion will kill a large man in a matter of moments." She remembered the mayor's horrified face and the look of death in his eyes, and she shuddered. The Code of the dark knighthood condoned murder if the act was done to advance the Vision. But if Takhisis was gone and her Vision with her, whose vision was Mirielle trying to advance? "Why? Why did you kill him?" she wanted to know.

The two women faced each other as if there were no one else in the room. The men and the servants were forgotten; the table sat empty except for the wineglasses and the trays of sweetmeats.

"I had no more use for him," Mirielle replied. "He was an obstruction that needed to be removed, and I chose the quickest, easiest method. Now that he is gone, nothing else stands in my way for a swift takeover of the Nerakan government. By morning, the city will be ours, and our troops will bring the populace to heel. It should have been ours in the first place. It was stupid of the council to just grant us the lands around Neraka."

She reached over and pulled the tray out of Sara's hands. "Thank you for this," she said, holding up the tray so the knife stood upright. "Your reflexes are still quite good." She smiled at Sara. This time the good humor spread across her face and lit her eyes with a genuine delight that made her look younger and as impish as a child.

"If you're quite finished with us, may we go?" the elder Targonne interjected.

The general tossed the tray to the table and rose to her feet. "Of course. How inconsiderate of me. Gentlemen, I bid you good night. Please remember our earlier conversations. The Knights of Takhisis are here to stay, and we seek to increase our advantage in every way possible. If there is something we can do for each other's benefit, do not hesitate to call on me."

Targonne bowed slightly and, gesturing to his son, he said, "Morham will bring the supply contracts to you in the morning. I think you will find them very advantageous."

The Jelek men bowed, too, and left wordlessly on the heels of the merchant lord. The Khur barbarian hid a smile behind his dark beard. He left a small bag of coins on the table and walked out, his silent bodyguard behind him.

Mirielle picked up the coin bag. Juggling it in her hand, she picked up the bowl of poisoned sweetmeats and tossed it into the fire. "By leaving this bag, the Khurs have agreed to bargain for wool and meat," she said, pleased with the success of her night. "All this with only one small bowl of candies."

Sara watched the firelight dance on Mirielle's

sculpted features. And she wondered, for what would
be the first of many times, what would have happened
if she had not stopped that knife.

Chapter 13

The morning blew in cold and raw on the heels of a bitter wind. The city of Neraka woke to find its lord mayor dead, his council under arrest, his mercenaries dead or switching sides as fast as they could surrender, and the Knights of Takhisis in firm control of all the city gates and watchtowers. The dragons who flew reconnaissance flights in the skies now flew over the city, reminding everyone who held the reins of power. A few ogres and draconians put up a token resistance in the streets with the knights, and a party of merchants sent a delegation to General Abrena to register a formal complaint, but overall the citizens of the city shrugged philosophically and went about their business.

General Abrena spent the day consolidating her position in the city. She fortified the area around her headquarters, doubled the guards at the gates, and moved a number of talons out of the tents to occupy the city. She met with the merchant delegation and the elders of Neraka to assure them that the change of leadership would not seriously affect the populace. Then she imposed a curfew and hinted that a "protection" tax to help pay for the upkeep of the military forces might be necessary.

The merchants looked resigned, and one suggested that she look in the lord mayor's personal treasury. The old mercenary had been collecting that tax and more for years.

Curious, Mirielle led two talons of guards to the hideous

structure the lord mayor had used for his palace. They drove out the mayor's retinue and searched the building from roof to dungeon. Sure enough, in a dank storeroom buried deep beneath the walls, they found boxes of steel coins, bars of iron and bronze, chains of gold, and enough jewels to keep a family of dwarves happy for years. As soon as they had stripped the place of its valuables, General Abrena ordered the slaves to demolish it. The palace, with its hideous colors and ridiculous design, looked like something put together by a committee of gnomes. It was too big an eyesore even for the knighthood.

Mirielle was pleased with her progress. In one swift stroke, she had removed her one rival, gained control of the city, and increased the order's struggling treasury. Now she had the headquarters and the foundation to begin the next stage of rebuilding the dark knighthood. The process would be a long one if it was to be done well, but Mirielle Abrena had learned patience and the art of doing things right the first time from her years as a senior knight before the war. Even then she had dreamed of leading the knights to victory.

* * * * *

If General Abrena was having a good day, "Knight Warrior Conby" was not. Exhausted after the dinner and standing guard at the Red Quarter's perimeter, Sara had gone to her tent and collapsed on her bedroll.

Two hours later, Massard beat on her tent walls with a stick and bellowed at his talon to rise and shine. They managed to rise, but even the sun wasn't shining. Stick in hand, he drove them at a jog-trot on a cross-country run across Neraka's plain to the distant hills and back again.

For a man who had been raging drunk the day before, he had made a speedy recovery and stayed with the recruits every step of the way, pushing them on with curses and insults. He paid particular attention to Sara and kept close to her to make sure she did not falter or fall back. Any time she stumbled or eased off, he slapped her back with the stick.

The run was torture for her. She hadn't run like that in years, and her stamina wasn't used to such long distances. By the time she stumbled into camp, her back was covered with welts and her legs had turned to lead. Sinking to a stool, she gasped for air, her face white. The younger squires watched her worriedly.

In the half an hour Massard gave them to eat, they fixed a rough breakfast and brewed tea for Sara. Jacson breathlessly told them about the general's dinner and Sara's act that saved Mirielle Abrena from the bodyguard's knife. Their growing respect for her jumped up several notches. Derrick brought the tea to her along with a hunk of bread and some hot bacon.

Sara waved her cup at the tent where Massard had disappeared to his own breakfast. "Is he always like this?" she asked wearily.

Derrick curled his lips down in a frown. "Vile or drunk. Take your choice."

"He must have changed," Sara mused, too tired to think carefully what she was saying. "He would not have lasted long under Lord Ariakan if he had been like that ten years ago."

"Why?" Derrick wanted to know.

"Ariakan believed in honor, skill, faith, and discipline. He taught his knights to respect the skills of their enemies and to train their minds and bodies to achieve their highest potential."

The other squires moved closer to listen.

"Like Steel Brightblade?" Kelena asked.

A jolt went through the older woman at the mention of her adopted son. She sipped her strong tea and looked far into the past. "Yes, like Steel . . ."

Kelena sat down beside her, avid to know more. "Did

you know him? My brother died in the Rift with him."

"I knew him. He was everything . . . everything Lord Ariakan wanted: strong, intelligent, dedicated, and honorable. He had a crooked smile, like yours," she said to Derrick. "And he lived to be a knight. It was all he ever wanted." Her voice trailed off as she stared into the depths of her tea.

She turned at a sound behind her and saw Massard leaning against his tent pole watching her intently through dark, brooding eyes. A tendril of fear crept around her heart. How much had he heard? Could he put her mention of Steel together with an old memory of her? He had only been at Storm's Keep for a short time before Ariakan posted him somewhere else, but he certainly had been there long enough to have seen her.

Finishing her tea with one swallow, she dumped out the dregs and climbed to her feet to face Massard. "What next, Knight Officer?" she demanded.

Massard grunted through his large nose. He had shaved that morning and changed his clothes, but nothing had changed his disposition. "Sword practice," he growled. He apparently had not made the connection yet.

Sullenly the recruits brought their weapons and shields to the practice field and paired off to skirmish. After a few desultory minutes of thrusts and parries, Massard shoved his thumbs in his belt and said, "You take them now, Conby," and left.

Sara stared at his back disappearing among the tents. "Who died and made him an officer?" she said incredulously.

"Experience and age," said Jacson glumly. "He's been a lazy brute for as long as we've known him, but now that you're here and competent enough to train us, he figures he can dump all the work on you."

Sara choked on a laugh. She had never taken the blood oath or the test or seriously trained as a knight while she stayed with Ariakan, yet here she was in Neraka, posing as a real knight and doing a better job of it than the officer in charge of her talon. It was ridiculous.

"All right," she sighed. "If that's what he wants, that's what we'll do."

To limber up her sore muscles after the long run, she first practiced every part of her daily sword exercises. The squires followed along, intrigued by the novelty of her maneuvers. Then they showed her some new advances and retreats and some defenses they had learned, and they put the entire regimen together and went through it one more time. Sara laughed. All they needed now was a troupe of musicians to accompany them.

While they finished the exercises, Cobalt appeared and settled down on the edge of the field to watch. Sara was delighted to see him. She paired the squires off again to put their skills to work, and this time she called on Cobalt to advise. The recruits were skeptical of the dragon at first. What dragon paid attention to the technical side of swordplay? Cobalt soon put their doubts to rest by telling Saunder how to use his longer reach to better advantage and telling Marika how to improve her footwork.

They practiced the rest of the dull, cold morning, and that afternoon, under the direction of Massard, they helped several full-strength talons move their gear into barracks in the city. Sara saw General Abrena several times at a distance, and she marveled at the woman's energy and organization. She seemed to be everywhere in the city, checking on everything, talking to knights and civilians, shouting orders, and keeping the work of occupation moving with her own sheer will. Sara envied her endurance.

Her own endurance and patience were nearly at an end. She was exhausted and sick to death of the smells and the endless noise in the city, and she thought if she had to listen to Massard's harsh voice scream at the young squires one more time, she would take his head off with the nearest brick. Half a dozen times she thought about slipping away to find Cobalt and fleeing Neraka.

She just couldn't bring herself to do it—not yet. She had not learned all of Mirielle's plans or discovered the true strength of the knighthood. Nor did she think the sentinel dragons would let them simply fly away. She needed a good excuse to leave the city that would give Cobalt time to put some distance between themselves and the vengeful anger of the knights.

Then there were the five squires. She hated to admit it even to herself, but she was beginning to like them. They were bright, enthusiastic, and searching for something to fill their lives. Although they had chosen the Knights of Takhisis, Sara wasn't convinced they were ready to totally dedicate their souls to the dark goddess. They seemed to lack a certain zeal for the truly evil. She could be wrong, of course; she had only known them for two days. But if there was a chance to show any one of them a different path, Sara asked herself, wasn't it worth staying in Neraka for a few more days?

So she bit her tongue and jumped to obey Massard's orders and kept her anger in check. Fortunately for her self-control, she stood the early watch that evening and afterward went to her bed for a much-needed night's sleep.

The days that followed assumed much the same pattern for Sara. The weather stayed dry and cold and drear. The talon remained in the tent quarter and divided its time between intensive conditioning and training in the mornings under Massard's abusive fist and serving the knights in the afternoons and evenings by performing whatever tasks needed to be done, followed by a turn at sentry duty sometime during the night. The schedule was strict and rigorous and varied little.

Sometimes Sara was able to take the recruits out on the dragons for reconnaissance flights, which everyone enjoyed, and once in a while someone would come to her and ask for help for a sick or injured animal. She appreciated these respites from the constant grind of physical labor, and she decided that if she ever returned home, she would never again complain about cleaning her house or digging her garden.

During those days, the newly designated Governor-General Abrena continued to consolidate the knights' hold over the city. A few more bands of surviving knights arrived in Neraka and were quickly assimilated into the new army. Recruits arrived, too, singly or in groups, and they were assigned to talons-in-training out in the tent quarters. Sara studied every new face she saw, and thus far her luck held. No one recognized her.

The general ordered her to attend as squire at several more dinners, but while Sara listened avidly, she learned little more about the general's future plans for the knighthood or how Mirielle intended to accomplish her goals. All she found out was the prices of goods on the black market, plans for the renovation of an interesting place called the Arena of Death, and how to charm city officials without actually saying anything meaningful.

Sara was going back to the Red Quarter one night after one of Mirielle's dinners when she saw Knight Officer Massard at the gate to the Queen's Way. There was nothing in his demeanor that caused her alarm, nothing that warned her of his intentions. He looked as if he had been drinking, but that was nothing new. She saw him leaning against a tavern wall just outside the gate, and for a moment she thought she could walk past him in the dim light without his noticing her.

He had no intention of letting her pass. She was just two paces away when his head snapped up. He lunged at her and his hand grabbed her arm. His fingers dug painfully into her muscle. "Come with me," he snarled, and he dragged her into the shadows of the deep alley beside the noisy tavern.

Sara had no choice. She could not break free of his powerful grip, and because she had been attending the general, she had no weapons with her. Her mouth went dry and her heart pounded painfully in her chest.

"I know you," he hissed in her ear. "It took me a few days to work it out. You're Ariakan's whore. The one who escaped from Storm's Keep." He shook her fiercely, his hands on both her arms. "What are you doing back? Why are you in Neraka? Who sent you here?"

"Nothing! No one!" Sara managed to gasp through the violent shaking.

He shook her again and slammed her against the wall of the building that loomed over them. "Don't lie to me. I know better than that. I'll take you before the General and let you tell her. I'm sure she'll be glad to pay a reward for a spy."

Something in what he said leaked through the pain, and a spark of hope lit in Sara's thoughts. "If it's only a reward you're interested in," she gasped, "perhaps I could find something you would like."

He chuckled and pressed her tightly against the wall. His foul breath fanned her face, and his rough beard rasped against her cheek as he whispered, "I'm sure you could." He rubbed a rough finger against her cheek. "I always wanted to see why Ariakan kept you around. Give yourself to me . . . and bring me fifty pieces of steel. With that, I can be quiet for a long time."

Sara shuddered from head to toe. Fury and repulsion surged through her. She knew, however, that without a weapon or help, she could not escape. She had to buy herself some time. "That's impossible. Where am I going to find fifty pieces of steel?"

He laughed again, the fumes of ale and spirits thick on his clothes and breath. His hand caressed her neck, then he circled his fingers tightly around her throat. "I don't care where you get them. If you want to live, you'll find a way. The knights don't look favorably on renegade spies. Think about that. Bring the coins and yourself to my tent before the end of three days and I'll forget that I ever saw you at Storm's Keep." He kissed her hard before he shoved her away and went laughing out of the alley.

Sara wiped her lips with her sleeve, spat on the ground to rid her mouth of his foul taste, and wiped her lips again. Abruptly her knees gave way and she sank down on a barrel.

Oh, gods, she cried silently, now what do I do? There was no possibility she would meet his demands. She could not beg, borrow, or steel fifty pieces of steel in this city, and there was no chance she would ever give herself to that brute of a man. She would prefer take her chances with the knights' adjudicator rather than submit to Massard even once. And she realized once would not be enough for him. Like most blackmailers, he was greedy. He had a powerful hold on her he could use time and again to twist her to his will.

No, she had to find another way to silence him. At least she had three days to devise something. Whatever she decided to do would have be handled carefully and discreetly. She did not want to jeopardize her position in Neraka if she could help it. There was too much at stake.

Cold and angry, Sara pushed away from the barrel and made her way back to the street. As she stepped out into the light radiating from the busy tavern next door, she glanced both ways to make sure Massard was gone. Warily she left the streets and alleys of the inner city and exited the main gates to return to the tent quarter.

On second thought, she angled out beyond the tents to where the practice fields lay wrapped in darkness. Cobalt, she knew, had dug himself a cave out in the highlands beyond the valley. When he was not hunting or spending time with her, he returned to his cave to rest.

He seemed to prefer the solitude to the company of other dragons.

Around her neck hung a leather cord she kept beneath her tunic. On the cord, she had strung three of Cobalt's sapphire scales, each about the size of a small child's palm. Satiny smooth and iridescent in the sun, they took the place of the lily brooch she gave to Mirielle as a focus for her ability to summon dragons.

When she conceived the idea, she didn't know if it would work without the magic inherent in the black lily. Fortunately dragons had their own kind of magic, and the scales bore enough vestigial power to be effective enough. She used that power now, coupled with her own mental energy, to send a call to Cobalt.

He came winging silently, like an inky shadow against the black sky, and landed beside her. "What's wrong?" he asked immediately.

Quietly she told him everything, and when she finished, she leaned against his leg and let his closeness sustain her.

The night lay cold and silent around them. Clouds still obscured the sky and blocked the light from the stars, so the only light came from the distant torches in the tent camps across the field.

"I could dispose of him for you," the dragon offered.

Sara smiled in the darkness. "I thought of that. But let's wait. His disappearance could be awkward, and if anyone pinned the blame on you, the other dragons would kill you."

"You could hire an assassin. There are probably dozens of people who would like to get rid of him."

Sara said glumly, "Doubtless. But first I'd have to find one in time, then I'd have to pay him—which I can't—and hope he'd keep quiet."

"Do you want to leave?"

"Not yet. But stay close." She rubbed a hand down his smooth scales and said thoughtfully, "I'd like to find something to hold over him, some way we could reach a standoff so he would leave me alone and I could leave him alone."

Cobalt dropped his head so his golden eyes glimmered close to Sara's face. "Massard does not seem to be a 'standoff' kind of human. Watch your back."

They did not talk anymore but curled up together in the night, Sara wrapped in the protective circle of Cobalt's neck.

* * * * * *

In the morning, Massard was back in the tent quarter, looking no worse than usual. He said nothing to Sara beyond a barked order for breakfast and generally ignored her while he took the talon on another cross-country run.

Sara was slowly getting stronger from the frequent endurance runs, and she could now keep up with the younger men and women without as much difficulty. Her new strength gave her more time to think as they jogged over the barren and frost-cracked ground, but try as she might, she couldn't think of a good solution to her problem with Massard. If only he would have the courtesy to fall into a bottomless fissure somewhere out on the valley floor.

That afternoon the talon was sent to the ruins of the Temple of Darkness to help with the excavation. Several other talons joined them, and Derrick explained to Sara that every squire and knight in Neraka came at least once a month to work on their queen's temple.

"Why?" Sara asked. "The walls of the upper temple are gone. What do they hope to find below?"

He cocked an eyebrow and confessed, "I don't know. They've never told us."

Nor did anyone mention a reason this time. The officer in charge, a Nightlord in gray robes, sent them off to sort through the rubble hauled out of the buried corridors by the slaves. Sara took one quick look over the wall at the deep cavern where the slaves still trudged out with their large buckets full of debris. Little had changed. The draconians in charge of the slaves looked like the same ones as before, and they cracked their whips with equal force. The slaves still moaned their monotonous cry.

The young squires, Sara, and Massard hurried on to the pile to get to work. They sorted rock into more piles, the small bits for use as filler in rock walls and foundations, the larger pieces for construction. Anything that was not rock was immediately turned over to the Nightlord for inspection. Whether it was a piece of bone, a jeweled necklace, or a hunk of armor, he examined it all minutely and placed it carefully in wooden crates for later study. It was tedious, backbreaking work.

In the brief moments when Sara had a chance to straighten her back and pay attention to things around her, she noticed Massard was staying rather close to her. He did not try to speak to her or look at her; he just kept a watch on her presence. It was disconcerting, and she found herself looking over her shoulder time and again to see where he was.

If the squires noticed any abnormal tension between their officers, they did not comment on it. They worked hard through the afternoon, although Jacson spent more time cracking jokes and entertaining his companions than moving rock.

When evening filled the city with gloom, the Nightlord dismissed the talons from their labor. Weary and sore, the recruits marched back to their quarter to rest and eat before standing their watches. Instead of retreating to his tent or going to the nearest tavern as usual, Massard sat down on a stool near the cooking fire and continued his sidelong observation of Sara.

"I wish he'd go away," Marika whispered to the older woman as they cooked strips of meat over a makeshift grill. "What's he staying around for?"

Sara could only shrug. She wished he'd leave, too. She wanted to search his tent or follow him somewhere to catch him doing something his superiors would frown upon. He had to be spending a small fortune at the taverns in Neraka, certainly more than he earned. So where was he getting the coins? Other blackmailing schemes? Illegal deals? She hoped fervently he was up to something. But she couldn't do anything—even make a pretense of collecting the fifty steel coins—as long he watched her like a guard dog.

Massard's presence dampened the entire evening for everyone. They were not accustomed to his dour, frowning company. Their conversation died to silence, and they sat shooting curious and disgruntled looks at his broad back.

Quickly they ate their meal and went about their business, leaving Sara to bank the fire and put the cooking equipment away. Finished at last, she went to her tent and tied the flap tightly behind her. Only then did she hear Massard retire to his own tent, and even though she listened for movement from his tent most of the night, the knight officer did not come out again until dawn.

The next day repeated the previous one almost exactly, except by evening Sara had blisters on her blisters, a permanent cramp in her back, and an intense desire to throttle Massard. He hadn't let her out of his sight the entire day. Now she had only one night and a day left, and she was no closer to solving her problem. By now the squires were starting to wonder about Massard's strange behavior and Sara's unspoken tension. Derrick, then Kelena, asked her what was wrong, and she had to pretend ignorance, an act she was sure Derrick, at least, did not believe.

Sara retired early to her tent that night, and even her frustration could not keep her awake. She slept soundly until Derrick woke her to take her watch late in the night.

The young man held up his small hand lamp and flashed his crooked grin when she came out, yawning and stretching. He nodded toward Massard's quiet tent. "Sounds like the old man isn't back yet."

Sara came wide awake. "Back?" she snapped. "Back from where? When did he leave?"

Derrick was startled by her intensity. "He left just before my watch. I don't know where he went. Probably a tavern, since he went to the city. Why? What's going on?"

She put her hands on his arms and looked up at his worried face. "Something I need to take care of alone, Derrick. Go to your tent and get some sleep. I'll see you in the morning."

He eyed her suspiciously, but a squire could not question an officer, even a junior one. "Be careful," he said at last. "Massard is dangerous and unpredictable."

Sara was surprised by his insight and pleased by his concern. She pushed him gently toward his tent, then she collected her sword, dagger, and a slender blade she tucked in her boot. She slipped on her black cloak and struck out into the dense darkness.

Chapter 14

She should have reported to the officer of the watch. He would be expecting her shortly, and her absence would be seen as dereliction of duty, an offense the knights punished harshly. But Sara did not believe Massard had gone to a tavern. It was too late, for one reason, and for another, she hoped fervently he had slipped away to do something he shouldn't. It was worth the risk to her to look. The trick would be finding him in the maze of streets and alleys both outside and inside the walls.

She had a bit of luck at the main gate. The officer of the watch at the walls was the young Knight Officer Targonne, who was a frequent guest at General Abrena's dinners. Sara had impressed him considerably by her actions to stop the assassin's knife, and he had altered his opinion of her age-worn abilities.

"Massard?" he replied to her query. "Yes, I know him. He went through perhaps an hour ago. Bundled in his cloak and reeking of spirits." The young man lifted his nose disdainfully at the memory. "He headed up that way, toward The Broken Barrel."

Sara gave him her thanks and walked up the road toward the notorious tavern. The Broken Barrel was one of those places where the patrons went for the brawls as much for the brews. There were usually more broken heads than broken barrels in the decrepit old place.

Despite the late hour, there were still some customers

in the tavern when Sara poked her head in the door. She quickly scanned the drunken faces and ducked out again before someone saw her. Massard was not there.

How far could he go in an hour? Where did he go?

Sara studied the street in both directions and saw nothing more than a couple of draconians walking into a distant building and a gully dwarf poking through a pile of trash. She heard rats scuttling in the alley behind her. A few lights gleamed in the windows of the crowded tenements.

She began to walk slowly along the street, keeping her eyes open and her ears attuned to the night noises around her. She nearly walked past the gully dwarf, then changed her mind and paused beside him.

The furtive creature saw the black-cloaked figure and backed away warily. "No hurt, no hurt," he croaked at her in Common tongue. "I only look for food."

"Don't be frightened," Sara said softly. "I'm just looking for a friend. I thought he might have passed by here a little while ago. A big man, a knight like me. He has a beard and walks hunched forward."

The gully dwarf peered at her face through the darkness. "Huh! Friend of yours, is he? Poor friends you have. He came. He kicked me. I hope he falls in privy!"

Sara couldn't help but chuckle. "To be honest, so do I. Did you see where he went?"

"Bad friend," the gully dwarf muttered, wrinkling his flat nose. His long, scraggly beard drooped down his chest. "When he kick me, I follow to see if I could help him down a privy. But he go in that shop, the one with three hands on sign. He not come out yet."

"Thank you," Sara said, and she gave him a copper coin for the information. She left him gleefully stuffing the coin into a ratty bag by his feet, and she hurried along the street to the shop he described.

It was there on her left, a new wooden building and one of the few of stout construction. Its shutters were closed, and the door, when Sara tried it, was firmly locked. The sign above the entrance showed three red hands in the form of a triangle and read "The Red-Handed Pawnshop."

Figures, Sara said to herself. The front of the shop was totally dark, but when she checked the sides of the building, she noticed a slip of light shining from one of the rear windows. She slipped noiselessly down the side alley and found a crack in the shutter of the window. When she applied her eye to the crack, she could see two men sitting at a worn table in what looked like an office. The men were drinking from flagons and engaged in a spirited conversation. Although she could not see the second man well enough to identify him, she recognized the first man immediately. She had found Massard.

Her excitement rising, she pushed closer to the window and tried to hear what the men were saying. It was difficult to hear them because they were across the room and the stranger had his back to Sara. She only caught a few words: "Nightlord" . . . "artifacts" . . . "good prices." It was enough to send her curiosity soaring.

Then Massard picked up a bag lying on the floor near his feet. He tipped it over and dumped the contents on the table in front of the strange man. A number of items of different sizes spilled out. Sara strained to see what they were.

The stranger moved his oil lamp closer to the objects to examine them, and the light gleamed on their surfaces. Outside, Sara's mouth fell open. She knew at least one of those items. She had found it herself that afternoon in the rubble removed from the temple and had given it to Massard to pass on to the Nightlord. She could not mistake it, a silver armband decorated with a geometric pattern of lapis lazuli. The other things appeared to be equally as interesting: a delicate silver cup, a tattered pouch full of rolled scrolls, some bits of armor, and a dagger encrusted with jewels.

The stranger looked pleased. Massard sat back and smirked.

Sara grinned. So that's what the old thief is up to.

She heard a sound behind her. Then something very hard hit her on the back of the head.

* * * * *

The first sensation she became aware of was a throbbing pain in her head. The second was of being carried by her arms and legs.

She heard a voice mumble through a thick fog, "Let's dump her in the ruins. The horax will dispose of the body."

She was dreaming. Surely this was a nightmare. It had to be.

She felt hands on her ankles and on her arms. Her body jerked and swayed. She heard footsteps pad on stone.

Suddenly she was falling. She hated dreams about falling. They always ended with a sickening crunch, and she'd wake in her bed sweating and panting. This time was different. This time she landed with a sickening crunch, and she woke to find herself on a dirt floor in total darkness.

Terror jolted her back to reality. Her first compulsion was to freeze. She could see absolutely nothing around her, no walls, no floor. She could not even see her own hands. She huddled on her stomach where she landed and felt panic build within her like the nausea rising in her stomach.

Somewhere, far in the distance, she thought she heard footsteps that quickly faded away. A heavy silence closed in on her. No! No! her consciousness cried. Don't leave me here!

But she knew it was already too late. Whoever had dropped her in this black hole had already left. She was alone.

She lowered her pounding head, too terrified to move. She wanted to scream, but some subconscious knowledge kept her quiet. There was danger here, wherever here was. She vaguely remembered hearing someone say something, something about . . . what?

In frustration, her fingers dug into the loose dirt and gravel under her. She paused and ran her hands through the dirt again. The feel of that crumbled earth and broken rock felt familiar, and the familiarity jolted another memory loose in her aching mind. The voice had said "ruins." That was it! They had dumped her in the ruins!

Ever so carefully Sara eased to her knees and reached her hands outward in a circle around her body. Far to her right, her fingers brushed a stone wall. Her breath came out in a sob of relief. It was something substantial in the endless darkness, a solid barrier against her growing terror. She scrambled close to the wall and pressed her back against it. With the comforting stone behind her, she could let her whirling thoughts slow down into some semblance of sense.

She put her pounding head between her hands. A large lump, sticky with blood, lay under her hair on the back of her head. Nausea still roiled in her belly. She took several slow, deep breaths and tried to think through the waves of dizziness that rolled through her.

She realized now she was in the ruins of the old temple—that blasted shrine so aptly named the Temple of Darkness. Just knowing that eased much of her fear. The lord mayor had said the work crews had only excavated a few of the lower levels. If all else failed, she could just sit here until daylight when the slaves returned to their labors.

But even as part of her mind took comfort in that, another scrap of memory intruded into her thoughts. There was something else the strange voice had said, something about a . . . horax? The name sounded vaguely familiar; she just couldn't remember why. Her head was still dazed from the blow, and her mind seemed slightly out of focus.

She inhaled deeply and began to take stock of her situation. The air was very cold and smelled of dust and old stone and dank mold. She realized her cloak was gone and her sword, too.

Her hand suddenly grabbed for the thong around her neck. Cobalt! If she could summon him, he could help her out of this hideous darkness. But the thong and the dragon scales were gone, and a burning sensation at the back of her neck told her it had been torn off.

She slumped against the stone, feeling terribly alone and vulnerable. Horax . . . a doubt nagged at her. What was a horax?

The cold began to penetrate her uniform, and she shivered. What she wouldn't give for a cup of tarbean tea and a light.

Sara dug her fingers into her knees. This was ridiculous. Why should she sit here the rest of the night and slowly freeze to death while Massard sat in his warm tent, counted his money, and laughed up his sleeve? That son of an ogress had done this to her, and by any god that still paid attention to Krynn, she was not going to let him get away with it! She had to get out. She had to confront him with his crimes and make him choke on his own arrogance.

She lifted her hands above her head and felt her way up the wall until she was standing upright. If there was a ceiling to this corridor or room or whatever she was in, it was beyond her reach. Keeping her hands flat on the wall, she extended her senses outward to seek any clue she could find that could help her find a way to go.

Slowly small details nudged into her awareness. There were tiny sounds she had not noticed before: the steady drip of water far away, the scuttling of a rat's feet on stone, and a very faint rattle, as if a bit of gravel had slipped loose and rolled down a slope. She also felt a slight movement of air on her right cheek. And where there was moving air, there had to be some sort of opening.

With infinite caution, she inched her way along the wall to her right, one tiny step at a time. Each time she moved, she extended her fingers and her foot forward to feel the stone ahead. It was slow going, but at least she felt as if she was doing something.

After a while, Sara decided she must be in a corridor. The wall was very straight, and there was no feeling of space around her. The air continued to waft gently past her, moving sluggishly through the blackness. She gritted her teeth and pushed blindly on.

After what seemed a very long time, Sara's fingers found the edge of a door and the end of the corridor. She felt all around the opening and discovered it was an arched entrance into an open space. Keeping her fingers on the stone wall, she stepped into the chamber.

Her eyes, so accustomed to the Stygian darkness, nearly passed over the faint luminescence. She blinked and looked again, and there it was, a ghostly blob of pale greenish light. Then she saw another and another scattered across the floor and walls of the large cavern. A largish patch gleamed like a will-o'-the-wisp on the wall several steps beyond her hand, so she edged over to take a look.

To her surprise, the phosphorescent gleam came from a round growth of lichen that clung to the wall like thick gray moss. The patch came off easily in her hands and lay on her fingers, softly glowing. Excitedly she looked around for more and found two other patches growing within her reach. She peeled them off, too, and fastened them into a ball with the leather thong from her hair. Their combined light barely lit the floor by her feet, but any light was a joy after the impenetrable blackness of the corridor.

She made her way across the floor of the chamber and added two more glowing clumps to her ball. At last she had enough illumination to take a look around.

The slaves had obviously done some extensive work in this room. The floor was cleared of almost all the fallen rock and debris, and only a few large pieces remained. The ceiling had been shored up by timbers in several places, and any artifacts and bones had been removed. Best of all, to Sara's mind, there was an obvious trail of booted prints leading through a layer of dust on the floor to a second entrance on the far side of the chamber. Her head-bashing friends, no doubt.

The skittering sound of falling gravel came across the room from the corridor she had left. Sara froze. Her blood throbbed in her head, and the hairs rose on the back of her neck. She felt it once again, that insistent warning that something was watching her.

All at once the hazy words came back to her: "The horax will dispose of the body." The horax. An image formed in her memory of something she had heard about years ago, of a large insectlike creature that lived in subterranean tunnels and fed off the living and the dead. Her breath rushed through her chest, and she hurried forward into the second hallway.

In the pale light of her lichen clump, she could see two pairs of tracks. One set led into the chamber the way she had come, while the other set led out along this other corridor. Sara stumbled forward gratefully.

With something to guide her, she could move faster through the ruined halls, though not fast enough to suit her. She had to move carefully for fear of losing the tracks in the darkness or falling into occasional fissures that split the floor. Other arched doorways led off the corridor, but Sara continued to follow the footprints in the thin layer of dust.

The strange scuffling sound came again, a little louder and a little closer this time. Something chittered in the dense darkness behind her.

Sara stifled the urge to look back and kept her eyes pinned to the tracks on the floor. She came to a flight of stairs and stumbled up the steps as fast as her shaking legs could carry her.

"Please let there be an opening. Please let me out of here!" she panted softly.

Another large chamber opened up before her. This one, too, had been cleared, and more clumps of glowing lichen grew on the walls and the high ceiling. A few rats poked their heads up when she entered, then slipped furtively away into the thick darkness.

The footprints led plainly across the wide room past a huge crack in the floor to an arched entrance. At the far side, where the tracks exited the room, they joined with a much larger trail of barefooted prints that came up from a staircase. That trail had to be the footprints of the labor gangs that were excavating the temple's levels.

The movement of air Sara had noticed earlier was noticeably stronger. A definite draft, similar to the smell of the city above, blew through this entrance, stirring her hair.

Sara clutched her ball of lichen and hurried forward.

Behind her, at the far end of the room, a long, slender shape, as black as the darkness around it, skittered in through the door. A second followed, then a third. Two more crawled out of the crevice in the floor. They met in the middle of the chamber, chittered among themselves, and all five scurried after the fleeing woman.

Sara heard them coming. The noise sounded dry and rattling, like the bones thrown by a soothsayer. Fear surged through her. She broke into a trot, then a run. She had to be close to the opening. The breeze was stronger, and the smells were different.

All at once, the ceiling opened up into a huge hole, and overhead she saw the gloomy night sky of Neraka and the faint reflection of distant torchlight. Dropping her bundle of lichen, she scrambled under the opening and looked frantically for the way out.

Her shout of joy died in her throat, for all she saw were the sheer walls of the hole. Paths came down the upper slope of the huge crater, but at the bottom, where the hole broke into the remains of the temple, there was a twelve-foot drop down to the old floor. Sara looked around frantically. There had to be something the slaves used to climb out of the ruin. She saw gouges in the dirt walls where ladders must have stood, but now there was nothing. No boxes, no ladders, not even a stepstool.

What a stupid arrangement! she cursed. They couldn't build a simple set of steps for the slaves to use?

Suddenly she whirled. Something moved in the darkness, its hard feet scratching against the stone. She could see nothing beyond the faint glimmer of the lichen on the floor where she dropped it. The thing moved again, then another thing clicked along the wall to her right. They sounded large and solid and quite at home in the darkness.

Sara's hand automatically flew to her sword, only to meet the empty scabbard. Her attackers had left her with no weapons. Or had they missed one? Her heart in her throat, she bent and reached for the slender blade in her boot. She cried with relief as her fingers found the stiletto still safely tucked away.

"Get out of here!" she shouted at the unseen things, and she brandished her knife in their general direction.

"There you be," shouted a voice above her. "Are you fine?"

Sara's head jerked up in surprise. "No, I'm not fine! Please, help me!" She searched the hole overhead and finally saw a small black figure perched on the edge of the drop-off. It appeared to be peering down at her. "Who are you?" she cried.

"I Fewmet, the gully dwarf. You give me coin and kind words. I see men drag you off, so I follow," came the raspy, hesitant voice.

Sara did not think she had ever heard a sound so sweet. "Fewmet, please, could you see if there is a ladder or a rope or anything I could use to climb out of here? There's something down here that wants to eat me."

"Oh, the horaxes. I no like them," commented the gully dwarf.

"I no like them either!" Sara shouted. "Would you please hurry?"

She heard a scrambling noise as the gully dwarf climbed out of the crater, then her attention flew back to the horax. They were scuttling closer from several directions. She stamped and shouted and waved her knife, and for a moment they seemed to hesitate. One edged warily into the glimmer of light from the lichen, and for the first time, Sara was able to see her pursuers.

Her breath caught in her throat. The thing in the greenish light was long and low to the ground, shiny black, and segmented like an armored centipede. It had six pairs of legs and short but powerful-looking mandibles that moved slowly back and forth as if the creature were tasting the air.

"Fewmet, hurry!" she shouted. She backed up until her shoulders touched the wall.

A horax made a feint toward her leg. Sara screamed and kicked at its head. The force of her blow sent it rolling back into the darkness. Chittering sounds echoed out of the silence and rattled around her head.

"Knight woman?" came the voice of the gully dwarf. "No can find the ladders. Men move far away. Did find this." Something long and thin fell out of the sky and crashed at her feet, just barely missing her already battered head.

"What is it?" she yelled.

"Torch!" he answered proudly.

Sara swallowed her frustration. "Fewmet, I don't have any way to light it."

"It already lit. Just blow on it."

Cautiously she reached out and picked up the torch. One end was very hot and glowed a faint red as if the flame had just been banked.

The horax suddenly chittered, and two of the creatures charged at her from left and right. Sara did not have time to think. She blew frantically on the torch, then whirled the end outward toward the horax on her left. To her surprise and the horax's, the torch burst into bright yellow flame. The horax chittered in rage and fell back, its eyes blinded.

The light was so bright to Sara's eyes after the blackness of the ruin that for several moments she couldn't see either. The creature on her right scuttled under her desperately waving knife and fastened its mandibles on her ankle.

Sara shrieked a cry of mingled pain and rage. She whipped the knife around to an underhanded grip and drove the point downward toward the black shape she could barely see by her leg. Her stroke fell true and pierced the horax just behind one of its eyes. The terrible pressure on her ankle relaxed, and the creature slumped to the ground, mortally wounded.

Furiously she kicked it in the direction of the other horaxes. One of them grabbed the body and hauled it out of sight. The others fell back to regroup.

Slowly Sara's eyes grew accustomed to the change of light. The torch burned merrily in her hand, throwing a myriad of dancing shadows on the wall of the corridor. The horaxes remained out of sight, although she could still hear them chittering and scuffling just beyond the torchlight.

"Fewmet?" she called hopefully. "Can you find a rope?"

Silence met her query.

"Fewmet!" she bellowed again. To no avail. The night above remained quiet; the gully dwarf had left. Sara fought down a surge of panic. Maybe the gully dwarf had gone for help; maybe he was seeking for a ladder somewhere else. Surely he hadn't just taken off to look for a snack in some trash dump.

A strange sound burst out of the darkness where the horaxes lurked. A high-pitched humming sound reverberated along the corridor and vibrated down into the depths of the ruin. It lasted several seconds, stopped, and started again.

Sara shivered. The noise sounded too much like a signal.

The humming stopped, and a deep silence settled back over the lightless chambers. Then, far away, from somewhere deep within the old temple, came an answer.

The woman gasped. She dropped the torch and made a desperate leap upward toward safety. She managed to jam the blade of her knife into a crack in the wall above her head, and she hung there trying to find purchase for her feet. But the walls were smooth stone at her level, and her body, weakened from the blow to her head, could not muster the strength to make the sheer climb. The blade of her knife slipped loose, and she tumbled to the ground beside the torch. She lay still, sick and dizzy.

The horaxes seemed to sense her weakness. Three of them moved closer, clacking their mandibles.

Sara managed to stagger to her feet. Her ankle hurt like fury and her head was ringing. She picked up the torch and waved it at the creatures. "Get away!" she hissed.

They stopped just out of her reach, but they did not retreat. They had her pinned against the wall and they knew it. They simply waited, their round, black eyes watching her every move.

Sara waited, too, her knife in one hand, the torch in the

other. Her eyes never left the shiny black horaxes.

Two sounds simultaneously registered in her throbbing head, a man's voice and the clatter of dozens of horax feet coming along the corridor.

"Is there anyone down there?" the man's voice yelled.

"Yes! I'm here! Hurry, please! They're coming!" she screamed.

"Sara Conby?" the man cried, amazed.

"Yes! Hurry! I need a rope!"

Shouts echoed down the crater. Someone called an order, and suddenly a rope snaked down. Before she could wonder how she would find the strength to tie it around her, another rope dropped down, and a man slithered to the ground beside her. He took one look at the horaxes, spat an oath, and grabbed Sara around the waist.

"Haul us up. Now!" he shouted.

The horaxes lunged forward. Sara threw her torch at the creatures and wrapped her arms around the man's chest. In the guttering torchlight, she realized she was face-to-face with Morham Targonne. The young knight grinned at her, and suddenly they were hoisted into the air.

Their bodies banged against the wall as they were dragged upward. Sara held on with all her remaining strength until she found herself lying on the path above the opening.

The knight chuckled. "You can let go now before you crush my armor."

Sara lay back on the dirt and gazed upward at the blessed sky. Dawn lit the eastern horizon with pale gray light, and the air was bitterly cold. A few snowflakes drifted down to land on her face. She smiled at the world. She had never seen anything so lovely.

A wizened face with a long beard blocked her vision, and Fewmet the gully dwarf looked worriedly down at her. "Knight woman all right? I find help."

For an answer, Sara threw her arms around him and hugged him, rags and all. Then the world whirled through her mind, and she slipped quietly into a peaceful darkness.

Chapter 15

Derrick told Sara later she slept for thirty-six hours.

When she first woke up, she had no idea how much time had passed. She lay dreamily on her cot, tucked beneath a warm blanket, and let her senses gradually return. Daylight glimmered through the walls of her tent, and someone had kept a small fire burning in her brazier, where her teakettle gently simmered over the embers.

Memories of her night's activities returned with total clarity, and she wondered what time it was. Was she too late to stop Massard from going to the general? At that moment, she did not worry that he had. She made a vow that she would make Massard pay somehow for that horrible night in the temple ruins. He wasn't going to get away with what he did to her.

She lifted her head gingerly from the pillow and was relieved to see her skull was not going to split apart. The tent didn't spin around her and her stomach didn't rebel. A dull headache was all that remained. She sat up and rested on the edge of the cot for a minute, trying to decide if she wanted to find the latrine or go back to sleep.

Voices began to intrude on her peaceful solitude.

She stretched her muscles carefully, pulled on her boots, and climbed to her feet. The voices outside grew heated, and all of them were familiar. Her curiosity was piqued.

A large shadow lay across the entrance of her tent, and at that moment, a faint rumbling began to vibrate in the air.

Sara shook her head. Going back to sleep was obviously out. She untied the tent flaps and stepped outside.

Cobalt sat blocking her exit, his bulk crowded in the space between the tents. His wings were tucked tightly around his body, and his tail was wrapped around the side of her shelter. His head was turned away from her so he could watch the squires and Massard standing near Massard's tent. An angry growl was building in his throat.

None of the people seemed to notice the dragon's ire or Sara's arrival. They were too busy shouting at one another.

Sara edged her way around Cobalt and put her hand on the dragon's foreleg.

Startled and angry, he slashed his head around to drive off the intruder. Then he recognized her and he yanked his muzzle back just in time. His teeth clashed on empty air.

"Sara!" he squealed in delight.

The arguing group stopped in midvoice and stared at her for a full minute before they closed in around her, everyone trying to yell at the same time.

Cobalt had enough. He rose to his full height and roared in their faces. The people fell flat on the ground. Alarms rang over the tent camps. Guards came running, their swords drawn.

"Now you've done it," Sara remarked casually.

The others raised their heads, brushed themselves off, and climbed to their feet as the guards charged in.

"It's all right," Sara said loudly. "He was just trying to protect me."

Knight Officer Massard bullied his way past Derrick and Jacson and shouted at Sara, "Get that dragon out of here! He is a nuisance and a—"

"No." Sara's refusal cut through his words and rang

over the voices of the others. The knights and squires suddenly became very quiet. No knight ever disobeyed a direct order without very good reason.

Massard's eyes narrowed. He had a great deal he wanted to say to this woman, but he knew this was not the time or place. Instead, he fell back on his rank as a superior officer to get back some control of a situation he felt was rapidly falling apart. "Remove that dragon, or I will have the other dragons do it for you."

Sara moved out in front of Cobalt, crossed her arms, and repeated "No" in a cold voice of adamant.

"Do you refuse to obey a direct order?" Massard snarled. A flash of anticipation gleamed through his muddy eyes like the flick of a fish's tail. There was more than one way to solve a problem.

Sara saw that gleam in his eye and understood then he had not yet exposed her secret. He was still looking for a way to turn things to his advantage. She had to strike now to silence him before he tried again to stop her. There were certainly enough witnesses for her purpose.

"I refuse to obey an order from an officer I believe to be incompetent and incapable of making decisions for the good of this talon. Therefore I challenge you to a duel for the right of your rank."

Massard's mouth dropped open. Never did he expect anything like this from this woman.

Derrick, Marika, Kelena, Saunder, and Jacson stared at her, appalled.

The other onlookers, the guards and knights, nodded in approval. A challenge for ranking was often the way inferior officers were weeded out.

"A duel," cut in the general's voice. "Are you sure you want to do that, Conby?" The crowd parted, and Mirielle Abrena strode through with Morham Targonne at her side. She ran an eye over Massard, then turned her sharp scrutiny to Sara. "Morham has told me an interesting story, Knight Warrior Conby. So I come here to see how you fare, and I find you challenging your officer to a duel. Is there more you wish to tell me?"

Sara's gray eyes were glacial when she faced Massard. "No, General. There is nothing more. Is there, Knight Officer?" Her words were as sharp and pointed as a dagger.

He caught her meaning instantly. For a heartbeat, Sara thought he might risk the extent of her knowledge and try to bluff his way clear, but then she saw him study her from head to toe and make up his mind. She could guess what he was thinking—here was an older woman, lighter, smaller, and poorly trained. She would be an easy kill. . . .

Massard visibly relaxed. "No, General," he added. "I accept her challenge."

Mirielle lifted her golden eyebrows in amusement. "Very well. Knight Warrior Conby, since you are the challenger, I will give you three days to recover from the concussion I hear you suffered. Knight Warrior Massard, you may choose the weapons. Do you wish to fight dragonback?"

"No," Massard answered quickly.

"Then we will meet at noon of the fourth day in the Arena of Death. Good hunting. Targonne, tell the officer of the watch that Knight Warrior Conby is excused from guard duty tonight. She does not look like she could guard a mouse." The general turned on her heel and left as abruptly as she appeared.

Morham Targonne bowed slightly to Sara. "I noticed the other night that your sword was missing. I will have another sent to your tent tomorrow." Ignoring Massard, he strode after the general.

His snub of Massard, a ranking officer, was so obvious that even the knight officer recognized it. He scowled at the young man's back.

After that, the crowd quickly dispersed. The guards returned to their posts, and the knights and squires from other talons drifted back to their own quarters. Soon only the Sixth Talon, its officers, and Cobalt remained.

Derrick and the other squires held back and waited while Sara and Massard faced each other.

The knight forgot all else but his own anger and self-righteousness. He slammed his hands into Sara's shoulders. "You piece of trash," he hissed. "What did you think you were doing following me?"

The force of his blow knocked Sara off-balance. She stepped back on the ankle the horax damaged and sucked in her breath as pain shot through her leg. She staggered and would have fallen if Cobalt hadn't put his foreleg out to catch her.

The dragon hissed in rage; his yellow eyes burned like twin suns.

"Cobalt, wait," Sara said softly. She rose to her full height and met Massard glare for glare. "We are even now. You hold the secret of my past. I hold the secret of your present."

His thick brows lowered. "Which is . . . ?" he rumbled.

"You are stealing and selling artifacts from the temple for your own profit. The Knights of the Skull—to which, I believe, General Abrena belongs—will not look favorably upon such activities."

His face twisted into a mask of hatred, and he raised his fist as if to hit her again. Only Cobalt's growl brought his hands back to his sides. "You can't prove it," he said sullenly.

Sara shrugged her shoulders. "I won't have to. If you turn me over to the knights, I will give the adjudicator names and places and descriptions of items, even witnesses, and let him find the evidence against you. And he will, you know." She leaned closer and added fiercely, "You should never have dumped me in the temple ruins. After horaxes, nothing you do can frighten me."

Massard actually blanched. "The ruins? I didn't know that. Red Erik just told me his men had found you and disposed of you."

Sara clicked her tongue and said, "Another name. Really, Massard. Forget secrets. They are too costly to pursue. A duel is the best choice for both of us."

The knight jerked his head in agreement. "Three days then, Sara Dunstan. They will be your last." He turned his back on them all and marched out of the camp.

Off to the nearest bar, Sara hoped.

The moment his black tunic disappeared, the five squires crowded around Sara, smiling and talking, their relief obvious on their faces.

"What was that all about?" Derrick asked.

"What happened to you?" Marika and Kelena said at the same time. "We've been so worried."

"What happened since I fainted last night?" Sara countered.

They all laughed.

"Last night! Sara, you've been sleeping a day and a half," Derrick informed her.

"The night watch brought you back from the city yesterday morning," Jacson said. "That Targonne fellow said some gully dwarf came running up to the gate jabbering about a woman who was pushed into the temple hole. They didn't believe him at first, until he described you. Then Targonne took some men and came to the rescue. He said they fished you out barely alive and told us to keep Massard away from you."

Saunder glanced back to where Massard had disappeared, his lean features dark with disapproval. "You should have seen his face when he saw them bring you in. He looked ready to kill." •

"Does this have anything to do with your challenge?" Derrick asked.

"Yes." Sara's tone was firm. "The rest is no longer important."

Kelena slammed her fist on her sword hilt. "But why do you have to fight him? He's bigger and—"

Sara cut in, "And meaner and uglier. I know. I challenged him because I believe it is my duty to defend my honor and do what I think is best for those I serve."

"Like General Abrena?" Jacson said skeptically.

"She is quite capable of managing her own affairs. No, I mean you five. You have been given to me as my responsibilities, and I want to do what I feel is right for our future."

The squires looked startled and even rather pleased at her intensity.

The thing that baffled Sara the most was she meant every word of it. These five young men and women were training to become members of the organization she despised, but for this brief time, they had become important to her, and she wanted to give them her best. Maybe one day they would change their minds about the knighthood.

Jacson still sounded doubtful. "Does that include getting yourself killed?"

"I don't believe it will come to that. Massard is basically an overweening, drunken coward. A poor combination for any officer."

No one could argue that.

"So," Sara said, smiling at their serious faces, "what were you all arguing about earlier?"

Their worry for Sara immediately coalesced into a unanimous contempt for their officer.

"Massard wanted to wake you up to stand your watch," Kelena said in disgust. "Cobalt wouldn't let him near you, so he was yelling at us to get you up."

Sara's eyes flew wide and she groaned, "Oh, no! I didn't stand watch the other night. The officer of the guard will have me on charges."

"Uh, well, no, he won't," Derrick muttered. His blue eyes twinkled. "I followed you out of camp, and when I realized you were going after Massard, I reported for your watch. I told the guards you were detained by our talon leader. Which was only a slight distortion of the truth."

Sara thumped his back gratefully. It seemed the Sixth Talon was going to look out for her, too. "It's all in your perspective," she said with a grin.

"My perspective tells me it's time to eat," said Cobalt. "If you're awake to stay, I will go hunt."

Sara scratched his muzzle lovingly and sent him off.

It was late afternoon, and a thick blanket of clouds hung over Neraka vale. A few snow flurries whisked around on the evening breeze, and twilight was closing in quickly.

Sara shivered. Despite a day and a half of sleep, she still felt weak and groggy. Her head ached, and her ankle protested every time she put weight on it. She was grateful General Abrena had given her three days. Often a challenge was accepted and the duel fought on the spot. Sara knew that, in spite of her bold words, she would've been an easy victim for Massard this day. In three days, she hoped she would be stronger and steadier on her feet.

She studied the dead fire ring, her lips pursed. What she really wanted was something hot and nourishing, and as soon as possible. "Are there any good places to eat in Neraka?"

"One," Saunder answered, giving his mustache a twist. "An inn in the outer city. Run by a woman."

"Let's go. I'm buying." Why not? Sara thought to herself. She had a few steel coins hidden away in her belongings. She thought she and the squires deserved an evening to celebrate.

Whoops of glee met her invitation. The five dashed off to get their cloaks.

Sara ducked into her tent, found a few coins and her cloak, and fished a small packet of herbs out of her bag. She sprinkled a spoonful of the herbs into a pot of water and let it sit on the edge of her brazier. By the time she returned, the infusion of feverfew and boneset would be ready to help treat her headache.

In a chattering group, Sara and the five squires trooped off to the tavern in the outer city for a hot meal. The tavern was crowded when they arrived, full of caravan merchants, travelers, and city folk, but a barmaid recognized Saunder's tall form in the doorway. She tweaked his mustache, smiled invitingly, and rearranged enough customers to clear a table big enough for the six of them.

At their request, she brought bowls of steaming stew, loaves of bread, butter, a plate of raisin cakes, and flagons of the tavern's hot spiced wine. It was a very quiet group that ate and ate until every bowl and plate was clean and everyone felt full to bursting.

Sara made it back to her tent on her own feet and drank her hot infusion of feverfew. Kelena and Marika helped her into her cot, wrapped her blankets around her, and added more coal to her brazier. By the time they left, Sara was already asleep.

* * * * *

A messenger from Knight Officer Targonne stood outside Sara's tent the next morning as the squires were rising for breakfast. They roused Sara apologetically and told her there was a messenger with a package for her. She rolled out of her cot, feeling sore and aching in every muscle and joint.

The messenger, a young squire, looked at her askance when she creaked out of her tent and identified herself.

Sara laughed inwardly. She guessed she looked dreadful, and here she had to greet this young man whom she could tell was destined for the knighthood. Tall, bound with muscles, steely-eyed, and humorless, he would make a perfect Knight of Takhisis.

"Knight Warrior Conby," he said, a taint of doubt in

his tone. "Knight Officer Targonne sent me to pass on his regards and to give you this sword with his compliments." He handed her a leather-wrapped bundle before he saluted briefly and hurried away.

Sara untied the strings holding the leather together and uncovered the sword that lay within.

"Wow," said Derrick, who peered over her shoulder.

Sara couldn't agree more. The sword was exquisitely crafted, elegantly simple, and well balanced. To her intense relief, the weapon was plain. There were no death lilies or skulls or other evil symbols adorning its surfaces. The steel blade had a diamond profile and a sharp point for thrusting through plate armor or bursting links of mail. The cross guard was copper gilt and polished to a sheen; the grip was made with black horn and ended in a fish-tail pommel. Sara was interested to see that the pommel had an empty space and four prongs in the butt, as if a stone or something had once sat there.

She gripped the sword in her right hand and hefted the blade. The weapon felt good, not too heavy, not too cumbersome. She wondered if it had originally been made for a woman. She switched the sword to her left hand and gave it a swing over her head.

"Come on," she called to the squires. "We have sword drills today."

Massard was nowhere around to gainsay her, so the talon went to the practice fields and spent the morning working on their fighting skills. Sara wrapped her ankle for support, then led the squires through their exercises and drills. When they finished that, she divided the talon into two teams and set up a mock battle. By noon, she was pleased not only with the new sword Targonne had sent her but with the squires as well.

After a quick meal, everyone went his separate way for the afternoon to fulfill his duties with other knights. Since Massard remained absent, Sara had no one to tell her what to do. Her morning's exertions had seriously tapped her slender reserves of strength, and she considered taking a nap. But there was something else she wanted to do, and she decided not to put it off any longer.

Strapping her new sword to her belt, she walked to the main gate and wandered into the streets of inner Neraka. Up one rough crowded street and down another, she wended her way past shops, taverns, and brothels, through the marketplace and along the few residential quarters. She looked in alleys and checked the trash dumps and looked behind every eating establishment. She knew Fewmet the gully dwarf had to be somewhere in the city, but she had no luck finding him.

Finally she had to ask a patrol of guards where the gully dwarves made their homes, and after they finished laughing and making rude suggestions, they pointed in the general direction of the city dump.

"Those gutter rats have a colony of some sort outside the walls near the dump. Look there, but take a mask with you," their leader said.

"Better yet, take an exterminator with you," advised one man before breaking into a fit of laughter.

Sara offered her thanks and left them shaking their heads at the foolishness of women. She walked to the Queen's Way leading out of the walled city and was about to turn toward the main gates when she changed her mind, and on the spur of a strange desire, she turned her footsteps to the center of the city and the ruins of the Temple of Darkness.

The slave gangs were there as usual, working under the whips of the draconian slave masters. A different set of talons was there that afternoon, and knights and squires alike sifted through the rubble for treasures and artifacts under the watchful eye of the gray-robed Nightlord.

It still amazed Sara that Massard had been able to slip

anything out of the sight of the sharp-eyed Knight of the Skull.

She stood for a moment at the entrance to the temple compound and took a deep breath. Her heart pounded faster, and a chill stole over her that had nothing to do with the frost in the air. Steeling herself, she walked forward until she could see over the wall into the crater itself. The black opening lay down at the bottom, like the maw of some buried monster. Large ladders poked out of the hole now, and the lines of slaves climbed in and out like ants.

"Do you have some purpose here?" said a deep voice beside her.

Sara nearly leapt out of her skin. She whirled, her eyes huge, her hands held up defensively.

The Nightlord stared at her from under the hood of his robe. The expression on his lean face was disapproving, and his eyes glittered dangerously.

"No. No, I just had to look," she stammered. Irritated at herself, she pulled herself together and asked in a calmer voice, "Why don't you build steps down into the corridor. It would certainly make it easier to get out."

The knight remained motionless as his dark eyes bored into Sara. "Exactly," he finally grated.

Sara suddenly laughed. She had to break the cold clamp of fear around her heart. "I see what you mean. There are some things best left in the dark." She heard footsteps behind her, and she and the Nightlord turned to see General Abrena striding toward them.

The general wore her knight's uniform that day, with her breastplate and greaves and a magnificent fur-lined cloak. On her armor, the skull emblem of her order gleamed like old bone in the pale afternoon light.

"I'm glad to see you did not lose your sense of humor down there," Mirielle said to Sara. She pushed her hair back with a restless gesture. She shifted on her feet, moving her body in a constant flow of small motions like a dancer who cannot stand still. She seemed to exude energy from every pore.

The Nightlord saluted the general and quietly withdrew. The two women were left alone.

Sara pulled her cloak tighter about her shoulders. Mirielle made her feel tired and very old this day. Wearily she turned away and let her gaze be drawn back down to the pit. "Did you know there are horaxes down there?" she asked quietly.

"Of course. They appeared last year shortly after we began the excavation. We decided to leave them alone. They do not bother the slaves during the day, for they are only active at night, and they have proven to be a marvelous deterrent for most would-be thieves."

"But not murderers," said Sara dryly.

Mirielle chuckled. "You are not the first to be dumped down there in the middle of the night. But you are the first to be pulled out alive. You were lucky. The horaxes are much slower when it's cold."

Sara shuddered and pulled away from the wall. Together the two women began to walk slowly across the compound toward a group of officers who were waiting for General Abrena.

"There are other kinds of thieves," Sara said deliberately. "You may suggest to the Nightlord to keep a closer watch on those who sift the rubble."

Mirielle pinned her predator's gaze on the woman by her side. They were very similar in height, so the general's golden-brown eyes could look directly into Sara's cool gray ones. Her expression warmed with understanding. "I will tell him."

Sara made up her mind to ask something she had wondered about for days. "What do you plan to do with the ruin? Are you just going to leave it for the horaxes?"

The general shook her head, her short blond hair blowing around her face. "We will build a new temple to be ready when Takhisis returns."

Sara was so startled by Mirielle's words that she tripped over a stone and would have sprawled on her face if the general had not caught her arm in a powerful grip. Swiftly Sara forced her face into calm serenity while she found her balance and stood up straight. Was this woman serious? And if so, where did she get her information? Or was it just wishful thinking? Whatever it was, the mere thought of Queen Takhisis returning to Krynn was appalling.

"Takhisis will—" she was horrified by the high squeak in her voice and tried again. "Takhisis will return?"

"We are planning on it, and when she does, we will be ready."

The conviction was strong in the general's voice, but Sara caught the words "we are planning. . ." So the knights do not know for sure, she thought, vaguely relieved.

Mirielle went on without a pause. "We have been here only three years, and already we have instituted a new training program, doubled the number of knights in this command, and gained control of the city. By the time our queen returns to us, we will once again be the most powerful force on Krynn." Her voice rang with pride, and her arms swept wide in a gesture that took in the whole world.

Sara was shaken by the woman's immense confidence. "What about the dragon, Malys? She is a force to contend with. She already holds the Goodlund Peninsula."

"True. But there are ways to deal even with the likes of her."

Sara's throat turned dry, and she had to force her words past a lump in her throat. "You have a grand ambition, General."

Mirielle corrected her. "That's 'Governor-General' now. The city elders saw fit to bestow the title on me."

They had reached the group of officers, and Sara felt six pairs of eyes regarding her intently. It was more scrutiny than she cared for when her guard was down and her mind was still shaken by Mirielle's revelation. She was terrified they would see through her fear to the reality of her deception. She saluted them in the manner of a proper junior officer and asked to be excused.

"Of course, Knight Warrior," the governor-general agreed. "I look forward to watching your duel in two days. Fight well."

Sara bowed and left as quickly as she could without actually running. At the gate of the compound, she broke into a jog and by the time she reached the main gate, she was running. She flashed a wave to the officer of the watch and flew down the road to the bare open fields that stretched to the feet of the distant mountains.

Outside the city, away from the reek and crowds of the streets, away from the dark gaze of so many eyes, Sara slowed down at last and fell to her knees, panting. The frozen ground chilled her to the bone, and the icy wind cut through her cloak and padded tunic like a knife, but she knelt there in the dead grass and sucked in the clean, cold air in great cleansing breaths. She felt like crying, except no tears would come. She had never felt so empty—empty and frightened and confused.

She had her answers now. She could go back to Solamnia, find the knights, warn them of the dark knighthood's resurgence, and go back to her village and her home. She would not have to face horaxes or drunken knights or megalomaniacal generals ever again.

Of course, she would have to leave Cobalt behind. She could never realistically hide him for long around Connersby. She would have to leave the squires in the Sixth Talon, too. But they were adults; they could make up their own minds. They would probably be horrified to know she wanted something else for them.

So why couldn't she leave? All she had to do was get to her feet and start walking. If the dragons caught her or a patrol stopped her, she could always claim dementia from her concussion. The going would be difficult without Cobalt, but she could make it. She simply had to move—if she wanted to.

Instead, she remained on the ground, her ankle throbbing, her head aching, and her body getting colder by the minute.

Sara sighed and said wistfully to herself, "This would be a good time for a god or a goddess to send a sign, a vision, perhaps, or a spiritual enlightenment, something to help me decide what I should do!" It was a shame they had gone and left the poor mortals to slog through the mires of indecision alone.

It was all so confusing. She couldn't see into the future to guide her path. There was no one she could talk to, no way she could tell if staying in Neraka would do any good. All she had was a deep well of tenacity, a stubborn pride, and the very quiet voice of her heart.

Be still, whispered the tiny voice in her mind. *Listen.*

She knelt in the vast solitude while the wind soared around her and the great arch of the sky slowly darkened toward an early twilight.

At last she put her hands on the ground and pushed herself to her feet. Her knees refused to unbend at first, and she had to work the joints loose from their stiffened position. Blood flowed back into her feet, making them tingle. Slowly she stood upright, turned around, and walked back to Neraka.

Her heart had known what to do all along.

Chapter 16

Sara found Fewmet eventually just outside one of the taverns not far from the ramshackle huts of the little Aghar colony and the mountainous city dump. The tavern's location was not auspicious for human business, but draconians and ogres did not seem to mind the constant low-level stench or the occasional ox-stunning odor that drifted over from the dump when the wind was right.

The stumpy gully dwarf was sitting on a wooden sidewalk, humming softly to himself and gnawing on a bone. When he saw Sara, he bobbed his head and offered her a shy smile, at the same time stuffing his bone out of sight in the rags of his shirt.

She squatted down beside him. "I've been looking for you," she said lightly.

He gazed at her in amazement. "Was I lost?"

"No," she chuckled. "I just didn't know where to find you."

He suddenly clutched his bone and glared at her suspiciously. "Why you look for Fewmet? No one look for gully dwarf."

"I just wanted to thank you for helping me the other night. That was very brave of you."

Fewmet's wrinkled face beamed. "Knight woman nice. Should not feed to horaxes."

Sara laughed. "No, I was very glad to get out of there."

The gully dwarf hunkered down and glanced both

ways before he said, "I hear you fight mean knight who kicks gully dwarves."

"News certainly travels fast around here," Sara observed. "Yes, I challenged him."

"Good. I no like. You remember this: Knight have bad knee. I see sometimes. He go to many taverns in city."

Sara's brow drew together in a frown. "I've never noticed that Massard had a limp."

"Not always. He try to walk straight. But knee is weak. Remember when you fight." He wagged a filthy finger at her.

Sara thoughtfully tucked that piece of information away. She expected Massard would choose swords for weapons, which meant she would have little opportunity to exploit the gully dwarf's information. But one never knew when such a tidbit could come in handy.

Ignoring the nasty looks and rude remarks of the draconian customers, she went into the tavern and ordered a bowl of stew, a wedge of cheese, and a honey cake. The barman, when he heard what she was going to do with the food, insisted she pay for the utensils, too. Sara shrugged and paid, then carried the food outside to the gully dwarf. The barman flatly refused to let him eat inside.

Fewmet was delighted. He never got to eat an entire hot meal all by himself. Sara stayed with him, her sword close to her hand, just to ensure no one tried to interfere with his repast. Other gully dwarves gathered close by to watch enviously, but they dared not bother him while the quiet woman stayed beside him.

He shoveled in his food with both hands, licked every utensil clean, and ate the honey cake in three crumbly bites. Watching him, Sara guessed he could probably get a second meal just by combing his beard. She presented the bowl and plate to him as a gift and solemnly shook his hand.

When she left, he was busy stuffing his new dishes into his bag and humming the same tuneless song.

* * * * *

The appointed day of the duel came with the first clear sky Neraka had seen in weeks. The sun climbed into a flawless sky, and for the first time in days, the cold eased to a bearable cool. By noon, the weather was positively balmy for Neraka in late winter, which brought the crowds to the Arena of Death in droves.

Challenges among the knights had been rare lately due to the scarcity of officers, so a duel between two of the older knights was cause for much anticipation. The fact that one was a man and the other was a woman just made it more interesting. Betting grew heavy the morning of the duel, and by noon, Massard was favored two-to-one.

In the tents of the Red Quarter, the members of the Sixth Talon hovered around their junior officer until Sara wanted to scream. She appreciated their solicitous efforts to feed her and advise her and prepare her for battle, but all she really wanted was a little distance and some quiet to settle her nervousness. Instead, Derrick insisted he should polish and sharpen her sword. Saunder had found a mail shirt that fit her and was repairing a broken link. Marika fussed over her tea and toasted bread; Kelena polished her boots, and Jacson paced back and forth, demonstrating defensive moves she already knew.

Sara tried to smile and be gracious, but it became so difficult, she finally took her food and her weapons into her tent and firmly fastened the flap shut behind her. The five knights-in-training exchanged mournful glances and counted the minutes until noon.

In her tent, Sara drank a cup of her tonic for headaches and lay down on her cot to rest her head.

Knight Officer Massard appeared shortly thereafter, blowing in like a thunderstorm. He stamped around the tents and shouted, "On your feet, you yellow-backed spawn of gully dwarves. You have work to do." He sneered as they jumped to attention. "Yaufre, put that thing down. Conby won't be needing it. Put out that fire! Clean up this mess! What do you think this is, a latrine?"

Sara, still in her tent, decided wisely to stay out of sight. Sometimes discretion was the better part of valor. From his overly loud voice and ugly behavior, she got the impression he was trying to lure her out into the open. But this was neither the time nor the place to pick a fight with Massard.

Massard charged around, snapped orders like bolts of lightning, and punctuated his demands with furious insults. When he was satisfied at last with the order of the camp, he lined the recruits up before his tent.

"Now that you're finished putting this dump in order," he growled, relishing every word, "you will report to Knight Officer Darcan at the stables. He has some muck for you to rake."

"No! We can't—" Jacson inadvertently cried.

Massard took one step forward to stand before the young squire. His eyes narrowed to mere slits, and before anyone could move, he viciously backhanded the youth across the mouth.

The blow sent Jacson reeling. Catlike, he caught himself before he stumbled into the fire ring, and he crouched, his hand reaching for his dagger.

"Jacson, no!" Derrick hissed. The bigger youth grabbed his friend's arms and wrestled him back into line.

Massard's black eyes glittered. "Wise," he said, his voice full of venom. "Now, move!"

They knew all the pleading in the world would not help. For some reason, Massard did not want them to accompany Sara to the duel, and because of his rank, they couldn't gainsay him. They shifted in their places. Jacson's face glowed red with fury, and Marika hunched her shoulders and clenched her fists as if ready to strike Massard's sneering face.

Derrick forced his hand to salute his talon leader. "Yes, sir," he said stiffly. He turned to the others and drooped his right eye in a slow wink. His gesture acted as a balm to the others. They understood and allowed themselves to relax. Still angry but resigned, they followed Derrick away from the tents and off to the western edge of the tent ring, where a large complex of paddocks and stables housed the knighthood's horses.

Massard watched them go. Worthless, the lot of them, he thought. He had never seen such a group of weak, spineless, whining children in his life. They were worse than goblins. Well, as soon as he dealt with that conniving, boot-licking tramp, he'd beat some backbone into those brats or kill them trying.

He wrenched off his sword belt and stomped to his tent. Flinging open the flap, he tossed his sword on the rumpled blankets of his cot and was about to leave when something caught his eye—a bottle, sitting on the stool near his bed. A familiar clay bottle, with the wax-sealed cork and the maker's mark of his favorite dwarf spirits. His mouth went dry. He should not drink, not this close to a duel in which he would have to fight for his rank and reputation. He realized the drink slowed his reflexes and did strange things to his vision.

Yet again, why should he worry? The woman he was facing was no knight. She hadn't trained for twenty years or fought with Lord Ariakan during that glorious summer the Knights of Takhisis conquered Ansalon. True, she could handle a sword, but he was certain she would not be able to survive what he had in mind.

His hand reached for the bottle. He pulled the cork and inhaled the earthy fumes with a sigh of pleasure. Without bothering to wonder why a bottle of dwarven spirits had been left in his tent, he tipped the bottle up and let the fiery liquid burn a trail to his stomach.

* * * * *

Sara woke with a start. A noise, a light scratching noise that sounded like nails on fabric, disturbed her. She sat up, dazed, and stared at the dim yellowish light that leaked through the tent walls. She had been doing this all too often since Red Eric's brigands cracked her head. Every time she sat or lay down, she fell asleep.

The scratching came again, louder this time, and the tent material jiggled under the pressure. Someone was at the door.

Sara groggily rose and opened the flap. A goblin face full of obsequious goodwill peered up at her. She recognized General Abrena's messenger in his filthy tunic and bits of purloined armor.

Her eyes flew to the sky to find the sun. "Oh, no! What time is it?" she cried.

The goblin peered upward, too, wondering what the fuss was about. "It's midday. High sun. General sent me to fetch you. She says almost time."

Rubbing her neck, Sara tried to calm down. She tied her hair back out of her way, then she picked up her new sword and her dagger and strapped them on. If Massard chose any other weapon, the general would supply one. She had no armor to wear—she'd never had more than the basic pieces she had worn during training years ago, and those were long gone—so she slipped on the heavy chain mail Saunder gave her. It was better than nothing.

She strode outside into the bright sunshine, the goblin at her heels. The camp seemed strangely empty without the squires. Now that the time had come to leave, she missed their noisy support. It was just like Massard's vindictive pettiness to send them to some onerous task instead of letting them witness the duel.

"Has Knight Officer Massard already left?" she asked.

The goblin shrugged his knobby shoulders. "Not in tent. Must have."

"Good." Sara pulled out her new thong decorated with dragon-scale disks. She had made a new one to replace the missing one the same day she woke from her long sleep.

"You won't need that. I'm right here."

Sara twisted around at the sound of the deep voice and saw Cobalt's horned head lying lazily on the ground beside her tent. The rest of the large dragon lifted himself off the ground from behind her tent and ambled around beside her. In the noon sun, his deep blue scales glowed with a richness all their own.

The goblin yelped and hid behind Sara's legs.

"Would you like a ride to the arena?" Sara asked the goblin in an effort to be polite.

"No," said Cobalt and the goblin in one voice. The goblin scurried off before she could make any more dreadful suggestions.

Cobalt waited while Sara quickly saddled him. He extended his leg so she could climb up to his back, and as soon as she was settled in the saddle, he thrust off with his powerful hind legs into the cool blue sky.

Sara was grateful that he did not question the wisdom of her challenge. All she wanted now was a few minutes of quiet. She ran her hand down his long sapphire neck, enjoying the smoothness of his scales beneath her palm. She could feel his life-force surge beneath the protective scales in a hidden current of power and energy. She was thankful more than she could say that he freely gave her his support and companionship.

The dragon winged over Neraka, past the main gate, the Queen's Way, and the temple ruin to the southeastern side of the city, where the Arena of Death sat just to the south of the ex-lord mayor's playground.

The arena, a remnant of Queen Takhisis's days in the city, was an oval-shaped coliseum used for various bloody entertainments and killing sports. Its attractions were quite popular with Neraka's residents and quite lucrative for officials, who charged a few coppers for admission, sold beverages and food, and ran a betting ring. Consequently the lord mayor, and now General Abrena, made a habit of presenting events whenever possible. A duel between two officers wasn't quite as exciting as watching a mass slaughter of captives by hungry tigers, but there would be enough interest to draw a crowd. Especially since the news of Sara's brush with the horaxes in the ruin had spread through the city.

Cobalt circled around to overfly the arena, giving his rider a chance to see it from above. It was no wonder there was talk of repairing the place. It was a wreck. Too many years had passed, too much blood had been spilled in the sands, too many overenthusiastic fans had trampled over the seats, hacked at the stone with their weapons, or broken every awning and railing in sight.

This day, a fair-sized crowd gathered in the dilapidated tiers of seats and cheered when the large blue spread his wings wide and coasted to the sand-covered floor of the arena.

General Abrena, several of her commanding officers from the Order of the Lily, and the Nightlord from the Order of the Skull walked across the sand to meet Sara. Lord Knight Cadrel carried the scepter of the adjudicator, the knighthood's judge in matters of contention.

Sara had seen duels often enough to know the procedure. She slid down from Cobalt's back, formally saluted the officers, and bowed to the Nightlord in his gray robes. "May Queen Takhisis walk with me this day and guide my efforts in her service."

"Fight with honor, Knight Warrior," replied the priest.

Governor-General Abrena frowned over Sara's mail shirt. "You wear no armor," she observed critically.

Sara stood straighter under the heavy mail. "My armor was lost, General. I have not been able to replace it yet."

"And yet you willingly fight a duel in simple mail?" She shook her head at the stupidity of certain knights. "I would prefer to keep you alive, Conby. Knight Officer Massard has not appeared yet; we have time to find you something better than that."

Cobalt suddenly growled deep in his throat. "He comes."

Another ragged cheer rose from the crowd as a lone figure entered the arena at the far end and swaggered across the open space to the group of officers. He tripped once but regained his balance and came to a halt in front of Governor-General Abrena. Knight Officer Massard saluted rather crookedly.

Mirielle's eyes narrowed, and her full lips tightened in disapproval. Her nose wrinkled suspiciously.

Massard suddenly belched. The reek of spirits on his clothes and breath reached out to them all. The adjudicator rolled his eyes. The others stifled mingled sounds of disgust and amusement.

"Knight Officer," snapped the general, giving him a withering glare, "you are a disgrace. Where is your pride? In the bottom of some latrine? How dare you show up here to fight a duel of honor in this condition?"

Massard planted his fists on his hips. "What difference does it make?" he bellowed belligerently. "I can fight her on one leg."

"Do you wish to let the challenge stand?" the adjudicator said in a hard voice.

"Blast it, yes! What'd ya think I came here for?"

"What weapon do you choose?"

"None." Massard turned his black gaze on Sara. "I'm gonna kill her with my bare hands."

Shocked, the knights began talking among themselves in harsh whispers. Bare-knuckled fighting was not considered an honorable alternative in duels. That sort of brawling was usually relegated to the lowest ranks of mercenaries and draconians.

Sara leaned back against Cobalt and tried to mask her emotions. The idea of fighting a big hulk like Massard with nothing but her fists scared her silly. At least with a sword, she would have a chance to wear him down and wound him. This way she wouldn't have a hope.

General Abrena obviously had the same thoughts, for she turned her swift glance to Sara and said, "No. Weapons must be chosen. I will not allow the duel for rank to be turned into a street fight."

Massard curled his lip. "Daggers, then. And that dragon must leave. I don't want to be scorched by him when she dies."

"I wouldn't worry about the dragon if I were you," Sara said caustically. "I'd worry about breathing near open flames. Your breath alone could kill an ogre."

Mirielle held up her hand to stem the gathering tide of insults. "Daggers are acceptable. Knight Warrior Conby, do you want armor?"

Sara noticed that Massard wore his usual tunic and padded leather vest. "My opponent is not wearing any. I will abide as I am."

The adjudicator held out his scepter for the crowd to see and shouted for quiet. As soon the audience settled down enough to hear, he continued. "The defender has chosen daggers. So be it. The fight is to the death. Let the dragon withdraw to the limits of the arena."

Whistles and cheers met his announcement. The knights withdrew to the walled seats above the arena floor.

Cobalt gently nudged Sara's arm. "He may be drunk, but he is strong and wily. Be careful," he warned in a soft hiss. She patted his neck in reply, then hooked her sheathed sword to the saddle and lovingly slapped his leg. He leapt up into the stands, crushing a few more wooden rails as he went, and took a precarious perch on the uppermost level of the coliseum, where he could see Sara but still be considered at the "limits of the arena."

All too quickly the expanse of the arena was empty except for Massard and Sara. A hush of anticipation settled over the crowd.

The adjudicator stood on a platform above the sands

and shouted, "You may begin."

Massard pulled his lips back in a sneer. Deliberately he drew his dagger and threw it into the sand. "I want to feel your death with my bare hands," he grunted to Sara.

Sara drew her own dagger, letting its blade shine in the sunlight. "You'll have to catch me first, you drunken lout," she taunted.

Like a bull, Massard roared in anger and charged forward. But the spirits were working deeper into his system, and their effects began to interfere with his vision. Suddenly he saw two identical women laughing at him. Before he could clasp either one of them, they ducked out of his grasp and ran around behind him. He staggered, caught himself before he fell on his face, and turned clumsily.

Sara looked into his eyes and recognized that unfocused look. "Massard, you're a fool!" she yelled. "Mushrooms are smarter than you. Ogres are better-looking. You couldn't fight a blind kender in a barrel."

The officer charged her again, and once more she slipped out of his reach. She hoped she could exhaust him by taunting him into these thoughtless rushes. As long he couldn't see her very well, she could easily stay out of his reach. She knew well he was so strong and heavy, he could kill her if he were to catch her.

They continued this deadly dance back and forth around the arena for some time, until Massard's face was flaming red and bathed in sweat. He breathed hard whenever he stopped, and his hands clenched at his sides.

Sara was tiring, too. The chain mail felt like a shirt of lead on her chest and shoulders and was becoming very hot. Her bruised ankle ached from the constant turning and twisting; her head had begun to pound.

Massard came at her again, his head lowered, his powerful legs thrusting his weight forward to crush her. This time she waited a fraction of a second longer, and as he bore down on her, she slashed outward with her dagger. The blade slid along his leather vest and skittered into the flesh of his upper arm. Blood had been drawn. Sara dropped and rolled away.

The crowd had grown restless during the charge-and-dodge game. Now they roared their approval and stamped their feet for more action.

Massard ignored the wound. It was only superficial, a mere scratch to him. He shook his head and mopped his face with his tunic sleeve. His vision seemed better; for the moment, he could see only one image of Sara.

He sprang for her again, but this time he slowed down and controlled his rush enough to see which direction she leapt away. As she dodged, he pivoted in the same direction and caught her by surprise. His fist swung up and slammed into her midriff. She staggered, wheezing with pain.

Massard punched her again and felt with tremendous satisfaction his fist connect with her cheek. The crowd roared with delight.

The impact knocked Sara off her feet. She fell flat on her back, while her head rang and her face felt as if something had shattered it. The flesh around her eye began to swell. Gasping for breath, she looked up and saw Massard take a flying leap to land on top of her. Desperately she wrenched her body sideways just as he crashed to the sand where she had lain. She managed to scramble upright and put some distance between herself and the knight.

Massard climbed slowly to his feet. Blood trickled down his arm and sand covered his clothes. "Almost," he said with a sneer. "Just lie down—you're good at that. Lie down and I'll kill you quickly."

Sara laughed in spite of the pain in her face. "At least I'm good at something. You never were, Massard. Isn't that why Lord Ariakan sent you away? Because you couldn't do anything worth an ogre's spit? Isn't that why you drink yourself into a stupor every day?" She snorted in contempt and finished with, "How did you ever get to be a knight?"

Massard's rage roared in his ears and his blood burned with fury. He lunged forward to catch her again, but this time, instead of trying to punch her in passing, he grabbed for her clothing so he could hold her down. His right hand closed on her upper wrist, and his left fingers caught a fistful of her chain mail. He forced her wrist back until she cried out in pain and dropped the dagger to the sand, then he dragged her close and pressed his lips to her mouth.

The audience in the seats laughed and cheered him on.

Sara spat in his face. She struggled wildly, trying to break his grip. Realizing that her panicked struggles got her nowhere, she forced her fear back and tried to think—quickly! Her son, Steel, had spent hours teaching her methods of self-defense, but she hadn't practiced them in so long, she had forgotten much of what she had learned. Leverage was everything, he used to say to her. Leverage . . . sparks of memory fired in her mind. Images became clearer. Phrases and words came back to her.

Another little snippet of information swam back into clarity. The gully dwarf had said Massard had a bad knee. It was too bad he hadn't told her which one.

These thoughts passed rapidly through her mind, and in the time it took for Massard to tighten his grip on her chain mail, let go of her wrist, and pull back his fist to punch her in the mouth, she decided what to do next.

Immediately she collapsed her knees and dropped to a crouch. Her move took him by surprise and forced his balance forward over his toes. Sara abruptly straightened her legs, driving her shoulder into his stomach. She grabbed his arm and, using his forward balance to assist her, deftly flipped him over her back. The knight crashed to the ground and lay gasping in the sand.

"Kill him!" The words echoed from one side of the arena to the other. "Kill him!"

Sara groped in the sand for her knife. Massard rolled over and staggered up. He pulled a second knife, a black stiletto, from his boot and reared back to stab her. Shifting her weight to her arms, Sara lashed out with a booted foot at Massard's left knee, the one she had noticed he favored in the past. Her hunch was right. The force of her blow slammed his knee sideways, and he fell like a stricken ox. His knife dropped to the sand.

But if Sara hoped he would lie on the ground and groan or nurse his knee, she was disappointed. Massard slipped beyond reason and the limitations of pain. Bellowing with rage, he scrambled over the ground and grabbed her leg.

Sara suddenly saw her dagger half buried in the sand, where it lay just beyond her fingertips. She tried to reach for it, only to be wrenched back by a vicious yank to her leg. Her face banged into the arena floor; sand ground into her nose and mouth and tore into her swollen skin. She spat out the sand with a mingled cry of pain and fury.

Somehow she twisted around to her back and used her free foot to kick at Massard's head. Her first kick missed, but the second connected solidly with his chin and knocked him backward just enough so his hands loosened their grip on her leg. With all the strength she had left, Sara jerked her leg loose and shoved herself back to her dagger.

The knight bellowed his anger. He threw himself forward over her, crushing her down into the sand with his greater weight. His hands grabbed for her neck.

She felt his fingers tighten around her throat like a noose. They dug into her skin, cutting off the flow of blood and air to her exhausted body. Her face turned a sickly red; her lungs burned from lack of air. The pain gripped her like a red-hot iron band around her neck and head. She wanted to scream, but she couldn't make a sound.

Terror welled up from the depths of her soul. Almost every conscious thought in her mind screamed at her to struggle, to fight back, to pry those killing hands from her throat. But a few strands in the cold, reasoning part of her brain held her terror at bay for just a few heartbeats, long enough to give her hand time to reach for the dagger. She could feel it still, under the small of her back. If she could just get her fingers on it and pull it out, she could get him off.

Massard screamed incoherent oaths at her as he squeezed the life out of her. He paid no attention to her drumming heels or the struggle of her left hand to claw at his face. Nor did he see her right hand worm its way under her back and laboriously pull out the dagger that Derrick had so carefully sharpened to a razor's edge.

Somewhere in the far distance, Sara heard the murmur of a crowd like the hum of insects, and even fainter, she caught the cry of a dragon. Cobalt, she wanted to cry. Cobalt, wait! The noises faded away into the thundering cry of her struggling heart.

Her eyes bulged as the world grew dark. The dagger felt like a bar of lead in her hand. It was so heavy she could barely lift it. She didn't waste time trying to aim for a killing stroke; all she wanted to do was get his hands off her neck so she could breathe again. With the last dregs of her failing strength, Sara drove the blade into his side just above his belt.

Massard screeched in pain and twisted around to grab at whatever jabbed his side.

Sara's chest heaved upward in a frantic effort to breathe through her constricted throat. She gasped and coughed as he struggled to pull out her dagger. The blessed air in her lungs brought back her vision and a trickle of energy. The black roar faded from her head.

Massard was weakening. She could feel his body sway. Her nose, free to breathe again, caught the odors of mingled sweat and liquor and the metallic smell of blood. He thrashed around so much, she couldn't reach her dagger. But she could reach his. The black-handled stiletto he had dropped lay just an arm's length away.

Her fingers groped for the handle. At that moment, Massard wrenched her dagger free from his side and raised it triumphantly above her, the bloody point aiming for her bruised throat.

Sara gathered the last vestiges of her strength. She closed her fingers around the black stiletto and brought it around and up. The slender blade slid deep into the knight's stomach and sliced upward behind his breastbone. A look of astonishment slid over his bearded face. He gazed down at the handle protruding from his abdomen as if he couldn't believe it was there. The dagger in his hand fell out of his nerveless fingers, clattered off her chain mail, and dropped harmlessly to the sand.

Slowly Massard toppled forward on top of Sara, crushing her into the sand. His weight was more than she had the strength to lift.

She sighed once and let the world go dark around her.

Chapter 17

If Sara actually killed Knight Officer Massard with the stroke of the second knife, no one ever knew for sure, because the moment he slumped over her, a frantic cry reverberated through the arena. The onlookers all clapped their hands to their ears and watched in amazement as the blue dragon lurking on the rim of the high wall catapulted downward to the sands. He sank his teeth into Massard's torso and flung the body aside. Torn and bloody, Massard crashed into the stone retaining wall with a dull thud and dropped to the sand.

"If that doesn't kill the old lush," remarked an officer to General Abrena, "nothing will."

The crowd waited expectantly. All bets were on hold until it was apparent at least one of the duelists survived.

On the sands, Cobalt gently nudged his rider. She breathed, he saw with relief. She looked bruised and battered, but there were no bloody holes, nothing obviously broken. He nudged her again with his scaly nose, and this time she groaned. One eye flew open. The other was swollen shut.

"Cobalt!" she exclaimed. "Where's Massard?"

"Over there," he said gruffly.

He held his muzzle steady so she could pull herself to a sitting position.

Cheers, applause, and a few jeers from losing bettors filled the stands. The show over, the spectators settled their bets, left their litter, and crowded through the exits.

Sara watched them in a daze. She didn't dare climb to her feet for fear of embarrassing herself by fainting again or giving in to the nausea that racked her stomach. Her face throbbed where Massard had punched her and every muscle in her body ached.

"Have some of this," Mirielle's voice said beside her. The governor-general handed her a flask filled to the brim with a pale golden liquid. Sara took a swallow and felt a fine, mellow honey mead coat her tongue and slide like liquid sunshine down her throat. Her rebellious stomach grumbled once and gradually subsided. She had another long drink and let her breath out in a long, heartfelt sigh of relief.

"You'd better get something cold on that eye," observed Mirielle. She offered her hand to help Sara to her feet. "Good fight, talon leader."

Sara's battered face broke into a smile. She had done it. She and the Sixth Talon were free of Massard. Her secret was safe for a while longer, and she had some breathing room. She took Mirielle's hand and made her way to her feet. Dizziness gripped her, forcing her to grab Cobalt's neck for support. Only grim determination kept her from fainting again at the general's feet.

Mirielle was pleased. This knight had pride and the courage she was looking for in her commanders. "Take her to her tent," she ordered.

The big blue was happy to obey. He scooped up Sara in his powerful forearms and carried her bodily into the air.

Pressed tightly against his chest, the woman looked up at the dragon's fearsome head and grinned lopsidedly at his worried expression. "It's all right now, Cobalt," she told him.

He would not relax, though, until he delivered her safely to her tent and saw her walk inside. As soon as she was lying down on her cot, he left the camp and flew around the city to the southwestern side, where the stables spread out beneath him. He knew he was not supposed to go near the barns to avoid panicking the horses. The dragon guards watched him closely, but he ignored them while he scanned the ground for any familiar figure. Far below, he saw Marika and Kelena emptying wheelbarrows of manure. He couldn't resist a single trumpeting cry of triumph.

The girls looked up, saw him, and pumped their fists. They had understood his message. Satisfied, he winged across the broad valley to the nearest snow-capped peak of the encircling mountains. Frigid air blew over his wings and nipped the ends of his nostrils. He snorted great gouts of steam as he landed in the deep snow near the summit of the massive peak. He paused just long enough to scoop up a big armful of snow and ice, then he dropped over a ledge and glided back down the mountain to Neraka's vale.

Some of the snow had melted or fallen away by the time he reached the tents in the Red Quarter, yet enough remained to make a giant-sized ice pack. Marika and Kelena met him at the camp. They had managed to get away from stable duty for a short meal break and had come racing back to find Sara.

Cobalt dumped his snow by Sara's tent and watched while the girls made an ice pack for her eye, brewed her tea, and talked to her about every move made in the duel. They had to go back to the stable to work, but their faces glowed with excitement when they left. They couldn't wait to tell Derrick, Saunder, and Jacson.

* * * * *

After two days of rest, Sara felt well enough to return to her duties. She was immediately struck by the change in attitude toward her, not only by the young men and women in her command but by the other knights as well.

The day after her duel with Massard, Governor-General Abrena sent her goblin messenger with compliments, a new rank insignia for her uniform, and an order to appear before the armorer for a new set of armor.

Chuckling at the irony of all this, Sara fastened the lily insignias to her sleeves, thanked the fawning goblin, and went out to greet her talon.

The five members snapped to attention and executed perfect salutes. New respect shone on their faces as they waited for their orders. They knew nothing about Sara's past life and the true purpose of her challenge to Massard. All they knew was that they liked this officer who treated them fairly, as individuals with their own strengths, and who had rid them of an odious dictator who had made their lives miserable. They stood a little straighter, their pride evident to all, and went about their work with pleasure.

On the third day, when Sara was able to move again without too much pain and the swelling around her eye went down enough so she could see, she took the talon out to train with their dragons. For the first time since the duel, she came face-to-face with other knights, both common and talon-ranked. Everyone she met, including knights who had never said anything to her before, had a word or two of congratulations or commendation, a salute, or a greeting. She guessed all this attention stemmed from the intense dislike Massard had generated during his time in Neraka. It never occurred to her that she had earned their respect on her own merits.

A further sign of her increased status in the ranks showed up several days later in the form of three more squires. They reported to Sara that morning and told her they had been reassigned by Lord Knight Cadrel to the Sixth Talon to bring it up to strength. She had them line up with the other five and studied them one by one.

The first, and by far the tallest, was Kazar, a barbarian from the Khur wastelands to the north. His face was comely but too hard and unforgiving to be pleasant. He did not seem pleased by his transfer and answered Sara's questions with curt replies.

Argathon had no idea where he was from originally. He had been orphaned in Jerek during the Second Cataclysm and wandered to Neraka simply because his father, a half-elf renegade and mercenary, had mentioned it a few times when he visited his son. Argathon's elf heritage was apparent in his short, slim stature and fair coloring, but his human blood gave him a trim, blond beard and a tendency to be short-tempered.

The last squire stared at Sara belligerently. "My name is Treb," she said in sharp, biting words. "I am Nerakan, born and bred, and I will take my Test of Takhisis next week."

"Congratulations," replied Sara dryly. She crossed her arms and examined the woman before her. Treb had to be the oldest of the squires, and she was like her name, compact and colorless. Her features were nondescript; her hair was lank and mouse brown. There was nothing drab about her attitude, however. She seemed to be trying to make up for a boring physical appearance with a tough, touch-me-not personality.

Treb's face darkened at Sara's tone. "I did not wish to transfer, but we were all that was left of our unit. Two deserted. The others failed their tests."

"I'm sorry," Sara said in regret. Those who failed the test for knighthood did not survive to try again. Derrick's friend, Tamar, had died that way.

Unfortunately her sympathy was wasted on Treb. The woman spat on the ground. "They were worthless." She raked her cold gaze over the other five squires. "Much like them. They probably won't make it either, and then I can be leader and get some real talent in this talon."

Sara stiffened, her gray eyes turned to granite.

Treb did not heed her silent warning. She went on venting her anger in spiteful words. "Our talon leader was old, too, but at least he knew how to train recruits. That Massard was a drunken bore. He couldn't train anyone to blow her nose."

Sara saw the squires stiffen with growing outrage. She jerked her hand down to stifle them. "And all but three of your talon deserted or died," she remarked. "Those are hardly the results of a good trainer."

Treb snorted indelicately. "I told you, they were worthless. I, on the other hand, could beat any of your children with any weapon, any time."

"Done," Derrick said suddenly, startling Sara. "But not yet. Squires cannot duel for rank. We will both take the Test of Takhisis. After we have been knighted, we will fight for the right to be junior officer."

"What?" Sara exclaimed, distressed by Derrick's impulsive challenge. Her cry was lost in Treb's loud acceptance and a chorus of cheers from Saunder, Jacson, Kelena, and Marika. "Be quiet!" Sara bellowed in her most commanding voice.

The talon hastily snapped into silence.

"Now, in case you have all forgotten, you must have my permission to apply to the governor-general for the test."

Treb said smugly, "Knight Officer Conby, that will not be necessary for me. I have already applied and been accepted. My mentor has arranged for me to take the test next Soldai."

"Then I will apply, too," Derrick put in, his tone reasonable. "Knight Officer, you cannot deny me. I am ready."

Sara's fists clenched. No, not yet. Not Derrick. If he passed his test and took his vows, she could lose him just as she lost Steel. He would give his soul to the Queen of Darkness and become one of those she hated. No, she couldn't let him! He was too honorable, too loyal, to be bound up in this evil knighthood. Surely there was something better for him somewhere else in Krynn, if he just took the time to look. But if he insisted on taking his vows now merely to satisfy a matter of pride, he could lose his chance to escape, maybe even lose his life.

Yet what could she do? Sara knew even as she looked at his strong, handsome face that she could not deny him, at least not here, not in front of his companions and especially not in front of Treb and the two new men. It would undermine his authority and be a severe blow to his pride that could drive a wedge between them. She had to play for time so she could have a chance to talk him out of it.

"Squire Yaufre, I am too new to this talon to be assured that you are ready. The Test of Takhisis is no game. It is deadly serious, and I will not take a chance on your life just to satisfy a recruit with more arrogance than sense."

Treb started to interrupt, and Sara cut her off with a fierce motion. "And you, Treb, will remember who commands this talon. Keep your mouth shut, your ears open, and learn to cooperate with your group. Even the Knights of Takhisis must work in unison in battle."

Treb opened her mouth again only to hear Argathon say cheerfully, "Pack it in, Trebbie. You won't get anywhere with this one. She's fought horaxes, remember? After those, you're just a mosquito."

The Nerakan's face burned like embers, and Sara quickly stifled a smile. The woman obviously did not like the nickname or the young man's rejoinder.

"Enough of this. We will discuss this later, Derrick. For this morning, we will go on a flight. Bring your flying gear, bows, a full waterskin, and enough food for a day. No swords."

She watched them break off to their tents to fetch their gear. Why in the names of all the absent gods did the order have to saddle her with three new recruits now? Her position was precarious enough without adding complications like these. She didn't intend to stay in Neraka indefinitely. When the opportunity arose to escape the city without pursuit, she would take Cobalt and go, and if she could convince some, if not all, of the five squires to go with her, she would.

But now Derrick wanted to take his test and be fully knighted in the service of Queen Takhisis. How much of his desire, Sara wondered, was a true calling, and how much was simple availability? Derrick had never expressed a deep devotion to Takhisis or her dark knighthood in Sara's hearing. He wanted knowledge, authority, power, self-reliance. But to devote his life to a missing goddess? Sara was not totally convinced. The problem would be to prove to him that he was not convinced either. She couldn't be blunt and deny him permission without causing a rift in their developing relationship. She had to find a way to show him that the Knights of Takhisis held nothing but darkness for his soul.

Sara drew in a long breath. The strife was too close to her heart. She couldn't think through this dilemma without remembering Steel and her failure to help him. At that time, she'd had help in the guise of Caramon Majere and Tanis Half-Elven, who helped her take Steel to the Tower of the High Clerist to see the tomb of his father, the hero Sturm Brightblade. But none of their efforts, or her pleading, or even the vision of Sturm's ghost had been enough. Steel returned to Lord Ariakan and took his vows.

This time she had nothing to rely on but herself. She ran her fingers through her short hair and thrust her thoughts of Steel aside for now.

She had an idea that might help ease at least one of the talon's problems. While she waited for the squires, she walked to the practice fields and summoned the dragons.

Cobalt came immediately, his presence reassuring to his troubled rider. A third dragon appeared with Squall and Howl, a young but fierce blue named Tumult. He was Treb's dragon, he told Sara loftily.

She had a quick word with them to warn them of her intentions. They squawked a bit until she told the younger ones they could watch from a distance, as long as they stayed out of sight. They agreed to that and were all innocence when the squires arrived to saddle them. The recruits had to ride double, since there weren't enough dragons. Cobalt, being the largest, agreed to carry the last two with Sara.

With everyone mounted, the dragons arrowed into the air. They turned west toward the heart of the rugged Khalkist Mountains. About twenty-five miles into the wilderness, they saw a valley that angled in the general direction of Neraka and wasn't buried too deeply in snow. A small stream flowed under a shield of ice, and trees grew in the sheltered dales. Water, shelter, and fuel. It was what Sara was looking for. She pumped her fist to signal the dragons and sent Cobalt gliding down to a landing in the snow. The three younger dragons followed.

"Everyone off," she ordered.

One by one the eight squires dropped off the dragons into the snow and looked around quizzically. The five originals and the new three instinctively splintered into separate groups.

Sara leaned her arms on the saddle. "One of the most important things you need to learn before you become a knight is survival. The second is teamwork. All too often, the skills go hand in hand. If you learn to work together as a team, you will stand a better chance of success. Therefore—" she waved at the dragons to take off, "—I am giving you the opportunity to practice what I preach. Work together and you'll get home. Neraka's that way." And before the startled recruits could protest, she urged Cobalt aloft. His leathery wings grabbed the cold air and sent snow whipping around the gaping men and women.

The big blue looked down at them and chuckled. "They don't look very happy."

Sara shrugged. Their dragons would be close by, out of sight, in case of trouble. She wasn't worried about their abilities to make it back to Neraka, only about their intentions to be knighted too soon. "I'll give them four days. They'll make it if they want to," she commented.

Those four days were the longest Sara ever spent. The other talon leaders laughed when they heard what she had done. Such tactics had been used before, usually to good advantage, and the older knights, who mentored the squires, heartily approved. They didn't like the hurried training they'd been forced to provide any more than Sara did, and they were in full support of anything that helped "toughen" the recruits.

Sara didn't really care what they thought. She was too busy searching her own heart and mind for some course of action. Should she stop Derrick or let him try? What if the others wanted their turn, too? The dilemma nagged at her every minute the talon was gone.

The turn of the new year came during their absence, and it was that night that Sara dreamed of Steel. He had walked in her dreams many times before, usually in the remembered image of the last day she saw him, when he mounted the blue dragon, Flare, and left her behind to face her own grief, loneliness, and sense of failure. This time she saw him in her dream's eye as a young man barely out of boyhood. He was standing in the open space before their two-room dwelling on Storm's Keep. A storm raged across the island, soaking Steel in a drenching rain. Wind buffeted him, but he just extended his arms to greet it and laughed. His long black hair flew around his face like the tatters of a minotaur's sail.

"Come in!" Sara tried to yell over the roar of the wind and the crash of the waves. "Come in before you catch your death."

Steel grinned his crooked grin and shouted back, "Not

yet, Mother. Be patient! It isn't time."

There was a tremendous crash of thunder. Sara bolted awake, trembling, the sound still ringing in her memory. The dark tent huddled silently around her. There was no wind or rain or thunder. No Steel.

Tears sprang to her eyes. She scrubbed her face with the rough blanket and pulled the bedding tighter around her. She hadn't cried for Steel in years, but the terrible loneliness that had held her in thrall in the months after he left returned with fresh, painful vigor. The tears broke loose and streamed down her cheeks. She buried her face in her blankets and let the tears come. There was nothing else to do. Even after eight years apart, Sara still missed him horribly. She cried for the child he had been, she cried for the years since she had lost him, and most bitterly of all, she cried for his death, which left an empty void in her soul that nothing would ever fill.

Perhaps if she had been able to have children of her own, her loss of Steel would not have been so wrenching. But even during the years she stayed with Lord Ariakan, she never conceived, and Steel became the cherished center of all her frustrated love.

Until this year. Now, in this cold, dark city in a tumultuous, frightening age for their world, she had found a group of young people who stirred her affections like none since Steel, and ironically enough, they didn't even know.

Sara suddenly chuckled at herself. She wiped her face dry and climbed out of bed to stoke her small brazier. A pot of water sat off to the side, where it stayed warm for tea. She brewed a cup of her favorite blend, dried and mixed from herbs in her garden in Connersby.

Back under the blankets, she sipped her tea and pondered her strange position in Neraka and the images of her dream. Steel had never been patient, which made it odd that she would dream of him cautioning her to wait. Perhaps he was right—or rather her inner self that conjured the dream was right. There were times when it was prudent to lie back and see what developed. Things could change in the blink of an eye.

She would bide her time and let events happen as they would. She just hoped that when the time came to jump, she would be ready. Feeling better, she lay back and slept dreamlessly the rest of the night.

Chapter 18

The squires straggled into Neraka during the afternoon of the fourth day. Squall flew in first to alert Sara, then the other dragons arrived. They, Cobalt, and Sara stood outside the main gates and watched the talon come in.

Sara breathed a silent prayer of gratitude. All eight of the squires were there, walking slowly across the flat plain in a ragged imitation of a patrol. Derrick had the point, and although he limped and had to lean his weight on a walking staff, he steadfastly led his group on the path for home. Saunder and Treb walked the flanks, and Kelena brought up the rear. The rest filled in the gaps, their bows slung over their shoulders.

Sara didn't say a word until the talon was lined up before her. She noted with pleasure that they stood shoulder to shoulder as a group, not as two factions. She doubted that friendship would grow among all eight of them, but they seemed to have found some respect for each other. That was all she asked. "Well done," she said proudly.

As exhausted as they were, every man and woman threw back his or her shoulders and stood a little taller before her simple accolade.

Sara stood aside. "There is soup, hot wine, and roast meat waiting for you at the camp. You are dismissed."

Irrepressible Jacson whooped his delight and sprinted toward the Red Quarter. Argathon dashed close on his heels. The others followed more wearily. They all looked as hungry as wolves and pale with patches of windburn on their faces.

Derrick gave Sara a twisted grin as he fell in beside her. "That was a nasty trick."

She returned his smile with one of her own. "True. Was it successful?"

"Eventually. Argathon is not so bad once he gets to know you, and if it wasn't for Kazar, we wouldn't be here. He has an uncanny ability to judge snow. But Treb has ambition and little tolerance. Kelena had to knock her into a snowbank before she would listen to anyone." He scratched some ice from the four day's growth of beard on his jaw. "I never thought I'd be glad to see this place," he muttered.

Sara glanced quickly at him, but his face was unreadable. "What did you learn?"

"Not to trust talon leaders," he chuckled. "Or dragons. We saw them following us once or twice, but they wouldn't come near us. Traitorous wyrms."

She pointed a finger at his limp. "How did you hurt your leg?" she asked.

He grimaced. "I twisted my knee falling down a hill."

Sara sensed there was more to it than that but did not press him. Instead, she merely said, "I'm glad you're back safely."

He leaned into his walking staff and said thoughtfully, "It wasn't so bad, really. We divided our food. There was plenty of firewood and ice to melt for water. The hard part was avoiding frostbite." His crooked grin shone on his dirty face. "We learned a great deal about one another huddled together through those bitterly cold nights. Did you know that Saunder has a dreadful snore, and Treb talks in her sleep, and Kelena hates to be crowded? All terribly useless information."

"That depends on how you use it," Sara said mildly. "If you were the leader of a talon, would you assign

Saunder to night guard or day guard? Would you trust Treb with vital information if you knew she could reveal it to others in her sleep? Would you send Kelena to a busy city or into the country to gather information? By knowing the people in your command, you can make better decisions that will ultimately be advantageous for all of you. Success improves your reputation. And that," she said, gently poking his arm, "is a good principle to follow wherever you go."

Derrick looked at the squires plodding ahead of him. "Point taken," he said.

They finished the rest of the walk in companionable silence. As soon as they reached the camp, Sara made certain every squire had his or her fill of hot food and drink. She listened to their reports and their conversation and was pleased to see that her earlier assessment was correct. The trek home had been long, miserable, and difficult, but it had forged a bond of mutual experience and a measure of respect among them all—even Treb. They knew now they could face difficult situations and work through them together.

Argathon was the first to hear the crunch of booted feet on the frozen ground. He glanced past the line of tents to see who was coming and hurriedly jumped to his feet. The others were just looking around when a tall, cloaked officer trod with slow deliberation into their midst. His hands were gloved, and his face was shadowed by a cloth hood.

Sara couldn't guess what would bring this particular knight out to their camp. She rose to her feet and saluted. "Good evening, Lord Knight Cadrel. Would you care to join us for a meal?"

The afflicted knight declined. "I came to see for myself that your talon returned intact. That is good. In two days' time, we are sending a new wing out for a training assignment south of here. Your talon has been ordered to accompany it."

Sara tried to hide her misgivings; Treb made no such effort. "But I am to take my test in two days," the Nerakan cried angrily.

Cadrel turned his hooded face toward her. His dark eyes caught the flicker of firelight, then vanished again in shadow. "Wait. You will be tested soon," he said in his gravelly voice.

Treb dropped her gaze from the hood that hid the ravaged face of the knight and was silent.

"You will all be tested soon," he continued. "Our order has too few knights. For a few years, we must speed up the progression in order to fill our ranks. You will finish your training on the fields of battle."

"Lord Ariakan would not approve," Sara said softly.

Cadrel clenched his maimed hand on his sword grip. "I am aware of that, Conby. But he is dead and we are nearly so. The knighthood must be adaptable to survive these dark days."

"By needlessly risking the lives of its recruits?" she demanded.

"If need be," he grated. "Be at the fields beside the Blue Quarter with your dragons at dawn on Soldai. This will not be a drill." He turned on his heel and stalked away, leaving behind a mingling of confusion and excitement.

As soon as he disappeared from view, the squires began talking at once.

"Where do you think we're going?" Marika asked everyone.

"Somewhere warm, I hope," Jacson threw in.

Treb snorted. "If we take the dragons, it will be very warm for someone."

Sara sat down on her stool and let them talk. She did not know whether to be relieved that the date for the squires' tests had been postponed or worried about what the lord knights were sending them into. It could not be pleasant.

She found out two mornings later.

A day of rest and the natural resilience of youth had brought the squires' vitality surging back. They came out of their tents at dawn joking and talking among themselves. They wore simple battle armor and carried their helms and a full complement of weapons. The black armor of the Knights of the Lily would not be theirs until their knighting.

Sara envied them for their enthusiasm and energy. She was still trying to recover from her concussion and her injuries from the duel with Massard. Thirty years ago, she too, would have bounced back to normal after only a day or two, but five decades had taken their toll on her resiliency.

She was not excited about this day either. She had spent a long night dreading the coming of dawn and an assignment that could not bode well. Then, to rub salt into the wounds of her anxiety, she had to don the hated black armor Governor-General Abrena had sent to her.

Feeling irritable, she led the talon to their practice fields, summoned the dragons, and took them around the perimeter of the ring to the Blue Quarter on the south side of the city.

Five talons had gathered in the open fields, forty-five knights and about twenty dragons, mostly blues. Sara realized their talon was the only one made up entirely of squires.

She was puzzling over that when an officer broke away from a group and strode to meet her. It was Knight Officer Targonne, looking fresh-faced and pleased about the morning. His armor, adorned with jewels and overlapping layers of dragon scales, gleamed with iridescent hues in the dawn's pale light. He greeted Sara cordially.

"Conby, come this way. Subcommander Torceth is briefing us now."

She walked with him and forced a smile for his benefit. "I did not have a chance to thank you for the sword you sent."

He waved it off. "It was a spare. I secretly hoped you

would blood it on Massard. I was glad to see him go. He was unfit to be a Knight of Takhisis."

A shiver ran down Sara's back at the cold disregard in the young man's tone. Charming he could be, but Sara also sensed a calculating cruelty lurking just beneath the urbane surface of this well-dressed young man. She guessed that he had probably pulled her out of the ruin on a whim, not for any eagerness to help.

They reached the group of talon leaders clustered around Subcommander Torceth. The others nodded to her, and Torceth shot a glance at her. "Ah, the squires. Lord Knight Cadrel told me to expect your talon. You're late." Of medium height and barrel build, Torceth made an imposing figure in his armor. He was a swarthy man with a heavy beard, thick lips, and a tendency to scowl.

Sara said nothing. She watched Torceth unroll a map and begin to explain their objective, punctuating his instructions with short jabs of his finger. Her heart sank. It was what she feared the most, a surprise attack on a strategic position that just happened to be at the site of an innocent village.

"The junction is south of here, about fifty miles along the Kortal Road," Torceth was saying. "There is a small troop of mercenaries stationed there by the Galiard family. They will be of little consequence. We will take the village and set up our own command post. We are to hold the area until further notice. Our wing will encircle the village from here and here."

He turned to Sara. "Conby, you will take your talon to this point on the road and hold it to protect our flank. I do not want to be surprised by a patrol from Kortal or a raiding party from the Galiards. Other than that, watch and learn. Is that understood?"

Sara could only nod. She returned to Cobalt and climbed to a seat in the two-rider saddle in front of Marika. Jacson clung to the back of the wooden frame.

The dragon craned his neck around to look at her mute

face. "Well?" he demanded. "Where do we go?"

"Follow the talons. We are to stay to the rear," Sara answered shortly.

"So what are we going to do?" Jacson insisted on an answer.

Sara refused to turn around. She watched the wing dragons leap into the air one after another. "We are going to attack a small band of mercenaries and a village that has the misfortune to sit at the junction of the trails from Neraka, Kortal, and Sanction."

Jacson looked quizzically at the wing that was now aloft. "They need all those knights just for that?"

"They seem to think they do," Sara said between clenched teeth.

Squall, Howl, and Tumult quickly followed the other dragons. Only Cobalt was left on the ground. Sara instinctively tightened her thigh muscles and wrapped her hands around the leather-wrapped pommel.

The dragon bunched his powerful leg muscles and sprang into the wind, the rush of his leap forcing his riders deep into their seats. The rising breeze caught his wing vanes and lifted him higher into the morning sky. He stretched out his neck and trumpeted his delight, huffing his breath out in great clouds of steam. He flew low over the windswept ground, then flapped his wings and rose to a higher altitude to join the Wing.

In a tight group, the heavily laden dragons turned south toward the mountains. Guided by an experienced scout, they found the trail leading through the snow-clad barren peaks. A volcano steamed gently to their right as they left the valley, its brown flanks the only bare rock in the vast panorama of snow and ice. The trail had been snowed over for more than a month now and, due to the danger of avalanches, had been closed to foot travel. Snowslides were certainly not an inconvenience for dragons, but keeping track of the narrow path through the mountainous wasteland wasn't easy.

Thin clouds obscured the sky and turned the day dull and spiritless. The air above the mountains was frigid and laden with plumes of tiny ice crystals.

The riders huddled close together for warmth. No one spoke. They wore their helms to keep their heads warm and wrapped wool mufflers around their faces to protect their skin from frostbite. Sara kept her gloved hands tucked under her heavy cloak.

Fortunately fifty miles, level as the dragon flies, does not take long on dragonback. Before the winter sun reached its zenith in the southern sky, the wing of dragons reached a particular humpbacked mountain that was a recognizable landmark along the Kortal trail.

Subcommander Torceth, on his blue, signaled to the six talons to split off and take their positions in preparation for the attack.

In groups of four or five, the great creatures separated and spread out along both sides of the trail. They tipped their wings and glided quietly upward, closer to the ice-bound mountain summits where they would be more difficult to see.

Sara glanced down. The trail had dropped down into a rocky valley dotted with pines and a few leafless groves of aspen. It curved in a broad sweep to the southeast between high walls of weathering granite. The dragons did not need their guide now to follow the trail. It lay below them like a long, unbroken white ribbon delineated by cliffs of gray stone and copses of gray-green evergreens.

All too soon the trail dropped down from the high mountains to the lower flanks, where the snow did not lie as deep and signs of civilization began to intrude. Small cottages could be seen here and there among the high pastures. A few goats grazed on a wind-scoured hill. The trail showed some evidence of use where someone had recently shoveled through a high drift.

Several dragons close to Sara's talon began to drift

downward.

Sara's heart started to pound harder. Her hands turned clammy inside her gloves. She wanted to stop this, to warn the village ahead, but unless she was ready to sacrifice herself and probably Cobalt, Jacson, and Marika, too, she could do nothing but wait and watch.

Below, a high ridge thrust out from the side of a mountain, forcing the trail to rise several hundred feet before it leveled out along the crest, then dropped down into another valley. This second valley was broader and less rocky and scattered with wide, open areas that in the summer were meadows of rich grass. At the base of the ridge, the trail continued a short distance toward a grove of large pines, where Sara noticed columns of smoke rising above the trees.

The first two talons landed their dragons on the ridge trail just behind the summit. The other groups continued on.

Sara told Cobalt to follow the southernmost group. Up and over the ridge they glided, as noiselessly as possible, in a wide arch that would bring them around behind the village on the eastern and southern side.

Sara saw the second path that forked off the Kortal trail. It went south through the heart the Khalkist range to Sanction, the port city on Sanction Bay. Another talon dropped down to guard that road. A moment later she spotted their objective, the eastern end of the Kortal trail, where it appeared again on the far side of the pine woods.

She pointed it out to Cobalt, and he led Squall, Tumult, and Howl in a quiet glide down to the ground. The last talon followed. The dragons landed heavily in a meadow out of sight of the village and immediately slid into the trees, where they could see the trail and the first few clusters of cottages. Sara and her squires took cover behind a deadfall covered with vines and brambles. Their four dragons hunkered down behind them in a thicker copse of pine.

The village had its origins in a single inn that had stood at the junction of the two trails for several generations. In time, people built a few houses, a livery stable, some storehouses, and a tavern that formed the nucleus of a thriving little village. More houses, shops, and a blacksmithy grew up around it. Beyond the limits of the huts and cottages were farms scattered along the valley, where farmers eked out a passable existence in terraced fields and small orchards. For most of the year, travelers passed through on their way to Neraka, Kortal, or Sanction, and shepherds from the lower regions around Kortal came in the summer, bringing their flocks to graze in the high meadows. It was a quiet, unassuming village that had the bad luck to be in the wrong place at the wrong time.

Sara looked around almost frantically for guards. Someone should have seen the great blue dragons landing. They weren't exactly silent. But she heard no horns of warning, no shouts or cries of fear. The village sat peacefully in its sheltering trees, unaware of the horror about to descend on it. A few people were out among the buildings, but most seemed to be indoors, where the warmth of a fire and a hot meal were more pleasurable than the cold, drear day outside.

The knights in the talon with Sara's slid off their dragons and unsheathed their swords. They waited impatiently, intent on listening for the signal.

When it came, a thundering boom echoed through the valley.

"That's it!" shouted the talon leader, and he charged up the trail toward the village with his knights close on his heels. Their three dragons roared their excitement. A stroke of lightning erupted from one of the beasts and exploded into the side of a cottage. The building collapsed, its wreckage already smoking. Flames licked at the dry wood and thatch, and in moments the ruin was overwhelmed with rushing, crackling fire.

That's when the screams began.

Several humans crawled dazedly out of the burning home.

The three dragons leapt forward through the trees. Their powerful legs toppled smaller trees and crushed the undergrowth. Their heavy bodies toppled the stone walls of several houses and demolished the wooden out-buildings.

Sara stared, appalled, as one dragon sank his claws into the struggling villagers and tore them to bloody shreds. The second smashed a stable and ripped a horse to pieces. It swallowed the animal, then grabbed a woman that came staggering out of the wreckage. Her terrified shriek died in a sudden burbling cough. The dragon shook her body fiercely and tossed her aside. Gleefully the three rushed on, their roars reverberating through the woods.

"Why did they do that?" Derrick shouted at her, his comely face rigid with shock.

Sara shook her head fiercely. "I don't know! They're supposed to capture the village, not raze it!"

Beside her, Treb licked her lips and watched every-thing with a wide-eyed stare. Her dragon, Tumult, squirmed impatiently.

From the buildings in the trees came more explosions and the sounds of terror. Cracks of lightning ripped through the chilly air, followed by thunderous crashes and the growing roar of fire. The columns of smoke Sara had noticed earlier changed to a dense, acrid pall. Tendrils drifted out through the tree trunks like ghostly tatters.

The squires could not see much of the village through the trees and the smoke, but it didn't take much imagi-nation to understand what was happening. What they could see and hear was ghastly.

The knights were supposed to attack the village from three directions while their dragons stayed at the perimeter. Sadly, the knights and dragons alike, goaded by excitement and the lust for blood, rampaged into the village, destroying houses and slaughtering everyone they caught. House by house, the knights forced out the inhabitants and inexorably drove them toward the center of the village. Most of the people were too over-come with dragonfear to resist. Only a few courageous people tried to make a stand and fight off their attackers, and they were quickly cut down with sword or axe. Nearly every building was on fire, and most of the out-lying homes were smoking ruins.

Where were the reported mercenaries? Sara thought furiously. Wasn't there anyone to defend this place?

Through a gap in the trees, she saw a small knot of six men and women slip through the flattened undergrowth where a dragon had already passed. They crept forward slowly, cowering with fear but determined to reach the trail and escape. They did not yet see Cobalt and the others.

Tumult started to edge after them.

"Hold him!" Sara snapped to Treb.

Treb rounded on her, her eyes strangely bright. "Why? Aren't we supposed to keep them from getting out?"

"We were only ordered to protect the flank from attack," Sara said fiercely. "Keep him under control."

Derrick's hands clenched into fists. "It doesn't matter now," he rasped.

Sara turned her head to see five knights charge after the villagers. Laughing with pleasure, they grabbed the unarmed men and hacked them down in front of the screaming women. Then their bloody swords slashed into the terrified faces of the women, and the screams were silenced.

Sara heard the sounds of someone being sick close by, but she couldn't turn to see who it was. Horrified and sickened, she watched the knights, their arms and faces splattered with blood, clean their blades on the dresses of the dead women and turn back to the burning village to find more victims.

From the center of the village rose a cacophony of shrieks and shouts and cries of agony. Dragons continued to roar through the trees and sear the remaining huts with their lightning breath.

"A knight must not engage in combat with an unarmed opponent," Sara hissed under her breath.

"What?" Kelena asked, her voice trembling.

Sara repeated the line from the Code for them all to hear. Then she yelled it with all her pent-up anger and frustration.

Tumult abruptly loosed a thundering roar and pounced out of his hiding place. He was a young dragon, and the smell of blood and the killing roar of other dragons was too much for him. In a frenzy, he bolted into the smoke toward the center of the village.

Sara spat a curse. She grabbed Treb's arm. "Come on! We have to bring him back! He has no business in there!" and she pulled the young woman out of their cover. Treb stood for a moment, looking confused, then she hefted her sword and started up the trail.

"You shouldn't go alone," Argathon cried. "Let us go with you."

Sara refused with a peremptory jerk of her hand. "Stay in position. Watch the road. I'll take Cobalt."

A sudden noise from the path made Sara whirl around. A large party of heavily armed men dashed up the road from the direction of Kortal. Their crossbows were already drawn, and even as Sara recognized their intent, they raised the stocks to their shoulders and fired their first volley at the squires and the dragons.

A tremendous wave of noise rolled over Sara: shouts and bellows of angry dragons, and the sizzling crackle of dragon lightning. Through it all, she heard one clear voice yell, "Sara, look out!" Then something crashed into her and knocked her to the ground. Her head, still healing from the attack days before, hit a tree root, and for a moment the sky seemed to fall in on her, and then all turned sickeningly black.

Chapter 19

Sara came to with a start. A heavy weight lay across her chest and face, making it difficult to breathe and impossible to see. Metal pressed against her nose and cheek, and something hard dug into her chin. A panicky jolt of fear galvanized her muscles, and giving a tremendous heave, she pushed the bulky weight off and reared upright. Her eyes flew open; air rushed into her lungs.

She brought her gaze to focus on the thing she had pushed off. Metal armor, a leather tunic, and a slender back met her eyes. Worst of all, a crossbow bolt protruded from a bloody hole just below the figure's shoulder blade. Her heart filled with dread.

"Oh, no. Oh, no," Sara cried softly. She thought she knew who it was, but to be sure, she turned him over to his side and carefully unfastened the helm with shaking fingers. The visor slid away to reveal an all-too-familiar face, already slack in death.

The youngest member of her talon would grow no older. Noisy, energetic Jacson lay limp and silent beneath her hands.

All at once Sara became aware of a clamor of noises around her. Someone groaned in pain close by, swords clashed in a desperate struggle somewhere out of her sight, and overhead, Cobalt hissed and steamed his fury and stamped his frustration into the trembling earth.

Climbing to her feet, Sara rapidly assessed the situation. Kelena lay an arm's length beyond her in the muddy snow, clutching at a bolt in her upper thigh.

The remaining squires, Treb included, stood shoulder to shoulder across the trail, locked in a desperate hand-to-hand struggle with a large party of mercenaries.

Four dead bodies lay strewn across the trail's clearing, two of them scorched and smoking from dragon's breath.

The other dragons were nowhere to be seen.

Cobalt, however, held his position. He had not yet noticed that Sara was on her feet, and he continued to hiss and stamp while he watched the melee and waited for a chance to help. At that moment, he could not aid the talon with his lightning breath because they were too close to the enemy, nor did he want to leave Sara until he knew she was alive.

"Where are Squall and Howl?" Sara yelled up at him.

Cobalt lowered his head, delighted to see Sara unharmed. "Derrick sent them after Tumult," he growled.

"Come on, then. We'll help Derrick." She bent down and sadly squeezed Jacson's arm before she drew her sword and dashed out of their vantage point and into the path.

Cobalt lumbered after her. Anxious to help, he plunged into the midst of the struggling fighters and knocked them all sprawling. His hind foot pinned one mercenary to the ground, and his tail swept Sara off her feet. As the attackers cowered back from the big dragon, he lifted his horned head and let out a thundering roar that shook snow from the trees and resounded through the smoking village.

The mercenaries dropped their weapons and groveled in the snow, paralyzed by dragonfear.

"Quick, get their weapons," Sara ordered as she struggled to stand up and get out of the dragon's way. Cobalt's tail swished by her again, nearly knocking her over a second time.

Derrick, Saunder, and Kazar scrambled to obey. Quickly they gathered crossbows, swords, daggers, and axes and piled the weapons beside a tree. Cobalt kept the soldiers flat on the ground.

"What do we do with them?" Treb wanted to know.

Sara took a moment to answer. First she checked the six squires to see if they were injured. To her intense relief, they had only minor cuts and bruises. "The men are our prisoners," she finally replied. "We'll keep them here until we can turn them over to Subcommander Torceth."

Saunder stood panting, glaring at the prisoners as if his eyes could strip the flesh from their bones. "They killed Jacson! They deserve to die!"

Sara strode over to the rangy squire. He refused to meet her eyes until she grabbed both arms and shook him hard. Only then did he turn his grief-stricken gaze to hers. "Listen to me," she said vehemently. "A knight will not engage in combat with an unarmed opponent. A knight will honor an opponent's surrender. Do you understand? It is from Lord Ariakan's Code of Honor that he adapted from the Solamnic Knights. Sometimes I think honor is the only difference standing between a beast and a Knight of Takhisis, and except for Jacson, I have seen precious little of it here today!"

Derrick and the others stared in surprise at her last heartfelt exclamation. No one knew what to say. A strained silence settled over the group.

Beyond the trees in the village, the sounds of the attack quieted to occasional shouts and the crash of a burning building. The dragons had ceased their roaring, and the screams that had torn the quiet of the day had faded into a dead calm.

Sara stepped back, her gray eyes like storm clouds. "Marika," she ordered. "See to Kelena. Derrick, you, Kazar, Saunder, and Argathon guard these prisoners. Treb, go find your dragon."

"Officer Conby!" a voice hailed her through the trees.

They all turned to see Knight Officer Targonne come striding down the trail toward them.

"Torceth sent me to check on you. . . . Oh, you found them!" he exclaimed when he saw their prisoners. "We've been turning the village upside down looking for the rest of these mercenaries."

"Was it necessary to do it by destroying the place?" Sara demanded. She could feel her anger building inside her. Anger at the needless killing, anger at Jacson's death, anger at the officers who had sent them on this so-called training mission.

To her fury, Targonne only shrugged. His cool expression never changed. "The men got a little carried away. They're new at this. But the village is ours, and that's what's important." He turned away from her, effectively cutting off any further argument. "Bring your prisoners to the inn. Subcommander Torceth will want to see them." He left the way he had come.

"And I want to see him," Sara grated. Leaving Marika to tend to Kelena and stay near Jacson's body, she led the remaining squires and their prisoners, about twelve in all, up the trail into the remains of the village.

All of them, even the mercenaries, looked around in stunned shock. The picturesque village was nothing more than a burning ruin. The dragons and the knights had destroyed everything. Only the original inn, sitting at the fork of the two trails, remained standing among the charred shells of houses, shops, and stables. Scattered along the paths, in the streets, and among the ruins of their homes were dozens of corpses, some charred and smoldering, others hacked and bloody. There seemed to be no one else alive but the wing from Neraka.

Sara looked ahead and saw a group of officers standing by the inn, Subcommander Torceth among them. Leaving the squires behind, she stormed up to the talon leaders and spat at their feet. "What sort of a 'training mission' was this supposed to be?" she yelled, her fury boiling over. "You were supposed to capture the village. Did anyone say wipe it off the map? What kind of officers are you that you allow your men to lose control like that? What happened to your vows? Where is the Code in an atrocity like this?" She was breathing so rapidly her breath hurt her sides beneath her ribs.

Torceth waved his hand as if swatting away a fly. "Ah, Knight Officer Conby. I see you found the rest of the mercenaries. I understand from the others they were out clearing the trail to Kortal. Excellent work!"

Torceth's total disregard of her questions made Sara all the more enraged. "Excellent work, my dragon's leavings! One of my squires is dead, another wounded. One of our dragons is missing, and while we fought your mercenaries, you were busy slaughtering unarmed civilians!"

Torceth pursed his heavy lips and frowned at her. The other officers took their cue from him and looked at her with disfavor.

Sara didn't care. She couldn't believe what she was seeing around her. Had the Knights of Takhisis sunk so low that they would turn a military objective into a slaughterhouse just for the fun of it? Lord Ariakan would never have stood for this sort of needless slaughter.

"Take your prisoners over there and leave them with those guards," Torceth ordered irritably. "Then return to your post."

Sara took a look at the guards he indicated. Four knights were standing by a blackened stone wall that had once been a comfortable cottage. The men leaned against the wall, chatting and laughing. Their weapons ran red with blood, and a pile of decapitated corpses were dumped close by. Sara shuddered.

"We will return to our post, sir. But I will not leave our prisoners with you. They fought well and deserve better than that." She jabbed a finger at the pile of bodies. "I will turn my prisoners over to Governor-General Abrena and no one else."

Torceth started to say something, but one of the older knights leaned over and whispered something in his ear. The subcommander paled slightly under his heavy beard. "Suit yourself," he growled to Sara. "I will hold you responsible for their care and conduct."

Sara rose on her toes, pushed her face close to his, and said fiercely, "And I hold you responsible for this massacre." She turned on her heel and strode away from them as fast as her legs could carry her before she did anything stupider than berating a superior officer.

The Sixth Talon stared at her in awe.

Derrick took one look at her face and herded the squires and prisoners after her without a single word.

The mercenaries, having seen the murdered villagers in the streets, followed willingly after their captors. They were quick enough to realize that their lives were safer in the hands of this outspoken woman knight.

By the time Sara returned to the clearing where Marika and Kelena waited, Squall and Howl had returned with a very contrite Tumult. Treb took one look at him and burst into a stream of invective that had even Kazar looking impressed.

"That's enough," Sara cut her off. Her patience was at an end with this whole terrible day. "Take the prisoners to those trees, Treb, and you and the dragons watch them carefully. No one is to interfere with them without my permission. Is that understood?"

Treb obeyed, albeit rather sullenly, and she and the dragons marched the prisoners to a large pine and made them sit in the snow. The men huddled as far away from the dragons as they could get, and Sara knew she would not have to worry about an escape.

She did worry about Kelena, though. Marika had stanched the flow of blood, but she had not tried to pull out the arrow. It was embedded too deeply for her simple skills. She had covered her friend to keep her warm and gave her sips of water to keep her from becoming dehydrated. She had laid out Jacson, too, and covered his face with his cloak.

Sara hesitated beside his body. She had not taken the luxury of time to think about what he had done for her. It was too painful. It was impossible to believe that his vibrant energy and talkative soul were gone from their midst. His sacrifice broke her heart. She couldn't think about it, could not accept it, not this soon. There was still much to do before she could try to reconcile Jacson's death with her vision of reality.

Turning away from the dead, she knelt by the wounded squire and took her hand. Kelena's blue eyes had faded to a watery gray. Her freckles stood out like tiny drops of ink scattered across parchment. Her breathing came in ragged gasps through her clenched teeth.

"Get it out," she begged. "Just yank it. I don't care."

Sara gently squeezed her hand. "I can do better than that," she reassured the young woman. "Hang on another minute or two." Hurrying to Cobalt, she found her healer's bag in a pouch on her dragon saddle and brought it back.

"Light a fire," she tossed over her shoulder to anyone who would listen. Derrick and Saunder nearly knocked each other over in their eagerness to obey. Quickly they cleared a patch of earth, built a fire ring, and started a fire using cut wood they found in the yard of a nearby burned-out cottage. Marika took a small cooking pot out of her gear and collected snow to melt for water.

Sara sorted through her bag while they worked. She had packed her bag specifically for treating wounds, and everything she needed for this operation was there. Deep inside she found a small package wrapped in soft leather. Within lay three glass vials of a precious liquid Sara had learned to make herself.

"Drink this," she told Kelena, pressing the vial to her lips. "It is a special syrup I make from herbs and flowers that will help you rest."

The syrup did its work, and in moments, the squire was asleep. With Marika's help and the concerned attention of Saunder, Derrick, and the others, Sara carefully cut out the bolt, packed the wound with a poultice to help prevent infection, and wrapped it with clean bandages. She saw, thankfully, that the tip of the bolt was not barbed and it had not damaged the bone or the artery in the thigh.

Sara gave her worried audience a smile when she was through. "I certainly miss the clerics' magic at times like this."

"Will she be all right?" Saunder wanted to know. For such a quiet loner, he was very attached to his friends.

"Barring fever, infection, bad weather, avalanches, or bloodthirsty knights, she'll be fine."

The others grinned at each other. Even Argathon and Kazar looked relieved.

"She's the first one I've ever seen knock Treb on her backside," Argathon said with a trace of respect.

Sara realized then the afternoon had slowly dwindled to twilight. She put the talon to work gathering firewood and erecting crude shelters from pine branches and whatever they could scavenge. She refused to let them take anything from the destroyed cottages or go anywhere near the corpses that still littered the ground. They could make do with what they had brought. She also had them build a fire and shelter for the prisoners and share part of their food with them.

No one tried to argue with her. It was a quiet and sober group that obeyed her orders and worked diligently to prepare for the night.

While the squires were busy, Sara had a quiet word with Cobalt. The blue's eyes gleamed greenish in the deepening darkness, and as soon as she finished her message, he slipped out into the open and took wing. Where she had sent him, she would not say to anyone.

They divided the watch, built up the fires, and settled back to wait for day. In the woods behind them, embers continued to smolder in the burned buildings, and every once in a while, the talon heard shouts of laughter and revelry coming from the inn.

For the six uninjured squires, the cold night passed very slowly. There was little sleep and much thought among the men and women. Only a few of them had been in actual combat before or faced the prospect of death so personally. They ran the events of the day through their minds time and again and found strength in the fact that none of them had flinched.

It was not so easy to contemplate the slaughter of the villagers. While many of the recruits had seen horrors during the Summer of Chaos, then it had some larger meaning. Few may have understood all that was happening to Krynn that summer, but most knew it involved the gods. This massacre was senseless. It had no reason, no motive, no unseen driving force. It was rooted in the boredom and cruelty and bloodlust of a group of untried knights. More than one of the squires found it difficult to reconcile what had happened that day to the Code of the Knighthood they had worked hard to learn. A few civilian casualties were expected in a take-over, but nothing like this needless carnage.

What would the governor-general think about this?

* * * * *

They found out what Governor-General Abrena thought the next day when she arrived midmorning astride her blue dragon, Cerium.

The first indication Sara had was Cobalt's return. He landed in the nearby meadow and smugly informed Sara that her message had been delivered and the general was spitting daggers. Apparently Subcommander Torceth had been slow to send a messenger back to Neraka, and Cobalt had arrived before him.

"Where is she?" Sara demanded, the gray fire creeping back into her eyes.

"She and Cerium landed in the field west of here, where the other dragons and part of the wing have made camp. She's reaming out several talon officers at the moment."

The squires had gathered around to listen, and Derrick spoke up. "Do we go to her?"

"No." Sara replied evenly. "We were ordered to remain at our post. She can come to us."

Despite her firm words and the sense of righteousness that bolstered her, Sara was nervous about seeing the general. She had disobeyed a superior officer on the subject of the prisoners, and she had blown protocol to pieces by sending her own message to Abrena over the heads of Subcommander Torceth and his talon leaders. If General Abrena was a stickler for discipline, Sara knew she could be in trouble.

Cobalt pricked his pointed ears. Hurriedly he raised his head to peer through the trees. "Here she comes," he hissed.

Sara ordered the talon back to their makeshift camp. Quickly she had them straighten their gear and stand in a line to await the governor-general. The mercenaries, sensing something important, climbed to their feet as well and stood in a ragged group under the watchful eyes of the dragons.

They could hear the general before they could see her. Her commanding voice rang through the woods, telling someone in no uncertain terms that he was an incompetent fool. Then Mirielle Abrena came stalking down the trail, Subcommander Torceth, Knight Officer Targonne, and the other talon leaders following her like a pack of chastised wolves. The general carried her helm under her arm and wore a long, fur-lined cloak. She was slapping her gloves against her thigh as she walked.

"Knight Officer Conby," came the sharp command. "Come here."

Sara detached herself from the talon and stood before the general. She leveled her gaze on Mirielle's golden eyes and refused to flinch before their fiery anger.

"I have heard Torceth's version of the attack on the village. Now I want to hear yours," demanded Mirielle.

So Sara told her everything she had witnessed and all that had happened to the talon. While she gave her report, the general's eyes studied details of the trail, the clearing, the prisoners, and the condition of the talon. She took in Kelena, still lying half-asleep on her blanket, and the shrouded figure of young Jacson. Mirielle had already heard Cobalt's message and the dragon's version of the massacre, but she wanted to weigh all sides before she acted.

Behind the general, Torceth fidgeted and shifted his weight from foot to foot. His heavy face grew darker by the minute, as if he wished to dispute Sara's words but was too nervous of the general to interrupt. Mirielle ignored him.

When Sara finished, she saluted the general and stepped back. It was in Mirielle's hands now.

The general did not keep anyone waiting. "Fine," she said abruptly. "Subcommander Torceth, it is my judgment that while you fulfilled the spirit of my orders, you allowed your men and their dragons to go out of control. The fact that they are new to the knighthood does not excuse them. I did not intend for you to destroy the entire village. We could have used the buildings and the people. This also sets a precedent for future attacks. Once news of this massacre leaks out, other locations may fight twice as hard and exact longer delays and higher casualties. Therefore, you will return with me to Neraka for adjudication of a minor violation."

"A minor violation!" Sara shouted, outraged. "He allows his men to slaughter an entire village and you give him a slap on the wrist? What about the knights? Aren't you going to punish them, too? What sort of justice is that?"

Mirielle's eyebrows curled down and her mouth hardened. "Mine," she said coldly. "And I will hear no more about it. I am short of knights and supplies. I need this village as a gateway to Kortal and eventually Sanction."

But Sara refused to give up quite yet. "And what about the people who lived here? They didn't have to die."

"No, they did not. But it is too late for them. We must move on. Take your prisoners and your wounded back to Neraka, Knight Officer Conby. Your talon has performed well." She turned to go, her mind already calculating her next move. "Knight Officer Targonne, you will take command of the wing until Subcommander Torceth returns. Tell your father that the gateway between Neraka and Sanction is ours. We will set up a trade route as soon as the passes are open."

Sara stared at the general's implacable face, and although her body still shook with anger and her mind was in a turmoil, she realized with a cold certainty she could do no more. Governor-General Abrena had given her orders, and unless she wished to jeopardize her position, Sara knew any further arguments were futile. Bitterly she returned to the talon and in tense silence watched the general and her officers march up the trail toward the inn.

The pensive quiet lasted long after the knights disappeared from view.

"Knight Officer," Argathon said into the hush, "why does the knighthood emphasize the Code so much, then let something like this go unpunished?"

His confusion was shared by them all.

Derrick threw his hands up in a gesture of frustration. "Why didn't the general do something about the knights who caused all of this? It isn't right!"

"Oh, grow up, Derrick!" Treb snapped. "What else could she do? What's done is done."

"I don't know," Sara said quietly, as if she hadn't heard Treb's remark. "I just don't know. This is not what Lord Ariakan had in mind when he built the knighthood. Steel Brightblade and his knights would never have done something like this."

Sara could make such a statement in utter sincerity. Although she hated the Knights of Takhisis, she had never found cause to doubt their strict Code and their discipline . . . until now. General Abrena seemed to be letting go of Ariakan's dark honor in favor of rapid training and lax recruitment standards to increase her army. This new trend in the development of the knighthood alarmed Sara.

Confused and pensive, Sara set the squires to work preparing to leave. If the general wanted them to return to Neraka, then Sara intended to get them all back to the city that day. She did not want to stay in this place another hour longer than they had to.

By enlisting the cooperation of the four dragons, Sara sent the talon and their prisoners back to Neraka in two shifts. The dragons made the first trip between the village and the city carrying a rider and two prisoners each. They returned just before nightfall to retrieve Sara and the remaining squires.

Kelena felt strong enough by that time to ride Howl, so they put a bound-and-gagged prisoner behind her saddle, bundled her in a cloak and gloves, and helped her onto the dragon's back.

Derrick and Saunder helped Sara put Jacson's body onto Squall's saddle. Squall, who had carried Jacson the most, asked for the honor and watched sadly as they tied the wrapped body in the second seat. Derrick climbed into the first seat to escort Jacson home.

At last they were ready to go. Sara had one prisoner

with her, a squat, muscular man. But she doubted she would have any trouble with him during the flight. His wrists were bound to the saddle, and he looked terrified to be on a dragon's back.

She gave the signal to Cobalt to take off, and one after another, the four blues launched into the darkening sky for the journey home.

On the western horizon, where the peaks of the great Khalkists reared up like a black fortress against the pale blue light of sunset, a sliver of the silvery moon hung in solitary grace.

A new moon, a new month. A new hope?

Sara doubted it.

Chapter 20

The talon returned to their usual routine the following morning: training, service, labor, and guard duty, to be repeated again the following day and every day thereafter until further notice.

In between duties, they buried Jacson in the hills by his talon-mate, Tamar, in a hole blasted out of the frozen ground by the dragons. They placed his armor-clad body on his cloak and put his weapons beside him. Sara laid the bolt he had taken for her sake in his hand, and, her eyes blurred with tears, she tied her last hair ribbon around his arm—a token of esteem from a lady.

The others left him tokens, too, small remembrances of his presence among them, then reverently they piled the dirt over his grave and stood back and watched the dragons build a cairn of stones over the mound.

Sara fervently hoped she would not have to add any more graves to this lonely hillside.

Two days later Governor-General Abrena returned to Neraka, and after dealing with Torceth and making sure the city's affairs were in order, she sent her goblin to summon the Sixth Talon.

He found Sara and the squires on the practice fields with another recruit talon practicing hand-to-hand fighting. He sidled up to Sara and, bobbing his head, delivered his message.

Annoyed, Sara called in her recruits. She had no desire

to see the governor-general and could not imagine what Abrena would want with them.

The goblin shifted nervously when she asked and grumbled, "Don't know. Governor-general say come."

Sara sighed and led the talon after him.

The goblin took them to the general's headquarters in the same house Sara had visited before. She had not been there in some time, since Mirielle liked to spread the honor of squiring her dinners among the knights.

They filed down a long hallway to a large room at the north end of the house. Sara felt her interest revive the moment she entered the room. Everywhere she looked there were maps hung on the dark paneling—ancient maps, recent maps, on parchment, on vellum, and even on bark—of every known part of Ansalon from the new Teeth of Chaos in the north to the massive Ice Wall Glacier to the south. The maps showed trails, high roads, villages, cities, fortresses, ruins, and landmarks.

Then Sara's eye was caught by a large table that stood in the center of the room. On the table sat the most amazing map Sara had ever seen of Neraka and its surrounding environs, from Estwilde in the north, as far east as the Blood Sea, down to Blode in the south and Throt in the west. Instead of being flat, the map was a three-dimensional relief map in bold colors of greens, blues, browns, and reds. Sara could identify the mountains and volcanic peaks around Neraka and Sanction, the towns and villages, the main rivers and ports, the realm of the Khur, and marked in red, the spreading domain of the dragon, Malystryx.

The map captured Sara's attention so completely that she did not pay attention to the four officers standing across the room from the talon.

Only when Governor-General Abrena moved to a side table to lift a wine bottle out of a bowl of snow did Sara look up. She recognized immediately that something of significance was about to occur. The first person she saw was Lord Knight Cadrel, his diseased face shadowed by a hood. In his left hand, he carried the scepter of the order's adjudicator, or judge. Beside him stood a gray-robed sorcerer, a Knight of the Thorn, and a grim-visaged woman wearing the emblem of the Order of the Skull. Three knights, three orders, and the general.

Sara's mental alarms began to clamor.

Mirielle refilled her glass from the chilled bottle, pushed it back into the slush, and turned to her audience, all with the graceful, deliberate movements of a hunter. She smiled now and said, "I understand several of your squires requested to take the Test of Takhisis."

Sara stiffened, her internal alarms in full howl.

Six of the seven squires exchanged uneasy glances.

Only Treb stepped forward gladly. "Yes, General. I was supposed to take my test the day we captured the village."

"Then you will be pleased to know that your involvement in the attack on the village was your test. For your valor, your skill, your adherence to the Code—" and here she quirked an eyebrow at Sara, "—we have found you all worthy to join the Order of the Lily."

Sara was flabbergasted. She stood and stared, too shocked to find the words she wanted to say. This was not how the test was usually applied! She couldn't believe these older knights actually agreed to this. These squires had not completed their training; they had not proven themselves in anything but one botched massacre, nor had they given an accounting of themselves before these ranking knights. What was Abrena looking for, knights dedicated heart and soul to Takhisis or whatever she could get tied by an empty vow?

Suddenly Sara heard the general say, "You will spend your vigil in solitary prayer to the Dark Queen this day. Tonight at midnight, if the priestess deems you worthy, you may take your vows. Please follow Lord Knight Atochia. She will take you to our new temple."

Treb moved first, her enthusiasm glowing in her face

as she joined the cleric. Saunder looked at Derrick, then back at Sara. The girls just stared at the floor.

No, Sara thought with all her being, don't go!

But whether they wanted to or not, they had little choice. To refuse at this stage, in front of the general, the adjudicator, and two ranking knights, would be blasphemy and cause for immediate execution.

Derrick knew this as well as everyone else. Nevertheless, he seemed to hesitate. His body swayed slightly, and he could not bring himself to look at anyone. Finally, just as the general's face was hardening into a frown, he moved slowly after Treb. The others fell into line behind him.

Sara's heart lurched. She clenched her hands into iron fists at her sides and concentrated on the pain of her nails digging into her palms. It was all that helped her contain her anger and grief. They aren't ready, her mind cried over and over. They aren't ready!

No, said her heart. I'm not ready. I'm not ready to lose them. Wordlessly she watched them file out of the room to go to the Temple of Takhisis for their vigils.

"Excellent," Governor-General Abrena said with satisfaction. "Knight Officer Conby, please stay. The rest of you may go. I will expect you tonight for the knighting ceremony."

The two officers bowed and departed.

Sara remained frozen in place. She had to steel herself not to cry or scream or vent her rage on the general. Emotions would accomplish nothing but disaster. "Governor-General, I wish to make it clear that I do not approve of testing my talon in this way. They have not completed every phase of their training, and the capture of the village was hardly a suitable test."

"Your complaint has been noted, Conby. Don't worry about them. They'll be fine. They can polish their training during the remainder of the winter with a new leader." Mirielle lifted her glass in a toast. "You have done well with them. You are a fine trainer. I have watched you since your return to the order, and I am pleased with your work and your progress. Therefore—" she strode to her map and gestured to Sara to come closer, "—I have a task I believe would suit you well and help the knighthood. I want you to go to Solace and visit the Tomb of the Last Heroes."

If she had said, "I want you to go to the Abyss," Sara could not have been more surprised. She knew her jaw dropped open, but she could do nothing but stare at the woman's intent face. "Why?" she croaked.

The general did not answer right away. Instead, she sipped her wine and gazed into a distance that went far beyond the surfaces of her map.

For the first time since Sara met Mirielle, she saw the general's calculating, self-assured mask slip slightly askew to expose a faint shadow of the uncertainty that lay beneath. Wondering, Sara moved to the table and let her eyes roam over the map. On it, she saw Mirielle's ambitious plans for Neraka mapped out for the next several years, including expansions in the outer ring, more permanent barracks, a new headquarters, improved training facilities, and the new temple built atop the ruins of the old Temple of Darkness. Beyond Neraka, Sara saw towns and villages marked in black in an ever-increasing sphere of influence.

"What you see here," Mirielle said abruptly, waving her long fingers over the map, "is a plan for the future, for the survival of the knights, and for the glory of our Queen. But without Takhisis's Vision . . . I feel empty. Do you know what I mean?"

Sara didn't, but she nodded anyway. She had not allowed herself to be sucked into the order so far as to receive the dark goddess's Vision, nor had Lord Ariakan ever suggested it. But she had talked to enough knights to know that the true magic of the Vision was that it was different for every person who received it and that it revealed each person's individual path to death or glory in Takhisis's grand scheme. Apparently, when Ariakan died and Takhisis fled the world during the Second Cataclysm, the Vision had faded from the minds of their knights.

Mirielle continued to sip her wine and stare at her map. She did not seem to notice Sara's silence. "The odd part is that I do not remember what the Vision was, only that it was once a part of me. Now it is gone, and I feel its loss every day." She swiftly straightened and turned her golden eyes on Sara. "That is why I want you to go to the tomb. I am hoping you will find a sign, a faint hope, a vision, something that will tell us that Queen Takhisis might return. Even if it is not in my lifetime, I would like to know that what we do here will be well received by our Dark Queen. Will you do this?"

Sara did not hesitate. This was her ticket out of Neraka. She would go to the Tomb of the Last Heroes to see Steel's resting place, but she would not return. The squires would be knights by tomorrow and would no longer need her. She had the information she wanted and permission to leave. "Yes, I will go as soon as you wish," she replied. Then a stubborn little wish prompted her to say, "If the talon is knighted this night, may I take them with me as an escort?"

Mirielle shook her head. "Too many people would attract attention. Take one. Then if something happens, perhaps one of you will make it back with news."

"When do you want me to leave?"

"As soon as the weather clears. My patrols tell me there is a snowstorm in the mountains west of here, and it is expected to come this way."

Sara saluted and left Mirielle studying the map on the table. As she came to the door, she noticed a metallic shield that had been polished to a mirrored sheen hanging on the wall. A glimpse of her reflection peered back at her from its bright surface. Sara grimaced. Her face had aged in the few months she had been here. She couldn't remember when she had looked so old and tired. More wrinkles had appeared on her forehead and around her eyes, and the blond coloring had faded from her hair, returning it to silver gray. She sighed wearily. She was too old to be a spy, running around Neraka pretending to be a knight. The effort had worn her out. It was time to go.

* * * * *

Sara thought about avoiding the knighting ceremony that night. She could hardly bear to face her failure or to see her squires received into the knighthood she loathed. Yet the thought of disappointing the young men and women with her absence proved stronger than her own weaknesses. Shortly before midnight, she gathered with the other knights before the Temple of Takhisis Mirielle had built just outside the old temple compound.

The storm from the mountains had made swift progress, and already a stiff wind roared among the black towers. A heavy blanket of clouds obscured the stars and turned the night darker and more forbidding. The cold grew intense.

A few snowflakes were beginning to fall when the waiting knights heard the clear notes of a trumpet on the gathering wind. Governor-General Abrena appeared in the courtyard of the temple, and the knights gathered in a circle around her. She threw her arms wide to greet the storm. Torches flared in the gusts that swept between the stone buildings. The yellow light danced on the knights' armor and threw shadows skittering across their faces.

The knights raised their arms with Mirielle and began a chant to their goddess.

In just a few moments, the men and women of the Sixth Talon would emerge from the temple where they had spent the day in prayer. If the priestess deemed them worthy, they would be invested in the dark knighthood and granted the status and rights of full Knights of Takhisis.

The snow fell harder.

In the growing storm, Sara lifted her arms beside the knights, but she only mouthed the words of the song of praise. Her eyes remained fixed on the door to the temple. She wasn't certain what she dreaded most, that all seven squires would emerge and be knighted, or that any of them had refused and been put to death.

The cold seeped into her bones and made her shiver.

The trumpet sounded again, ending the knights' chant. A silence settled over the courtyard, and all eyes turned to the temple. Someone flung open the door from the inside. A priestess in robes of black emerged. The wind whipped her long black hair about her face and sent her robes snapping. "They have been accepted," she cried in a high, clear voice.

Well, of course they have, Sara thought cynically. Abrena said take them, and Takhisis was not around to argue.

In single file, Derrick, Saunder, Kelena, Kazar, Marika, Treb, and Argathon emerged from the temple, each carrying the skull-shaped helm of a Dark Knight. In full armor, they knelt before Governor-General Abrena.

Sara closed her eyes, not wanting to see the black lily of death and the bloody axe that adorned each black breastplate. She listened, her teeth clenched so hard her jaw ached, as the general heard the initiates' blood oaths that joined each squire body and soul to the cause.

Using her own sword, Governor-General Abrena touched the blade to both shoulders of each squire and named them Knights in the Order of the Lily.

Sara did not stay to see more. Before the trumpet sounded dismissal, she turned her back on the ceremony and fled into the rising storm.

The wind and snow were bad enough within the city

walls, but outside the main gates, the cold took Sara's breath away. The snow, driven in horizontal sheets, struck her like needles of ice. She pushed forward toward the ring of tents she knew to be out there in the wild, swirling darkness. Only for brief instants, when the gusts parted the curtains of snow, could she see faint glimpses of torchlight from the camps.

Sara pushed on into the blinding storm while the wind roared its wild melodies around her. Her cloak whipped around her, sometimes wrenching at her neck as the wind tried to pull it off. Other times it wrapped around her legs so suddenly it made her stumble.

It seemed the cold and the winds, the noise and the smothering, scratching snow would last forever. But at last Sara saw the dark humps of the tents through the blinding snow, and she stumbled gratefully into the meager windbreak provided by the camp. The guards, huddled in the shelter of a low shed, merely nodded to her.

She worked her way across the open quadrangle to the talon's section of the camp. In the whipping snow and darkness, she did not see Cobalt until she fell over his tail.

Sleepily the blue dragon lifted his head from beneath his wing. He lay curled around Sara's tent, his big body protecting her shelter from the ravages of the wind. Already a thin layer of snow blanketed his blue hide. He blinked at her. "Are you all right?"

Deeply touched by his concern, Sara threw her arms around his neck. She inhaled his pungent, reptilian odor and felt the slickness of his scales on her cheek. He felt cool to her touch, which accounted for his sleepiness, but Sara knew he could easily sleep out in a storm like this without discomfort. As long as he could feed in the morning.

"General Abrena is sending us to Solace as soon as the weather clears," she told him.

He tilted his head curiously. "What for?"

"To go to the Tomb of the Last Heroes."

"All right," he answered, too drowsy to really care. He nudged her good night, tucked his head back under his wing, and went back to sleep.

Sara made a quick round of the other tents to tighten storm ropes, check pegs, and make sure there was plenty of coal for the braziers. At last she stumbled into her own tent. She had to stand for a minute, taking deep breaths, before she could peel off her snow-crusted cloak and stoke up the banked embers of her own brazier.

In the ruddy glow of the little brass heater, she boiled water for tea and warmed her numb hands. She heard the newly knighted talon return to camp, but she did not go out to greet them. She could not face them, not yet. She knew she would have to soon, but tonight she needed the solitude of her own thoughts.

Derrick called to her once, and she stood still, hoping he would think her asleep. Cobalt grumbled sleepily at him, and Sara heard his steps crunch away until there was nothing left but the whining song of the wind and the creak and flap of the tent around her. She hung her cloak to dry, then bundled herself in the warmest clothes she had and crawled under her blankets.

As soon as the storm ended and she could say good-bye to the recruits, she would leave. She would put Neraka behind her forever, tucked away in the dark corners of her mind with her memories of Storm's Keep and Lord Ariakan and Steel Brightblade.

Chapter 21

The storm lasted through three long and miserable days. The snow fell heavily, and the wind, which continued to blow with a ferocity that cut through the warmest clothes, built the snow up into towering drifts. Powerful gusts shook the tents, sent snow swirling in blinding ground blizzards among the camps, and made cooking outdoors impossible.

During that time, the new knights stayed together in their tents or fought their way to the nearest inn for a hot meal and a bit of warmth. There was no practice, no training, and very little work beyond the effort of survival. They still had to haul coal, check their tents for wind damage, cook their meals, and shovel through deep snow that clogged the paths.

Cobalt brought the other dragons to help the knights build windbreaks around their tents, and they plowed through several drifts that piled up in inconvenient places.

Sara helped them as well, but she kept a distance between herself and the others and spent most of her time in her tent. She congratulated them all with an obvious lack of enthusiasm, then refused to speak any more about the knighting. She also told them she would be going to Solace on the general's business.

The young men and women wondered at her behavior and worried.

The snow stopped on the third day, but it was two days later before the sky cleared and the wind died to a breeze. In the crystal light of morning, the general's goblin brought the order for Sara to go.

"Governor-general sends you map. She say you have a fortnight. Return to her by time moon is full to report."

Sara snatched the map out of his clawed hands. "Thank you," she said, shooing him out.

The young knights, attracted by the goblin's arrival, crowded inside the tent's entrance.

Sara shoved the map in her belt. The map wasn't really necessary. She had a complete knowledge of Ansalon's continent from her time at Storm's Keep. What she needed now was a spiritual guide to help her get through the next few hours. She looked at the expectant faces around her and managed a smile.

"I have permission from the general to take one of you with me on this quest." She had spent hours debating this question, but in the end, the choice was inevitable. She chose Derrick for his grin like Steel's, his youthful courage, and for the mantle of loyalty and honor he wore that, to Sara, did not seem to have a place among the Dark Knights. She had tried once to sway a young man away from the darkness by taking him to a tomb and had failed. Perhaps this time she would be more successful.

A puzzled look flashed over Derrick's face so quickly Sara thought she had mistaken it. Then it was gone, and he grinned, pleased by her decision.

"All right. It's time to go, Derrick. Pack your gear. We'll take just Cobalt—one dragon to sneak into Abanasinia. We'll need several days of food, two water-skins, and a camp tent. Bring something to wear besides your armor. You can't get into Solace sporting that death lily." Sara knew she was talking too fast and too much to hide the unexpected surge of emotions that made her fingers tremble and her voice shake. She was leaving this hateful place at last, leaving the foul city, the dangerous citizens, and the bloodthirsty knights. Yet she studied the faces peering in at her and knew she would miss them horribly.

"Knight Officer, now that you're leaving and we're getting a new talon leader, I want to request the position of junior officer," Treb said loudly.

Well, Sara thought, all but that one. "Take it up with your new leader, Treb. If you want it, you will have to earn it."

"Over my dead body," Kelena muttered darkly.

With the help of the talon, Sara and Derrick gathered their gear. Sara had brought little with her, so the knights did not think it odd when she left her tent, that there was nothing remaining inside but the original contents. They loaded the bundles behind Cobalt's two-seat saddle and stood in a row to see the travelers off on their quest.

Only Sara knew this good-bye was permanent. She held on to her tears with an iron grip. This wasn't the time to weep. Yet the leave-taking was harder than she imagined. *I should never have allowed myself to become so close to these young people,* she thought wearily.

Forcing a smile to her face, she gave the talon the knight's salute and scurried up Cobalt's leg into the saddle. Derrick climbed up behind her, his expression blank. He saluted his talon mates and held on as Cobalt spread his wings.

The dragon was eager to be off. At Sara's word, he sprang into the air, his powerful wings lifting them swiftly into the morning sky.

The dragon patrols circling the city curved by them and waved them on.

Cobalt climbed rapidly into the frozen air and angled his flight to the southwest, across the Khalkist Mountains.

Sara planned to avoid as many populated areas as possible by flying north of Sanction and across the New Sea to Abanasinia. It was the route she had flown before, many years ago, on a different dragon, but with a similar purpose. With luck, they would make the flight without a stop. She did not want trouble in any form from sharp-eyed townsfolk still irate at the Knights of Takhisis, or hill dwarves, or even other dragons looking for a fight.

Nor did she want to announce her arrival in Solace. She decided to leave Cobalt hidden somewhere, and she and Derrick would slip in like any other pilgrims to the tomb, pay their respects to the dead they revered, and slip out. After that, she did not know what would happen.

Sara huddled deeper into her cloak and tightened the muffler wrapped around her lower face. She was glad she had dressed warmly for this part of the flight. The westerly winds swept over an endless range of snow and ice below and lost any hint of warmth they might have brought from the wastelands. The wind stung her flesh and cut deep into her bones. Breathing was difficult and talking was almost impossible while the dragon flew above the frozen mountains.

Eventually the mountains fell away to a valley that rolled placidly to the sea. Only a light coating of snow lay on the ground, and the air lost much of its bitter cold. To the south lapped the blue waters of the New Sea. In a matter of moments, Cobalt left the land behind and soared out over the waters of the inland sea.

Clear weather followed them southward. Sunlight sparkled on the water and warmed the air currents that flowed like water around them. Far to the south, Sara could see the peaks of the southernmost Khalkist ranges and the verdant grasslands of Blodehelm.

This portion of the New Sea they flew over narrowed to a strait before widening into the main body of the sea. Due southwest, perhaps an hour's flight, lay the isle of Schallsea, and just beyond it was Abanasinia.

Warm at last, Sara and Derrick came gradually out of

their cocoons. They unwrapped mufflers, removed their fur-lined cloaks, and took off their gloves. Without the cold to shrivel their noses and freeze the air they breathed, they could talk over the rush of the wind and the rustle of Cobalt's wings. For a while they talked of simple things, of the snowstorm in Neraka and the fun the talon had sledding down a hillside on their shields, of Derrick's home in the mountains near Jelek, and of their memories of Jacson.

But there were too many unsaid things between them that neither were ready to broach, and so eventually they retreated into a long, unbroken silence.

Cobalt kept one ear cocked back to listen and made no attempt to interrupt their stillness. Dipping south to bypass Schallsea, he winged over the northernmost tip of New Coast, an area of flat grasslands and rich pastures.

At Sara's signal, Cobalt found a place to land on a broad strip of beach along the coast just to the north of the ruins of Sithelbec. A small creek provided fresh water, and a clump of trees offered cover and some shade for a quick meal. The dragon touched down heavily on the sand.

Sara slid down, glad to stretch her legs. Derrick unpacked the food, and together they sat under the trees to eat their lunch. Cobalt had eaten a fat cow before they left, so he entertained himself digging in the sand like a huge overgrown reptilian puppy.

Sara and Derrick watched him and ate their meal in the same contemplative silence.

A stiff wind picked up by the time they were ready to leave again, and clouds had begun to gather in the northwest off the Straits of Schallsea.

Cobalt snuffed the wind and tasted its moisture on his tongue. "There's a storm building," he warned Sara.

She nodded. "Do you want to risk the last leg across the open water?" she asked him.

The dragon appreciated her question. Her respect for

his abilities was one of the things he loved about her. "It is near, but we shouldn't have any problem reaching the coast."

Without further delay, the two humans climbed atop the dragon and took their seats in the saddle. The big blue pushed off immediately and pumped his wings to gain altitude. As soon as he reached his preferred cruising height, where he could catch the best drafts, he leveled out and pushed hard to race the storm across the wide stretch of water.

Sara and Derrick kept a watch to the northwest and said little.

Derrick was the first one to scale the wall of silence. "Knight Officer Conby—"

She interrupted him. "Please call me Sara on this trip. A title like that might be a giveaway to the wrong people."

He chuckled. "I'll try to remember that." Then his tone turned serious again. "I . . . I mean we . . . were wondering if something was bothering you? Were you not pleased that we became knights?"

Sara stiffened in a sudden chill that had nothing to do with the wind. She clasped her hands together to hide their sudden trembling. "I'll match you your question and raise one. Are you happy to be a Knight of Takhisis?"

He looked at her keenly, considering how he should answer this. "I thought I would be."

She heard the unspoken hesitation and swiveled around to look at him. "But?" she prompted.

His eyes were shadowed, like the dark depths of a grotto. "But . . . now the truth eludes me. I don't know."

"Why did you take your vow?"

He snorted. "What choice did I have? Besides, I thought it was what I wanted. I thought it was what you wanted."

"Me!" Sara cried, more astonished than she had ever been. "By my sweet grandmother's knucklebones, whatever gave you that idea?" She was appalled to think the squires had even considered taking their vows to please her.

He stared at her as the blood drained from her face. "You did! By your training and your duel with Massard and the way you helped us. Isn't that why you were there? To make us into knights?"

Something shattered in Sara. Of all the things she had worried about and imagined, this possibility never occurred to her. She leaned over, wrenched her skull helm loose from its bindings, and, giving an anguished cry, threw it into the sea.

The young knight behind her stared, stupefied, at the helm as it fell and splashed far below.

"I didn't want to train anyone!" Sara said miserably. Her gray eyes glistened with unshed tears. "I came only to see what was happening in Neraka. But we were found and brought to the general, and all I could do was go along with the masquerade. She put me in charge of a training talon, thinking my experience would benefit you all," she ended bitterly, spitting out the word "experience" like a foul taste.

Overhead, the clouds drew together in a thick canopy and brought a chilly, wet wind whistling by them. Cobalt pushed harder for the coast. With his keen dragon eyes, he could just make out the distant line of land in the thickening mist. His riders paid little heed to the worsening weather. They concentrated on each other and the truth that finally gnawed its way out.

"I don't understand," said Derrick. "Are you not a Knight of Takhisis?"

Sara turned again to face him, and her heart jumped painfully to see him. His shoulders were slumped and his proud face looked bewildered. "No, I am Sara Dunstan. Steel Brightblade was my adopted son, and I spent ten years with the dark order trying to convince him to leave it."

Derrick jerked upright. A cloud of anger scudded across his features. Words and phrases she said became clear and stabbed like knives into his pride. He had respected her, admired her! For nothing but a sham. Without probing deeper into her motives or her feelings, he lashed out with his own bitter hurt.

"You lied to us!" he said savagely. "You spoke of honor and courage, all the while hiding behind a mask of deceit! You're just a filthy spy. All you wanted was information. You probably laughed at us while we worked so hard to earn your approval. We thought you were one of the most honorable knights in Neraka. We wanted to be like you. Like you!" he shouted furiously.

Sara stretched out her hand to him. "No. No, Derrick, it wasn't like that at all."

But he would not listen. His lean face turned cold and hard. His green eyes glittered like brittle ice. "Worst of all, you're a traitor. You betrayed the order and betrayed us. Why are you going to the tomb at all? Or are we? Cobalt!" he yelled at the dragon. "Where are we?"

"Just off the coast of Abanasinia," came the reply.

"Good! Put me down at the first land you come to."

Sara started. "No, Derrick. Please listen to me!"

"I've listened to you enough," he said, his tone implacable. "I want off. I'll go my own way."

Sara whipped around to shout at the blue. "Don't land, Cobalt. Keep flying to Solace. Maybe the Majeres will talk to him."

"Sara, I am going to have to land. I can't see where I'm going."

At once Sara saw what he meant. While she and Derrick were talking, the storm had moved in with winter rapidity. Already the dragon was being buffeted by strong winds, and the visibility dwindled rapidly in an approaching squall of flying rain.

Sara bit her lip to keep from crying. There was no choice. Unless the squall blew over, Cobalt would have to land soon. She turned to reason with Derrick one more time and saw him untying his gear and yanking it loose.

"Derrick, I never laughed—"

He cut her off with a vicious gesture. "I don't want to hear it. You'll only lie to me again."

Sara tried desperately to regain some composure, to talk reasonably to him. "The only lie I ever implied was that I was a knight. Everything else was from my heart. I care about all of you. Especially you. You remind me of Steel in so many ways, except I do not see the darkness in you that shadowed his life."

If he heard anything she said, he gave no sign. He continued to collect his things, his bow, his pack, the sword strapped to the saddle. "Do you know what really burns me up?" he said, without looking at her. "It's that Jacson died to save you and your treachery. I hope you're satisfied."

The verbal blow struck Sara brutally hard. She gasped, and her thoughts went cold. Before she could think of something to say, Cobalt informed her, "I see the shore just ahead. Hold on."

Just as he said that, the rain caught up with them and lashed down in a dense downpour.

"Don't go," Sara pleaded to Derrick. "Please talk to me. This is all wrong. You have to understand."

The young knight ignored her. He gripped his belongings in a fierce embrace and braced himself for the landing.

Cobalt came down so fast that the jolt of his landing threw Sara into the high back of the saddle. Twisted as she was, the impetus strained her back muscles and slammed the side of her face into the wooden frame. Blood poured out of her nose. Half-stunned, she tried to right herself to stop Derrick, but he moved too fast. Slick as a weasel, he slid out of his seat, dropped to the ground, and took off at a run.

"Cobalt, stop him!" she cried. Her tears slipped loose and mingled with the blood and rain on her face.

"I didn't see where he went," Cobalt replied. He searched through the pouring cascades of rain and saw nothing but a flat area of fetid bog. "Sara, I think we're on the fringes of the swamp around Xak Tsaroth. We need to move farther inland."

"Not without Derrick," she cried frantically. "We can't just leave him. Xak Tsaroth may be a ruin, but it's full of goblins and other things." Wiping her face on her tunic, she slid down the wet dragon and landed in soft, shallow mire up to her ankles. Cobalt's weight had sunk him to his knees. He was right. If they didn't get out of that spot soon, the dragon could be mired.

She ran forward into the rain, looking desperately for some sign of the knight. There was nothing. All she could see through the driving rain were tall clumps of reeds and copses of twisted black trees intertwined with sprawling vines and underbrush.

"Derrick!" she tried, but her cry was swept away by the wind and lost in the rush of the rain.

"Sara, can we go?" Cobalt trumpeted. "I'd rather fly in the rain than sink in the mud!"

The woman stopped, blinded by tears and the driving rain. "I've got to find him!" she begged.

"Not now. He's gone. I will take you to Solace. You go to the tomb, and I will come back and see if I can find him."

Sara came slowly back, her expression devastated. "I lost him. I lost him just like Steel," she mourned.

"I'll do my best to find him. Maybe he'll listen to me," Cobalt suggested gently. He curled his neck around her back and guided her gently to his side.

It wasn't what she wanted. She wanted to search for Derrick, but she could not selfishly put Cobalt in jeopardy. She took one last look around, checking to see if the rain would ease soon. There was little hope. The storm showed no sign of letting up. In fact, it was getting colder and night would soon be at hand. Sick at heart, she climbed up to the saddle.

As soon as she was seated, Cobalt pulled his front legs free of the mire and spread his wings. He jerked his back legs free at the same time he pumped with his wings and lumbered into the air. Flying low, he skimmed westward toward the Sentinel Peaks.

He did not like flying in this murky weather so close to mountains he could not see. He had to strain all his senses to seek out the terrain below and read its rising and falling. Unfortunately the closer he drew to the mountains, the colder the temperature dropped. Soon the rain turned to sleet, and the sleet gradually soaked through Sara's already wet clothes. She put on her cloak, which helped for a while, but she was badly chilled and shivering uncontrollably. Cobalt knew he had to get her to shelter soon.

Like a great eagle, he warily picked his way between the peaks of the eastern side of the Sentinels. The light grew dim under the lowering clouds, and dusk loomed on the horizon. The sleet turned to snow that whirled around the flying dragon in white streams.

After a short while, he passed over the mountains and flew above a broad strip of flat grasslands. The snow slowed a little, granting him better visibility, and he was able to fly faster. Then he entered the second range of mountains and was forced to slow down to navigate between the towering ramparts.

The way to Solace from the coast was not long by dragon wing, and yet it seemed to take forever to Sara. The cold wind only added to the misery begun by Derrick's anger. She had to find him again, to make him understand. Surely when he calmed down, he would be willing to listen. Cobalt could locate him better than she, and he would bring the knight to the tomb where, in that revered place, she could explain about honor and pride and sacrifice.

She held on to that thought like a lifeline, unaware that her hands held on to her saddle with a bloodless grip.

Blessed lights suddenly twinkled through the murk ahead, and Sara realized they were nearing Solace. The mountains below them fell away into a magnificent valley, where Crystalmir Lake lay like a deep blue jewel in the snowy breast of the mountains and the town of Solace perched in its rare and beloved vallenwood trees.

Cobalt found an open hillside where he could land out of sight of the town. Gently he touched down and waited for Sara to slide off. "Do you want me to come back at sunrise or wait for your summons?"

Sara forced her hands to let go of the saddle. Her fingers were swollen and cold and gave her no support as she dismounted. She fell heavily onto her feet and barely stifled a cry of pain. Her feet, too, were aching with cold and she could barely feel her legs.

She limped around the big dragon to his head. "Keep looking for him. If you find him, bring him here. Otherwise I will summon you when I am finished." She tugged his head down to her level and gently scratched his eye ridges. "Be careful. It's almost dark."

"Yes," he rumbled. "And you're nearly frozen. There is an inn here I've heard about. Go there and get warm."

She smiled a sad, bitter grimace and watched as he flew out of sight. She knew he did not like to fly in this miserable weather, and she appreciated his willingness to go more than she could say. Fortunately the wind had slowed and the snow had dwindled to a light fall, which would make flying easier for him, and without a rider, he could fly higher above the mountain slopes.

She found a path that led down the hillside toward Solace and carefully made her way to the valley. Not far away, the vallenwoods, splendid in their winter browns and grays, reared their tall crowns through the dusk. Lamplight gleamed through the silent snowfall from the houses high in the trees, and from the largest building in

Solace, the Inn of the Last Home, owned by Caramon and Tika Majere.

Sara stumbled to a stop. Memories bitter and sweet flooded into her mind of the time so many years ago when she fled to that inn late in the night and begged for help from a man she knew only by reputation. She had stunned Caramon Majere with her news of a nephew, young Steel, yet despite his reluctance and his shock, he had come with her and given his best to help a total stranger. For that and for the days after Steel's departure, when Caramon and Tika took care of her, she was deeply grateful.

But some strange reluctance held her back from the inn. She didn't want to go there just yet. As cold and wet and shivery as she was, she wanted to go first to the tomb to spend a few minutes alone with her son.

Sometimes she wondered if he had ever forgiven her for kidnapping him that night. Sara knew she could not bear it if he had hated her all those years before his death. Although it was too late to ask for his forgiveness, she could offer her own love at his tomb and perhaps let him know that nothing had ever changed her devotion.

She looked around to get her bearings and spotted a wide field close to the vallenwoods. Through the glimmering snow, her eyes were drawn to the pale shape of a building unlike any other in Solace. It had not been there nine years ago.

Automatically her legs moved forward off the path and toward the field. The snow wasn't deep enough to make the going difficult, and she soon came to another path leading directly to the building. Pale and numb, she came at last to the Tomb of the Last Heroes.

Chapter 22

The tomb had been built three years ago, after the Second Cataclysm, to honor both the Knights of Solamnia and the Knights of Takhisis who died fighting Chaos in the Battle of the Rift. People from all over Ansalon had gathered together to pay their respects and erect a tomb of stone worthy of the knights' sacrifice. Built of polished white marble and black obsidian brought from Thorbardin by dwarven artisans, the monument was simple, elegant, and ageless.

Around the tomb grew a row of trees lovingly brought by the elves of Qualinesti and Silvanesti. Although they were only saplings, the trees were tall and strong and full of health. Sara could imagine them a few summers from now in full leaf, giving their shade to the pilgrims who visited the tomb.

This night there was no one else about. The tomb lay silent in its snowy shroud, alone in the darkness except for Sara.

Well, not totally alone. Away to her right, she saw the ghostly glimmer of lights shining through several small tents. A party of kender had camped in the field close by to visit the memorial of their hero, Tasslehoff Burrfoot. But even the inquisitive, irrepressible kender had retreated to their shelters in the cold, wintry night. Sara had the tomb to herself.

The path she had found followed an oblique angle

down from the hills to the north and ended on the low steps at the front of the tomb. Exhausted beyond measure, Sara sank down on the steps, too tired to care about the icy chill that seeped up from the stone. Bleary-eyed, she looked around the entrance to the tomb.

Two brass lamps hung on either side of the double doors and burned perpetually through the night. Their clear light illuminated the images carved on both doors by the Knights of Solamnia. The gold door bore the rose of Solamnia; the silver carried a death lily. On blocks of stone around the doors were engraved the names of the knights who lay within and the knights whose bodies had never been found. One name was chiseled alone above the door with the image of a kender's hoopak. It was to honor Tasslehoff Burrfoot, a kender of boundless courage and wondrous adventure, whose small body was never recovered from the rift.

Sara let her breath out in a slow sigh. Wearily she rested her arms on her knees. She lifted her eyes to the names chiseled into the walls and began to read them until she found the one closest to her heart: Steel Brightblade.

Oh, my dearest child, did Takhisis honor your soul when you died? Did she grant you anything for the supreme sacrifice you made? Or had she already abandoned you?

Sara's head drooped to her arms. Her eyes closed, and a tear slid down her cheek.

How long she stayed that way, Sara never knew for sure. The silence of the tomb gathered close around her in a deep, boundless peace. She felt it as a comfort and let the soundless company of the dead lull her into tranquility. Her worry and grief fell behind, her confusion vanished. For this moment, there was only the contemplative stillness of her own heart. Listen, the silence told her.

Something clicked beside her.

Sara lifted her head, curious to see what had disturbed the profound quiet, and saw that the silver door of the tomb had opened a crack. Surprised, she climbed stiffly to her feet. She had heard the tomb was sealed to protect the bodies of the knights within. Yet the door stood open.

She laid her hand on the silver edge and gently eased it toward her. The darkness within was complete. She saw nothing beyond the lintel but blackness. Strangely, she felt no fear. She knew without a doubt there was nothing inside that meant any harm to her.

Removing one of the lamps from the wall, she stepped to the open doorway. Perhaps she wasn't supposed to go in there, but at that moment, Sara didn't care. She wanted to see her son.

She lifted the lamp above her head and stepped beneath the lintel. The small brass lamp made a golden ball of light from her hand to the stone floor and gleamed like a tiny star in darkness that had not seen light for three years.

Three paces within the door, Sara reached the first of a long row of low stone biers. The body of a knight lay on the bier. His sword lay by his side, and a shield bearing the rose of the Knights of Solamnia rested on his chest. His face beneath the visor of his helm looked as if it had been carved from marble.

Beyond him, on the second bier, lay a Knight of Takhisis, his skull helm leering up at Sara in the faint light. She nodded once to him and moved on. A second row of biers sat to her right, and Sara realized there was no order among the dead men. The knights of the light and the dark rested together as they had fallen.

Soundlessly Sara walked deeper into the tomb. Points of light reflected from swords, shields, breastplates, and helms played across the dark ceiling. She was surprised to see there was little dust and no smell beyond the odors of old leather and cold stone. The bodies seemed to be remarkably preserved in the cold, dry air.

The reason for their preservation appeared a moment later in the gloom. Two stately pedestals stood to her left and right between the rows of biers. If Sara could have seen the entire interior, she guessed she would see a complete circle of these pedestals, each bearing a polished orb of bloodstone. Many years ago she had seen such stones, spelled with magic and set in a tomb to preserve a body. These stones, carved by the loving hands of the dwarves, were large and polished to a sheen that set their flecks of red gleaming like drops of blood.

Sara passed the pedestals carefully and moved deeper toward the center of the room. Something large and black loomed out of the darkness, a larger catafalque crafted from black marble. A knight clad in black armor rested on the stone, his father's antique sword in his lifeless hands.

Steel.

His face was as pale as granite and hollowed where the skin had sunk around the bones, and yet even after three years of death, Sara could still marvel at the look of peace on his face. The internal battle between his mother's evil and his father's good had finally come to an end and left their son in peace.

Just beyond Steel's bier, at the edge of her light, Sara saw a second large catafalque, this one made of white marble. On it, she recognized the noble form of Tanis Half-Elven. His body was clad in green leather, and a blue crystal staff lay by his side, a gift from the children of his friends, Goldmoon and Riverwind.

Sara bowed her head to the grief that welled up within her. Her arm holding the lamp faltered and dropped to her side. She was stepping closer to Steel's catafalque when the edge of her cloak caught on the stone corner of another man's bier. The cloak wrenched her off-balance, then slipped loose from the stone, sending her stumbling up against the black marble. She fell to her knees at its base. Her hands reached out to stop her fall into the stone table, and her fingers inadvertently touched Steel's gloved hand. The light crashed to the floor, flickered once, and went out.

Everything stilled.

Out of the intense darkness, a light began to glow, as if at a great distance. Tiny as a firefly, it pulsed with life and color, and with each pulse, it grew larger while the darkness coalesced around it, like the walls of a deep well. Sara stared down the well, marveling as the light and color filled her vision with a panorama of brilliant forms and hues that blurred and ran together like watercolors.

All at once the colors and forms took shape and became a recognizable portrait of a swamp—or rather the edge of a swamp, where the land met the water and gradually vanished into a world of dark fens and peat-colored meres. Sara choked on a cry. She knew that dismal-looking swamp was the one surrounding Xak Tsaroth.

As soon as she made the recognition, the vision before her began to move. Wind swayed the rushes and the scrub willows, water birds soared above the trees, and something black slithered out of the shadows of a clump of swamp grass into the dark, noisome waters.

The time could have been that day or the next, for the land was locked in winter's grip, its water edged in ice and its rushes browned by frost. Daylight filtered down through a slate roof of clouds. A few lonely snow flurries drifted on the wind.

Unnerved, Sara gazed wide-eyed at the vision before her. She could see everything so clearly, yet the images were strangely silent.

She saw a rustle of movement in a tall stand of grasses,

and a knight on foot appeared out of the underbrush, bent low over a trail he followed along the rim of a grove of trees. It wasn't until he straightened and rubbed his neck with one hand that Sara saw his breastplate bore the rose design of the Solamnic Knights.

Suddenly he crouched low, alert, and his hand flew to his sword and slid it loose from the scabbard in one flowing movement.

A second knight stepped out of the trees, a tall, dark-haired knight in black armor. Derrick.

Sara wanted to cry out to him, but she couldn't move or make a sound. She was locked in place as the vision unfolded before her.

Aching, she watched Derrick approach the Solamnic with his hands outstretched in a gesture of peace. The older knight took in Derrick's muddy boots and his tunic, torn from thrashing around in the swamp, and he relaxed enough to let him come close to talk. A long, animated conversation ensued. The Knight of the Rose seemed very agitated about something, for he continually pointed toward the south and then to the trail in front of them.

Derrick bent his head to examine the ground and listened intently to every word. Concern hardened his lean face.

Soon it became apparent the knights had reached some accord. The older Solamnic and young Derrick set off together, single file, down the winding trail deeper into the swamp. They walked warily, their swords drawn, their eyes on the trail and the swamp ahead.

They passed a huge skeleton of what could have been a dragon half-submerged in a slimy pool. More bones, dented rusting armor, and bits of junk littered the trail. Here and there a shattered tree lay to the side as if something large had kicked it aside.

Sara felt her heart beat faster.

Ahead of the knights, the trail widened into a large,

egg-shaped piece of land surrounded on three sides by the dark waters of a mere. Grasses and shrubs had been trampled flat or uprooted; bones lay scattered everywhere.

In the clearing sat the most peculiar and hideous structure Sara had ever seen. A huge rounded dome, similar in shape to a beaver's den, straddled the center of the stripped earth. But this domicile had none of the careful engineering and only a few trees in common with a beaver's house. The rest of the material consisted of anything some foul creature had tossed there: bones, armor, wagon wheels, half-devoured cows, plowshares, battered shields, a child's doll, rags, a broken chair, pieces of a raft, a headless ogre, a dragon's skull, and those were only the things Sara recognized. A crude doorway penetrated the revolting structure, and from the height of it, the owner had to be abnormally tall.

Sara watched the two knights separate and approach the hut cautiously from two directions. Although she could not hear a sound, she guessed from the tension in the men's faces that their quarry was at home.

All at once Derrick and the second knight scrambled back as two small girls in ragged dresses came pelting out of the doorway, their faces contorted in terror. A third form, a young man, flew out behind them, though it was obvious, even from Sara's position, that the man had been flung out. He landed in the mud in front of the girls and lay spread-eagled, shattered beyond hope of life. The two girls slid to a frantic stop and turned to bolt in another direction, unaware that the two knights were close by.

Abruptly a huge shape paused in the doorway, then burst into the open, its face contorted with fury.

Sara's stomach lurched in reaction. She had only heard about such brutes in the past few years, since it was rumored that the monstrous manlike things were spawns of Chaos, sprung from the earth during the Second Cataclysm. Chaos giants, they were called, and they were three times the height of a man and three as broad.

This one looked as if it had eaten well. Its heavy body was ponderous with muscle and fat that rolled and bulged like cooling lava. Its great hairless head hunkered on its shoulders like a monolith crudely carved with thick, bulbous features. It saw the two knights immediately. It stamped the earth and bellowed its fury at the puny intruders.

Derrick shouted something to the girls. They stared, stunned by the sudden appearance of the men, then the elder grabbed the younger's hand and fled up the path into the swamp.

Both knights attacked the giant at once.

The battle raged around the clearing. The giant, like a bull besieged by dogs, charged after first one assailant, then the other, and each time it thundered after one knight, the other harried it from behind. Again and again the giant rushed to catch one man in its crushing hands, and each time the knight slipped away.

Alone, neither man could have fought the superior strength of the giant and survived, but together they worked as a team and wore the brute down to a staggering exhaustion.

At last, bleeding from a dozen sword cuts and drenched in sweat, the giant stumbled to one side, lost its balance, and toppled over. The ground shook from the impact.

Derrick and the Solamnic knight threw themselves at its prostrate body before the gigantic creature could get up and stabbed their swords through its eyes deep into its brain. The giant bawled in outrage, shuddered violently, and lay motionless.

Sara exhaled in a slow breath. It was over.

The knights, pleased with their success, shook hands

and slapped each other on the back. Both looked tired and battered, but neither man was seriously injured.

They rested for a few minutes before the Solamnic Knight walked over to the bizarre hut and gestured to Derrick. They entered the shelter. Then Sara saw them come out carrying a wooden strongbox. Back inside they went and brought out more boxes, some leather bags, and a few pieces of finely crafted weaponry and armor. Soon they had a goodly pile of spoils from the beast's lair.

They fell into conversation again, this time over the heap of treasure and valuables. Sara watched in growing alarm as the talk grew heated. Both men argued their point with increasing aggression and animosity. Their faces darkened, their gestures turned sharp and savage.

Suddenly swords were drawn. The blades angrily clashed above the heap of spoils.

Stop it! Sara tried to cry, but she could not move her lips.

Once they crossed swords, neither knight would surrender to the other. They were too evenly matched and too stubborn with pride. Ferociously they fought across the same ground they had struggled over together. The Solamnic drew blood first, cutting Derrick deeply across the thigh. The Dark Knight crashed back against the giant's body, his face contorted in pain. Blood flowed freely from the wound.

Stop it! cried Sara's soul.

Neither knight could hear her. Derrick threw himself forward and brought his sword whistling around in a vicious undercut toward his opponent's ribs.

The Knight of the Rose was too exhausted to avoid the blow completely. He swerved left just enough so Derrick's blade missed his ribs, but the sharp edge slid across the chain mail and caught him under the armpit, where the mail did not protect him. Blood soaked his tunic and mail.

Now both men bled freely. They swayed and staggered across the slippery mud and hacked at each other in clumsy, brutal blows that became automatic. There was no thought left in either knight, only the primal need to kill.

There could be no victor in a battle such as this. While Sara stared, wracked by grief, Derrick struck a heavy blow to the Solamnic's leg. The knight could not evade it. The blade slashed deep into the muscle just behind his knee.

The Knight of the Rose could no longer hold himself up. Disbelieving, torn by pain, he toppled over and crashed into the mud.

Derrick looked stunned. He sank slowly to his knees, unaware of the blood that soaked his leather leggings. The color drained from his face. He tried to lean his weight on his sword, but he had no strength left. His eyes rolled up into his head, his hands slipped off the bloody sword, and he fell sideways beside the other knight. His ribs rose and fell, then sank slowly into stillness.

The vision stopped on this scene, everything held in place as if a sorcerer had frozen an image in a mirror.

Sara stared frantically at the two knights for some sign of life until her head pounded and her eyes burned with tears. The picture blurred and wavered; the dark well of her vision swirled inward.

"No," she cried out loud. "He can't be . . ." Somewhere within her, she was aware of pain, deep and biting, and of anger at the senseless waste.

"Mother," a voice whispered beside her.

The image of Derrick dissolved into dark motes and was blown away on a sudden gust of wind.

"Mother."

Steel? Sara raised her head, her hope raw in her heart at the sound of that beloved voice. Her fingers clutched at the cold stone, and she pulled herself to her feet.

"Steel?" she cried brokenly, and her hand came to rest again over his cold appendage.

A dazzling light flared beside her. She blinked and rubbed the spots in her eyes, half-blinded by the unexpected light. By squinting hard, she adjusted her sight to the new radiance and finally saw its source.

Steel stood at the foot of the catafalque. Or something did. His lifeless body still lay supine on the marble, yet his image stood before her, his form bathing her in soft white light. The vision looked so real, Sara reached out her hand to touch him, then jerked it back, afraid to learn that the image might not be her son.

He smiled at her then, his crooked grin filled with love and understanding, and Sara lost any doubt. Sometimes a mother's love sees clearer than fallible eyes.

She did not try to speak. She simply filled her gaze with him, his fine features, his black hair, the line of his jaw, the angle of his shoulders. She soaked in his presence like dry earth absorbing a spring rain.

He lifted his hand, and his fingers closed around something. A second light, pure and white, welled from his fist. Steel reached out to the only mother he ever had.

Sara was shaking like a leaf. Instinctively she held out her hand, palm up.

"Mother," Steel said, his words ringing in the dark tomb. "All we have is each other," and he dropped the white light into her hand.

The light pulsed like a tiny star, dazzling and exquisitely beautiful. A sudden burst of radiance surged through Sara and sent her senses reeling.

"Steel!" she cried frantically. She could no longer see him, could no longer feel the stone-coldness of his hand. The light became a darkness so complete that Sara could not bear it. She staggered and fell onto something frigid and unrelenting that sapped away what little strength she had left. She tried once to push herself up and found she had not the energy to move her arms or legs. She sagged down to the stone floor and lay there while the cold seeped insidiously into her limbs.

Unable to move, unwilling to leave, she closed her eyes. Her breath fluttered out in a sigh, and her weary spirit fled to the comfort of sleep.

Chapter 23

"Do you think she enjoys sleeping on snow-covered stone?" the first voice murmured.

"Sure. Why else would she do it?" answered a second.

"It is rather cold tonight. We might find her frozen stiff in the morning."

The second voice sounded pleased by that prospect. "Do you think so? They'd have to pry the body off the step. That might be interesting to watch."

Sara listened to this conversation in an offhand sort of way. It meant nothing to her.

"Do you think she's dead already?" the second voice added hopefully.

A finger poked Sara's shoulder. "No. Look, she's warm and still breathing, too."

Small hands patted her belt and her clothes. "See this?" said the first excitedly. "She's a dragon rider."

"Ooooh, I wonder where her dragon is. I'd love to see a dragon. I haven't seen any dragons since the summer it got so hot."

"That's probably a good thing. There are some dragons I never want to see."

Something about the talk of dragons set off a nagging spark in Sara's exhausted mind. Dragons? No, just one dragon. A special one of deep blue. Flare? No, her memory told her, Flare was dead. Cobalt, then. He was alone, looking for someone.

"He will be back," she whispered to the two voices.

"She said something!" the first voice cried in excitement. "Maybe she'll wake up now and talk to us."

A finger poked her shoulder harder. "Hey, dragon rider, are you asleep?"

The voices, Sara noted, were childlike and pleasant, too high-pitched to be human. She groaned, then hauled her eyes open and found herself literally nose to nose with two kender bent over her face.

"She's awake," yelped the first voice. This voice belonged to a slender female with a round apple face and a bountiful topknot of nut-brown hair. She grinned at Sara.

Her companion, a young male kender, asked without preamble, "Why are you sleeping on the stone steps? Is it an adventure, a penance, a bet? Is it fun? Could we try it with you?"

Sara gazed at them, unblinking, for several long minutes. Bits of memory, odd visions, and the feeling of something urgent floated around in her mind. "I don't know . . ." she replied, her thoughts fuzzy. "I didn't mean to."

"Ahh! Of course," the female kender snapped her fingers. "She's sick."

Sara noticed she was lying across the stone steps of some building at such an angle that the steps were digging into her back and shoulders. It was dark and a light snow fell around her. What an odd place to be, she mused. So thick and unwieldy were her thoughts, she gave up trying to make sense of anything and turned her attention toward making her body move.

The male kender patted Sara's shoulder and proffered a small hand to help her up. He was about the same height as his companion. He had the same apple-round face, bright brown eyes, and an abundant head of red-brown hair tied in a topknot with a strip of yellow leather.

"My name is Badger Coltsfoot, and this is my sister, Lemmi. Who are you? You don't look sick, but you look awfully tired. Do you know someone in the tomb? Is that why you're here? We don't get many dragon riders around here."

Sara shook her head to stem the flow of questions. "Is Badger your name or what you do?" she asked with a small chuckle. She took his hand and let him slowly pull her up to a sitting position.

Her head suddenly reeled, and for a moment she thought she would faint. She leaned her head between her knees and took several deep breaths.

"Oh, what do you have in your hand?" Lemmi asked curiously. "It's beautiful."

Sara didn't know she had anything in her hand. Curious, she looked down at her right hand resting on her lap and saw that her fingers were tightly clenched over something small that glowed with its own soft white light. The light leaked between her fingers and made her skin glow red from the blood within.

Sara choked on a cry. Her fingers opened, and there on her palm lay an elven jewel, carved in the shape of a star and hung on a slender steel chain. The only time she had seen that jewel before was the day Steel received it from his father, Sturm Brightblade, in a vision at the tombs in the High Clerist's Tower. As far as she knew, he had carried it ever since.

Like the flare of a lamp in a darkened room that lights everything around it, the star jewel pulsed through the dark confusion of her brain and illuminated her thoughts and memories with pure clarity. Everything fell into place.

Yet it all seemed so unreal. She twisted around and saw that the silver door to the tomb was closed tightly and the lamp was back on the wall. If it were not for the star jewel in her hand, she would have thought she had dreamed the whole thing.

Sara realized this was too important to deal with alone, and besides, she could barely sit, not to mention stand or walk or summon Cobalt for a ride. Her legs were numb, and her hands were patched white with frostbite. She was trembling so badly, she could barely hold the jewel. She needed help.

The young kender watched her expectantly.

Remembering who she was dealing with, Sara slipped the steel chain over her head and tucked the jewel into her tunic. Badger looked slightly disappointed.

"Do you know the Inn of the Last Home?" she asked both kender.

Their faces lit up and Lemmi giggled. "I should say we do. The innkeeper just threw us out a little while ago."

Sara frowned. That did not bode well for a message she wanted to send. Nevertheless, she didn't have anyone else. "Could you please go to Caramon Majere and tell him I'm here? Tell him my name is Sara Dunstan and I need his help. Again."

Badger shrugged lightly. "Sure. Need anything else? Our tents are right over there. We're camping here for a few days while we visit the tomb and pay our respects to our Uncle Tas. We've met some fun people here. There was—"

Lemmi tugged his arm, cutting off his enthusiastic explanations. "I think we'd better go see Innkeeper Majere, Badger, before it gets too late. We can tell Sara about our new friends later."

Sara silently blessed the more practical Lemmi. She watched the two kender trot off into the darkness toward the distant lights of Solace. Now she could only sit and hope that Caramon or Tika would listen to the kender and come find her.

Time lost all meaning for Sara, sitting by the tomb in the snowy night. She paid no heed to the cold or the darkness or the fact that her feet had no feeling. All she could think about was Derrick, Steel, and the jewel that

hung about her neck. She did not even see Caramon and
Tika come huffing out of the darkness.

"Look!" she heard Tika Majere call. "It is Sara! Blessed
Paladine, what are you doing out here?"

Sara looked up at the faces of her rescuers and burst
into tears.

* * * * *

An hour later she was comfortably ensconced in a
large chair in front of a roaring fire in the main room of
the Majeres' inn. Tika had replaced Sara's damp, frosted
clothes with dry ones and wrapped her in blankets while
Caramon carefully removed her boots and set about
treating her frostbitten hands and feet with warm water
and gentle massage. She sat back in her chair and
grinned stupidly while the two bustled around her and
exclaimed over her condition. A mug of hot mulled wine
was pressed into her hand, and Tika brought her a plate
heaped with Otik's famous spiced potatoes, heaps of
roasted meat, a wedge of golden cheese made only in
Solace, and enough spice cakes to feed an army.

The two kender who brought the Majeres naturally
had to see what was happening, so they had followed
Caramon, with Sara in his arms, back to the inn and
made themselves at home near Sara. She was too grateful to them to ask them to leave, so she pushed several
spice cakes in their direction and fell on her own meal
like a ravenous wolf. It was the best food she'd had since
leaving Connersby.

Once Sara's immediate needs were seen to, Tika and
Caramon pulled chairs to her table to join her. She
grinned her appreciation at them between bites and took
the opportunity to study her friends.

She had met both Majeres that night nine years ago
when she came begging Caramon for his help. Despite
her ties to the Knights of Takhisis and her wild tale of

Steel's parentage, he had believed her, and with his friend, Tanis Half-Elven, had taken Steel to the High Clerist's Tower to see the body of their friend, Sturm. It was during that visit that Steel was met by the spirit of his father and given the elven star jewel.

Although the visit had not persuaded Steel as Sara hoped it would, she had been indebted to the Majeres for their trust and help. She stayed with them for several months after Steel returned to Storm's Keep and left only because she did not want to endanger them with her presence. She decided a small, isolated village far from Solace would be safer for them all, so she had wandered to Solamnia and eventually found Connersby. She had not seen the Majeres again until this night.

She was pleased to see they had not changed very much in the past nine years. Tika's bright red hair had mellowed to a rich roan of gray and red, and her face had more wrinkles than Sara remembered, but her figure was still youthful, and her beauty had ripened to a full blush.

Caramon was much the same as ever—bluff, hearty, and softhearted. If the big man was a little rounder in his barrel chest and a little more worn around the face, Sara put it down to the years and to the grief of losing his two oldest sons during the Summer of Chaos.

When Sara finished her plate at last and pushed it away with a sigh of contentment, Tika whisked it away and came right back to the table. The Majeres exchanged a glance between them to see which one would speak first.

It was Tika who refilled Sara's mug and said bluntly, "Sara, we are so glad to see you. But what are you doing here dressed in the clothes of a dragon rider?"

With that simple question, Tika opened a floodgate in Sara's reserve. She had been so careful, so contained while in Neraka, she hadn't realized how much she missed having someone safe to talk to. She wrapped her hands around her mug and said to warn them, "It's a long tale."

"We've the time," Caramon told her.

So Sara told the Majeres everything, from the first night she dreamed of Cobalt to her departure from Neraka. She explained her motives for going, described the squires and Governor-General Abrena, and detailed the garrison at the city.

They listened, fascinated and stunned in turns. Caramon paid careful attention to her information about the dark knighthood and its new leader; Tika listened to the deeper emotions Sara revealed when she talked about Derrick and the squires, and she nodded in understanding.

Sitting by the fire, the two kender sat wide-eyed in delight. This was the best tale they had heard in years.

At last Sara came to the part of her story that happened in the tomb. Her words slowed to a trickle, and her gaze lengthened into the distance beyond the walls of the inn. She told what occurred succinctly and without expressing the changing emotions that ebbed and flowed through her.

"He stood by his own bier," she said softly. "He said nothing more than, 'All we have is each other.' Then he handed me something and was gone. The next thing I remember is waking up outside the tomb."

Tika, practical and pragmatic, eyed their guest dubiously. She knew Sara to be honest, courageous, thoughtful, and determined, and she accepted that Sara believed she had been in the tomb and seen Steel. But the mind can be deceiving. Dreams and visions can seem quite real to someone who is exhausted and numb with cold.

Tika glanced at Caramon and recognized the vague look he often got when deep in thought. Caramon was often slow to react, not because he was dull-witted, but because he always looked carefully at things from every angle before making a decision or reaching a conclusion.

The slowness of his ponderings often drove some people to make the wrong judgment about his abilities, but once he made up his mind, he often found insights or details other people missed.

To give him time to think, Tika fetched two small glasses and poured hot cider for the kender. She ran a swift eye over the silverware and nearby knickknacks and was relieved to see everything was still in place.

Badger and Lemmi had been so enthralled by Sara's story, their instinctive tendencies to "acquire" things had been stifled. Nothing extra had found its way into the collection of pouches at their belts. Brother and sister sat still in their chairs by the fire pit, their short legs dangling down, their faces bright with curiosity.

Tika smiled at her guests and asked, "When you found Sara, did you see anything different about the tomb?"

Delighted to be involved in such a mystery, Badger nearly fell out of his chair in his haste to answer. "You mean was the door open or any ghosts hanging about? No. The lamp was on the hook, too."

Tika pursed her lips and posed another question. "Did you see any footprints in the snow by the door?"

Lemmi thought for a minute and shook her head. "No. There wasn't any snow by the door. I guess the wind blew it away. Sara was just lying there on the stone."

Sara nodded. "I don't even know how I got out of the tomb, but somehow I must have," she said, with a defiant glance at her hosts. She knew what they were thinking. "I thought at first I dreamed it all. But there is more to it than that. Steel wanted to tell me something, to give me hope for the future. This is what he gave me." She took hold of the steel chain and gently tugged the elven star jewel off her neck. Laying it on the table, she sat back to watch the Majeres' reactions.

Tika clasped her hands together, her eyes huge.

Caramon leaned forward, his face alight with fascination. "That is Sturm's jewel," he observed. "The one

Alhana Starbreeze gave him as a gift of her love. I remember that. Sturm gave it to Steel in the tower. . . much like your vision." He touched the jewel gently with his forefinger, marveling at its beauty. This was no dream. It felt hard and warm beneath his finger. "When the remnants of the Solamnic Knights returned to the ruins of the tower after the Battle of the Rift, they found the jewel on Sturm's bier where Steel had left it. They returned it and put it around Steel's neck before the tomb was sealed."

A thoughtful quiet settled over the small group while everyone stared at the white jewel glittering in the firelight.

"What do you think Steel wanted to tell you?" Tika asked softly.

Sara sagged back in her blankets. The warmth, the food, the feeling of being safe—it had all caught up with her and pulled her down into a deep, soft well of exhaustion. "I don't know yet. I have to put it all together. There is something here I feel is vitally important, but I can't see it yet." Her eyelids drooped and she yawned. "Forgive me," she murmured. "I am so tired."

The next thing she knew, Caramon's strong arms lifted her out of the chair, took her to one of the small rooms reserved for guests, and set her carefully on the bed. She smiled at her friends and fell asleep before Tika covered her with the blankets.

Sometime late in the night, when the inn was dark and silent, Sara sat bolt upright in bed. Her eyes flew open wide in wakefulness and stared, unseeing, into the night. Of course! That's it! she told herself over and over. Her body tingled with the energy of inspiration; her mind raced ahead to the future and to plans for immediate action.

Steel had fought good and evil within himself his entire life until at last he set them both aside and did what he believed was right. Only then did he achieve success, glory, and the peace he so desperately sought for.

She understood that, but she had not made the right conclusion until she looked at the vision of Derrick and the Solamnic Knight from a less personal angle and made the connection.

Each knight represented his order, the good and the evil, the light and the darkness. Their battle in the clearing, as well as her own knowledge of General Abrena's plans, pointed to more conflict in the future. Sara was terribly certain that whatever good the Solamnics might do, the Knights of Takhisis would undo.

There had to be a middle ground. A third party that would not worry about absent goddesses, or strict codes and measures, or ambition and power, or self-interest. A group that would serve the people. Steel's statement echoed her own deep-rooted belief that the destiny of Krynn lay in the hands of its people, working together. "All we have is each other."

Sara never did return to sleep that night. At dawn, she bounced out of bed, threw on her dried clothes, and hurried into the inn's kitchen.

Tika was already there, cooking eggs and sausages and baking bread for the day's customers. She wiped floury hands on her apron and poured a cup of tarbean tea for Sara. Her expression brightened at the look of energy and determination on Sara's face.

"I have to make a short trip," Sara announced. "I hope I won't be long. When I come back, may I leave a friend with you?"

"Of course," Tika replied, puzzled by Sara's request. "Where do you have to go in such a hurry?"

"The knight I saw in my vision is close by. If I can reach him before he fights, or . . . before he dies, I want to bring him back here."

Tika paused, her hands poised over the frying pan. "The Dark Knight?"

"His name is Derrick," Sara said firmly. "He looks like Steel and has his sense of honor. I don't believe he will make a good knight of evil."

Tika eyed Sara shrewdly. "All right. If you say he needs to come here, I will take him. And you, too. You cannot return to Neraka."

Sara's reply was ambiguous. "We'll see what happens. I want to find Derrick first."

The doors of the kitchen slammed open and Caramon came in, stamping snow from his boots. The big man grinned as he hung his cloak on a peg and came over to join Sara. His wife handed him a mug of steaming tea and his breakfast.

"You look better this morning," he observed after eyeing Sara from head to foot.

She agreed. She felt better, too, better than she had in a long while, filled with energy, enthusiasm, and an inner joy that simmered in her gray eyes. Something had happened to her during the night that she could not entirely explain—yet. She needed some time to think it all through.

"I walked around the tomb this morning at first light," Caramon said. "The tomb is sealed, as always. If there were any footprints by the door, those kender of yours trampled all over them."

Sara laughed, and Tika, watching her, thought twenty years fell away from her face.

"It doesn't matter if I was in the tomb or not, Caramon," said Sara. "What matters is that Steel gave me his message and his star jewel for a purpose. That jewel has always symbolized one's love for another, an unspoken pledge of mutual protection, and it is now up to me to put it to use."

Caramon looked puzzled. He glanced at Tika, who merely shrugged her shoulders. "What are you going to do?" he asked.

"First I am going to summon my dragon and go find my companion before he does something stupid. When I think through the rest of it, I'll let you know." Impulsively she leaned over, gave Caramon a kiss on the cheek, hugged Tika, and flew out the swinging doors before they knew what blew by them.

"Was that the same woman we brought in last night?" Caramon asked in wonder.

Chapter 24

Outside, Sara paused to throw on her cloak and fill her lungs with the crisp morning air. From her vantage point high in the vallenwood tree, she could see most of Solace and out to the fields beyond where the tomb glistened in the early sunlight.

The Inn of the Last Home was the largest building in Solace and sat nearly forty feet off the ground in the secure branches of a tremendous vallenwood tree. The Majeres had taken loving care of the inn and its tree over the years, and their attention had been rewarded by a steady stream of customers that came to enjoy Caramon's brown ale, Tika's inestimable cooking, and the inn's excellent service.

A broad set of stairs wound down the convoluted tree trunk to the ground, and Sara went down as fast as her legs could carry her. A euphoria of joy, of power, of direction energized her muscles and sent her racing across the snowy fields. Without stopping, she pulled the dragon-scale thong out of her tunic, clasped her hand around it, and sent her mental summons winging out to find Cobalt.

She wanted to go to the Tomb of the Last Heroes to see it in the daylight while she waited for her dragon to come, so she turned her racing steps toward the tomb. She felt so strong, she ran three times around the large building before coming to a breathless halt on the stone steps.

In the clear morning light, the marble building gleamed as pure and white as the new-fallen snow around it. Nothing looked different. The gold and silver doors still shut in the darkness behind them, the small lamps still hung on the wall, the names of the dead still made their dark lines against the flawless stone. Yet something had changed in Sara. She felt it and relished the change. The emptiness she had carried within her for almost nine long years was gone. The purposelessness she had dragged with her like an empty shell had cracked off and fallen away. Steel loved her and forgave her; Steel had given her a reason to continue.

Excited voices drew her attention away from the tomb, and she turned to see two small figures dashing toward her. Badger and Lemmi grinned from ear to pointed ear to see her.

"Sara!" they shouted. The two kender were dressed warmly against the winter cold in fur jackets and thick leggings of brilliant yellow. Their cheeks glowed apple red and their eyes, she noticed in the daylight, were summer green. They looked so bright and cheerful, she laughed to see them.

"When can we see your dragon?" Badger wanted to know before she could draw breath to say hello.

"In just a few minutes, I hope," Sara replied. "He's on his way."

"You're calling him here? Just outside of Solace? He's a blue, isn't he?" Lemmi asked. "Is he mean?"

Badger bared his teeth and imitated a rather high-pitched dragon growl. "Of course he is, you doorknob. He's a blue. They're all evil."

Sara held up her hand. "Well, some are worse or better than others. Cobalt was badly injured last year and almost died. He is much calmer and more mellow than when I knew him years ago. He may wait to say hello before he eats you."

Badger's eyes widened with excitement. "Could he

give us a ride first?"

"I'll have a talk with him. He may be grateful for what you did for me. If he's in a good mood, he just might."

Both kender looked delighted with the suggestion and settled down to wait with Sara for the dragon's arrival.

"Did you know your dagger is missing?" Lemmi asked after a moment of quiet.

Sara glanced down at her belt and noticed for the first time her empty sheath. A little suspicion jiggled in her thoughts. "Well! I wonder how that happened. I must have mislaid it. I don't suppose you know where I could find another one to take with me while I look for my friend."

"Oh, I've got one!" Badger offered, pleased to be of help. He searched through his pouches and pockets and belt loops until he found what he was looking for. "Here, you can have this one. I found it somewhere. It's a very nice one," and he handed Sara a dagger that looked exactly like her old one.

The woman shook her head. What would Krynn be like without the irrepressible, sticky-fingered, guileless, child-hearted kender?

Lemmi suddenly pointed her finger toward the east and exclaimed, "There he is!" and out of the rising sun came a dark shape winging fast on the rising breeze.

Large wings rustled overhead, and a gust of wind nearly knocked the kender over. The ground trembled as the big dragon settled to the ground.

"Sara!" he trumpeted. "Are you well? What's happened? Your summons came so fast and so strong, it nearly knocked me out of the air."

Taking a running leap, she sprang up his leg and into his saddle before she explained. "Yes, I'm fine, Cobalt. We're going to find Derrick. I think I know where to look." She threw her arms around his neck. "I am so glad to see you."

Her eyes happened to glance down at the two kender,

and she saw the crestfallen looks on their faces. "We'll be back soon," she called down, "and I promise I'll talk to him."

Their expressions brightened considerably, and they waved as the dragon pushed off into the air.

"Talk to me about what?" he asked suspiciously.

"About taking them for a ride," Sara said. She had to purse her lips hard to keep from laughing.

"Absolutely not!" the blue roared, pumping harder toward the mountains. "I will not carry those little pickpockets. They're worse than children, and I hate children."

Sara ran her hand down his neck to placate him. "Hear me out first, then you can decide." Knowing her experience and her decisions would affect him, too, she told him everything that happened from the moment he dropped her off on the hillside.

He listened quietly from beginning to end, his ears cocked back to catch every word. They were over the mountains and approaching the swamp before she finished. He stayed quiet for some time after, his mind carefully ruminating over her tale.

Whether he believed it or not did not matter to him. What made him accept her story was the change he sensed in her, in her voice, in her happiness, in the new strength he felt coursing through her. Cobalt had long ago given up any thought of serving Takhisis. When the dark goddess abandoned the world and his first rider died, a part of Cobalt died, too. Or rather, with Sara's arrival, a part of him was reborn. Now he cared only for her, and for her he would give his life if he needed to. If she said her adopted son left her a legacy and she intended to use it, then by all the powers of Krynn, Cobalt knew he would stand with her.

"All right," he said at last. "I'll give those kender a ride—a short one, that is."

Smiling to herself, Sara guided the dragon over the swamp. Although she did not know the exact location of the clearing where the giant dwelt, she thought she could spot the place or even the trail leading to it from the air. In the morning sunlight, trails and landmarks were fairly easy to spot from the air.

Cobalt swept low over the swamp and began a systematic sweep of the borders. It was nearly noon before Sara saw what she was looking for—a trail beaten through the undergrowth and trees. She pointed it out to Cobalt, and he tilted his wings and glided lower over the path.

In minutes, they overflew the clearing. Sara groaned her dismay. She hoped the battle with the giant had not yet taken place, or that it truly was nothing more than a vision of possibilities, and she would find Derrick still fuming in the swamp. But just as she had witnessed in her vision, the giant's body lay sprawled in the trampled mud. Close by lay two smaller bodies, clad in armor.

"Sara, there are goblins down there," Cobalt hissed.

She took a closer look and saw what he meant. A party of perhaps ten ill-clad, unkempt goblins was creeping along the trail into the giant's clearing. Several of the boldest ones were already pawing over the pile of spoils. They looked up in alarm as the dragon's shadow passed over them.

Cobalt did not need to wait for instructions. He folded his wings and dropped like a stone into the clearing, where he landed heavily on top of the dead giant. The electrical energy of his dragon breath surged within him. He held his breath for as long as he could, then belched forth a tremendous bolt of power that seared into the largest cluster of goblins. A clap of thunder shook the clearing.

The massive stroke of lightning slammed into three goblins and sent their charred bodies flying into their companions. The other goblins squealed in terror. They could face dead giants, but not living dragons that spit lightning. They scrambled madly over one another in their effort to escape the clearing. The three by the pile of treasure cowered down behind the boxes, too terrified or too greedy to run.

Sara pulled her sword free from its scabbard on the saddle and slid off. The three goblins by the piles were too close to the knights' bodies for Cobalt to sear them, so she went after them herself while the dragon dealt with the rest of the mob.

The goblins saw her coming and drew their own small weapons. One lone female human was more to their liking. But if they hoped to dispatch her quickly and flee out of the clearing while the dragon was distracted elsewhere, Sara immediately dashed their hopes. Giving a furious yell, she charged the three creatures and lopped the head off the nearest one. The others took one look at the head rolling at their feet and whirled to flee.

"Oh, no, you don't!" Sara shouted forcefully. She caught the second in three running strides and cut him nearly in half as she passed by. The last goblin dashed as fast as his bowed legs could run across the muddy clearing toward the trail.

Sara stopped, pulled the dagger from her belt, and hurled it toward the running goblin. The knife caught him neatly between the shoulder blades and knocked him sprawling. The clearing fell silent.

Sara looked around in satisfaction. The goblins were gone or dead, and Cobalt was busy cleaning up. A night of searching the swamp had made him very hungry.

She hurried to the two knights where they lay near the treasure they had fought over. One quick glance told her the Solamnic was already dead. His face was white and rigid with death; a pool of blood congealed under his body. Sadly Sara covered his face with his cloak.

Afraid of what she might find, Sara slowly knelt by Derrick's body and checked his pulse under his jaw. To her everlasting delight, his skin was still warm and pliable, and a weak heartbeat fluttered under the pressure of her fingers.

"Cobalt!" she shouted.

The dragon hurried to her summons. Swiftly Sara bound Derrick's wounds, then bundled the young knight in her own cloak. With Cobalt's help, she lifted him into the saddle. She held him tightly as the dragon flew back to Solace.

Cobalt gave the citizens of Solace a terrible fright by landing at the edge of the vallenwoods. Voices rose in shouts of warning and fear at the sight of a large blue dragon dropping out of the sky. People came running to investigate. Ignoring the hubbub, Cobalt delivered Sara and the wounded knight to the foot of the inn. As Caramon and Tika rushed out the door, he lifted his head, gave them a wink, and flew away before the people decided to take arms against him.

Tika threw aside her initial shock and ran down the stairs to help Sara. Caramon followed more slowly. Together the three carried Derrick up to the inn and put him to bed. After a careful examination, Tika and Sara found the young man was very lucky. He had had enough sense to put a tourniquet on his leg just long enough to stop the bleeding before he passed out. He was still unconscious, pale from loss of blood and exposure, but with care, food, and bedrest, Tika thought he would survive.

He was sleeping soundly, his leg bandaged and his minor wounds cleaned, when Sara left him in Tika's care and went to call Cobalt again. There was one more thing she wanted to do before sunset.

They flew back to the clearing and collected the Solamnic's body and the pile of spoils from the giant's hut. The knight had fought well against the giant, and Sara felt he did not deserve to be left as carrion for goblins and swamp creatures. Although the combination of two humans and a pile of boxes made a heavy load for the dragon, Cobalt carried it all without complaint back to Solace.

By this time, Caramon had explained to the town's elders that the blue dragon who kept popping in and out was not dangerous and was actually helping a friend of his. When Cobalt returned with the dead man and the treasure, there were wary but willing volunteers to help Sara untie the body and the collection of bags and boxes. The giant's spoils were put in the inn for safekeeping until Sara could decide what to do about them. The Solamnic knight was buried with honor in a small grave-yard just outside the town, near the graves of Sturm Brightblade and Tanin Majere.

The last thing Cobalt did before retiring for a well-deserved rest was take Lemmi and Badger Coltsfoot for a ride. Keeping his grumbling to himself, he flew them over Crystalmir Lake, circled Solace, and passed over the edge of the vast Darkenwood. By the time he landed, the two kender were nearly incoherent with excitement.

Sara scratched his eye ridges in thanks. "Rest well, my friend," she said softly. "I promise not to bother you again, at least tonight."

The dragon huffed a cloud of steam. "Was no bother," he said gruffly, and he left to seek a secluded cave for some peace and quiet.

That night Sara stayed in a chair beside Derrick, keeping watch by his side.

Day was creeping soundlessly into the inn when the young knight woke up to find himself in a bed in a strange place, with no idea how he got there. He lay still and gazed at the ceiling for a long time. He remembered the hateful circumstances that brought him to death's door, but he could not remember anything beyond tight-ening the tourniquet on his leg. He should be dead.

Someone moved beside him, and he turned his head to see Sara in the chair by his bed. Her eyes slowly opened, like curtains pulled back on a sunny window. He stared at her in astonishment. Something had happened to her that had erased years from her face. Her gray eyes were brighter and more full of life than he remembered. Lines of worry were gone; the drab color of her skin had freshened to sun-kissed peach; the tension he had always seen in her expression had softened to a shimmering joy. Instead of the condemnation he expected to see in her face, she gave him a dazzling smile.

She moved her chair closer and took his hand in hers. "Derrick . . ."

"I'm sorry," he blurted out. "I shouldn't have left like that."

Her fingers tightened over his. "No, probably not. But I understand why you felt betrayed." She leaned forward to rest her elbows on the edge of the bed so she could see his face. "Derrick, please believe that I never intended to deliberately mislead all of you. I came to like you all much more than I ever imagined, and I saw a great deal of potential in each one of you." She shook her head at the irony of her emotions. "I was hoping that if I stayed just a little longer in Neraka, I could help you see that the Knights of Takhisis cannot offer you what you want, that there is more that you can do for this world than serve a missing goddess."

He gave a grim laugh and threw his arm up over his eyes. "I can't even be good at that. I turned on a partner, Sara. I fought him for mere treasure simply because he disagreed with me and because he challenged me. And I hated it! But I couldn't stop myself. Is that what the Dark Knights have done to me?"

He lowered his arm and met her sympathetic gaze with bitter eyes. "I killed that knight, didn't I?" When she nodded, he gritted his teeth as if in pain. "We shouldn't have fought over something so insignificant. All we wanted to do was dispose of the spoils so the goblins wouldn't get it. But neither of us would budge. A compromise seemed so weak. All I could think of was trying to obey the Code and my oath to the knighthood and how that treasure would help the talon buy new weapons and food."

"What did the Solamnic want to do with it?"

"Give it back to the victims. I told him that would be impossible. Much of the treasure had been there for years. Many of the victims were probably in the walls of that foul hut. He still insisted he knew some of them—like those two girls who fled when we attacked the giant. But he wanted it all! That didn't seem fair. I had fought for it, too."

Even as he tried to explain, Sara heard the edge of anger creeping back into his voice. Derrick heard it, too, and bit off his last complaint. "Gods, I sound pathetic. I'll never make a good knight."

"No, I don't think so either," Sara said lightly, and she laid a finger on his lips to stem any response. "Despite what you think now, you are too honorable for Takhisis. You made a mistake, but you have survived to rectify it. Now, since you cannot move from that bed, you will lie there and listen to me. There is something else I think I can offer you."

First, to clear any lingering doubts between them, she explained her reasons for going to Neraka in the first place, then once again she told about her experience in the tomb. Derrick lay still at first, then struggled upright and stared at her in growing wonder.

When she finished, she pulled out the star jewel from her tunic and laid it in his hand. "I am going to use this sign from Steel as a beginning, and I want you to join me. I am going to form a third order in Krynn, a legion if you will, of men and women who are dedicated to selflessness and service. We will help where we are needed, and we will strive to do what is right, not what some power-hungry general or antiquated code demands we do. It will have to be a secret order for now, to protect our members. If you leave the Knights of Takhisis, you will be condemned as a traitor, as I am. But if you join me, we will do what we can to help the people of Krynn in a way the Knights of Takhisis and Solamnia never could."

Sara heard a slight sound at the door and swiftly twisted around to see Tika and Caramon standing in the doorway, their expressions frozen in rapt attention. Tika held a forgotten breakfast tray in her hands.

"Great gods of Krynn, Sara," Caramon said slowly. "Is this something you really want to do?"

"More than anything." She rose to her feet and faced her friends. "For the first time since Steel left, I have something to believe in again. This is something I can do for Krynn, not just for me or for Steel. I believe it will work."

Derrick cleared his throat. "You could call it the Legion of Steel."

Sara's fingers touched the star jewel in his hand. "That will do perfectly."

"Legion of Steel," Tika murmured. "I like it."

Caramon didn't say anything, and Tika could see his mind was at work. She brushed past him and set the tray of food on a small table beside the bed. She left again to fetch some tarbean tea, and by the time she returned with it, Caramon was still standing by the door.

He seemed to stand a little straighter, and his face glowed from an inner resolution. "It's been done before, you know," he was telling Sara and Derrick. "In fact, both knightly orders began with visions and quests. Why not a third? Stay here, Sara. Make Solace your headquarters. My inn and my aid are yours for the asking."

Tika couldn't have been more pleased. She was an excellent judge of character and circumstance, and something about this whole vision and legacy seemed right. Echoing her husband's enthusiasm, she carried the teapot and mugs to the bed. "You would do well to follow her, young Derrick. You may not find wealth or glory in her service, but you will attain honor and self- respect and perhaps do some good for this war-torn land."

A hint of a smile erased some of Derrick's sadness. "That was all I wanted from the beginning." He held out his hand to Sara, who clasped it fiercely. "If you will have me, I will join your legion . . . heart and soul."

* * * * *

And so it happened that the Legion of Steel began with one and doubled its size in just one morning. But Sara was not content to leave it at that. She decided to try to increase her numbers—by returning to Neraka.

Caramon and Tika were appalled when she gathered her cloak two mornings later and told them what she was going to do.

Caramon thrust himself between the door and Sara and crossed his arms, an immovable wall. "Sara, don't be a fool! If you go back to Neraka, they will kill you. Then your legion will be nothing more than one wounded renegade boy!"

Sara lifted her eyebrows. "I don't think so," she said mildly. "General Abrena sent me here in the first place. She is expecting me to return. I will go back just long enough to talk to the members of the talon. I have a feeling one or two others would make better legionnaires than Dark Knights. After all we have been through together, they deserve a chance to change their minds."

"But how will you escape the city again? You yourself said the fortress is heavily guarded," Tika pointed out.

Caramon jabbed a thick finger at Sara before she had the opportunity to reply. "And how would you keep the ones who do not join from betraying you?"

Tika nodded vigorously and added her own protests. "And how do you know the lord knights have not already learned of your treason? You could be arrested the instant you stepped foot in the city."

"I know, I know!" Sara held up her hands to ward off the barrage of questions. "Or, rather, I don't really know.

I am aware of the danger. I've spent more than three months in Neraka! But this is something I have to do. For them. For me. To prove to them that I did not deceive them, that honor can be one's life."

Caramon slowly pulled his lips up in a smile. "Sturm would have liked you."

Tika looked from one to the other and knew the argument was lost. She had rarely known anyone with Sara's persistence, and if Caramon was ready to back down this quickly, there wasn't much point in continuing alone.

"Well," she said, rummaging briskly around the bar, "if you are going, you'd better take some food with you. Don't worry about Derrick. We'll get him back on his feet. Just keep that dragon close to you. I've never seen a blue as devoted as that one." She shouted the last sentence as she walked into the kitchen and returned carrying a small loaf of bread.

Sara watched, bemused, as she packed the bread, a bottle of ale, cheese, and some dried apples in a bag and walked across the floor. "What do you want to do with that pile of boxes from the giant's hoard?"

Taking the bag with a word of thanks, Sara said, "Let Derrick decide." She pulled on her fur-lined cloak. She was about to walk out the door, then hesitated and stopped in front of Caramon. "Caramon . . . if something happens so I don't make it back . . . will you take my information about General Abrena and the knights to the remnants of the Solamnics?"

He regarded her gravely before moving aside. "There are some I know in Sancrist. I will tell them."

"Thank you, my friends," Sara said and left before either Caramon or Tika had another chance to change her mind.

Chapter 25

Sara and Cobalt returned to Neraka shortly after noon the next day. Little had changed in the sprawling fortress. The filthy snow still clogged the streets, smoke still rose in grayish pall from hundreds of stoves and campfires, and the population of ogres, goblins, draconians, and humans still eked out an existence like maggots in a corpse. Despite Sara's fondest wish, the city had not been swallowed whole by a bottomless chasm while she was gone.

The winged guards still flew above the city as well, and they were quick to escort Cobalt to the open court next to the governor-general's palace.

Sara patted the big blue's shoulder after dismounting. "You may go feed if you wish."

"I wish to stay close by," he rumbled softly, his head close to hers. "Only a crazy human would walk back into a trap like this." Cobalt had not approved of Sara's plan to fly back to Neraka, but when she threatened to take a boat back across the New Sea, he reluctantly agreed. On his back, at least she wouldn't drown.

"I will be as quick as I can," she promised.

"Humph," he snorted and settled down to wait.

Governor-General Abrena had received word from her guards of Sara's arrival and waited for her in the map room. Her sleek blond hair gleamed in the light of a roaring fire, and her body moved sensuously in tight, pale-gold leather.

Sara rarely disturbed herself with matters of appearance, but the lithe general always made her feel plain and rather dumpy, especially when she had to wear that hideous black uniform.

Stifling a chuckle at herself, Sara saluted the general.

Mirielle stood at her table, staring down at the map model. She paid no attention to Sara's salute. "You're back quickly. Did you have success?"

Sara had plenty of time to concoct an explanation. "We reached the tomb with no difficulty and stayed close by for several days. We saw nothing more than plain walls and some names on the stone. There is little there for you, General, beyond the reminder of what it is to live with honor."

Mirielle shot a swift, hard glance at Sara. "And they died with it," she snapped. "Now we take what they left for us and move on. So Takhisis did not deign to give us a sign. . . ." She smacked her palm on the edge of the table and began to pace irritably in front of the fire. "You are not the first to fail. I have sent others to places of importance to our cause, and they all report the same—silence. Perhaps our goddess is gone for good after all." She glared balefully at the fire. "Why did you not stay longer? Where is the knight who went with you?"

"He was killed," replied Sara without emotion. "A party of elves came to the tomb and discovered who we were. They drove us away." She thought elves would be a good choice, since the Dark Knights hated them with a passion and would accept any sort of hinted elven villainy.

Mirielle curled her lip. "Elves." The word was a curse on her lips. She waved Sara away. "You may go. Report to Lord Knight Cadrel for a new assignment."

Sara made a mental apology to elves everywhere for maligning their reputation, turned smartly on her heel, and exited the room before the general thought of something else for her to do. She hurried back to Cobalt.

"Do we leave now?" the blue asked when he saw her coming.

"Not yet. I'm supposed to report to Lord Cadrel."

"That festering old grump?"

"Fortunately the general did not say when, so let's go find the talon and see if we can talk to them now."

Cobalt was off the ground and winging into the air so fast he nearly blew Sara out of the saddle. Soaring over Neraka, he spotted Squall and Howl out beyond the practice fields near the Red Quarter and flew to join them.

Marika, Kelena, and Argathon were there with the dragons and several others practicing the use of the lance. Sara was disappointed to notice the others were not present.

The girls came running to meet her, their pleasure clear on their unguarded faces. Argathon followed more slowly, as if hesitant of his welcome. Sara made sure to include him in her warm greetings. She liked the fair youth and had a suspicion that he, like Saunder and the girls, did not have the brutal core or the drive necessary to be a devout follower of Takhisis.

"How was your journey?" Kelena asked.

Marika said at the same time, "Where's Derrick?"

"Are you here to stay for a while?" Argathon inquired.

"I will answer all of your questions as soon as everyone is all together. Where are the others?"

Marika told her, "Saunder and Kazar are on patrol with Knight Officer Treb."

Sara's eyes narrowed. She didn't like the sound of that. "Knight Officer?" she repeated.

Kelena grimaced. "We heard she slept with Lord Cadrel to get the position."

Sara was shocked. "Oh, even Treb wouldn't do that."

"Sure she would," Argathon said with a cheerful smirk. "Treb plans to be a lord knight someday. She'd do anything to accomplish her goal."

Sara shook her head, her eyes thoughtfully on the afternoon sun. "I need to talk to all of you. Is there somewhere to meet . . . while Treb is busy?"

Marika and Kelena thought a moment, then Marika shoved a strand of brown hair out of her face and replied, "Treb has guard duty at the main gate tonight at sunset. The rest of us have a break then before we start our shifts. How about then?"

"Good. Tell Kazar and Saunder for me."

From Cobalt's back, Sara waved to the three knights and watched them dwindle to small figures as the dragon flew up over the city.

"Now what?" grumbled Cobalt.

"There's no help for it. I'll have to report to Lord Cadrel," Sara said. She did not want to. The less involved she became in this routine of the knighthood, the easier it would be for her to escape again. On the other hand, Cadrel was probably expecting her by now and would grow suspicious if she did not obey the general's orders.

Sara's head began to ache from the tension. She was growing nervous and edgy about all of this. It seemed to her that every eye that beheld her could see through her flimsy facade. She made up her mind that if she could not convince any of the talon members to join her, she would leave tonight.

Cobalt angled over to the gates and came to earth near the buildings where the lord knight of recruitment had his office.

Sara was surprised to see another large blue dragon crouched outside the buildings. The dragon looked vaguely familiar, yet one she had not seen in Neraka before. He was slightly larger than Cobalt, darker in color, and he wore an air of sullen disinterest. He was obviously an old veteran, for his body bore the scars of numerous battles, and the tip of his wing sail was tattered.

He paid no attention to Cobalt, but simply stared morosely into the distance.

Sara slid off her dragon on the opposite side so the old blue wouldn't see her. Something about that dragon bothered her deeply.

She strode forward into the building, stepped through the door, and came face-to-face with another knight. This one she recognized instantly, and her heart nearly failed. It took every fiber of muscle control in her face to keep her expression bland and her eyes blank.

He started in surprise and stared at her features, a question of recognition in his lowered brow. He had been one of Ariakan's staff officers, a mediocre warrior but a better administrator. From the look of his tattered clothes and worn face, he had been struggling to survive the past few years.

For just a heartbeat, Sara thought he was going to accost her. She forced her head down in a civil nod and kept her hand close to her sword.

The knight hesitated, shook his head slightly. Ridiculous, he seemed to say to himself. He barely nodded in return and pushed past her out to the old, surly blue dragon.

Sara tightened her hands around her belt to hide their shaking. She inhaled long and deeply and released it in a relieved breath. Great Paladine, that was close. The sooner she left Neraka, the better!

Still trembling, she entered Lord Cadrel's office. The afflicted knight sat at his table as usual, working on lists and scrolls and piles of records. He wore light leather gloves that day to protect his diseased hands from the cold.

"You're back," he said without looking up. "There's a new talon of recruits in the Black Quarter. They're yours for training as squires. I have one more to add this afternoon, then you take them tomorrow."

"Yes, sir," Sara responded as expected. "Lord Knight," she added, "who was the knight who came in before me?"

He replied without a pause, "Knight Officer Chekon. He just reported in from the east. Seems that cursed Malystryx is expanding her domain again. Blasted dragon." He continued to work, his pen scratching across a piece of parchment.

When he did not bother to speak to her again, Sara saluted and hurried outside to Cobalt.

"I know that dragon that just left," Cobalt informed her.

"And I know his rider," replied Sara worriedly.

"Does that mean we're leaving now?"

"No. He didn't seem to remember me. Maybe he won't. I want to keep my meeting with the talon. Then we'll leave."

"Promise?"

"On my word."

Cobalt grumbled something unintelligible and lifted himself and his stubborn rider into the air. For the rest of the afternoon, he and his rider made themselves as unobtrusive as possible. They went out to the hills to hunt a meal for Cobalt and stayed out of sight as much as they dared. Sara knew the dragon patrols realized where they were, but as long as Cobalt fed and slept the others would not disturb him and she would not be available for unnecessary tasks or unwanted reunions.

Dusk was gathering in thick blue shadows when Sara had Cobalt fly her back to the Red Quarter. Campfires twinkled below them like stars.

"Stay close," she advised Cobalt. "But if I am betrayed or captured, keep your wits. A fight among the tents could only hurt you or one of the talon. Keep out of sight and bide your time."

The dragon reluctantly agreed and landed in the open quadrangle near the Sixth Talon's tents.

Saunder came out to greet her. The grave young man saluted her, then gave her his quirky smile that crinkled the skin around his pale eyes and shone with honest pleasure. He took her to his tent, where Kelena, Marika, Argathon, and Kazar waited.

Kazar's face was dark and impassive in the dim light of Saunder's brazier, but the others sensed something was different about their leader, and they watched her curiously, waiting for her to speak.

Sara sat on the edge of the cot. The young knights squatted or stood on the floor around her.

Sara took a deep breath as she looked around at their intent faces, then she plunged into her tale, beginning this time eight years before, with her journey to save Steel's soul. She explained her reasons for returning to Neraka and finally told them of her vision in the tomb.

It was a credit to Sara that out of their respect for her, they did not interrupt her once. They listened, fascinated from beginning to end. When she finished, she pulled out the star jewel for them to see. Kazar said nothing, but the others burst into a flood of comments and questions.

"Derrick is still alive and he agrees to this?" Saunder asked carefully.

Argathon exclaimed, "I can't believe you came back here after all of that."

"You were Steel Brightblade's mother? And you're not a real knight?" Marika asked, incredulous.

Kelena suddenly held up her hand. "Quiet! I hear something outside."

The others abruptly fell silent. Although they strained to listen for several minutes, they heard nothing more than the usual sounds of the camp at night—a few distant voices, a barking dog, the creak of tent ropes. They visibly relaxed.

"Knight Officer Treb will be back any minute," Kelena reminded them, scorn heavy in her voice.

Sara looked at them all one by one and said softly, "I know this is a great deal to ask you to think about, but I wanted you to know what has happened and how I feel about all of you. I want you with me in this new order. I think your talents and strengths will be wasted in the Knights of Takhisis. Please think about it."

She rose to her feet and put a hand on Saunder's shoulder in thanks. "I cannot stay. A knight whom I recognized arrived today. It's only a matter of time before he remembers me. If any of you decide to come with me now or twenty years from now, you will be welcome."

No one moved to go with her. They watched her with eyes full of confusion and hearts too uncertain to decide. She knew how they felt.

Bidding farewell to them, she stepped through the tent flap and walked past the fire ring toward the quadrangle where Cobalt waited.

"Knight Officer Conby," called a guard. Immediately three heavily armed knights strode out of the shadows and surrounded her.

"Your sword, please," said the officer in charge. "You are under arrest."

Fear, dismay, dread, crowded into Sara's thoughts. The bitterness of defeat was sharp in her mouth, but she kept her face impassive. Slowly she unbuckled the belt with the sword and its sheath and handed it to the officer. She turned once and saw the young knights crowded into the tent's entrance, staring at her in dismay, their faces pale and grim.

"Tell Cobalt to be patient," she called to them.

"This way," the officer directed. "Governor-General Abrena wants to see you."

Sara set her jaw. If Mirielle ascribed to Lord Ariakan's policy that "discipline must be swift to be maintained," then she would try Sara tonight and probably convict her.

The guards marched her immediately to the governor's palace and into the dining hall, the room that served so many purposes. The long blackwood table sat before the fireplace as usual, but it was not set for a convivial dinner that night. Governor-General Abrena and

Lord Knights Cadrel and Gamarin sat at the table facing the doorway. A crowd of officers, aides, and knights waited at one end of the room.

The guards escorted Sara to a place in front of Mirielle and the two lord knights.

"Knight Officer Karn, reporting as ordered with the prisoner, my lords." The officer of the guard laid Sara's sword on the table in front of them.

Governor-General Abrena turned her predator's eyes on Sara. Mirielle was known to be a cold but fair judge under normal circumstances. This, however, was not normal or acceptable to the general. She had been duped, and there was no mercy, no compassion in her gold eyes. "The accused, Knight Officer Conby, stands before us. Stand forth, accusers," she ordered in a voice harder than steel.

The old knight Sara recognized from that afternoon walked out of the crowd, closely followed by a second knight, who came around from behind him and assumed an aggressive stance in front of the table. She crossed her arms and threw a contemptuous glance at Sara. It was Treb.

"We are the accusers, my lords," the older knight stated.

"Knight Officers Chekon and Treb, state your charges against this knight."

Chekon jerked his grizzled chin toward Sara. "She was no knight, my lords. I knew her as Sara Dunstan, the adoptive mother of Steel Brightblade. She served Lord Ariakan for years until he discarded her. I heard she was exiled."

Sara stood motionless, her back erect, her hands at her sides. She kept her eyes straight ahead.

Mirielle lifted an elegant eyebrow. "Lord Ariakan's mistress," she growled, much like a cat about to pounce. "I heard you were dead."

Sara said nothing.

"Do you deny the charges?" the general demanded, her fingers curled into claws.

Treb curled her lip and spoke up. "She cannot, my lords," she stated, her voice full of triumph. "I heard her tell the others in the Sixth Talon the same thing. She came to Neraka to spy on the order. She's not only a renegade, but she's also a traitor!"

Sara felt a deep chill. Obviously Treb had been listening outside the tent. Just how much had she overheard? Did she know Derrick was still alive or that Sara had asked the others to leave the order? Sara guessed not, or Treb would have already brought out such news in the hope of further advancing her ambitions. Sara leaned on that hope and ignored Treb's derisive sneer.

The crowd of watchers by the wall exclaimed among themselves in a disapproving mutter.

Mirielle's angry frown deepened. Her disappointment in Sara's perfidy was a bitter gall. But worse, the general did not like to be made a fool of, especially in front of her army. She had liked this woman knight, her courage and sense of honor, her ability to train and engender loyalty in her underlings. She had trusted her, too—as much as Mirielle trusted anyone. After all, the woman had saved her life. The fact that Sara deceived her and was in reality a traitor and a spy filled the general with unremitting rage.

"What do you have to say for yourself?" Mirielle insisted.

Sara kept her face expressionless. What could she say? They knew the truth. If she tried to deny it or bluff her way out of it, they would never believe her. They could even drag Kelena or Marika or one of the young men into the trial and force one of them to reveal her whole story. She had to do something quickly to distract the knights and buy herself some time.

Wrenching free of her guards, she marched to the table, put both hands on the edge, leaned over to match

Mirielle glare for glare, and said flatly, "It doesn't matter what I say. Let my deeds speak for me. I demand the right to trial by battle."

Lord Knight Cadrel looked startled by such a suggestion. There was rarely any point in a trial by such means when the accused was so obviously guilty. They should just take the woman out and behead her on the spot.

Mirielle did not see it that way. A trial by battle suited her perfectly, allowing her to redeem the respect she had lost through Sara's deceit. She would personally see to it herself. "Very well, Sara Dunstan—or whoever you are—you may have your trial by battle. I will stand as champion for the accusers. If you are defeated and are not yet dead, you will be executed immediately."

"And if you are defeated, I will be exonerated and allowed to go free," Sara said loudly, so everyone could hear her.

A feral gleam lit in Mirielle's narrowed gaze. Since there was no possibility that an older, untrained rider like Sara could defeat her, she was willing to agree to that condition. "Of course." She rose to her feet and announced to the watching knights, "The battle will take place tomorrow at noon. We will fight on dragonback. Until that time, Sara Dunstan, you will remain a prisoner and will be held under guard in the prison cells until an hour before the battle. You will be released then to give you time to prepare." Mirielle gestured toward the door. "Take her downstairs," she ordered.

The guards bowed and took Sara out of the room. The surge of noisy comments and opinions died behind them as they entered a stone stairway that wound down into the subterranean floors beneath the palace. Down they went, past the storage levels, to a dank, cold, stone-walled dungeon where the prison cells were carved into the bedrock under the city. Torches sat in brackets on the walls and cast a dim, guttering light on the damp floor.

The guards unlocked one door in a row of doors and

pulled open the stout wooden hatch.

Sara peered into the intense darkness, and when she hesitated a moment too long, the guards shoved her inside.

She stumbled forward, tripped, and fell sprawling across the slimy stone floor. The door slammed behind her, and darkness, black and impenetrable, closed around her.

Memories of her journey through the temple ruin reared up on wings of terror, and for several interminable minutes, she fought off a fear that threatened to suck her down into mindless panic.

She kept repeating over and over, "I know where I am. This is a small room. I know where I am." Her words sounded feeble in the darkness, but the litany gave her strength.

Trembling, she reached out a cautious hand, and suddenly she realized she could see it. A tiny light, soft and white, gleamed from somewhere close in front of her. Her eyes traveled down to the front of her tunic, and there, glowing under the fabric of her shirt, was the star jewel. She tugged it out. Freed of the material, its light glowed brighter, like a tiny star cupped in her hand.

Sara's fear evaporated. The star jewel drove away the darkness and illuminated her in the power of Steel's love. As it had for Steel and his father before him, it reminded her that she was not alone, that she still had something to believe in.

In the light of the jewel, she found her way to the single stone shelf that served as a bed and sat back against the wall. Her hand closed around the star jewel and pressed its light to her heart. Now she only had to wait for day and for the battle that would either kill her or free her.

Chapter 26

The guards came an hour before noon, as promised, and escorted Sara outside. They expected her to be weakened from exhaustion, cold, and hunger, but they were disappointed. She walked out of the palace with a strong, determined stride and paid no attention to their crude remarks and insults. Nor could they find any sign of fear in her calm expression. Shaking their heads, they returned her sword to her.

"Be at the Arena of Death in one hour," one guard told her. "You are on your honor not to escape."

"Of course," she said coolly. Escape was the last thing on her mind.

A more pressing desire was the need for food and drink. She had not had anything to eat or drink for nearly a full day, and the need for liquid was growing crucial. She turned her back on the guards and walked through the walled gate into the main streets of the city. The streets were as busy as ever, and as noisy, filthy, and dim. Ogres and draconians crowded past her, and goblins scurried by underfoot. Sara had to push her way through in some places, and once or twice she had to throw herself against the wall of a building to keep from being trampled by a passing team of horses or a patrol of guards who paid little heed to the people around them.

Sara was so intent on working her way out of the city, she never would have noticed the small gully dwarf by her side if he hadn't touched her sleeve.

She looked down into a grungy, bewhiskered, familiar face. "Fewmet?" she asked, astonished. "What are you doing here?"

He gestured around with a hand even dirtier than his clothes. "Me live here," he said, astonished that she would ask such an obvious question.

"I know," Sara said patiently. "I was just surprised to see you."

"Are you hungry?" he asked, a hopeful light in his eyes.

Sara sighed. "Yes, as a matter of fact, I am. I don't have much time, but I would like to eat."

They went to the inn where Sara had bought him a meal the last time, and Sara purchased two bowls of soup, bread, and an apple tart. The innkeeper told her in no uncertain terms that gully dwarves were not allowed to eat indoors because their eating habits tended to drive out the other patrons, so once again Sara obligingly took the food outdoors and sat under a tree with Fewmet.

Sara ate her own food and tried to ignore Fewmet's loud slurping and belching. She wasn't sure why she was spending her last hour in the company of a gully dwarf, but it seemed better than eating alone.

At last he wiped his mouth on his greasy vest, which did nothing to clean his face, and tucked the dishes in his bag. "You nice for human," he told her. "Come. I know where your dragon is."

Sara looked startled. "How do you know that?"

"I see lots of things," he said mysteriously. He tugged on her pants leg and led her down the street toward the outskirts of the city.

"I know you fight again," Fewmet said, his tone serious. "Last time you fight bad knight I tell you something. I see fight. I see you knock bad knight down. What I told you helped."

"Yes. Yes, it did," Sara responded thoughtfully. What

was he leading up to? she wondered.

The gully dwarf took her past the main gates and toward the open fields near the Red Quarter. His stumpy legs had to take three strides to her one, but he trotted gamely beside her and continued to talk breathlessly.

"People pay small attention to gully dwarves," Fewmet went on. "We get kicked or hit or people drive us away sometimes. Most times they not know we are there. We see many things." He looked at her sideways through his greasy forelock. "I see general fight. She is good. She is best. But her dragon hurt long ago. His right wing is not strong."

Sara stared at him as the information sank in. "Fewmet, if I survive this battle, would you like to come with me to Solace? You can leave this city and come where people will appreciate you."

He broke into a cackling laugh. "People not appreciate me anywhere. Only you have been nice to Fewmet. I have never left city. I would not know what to do in strange place. Thank you, Sara. Dragon over there. Fight well." He sketched a bow and trotted away.

Sara watched him go and sent a silent blessing after him. Perhaps it was for the best. She couldn't imagine how she would have convinced Cobalt to carry a gully dwarf.

She found the blue dragon waiting for her near the ring of tents. He crouched on the ground, his head held high to look out for her, his tail twitching with agitation. As soon as he saw her, he lumbered toward her. Steam curled from his nostrils, and his yellow eyes burned like fire.

"Be patient, you said," he hissed at her. "Be patient. That was all! If I had not overheard that rat dung, Treb, tell everyone all about the trial, I would have torn the city apart looking for you."

"And been killed by the other dragons for your pains," she said. She tugged his head down and hugged his neck, then scratched his ears soothingly. "I would have gotten a message to you if I could, but they put me in a dungeon cell until just a little while ago."

"I know," he grumbled. "Treb said—" The dragon paused, and his eyes burned whiter in anger. "She's had the others arrested, all but Kazar."

Sara did not indulge in any exclamations of anger or curse words heaped on Treb's head. Anything she could say now would be a waste of effort. But her anger ignited to a slow burn and began to build within her like a firestorm about to erupt. "Do you know where they are?" she asked between clenched teeth.

"They're in camp, under guard. They're to stay in their tents until after the battle. Then Treb intends to take them before the adjudicator for violations of the Code." Cobalt lifted his lips in a draconian sneer. "Before we leave here, I would like to eat her liver."

"All that bile would probably give you indigestion," Sara said. "We will deal with her later." She hesitated before broaching her next question. Dragons could be haughty at times, and they preferred to work with their riders as partners or allies. Sometimes they refused to fight if it did not suit their purposes. If Cobalt was not willing to fight in this trial, she could be in a real predicament. After a moment's consideration, she asked, "So Treb mentioned the trial by battle?"

"Yes."

"Did she say it is on dragonback?"

"Yes."

She tilted an eyebrow and looked up at his reptilian face. "You're not making this easy for me."

He tilted his nose up and looked smugly down at her. "Serves you right for scaring me like that."

Sara laughed. "True enough. Will you fight with me?"

For an answer, he turned sideways so she could see his dragonsaddle. The two-man saddle she had used to go to Solace with Derrick and had ridden back was gone. In its place was a one-rider fighting saddle fashioned of lightweight wood and leather and fully accoutred with a rider's lance, a shield, and a crossbow. A breastplate and a helm hung from the saddle's straps.

Pleased, Sara ran a hand over the armor. It was old and well worn, but someone had taken the time to polish it and replace the straps with new ones. Best of all, it was unadorned. It did not bear the hateful death lily or any of the emblems of the dark knighthood.

"Who helped you?" Sara asked.

"General Abrena," Cobalt answered briefly. Sara looked so startled that he elaborated. "The general wishes this to be a fair battle. She wants to kill you in a matched fight, not in an execution. A matter of pride."

Sara did not ask more. She knew Mirielle enough to know she could trust the weapons and armor provided for her.

Swiftly she donned the armor and was glad to see it fit well enough. She pulled the fighting helm over her silver hair. It was nearly noon.

Before she mounted Cobalt, she paused and touched the star jewel hanging on its chain against the metal breastplate. In the past, before the Second Cataclysm, she had been in the habit of saying a prayer or two to Paladine when she felt in need. Even after the gods' departure, when she had felt empty and bereft, she had prayed in the hope they would hear her somehow. But after that night in the Tomb of the Last Heroes, she no longer felt the need to petition a vanished god. She had found a strength in herself, a cause to believe in. It did not make a difference to her how Steel had come or who had sent him. The only thing that was important to her was that he had come, and he had left her his token so she would know his love would always be with her.

Sara climbed to Cobalt's back and drew her sword. This battle she was about to fight was not just to save her life. It was also the first test of the validity of her vision.

The Legion of Steel was going forth to face its first real challenge, and if it was to survive, she would have to emerge victorious.

Cobalt spread his great wings and took to the sky. He winged south, skirting the inside edge of the tent ring, and flew over the city wall and into the Arena of Death. The sand floor of the arena was empty, which Sara expected. The haughty governor-general would certainly want to make her own entrance.

The seats of the arena were crowded again, and hawkers were doing a thriving business in the stands. A few groups cheered Sara; many more jeered her.

She instructed Cobalt to land at one end of the oval. He descended with a roar and a rush of wings that sent dust swirling into the stands and crowds of people rushing back from the wall.

The dust raised during Cobalt's landing had barely settled when a shout went up from the audience and a large shadow passed swiftly over the arena. At half speed, Mirielle's dragon, Cerium, circled around and cruised over the arena a second time. Every eye was upon him. Coming in to land across from Cobalt, he beat his wings and stirred up a great cloud of dust and sand that whirled through the arena.

Sara clapped a handful of sleeve over her nose and mouth. She could hear Mirielle laughing. When the dust settled, Sara finally had a close look at the veteran dragon who bore the governor-general.

Cerium was a mature male, slightly larger than Cobalt at more than forty-eight feet in length, and bulky, with bulging muscles. His thick horns were the color of polished steel, and his hide was an iron blue. He stamped his powerful forelimbs and dug out great gouges of dirt with his claws. His scaly frill flared out around his wedge-shaped head to show off his fearsomeness. His roar shook the arena.

Cobalt was not impressed. He returned the challenge

with a roar of his own. His tail lashed back and forth in fury, and his own spiked frill flared around his head. His horns stood straight out from his head.

Sara raised her sword in salute to Mirielle. The general returned the gesture. She then shouted to a group of staff officers waiting in the stands. They saluted and hurried to a platform, where one knight stood holding the general's black standard. At a word from an officer, the knight slowly dipped the standard toward the ground.

That was the signal to begin. A chorus of cheers from the crowd mingled with matching roars from the dragons to make a swelling wave of sound that crashed over the arena.

Usually at this point in a duel, dragons cast their spells while still standing on the ground, but in a trial by battle, magic was forbidden. Cobalt and Cerium would have to rely solely on their teeth and claws, their lightning breath, their natural strength, and their riders.

Cerium moved first. He crouched and sprang forward with unexpected agility, hoping to take the younger dragon by surprise. Cobalt reared up, taking the force of the dragon's charge against his powerful chest. His head sloughed around and he snapped at Cerium's wing, tearing the fine membrane at the tip. Forelimbs scrabbling, the dragons wrestled with tooth and claw while their riders held on frantically.

"Go aloft!" Sara shouted. "Fly!"

Suddenly Cobalt broke loose, swept his wings upward, and sprang into the sky. With unbelievable speed, he was airborne above the arena.

In the blink of an eye, Cerium was after him, his massive wings lifting him rapidly after his opponent. The iron-colored blue spat a jolt of electricity that for the most part passed harmlessly under the speeding dragon. Only a tendril of energy caught Cobalt's tail and burned the scales where it struck.

Cobalt roared his defiance. He soared quickly above

Cerium, arched around, and furled his wings into a dive. Sara raised her shield as the older blue fired another bolt of lightning. The energy seared around her and rebounded off her shield. Cobalt responded with his own blast that struck Cerium on the foreleg and rocked Mirielle back in her saddle.

Diving and darting in intricate patterns, the dragons climbed ever higher into the sky. For the most part, their riders could only hang on and try to avoid the blasts of lightning that scorched the air around them.

Sara twisted her head back to look at Cerium and Mirielle. The older dragon definitely had more experience and endurance for this kind of battle. Cobalt had more speed and agility, but so far he was just fighting a defensive skirmish. She had to get him to take the offense.

Sara shoved her sword in the saddle scabbard by her leg and unfastened the crossbow. It was already cocked and needed only a dart to fire. She loaded it and waited for her chance.

"His right wing is weak," she yelled to Cobalt. "If you can get me closer, I'll try to shoot him." She could try to shoot Mirielle, and the thought was very tempting, but the dragon presented a much bigger target for a weapon inaccurate as a crossbow in midflight.

Cobalt only grunted a reply and pivoted sharply around to pass underneath Cerium.

The older blue sensed his danger immediately and plummeted straight toward Cobalt. Sara had only a second or two to aim the crossbow, fire the dart toward Cerium's shoulder, and duck as Cobalt furled his wings and rolled to the left out of the way of the other dragon.

The dart must have hit something, for Cerium shrilled in pain, but it did little to slow him down. Furiously he flew after Cobalt. The younger dragon managed to lash him in the muzzle with his tail before looping around and slipping away. He circled around again and headed straight for Cerium.

Sara could see Mirielle holding her own crossbow, but there was little she could do to disarm the general at that moment, for the other blue trumpeted his rage and charged forward at a blinding speed.

The two dragons clashed in midair, craving for the glory of the kill. Their wings pounded each other's heads; their claws raked each other's chests and sides. Their blood mingled across their blue hides. As each strove to outdo the other, their wings became befouled, and suddenly both dragons began to plummet toward the ground.

Calling on hidden reserves of strength, Cobalt wrenched away and spread his wings to pull himself up.

A pain, brilliant red and agonizing, shot through Sara's leg. Taken by surprise, she clutched at a crossbow bolt buried in her thigh and screamed. Her cry of pain jolted Cobalt's attention. He jerked his head around to see his rider collapse against his neck, and in that moment of inattention, Cerium lashed out with a hot streak of lightning.

The bolt was poorly aimed due to the rapid descent of the dragons, but some of the furious energy caught Cobalt across his haunches and lower left wing. A section of his wingsail burned to tatters. Scales melted across his back, and blood welled up through the wound. Cobalt snarled in pain and rage. Memories of another rider, another battle, filled his thoughts. This general had contributed to the death of Vincit, and now she had killed Sara.

Pain blurred the edges of reality, and his only desire became revenge. Instead of avoiding the bigger blue, he turned into him and sank his talons into Cerium's left wing. The right was the weakest, Sara had said. It would never hold. Snapping and snarling at Cerium's head, he held on with all the strength and tenacity he could muster and furled his wings tightly against his body.

Locked together, the two dragons tumbled like dead birds toward the ground. Cerium did not have the strength to stop his descent with an extra dragon weight fastened to his strong wing. Although he struggled frantically to tear away from Cobalt, Cerium could not escape. Cobalt seemed determined to take them all to their deaths on the frozen ground.

Mirielle desperately hacked at Cobalt's neck with her sword, but the blade had little effect on the dragon's tough scales.

He closed his eyes and ignored her, ignored the pain.

Sara lay across Cobalt's neck and stared dizzily at the earth whirling up to meet them. The dragons had risen to a high altitude before beginning their fall, but that distance was rapidly melting away. If Cobalt didn't break off quickly, there would be no time to pull up. She tried feebly to move and discovered the crossbow bolt buried in her upper thigh had pinned her leg to the saddle.

"Cobalt!" she cried. "Cobalt, let him go!"

The blue's eyes popped open. He thought Sara was dead.

"Cobalt!"

The dragon responded. Summoning his last vestiges of strength, he stretched his wings out over Cerium's and dug deeply into the rushing air to slow their fall. At the same time, he wrenched his head up, pulling Cerium's wing up at a sudden and unnatural angle.

The combined forces of the abrupt slowdown and Cobalt's weight on his wing were too much for Cerium's wing. The bone snapped near the shoulder. The dragon screeched his agony and fury. Unable to hold his weight up and sustain flight with only one wing, he plummeted toward the fields below.

Cobalt let him go. Now he had to save himself and his rider. His own wing was tattered, and his back was badly burned from Cerium's lightning breath. His strength was nearly gone. He pumped madly to catch the air and slow his breakneck fall, but the ground was so close that he and Sara could see the people running out to the fields just outside of Neraka to see the dragons land.

Sara held on to the saddle. The cold wind roaring by brought tears to her eyes. Out of the corner of her vision, she saw Cerium twist weakly around to land on his belly and crash to the earth with crushing force. He twitched once, then lay still on the cold, frozen ground.

Then all her attention focused on Cobalt. He flapped his wings with all his remaining might. He was still dropping at a terrifying speed, but gradually his fall slowed and his wingsails caught enough wind to bring his body to a level, controlled descent. He landed heavily on the field, crashed forward onto his chest, and slid ignominiously across the snowy ground. He came to a stop in an undignified heap. But he was alive, and he rose to his feet and shook the snow from his head and tail.

Surprisingly, Knight Officer Morham Targonne was the first one to reach Cobalt's side. Without asking permission, he vaulted up the dragon's leg and swiftly checked Sara's condition.

Cobalt did not complain. He was too frantic to know if she was all right.

Sara stared blearily at the young knight. "Is the general . . . still alive?"

He shot a glance at the other fallen dragon and saw Mirielle climb out of her saddle, apparently unhurt. He nodded his answer.

"Then pull it out," Sara ordered.

Morham looked at the bolt in Sara's leg and shook his head. "You could bleed to death," he warned.

"Pull it out!" Sara demanded again. "I have to finish this." Technically the trial was not over until one of the opponents was dead or had surrendered.

Morham shrugged, but he gently worked the bolt tip

out of the saddle leather and, placing a booted foot against Sara's leg to hold it in place, used both hands to pull the bolt quickly and smoothly out of Sara's thigh.

Sara bit off a scream. Clenching her teeth, she leaned into Cobalt's strong shoulder until the worst of the pain passed. Finally she gulped some air and managed to sit up. Fortunately the bleeding wasn't bad, assuring her that the bolt had not struck the large artery in her leg.

Sara patted Cobalt's neck. "Thank you, my friend. You are one glorious dragon."

Cobalt chuckled. "Of course."

"Rest here. I must finish this. Then we will go." While Morham watched, Sara pulled her sword out of the saddle scabbard and climbed down Cobalt's side to the ground. She limped unsteadily toward the body of the other blue where he had slewed into the snow.

Looking at Cerium, Sara knew he would fly no more. The dragon, in his attempt to save his rider, had broken his neck in the fall. He lay motionless in death, his color already fading.

The people gathered around Cerium saw Sara coming and silently stood aside. With the dragons out of the fight, the battle had to be continued on foot.

General Abrena hefted her own sword and strode forward to meet her. Her eyes glittered with the prospect of a kill. "Your dragon fights well," Mirielle shouted. "Can you do the same?"

With a wounded leg, against a well-trained, ruthless fighter? Sara doubted it. But she thrust every vestige of fear, pain, and doubt aside and emptied her mind of everything but her enemy and the feel of the sword in her hands.

The spectators, who had followed them from the arena, formed a large circle around the two women in the snowy field and kept up a steady chorus of cheers, jeers, opinions, and advice.

Mirielle and Sara ignored them. They circled each

other for a few tense moments, their swords raised, their faces intent on each other. They moved at the same instant and came together in a clash of blades. Back and forth they struggled across the circle, hammering at each other with a rain of deadly blows.

Time and again Sara silently thanked Knight Officer Massard for the conditioning he had given her. Without the months spent in Neraka running and training and strengthening the talon, Sara knew she would not have survived the first five minutes of the duel. Her own years of practice served her well, too. As the blood soaked down her pants from her leg wound and her body grew weaker, more and more often her muscles reacted automatically with an oft-practiced defense against a vicious thrust or a heavy upward slice.

"You are weakening, Ariakan's woman," Mirielle taunted. "You were never worthy to be a knight."

"No, thank the gods!" Sara panted between breaths, and she brought her blade around in a swift parry.

Their swords clashed again, and for just a second, Mirielle's grasp on her leather grip appeared to slip. She recovered quickly and continued her attack, but Sara sharpened her focus on the general's physical condition, and for the first time, she recognized pain in Mirielle's golden eyes. Cerium's crash landing had battered his rider more than she let on, and the duel was taking its toll on her as well. Her face was slick with sweat and red from her exertions, and her lithe movements were growing clumsier.

As Sara watched the general, she realized the woman was favoring her left arm. Before she had time to act on that knowledge, however, Sara's foot slipped on an icy patch of snow. Her wounded leg couldn't catch her weight, and she stumbled sideways.

As fast as a cat, Mirielle leapt to attack. Her blade slid around Sara's and knocked the sword out of Sara's hand.

Sara did not even hesitate. In the back of her mind, she

had anticipated such a possibility, and the moment she felt the sword leave her clasp, she scrambled upright and, with her last strength, ran away from Mirielle toward the edge of the circle where Cobalt crouched.

"You coward!" Mirielle screamed furiously. She charged after her quarry across the trampled snow.

The crowd hooted in derision.

"Cobalt!" Sara yelled. "The lance!" The short rider's lance she had taken into the battle was still attached to Cobalt's saddle. By trial law, it was still considered an acceptable weapon in the duel.

The blue dragon trumpeted his understanding. Shoving aside draconians and knights, he lumbered into the open circle and turned so Sara could reach the lance.

She scrambled up his leg, wrenched the lance free, and dropped to the ground just as Mirielle reached them. Cobalt reluctantly backed away to let Sara finish the battle alone.

The general skidded to a halt, her words of scorn congealing on her tongue. Her eyes narrowed as she tried to reassess this new weapon in Sara's hands.

Sara gave her no more time to think. As the general raised her sword to resume the attack, Sara furiously hefted the heavy lance and swung it as hard as she could at the general.

Startled by such a basic move, Mirielle tried to block the wooden shaft with her blade. The sword's edge sank into the wood and stuck there, and the momentum of the lance wrenched the sword out of Mirielle's hands. The lance, weighted by the sword, crashed into the general's left arm with an audible crack. The lance tip broke and the sword tumbled free, but Mirielle could not pick it up.

She fell to her knees, clutching her left arm, her face racked by pain.

Sara stumbled forward, picked up the general's sword from the ground, and held it to Mirielle's throat. "Surrender or die."

The general saw no mercy in Sara Dunstan's face. She meant every word she said. Briefly Mirielle weighed her choices and accepted her decision. What profit was there in dying by the hand of an exiled renegade? Sara had won the victory this time, but there would be another time in the future when the traitor would not be so lucky. Mirielle would be certain of that.

"I surrender," Mirielle said between clenched teeth.

Sara hauled the Dark Knight to her feet. "I have won my freedom, but I have not finished my task. Tell your knights to leave us alone, or I will kill you."

At the general's sharp command, the knights in the crowd moved away from Cobalt. Sara limped back to the dragon, taking Mirielle with her. The big blue stood unsteadily on his feet, waiting for her. Sara knew they both needed rest and medical attention, but she wanted desperately to see Kelena and the others before she left Neraka. "Could you carry us for a short while?" she asked the dragon. "We need to get to the Red Quarter."

Cobalt tested each leg and wing in turn and decided that indeed he could walk without too much difficulty. He waited patiently while Sara urged the general up into the saddle at the point of her own sword, and he carried the two women as quickly as his burned back would allow to the Red Quarter and the tents of the Sixth Talon.

They found a talon of armed guards clustered around two of the tents, and Squall and Howl crouched close by, looking very disgruntled. The two dragons perked up when they saw Cobalt, and they bellowed a welcome. Four heads poked out of the two tents, and four pairs of eyes took in every detail of the scene.

The guards saw General Abrena and several approached to greet her.

"Stay back," she commanded, prodded by Sara's sword. "Put your weapons down and back away from the tents. I am releasing the prisoners." Surprised, the guards did as they were bade and backed away from the dragon and the tents.

"No!" shouted a voice. Treb came running from the direction of the fields. "Governor-General, don't do it!" she protested. "They are all traitors!"

Kelena, her freckled face dark with anger, charged out of one of the tents and knocked Treb into the snow face first. Skillfully she disarmed the knight and left her lying in the snow. "You would risk your general for the likes of us?" she said in derision. "Curb your ambitions, bootlicker!"

Saunder, Marika, and Argathon came out of the tents and, with Kelena, gathered before Cobalt.

"We've been talking," Saunder said before Sara had a chance to say anything. He glanced at the others, who nodded to his silent question. "If you will have us, we want to go with you. Squall and Howl have already agreed to carry us to some place beyond the Khalkists."

Sara stared at Saunder in dawning hope. "Are you all going with me?" she asked incredulously. This was more than she ever hoped for.

Argathon shrugged. "All but Kazar. He prefers to stay here. We are no longer welcome."

"You were right," Kelena added seriously. "The Knights of Takhisis are no longer what they were. Their honor is fading. We would rather follow you and your legacy."

Sara looked from face to face and saw in their eyes the same glow of determination. Her hand closed over the star jewel and she breathed a silent word of gratitude.

"Then let's go," she said, "before we lose the advantage of surprise."

Quickly, efficiently the four knights loaded their gear on the two dragons and helped Sara into the saddle of Squall. Kelena gleefully tied up Treb in a tent and bound General Abrena to Squall's saddle in front of Sara.

Cobalt rested while they worked, and by the time they were ready to leave, he felt strong enough to fly with the two blues for a short flight over the mountains.

No one tried to stop them. The knights were too afraid for the safety of their general, and even the dragon guards retreated at General Abrena's order.

The journey over the mountains was soon accomplished and as agreed, Squall and Howl dropped them off near a village where they could seek help and supplies. The four young knights unloaded their gear while Sara climbed painfully to the ground.

At last only Mirielle was left sitting on Squall. She glared down at Sara over her slender nose. "Watch your back, traitor. The Knights of Takhisis do not forget."

Sara suddenly smiled. "Then remember this, Knight of Takhisis. I am the commander of the Legion of Steel, and I promise you, we will fight your evil every step of the way, in every city and every realm. The gods are gone, Mirielle. We have no one left but each other."

The general looked down at her and saw for the first time someone more than a mistress or an underling or a traitor, and she felt a grudging measure of respect. She turned her face away and fell silent.

The two dragons, Squall and Howl, said their farewells. They had no desire to follow the legion to Solace; they would take Mirielle back to Neraka.

Sara gave them her thanks, and when they had flown away into the gathering dusk, carrying Governor-General Abrena with them, she turned to her new legionnaires and said, "Let's go. We have a lot of work ahead of us."